Book of the Year 2002 — ForeWord Magazine's first place gold winner for science fiction: Chronicler's Edition

Best Books of 2002 — Made January Magazine's list of their top 92 books across all genres. One of six picks in the science fiction/fantasy genre.

Book of the Year 2015 — ForeWord Magazine's bronze winner for science fiction: 2013 Edition.

PRAISE

"Scifi at its best. Conflict abounds, characters are larger than life, and the technology projections are superb. This will be a classic work on the scale of [Asimov's] Foundation series. Our best Five Hearts rating."
— *Heartland Reviews*

"Highly imaginative."
— *Publishers Weekly*

"A rip-roaring good tale ... a story for all ages. Better put, a story for all people hip enough to 'get it.'"
— *Locus Online*

"An impressive, sprawling tale. World-building is top-notch and the sociological satire is both funny and believable, as are his inventions.
— *SF Reader*

"*The Luck of Madonna 13* signals the arrival of a new force on the fantasy and science fiction scene. What a story!"
— *Blue Ear*

"*The Luck of Madonna 13* is quite wonderful, and original enough that it begs for its own genre."
— *January Magazine*

"Ellison is a hugely inventive storyteller with a wry sense of humor, a satirical bent that verges on Swiftian and a talent for making wacky and bizarre ideas completely believable."
— *The Mountain Signal*

Books by E. T. Ellison

In THE LAST NEVERGATE CHRONICLES:
The Luck of Madonna 13
The Mask of Madonna 13
The Ghost of Madonna 13
The Ashes of Madonna 13
The Axe of Madonna 13
The Cult of Madonna 13

Genesis ... and Then Some
The essential companion to the Last Nevergate Chronicles

In the FALLING SKY series:
The Deadly Crocus
The Well of Life

TRAVIS ONE-SHOE thrillers:
Treasure of the Holy Quincunx

The LUCK *of* MADONNA 13

E. T. ELLISON

© Copyright 2019 by E. T. Ellison

ISBN 978-0-9965822-3-0

Book and cover designs by E. T. Ellison. www.etellison.com

Published by Clownbox Press
216 Mt Hermon Road, Suite E-233
Scotts Valley, CA 95066

022060

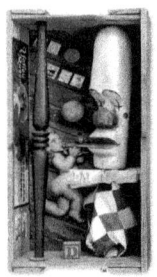

cLoWNboX
P R E s s

For my family. Their generous support and their ability to humor me with such good humor all these years has been nothing short of legendary.

QUINCUNXIFICATION

QUINCUNX IS A WORD you'll encounter in this book ... and not infrequently. While it's picturesque as words go, it does not exactly make an elegant swan dive off the tongue. At least that's been my tongue's experience. Although it's pronounced exactly as it's spelled (kwin-kunks), the people of St Coriander take no more pleasure in its elocutionary gymnastics than you or I do. So they have been known to cheat. In everyday conversation they often say "quinkess" or even "quinks." For a time, "kwunks" (they wrote it "qunks") was a fashion amongst the students of both Eastac and Westac, to the annoyance of school authorities, who feared the more formalistic members Fatherhood might take offense, although they rarely did. "Ah youth," they'd say.

Some readers don't even bother to mentally pronounce it; they acknowledge they know what meaning it stands for, and then move on to the next word. My authorial recommendation is to do whatever you want.

A FRIDAY THE 13TH ENCOUNTER

This [long, convoluted] odyssey called the Last Nevergate Chronicles might never have been finished were it not for that singular event of Friday, September 13, 2013. That's when a stranger knocked on the door to my studio.

A prank, of course. My studio at the time was in a building that was once a granary when the place was a working dairy farm in the way-back-when. In late 2013 it still looked abandoned and probably haunted, and the next house is half a mile away. Who would dare come here uninvited? Jehovah's Witnesses? LDS missionaries? Running out of obvious culprits, I just opened the door.

A man was standing on the top step holding out a white card. "Mr Ellison? E. T. Ellison? Author of *The Luck of Madonna 13*?"

He was tidy, well groomed, hard to place age-wise, but seemed normal in every respect. His most remarkable feature was a serious Men in Black suit. An IRS agent? I took the card, donned my readers, noted the stern black Copperplate Gothic typesetting, and read this: "Amalgamated Guilds of Fictional Personas, V. Michael Smith, Agent."

"It's a joke, right? Very cool though ... whoever put you up to it gets a double kudo. Remind me to write that organization into a blog post someday, Mr, ah, Smith. Seriously, though, what can I do for you?"

He held out a folded sheet of paper sealed with a genuine wax seal. Red. "The characters of your incomplete fictional work, 'The Last Nevergate Chronicles,' have filed a formal plea."

"Awesome. It just keeps getting better. I'm really glad I opened the door. So what happens next? Today's Friday the thirteenth, right? So somebody's hiding around the corner with an unbirthday cake with 13 uncandles?"

"The next step is up to you; I just serve the notices. Good day to you, Mr. Ellison."

That was it. Mr V. Michael Smith just walked past the defunct swing set, down the long driveway and through the open gate.

It wasn't a joke.

The single sheet of paper didn't have a lot on it. It said, "Dear Chronicler: We loved being in *The Luck of Madonna 13*, but we've been waiting to get back to work for more than a decade. Finish our damn story, ET!" The signatories were mostly human characters, but also included a ground squirrel, a chuckwalla, a Cametto-5 dragon, a wyvern, a dunnikin, a satellite brain in a variable geosynchronous orbit and a Nevergate. I recognized all the names, so at least I couldn't be faulted for totally forgetting them.

Truth is, those characters and the world they romped in had actually been on my mind a lot at that particular time, thanks to having spent the previous year creating a new and improved edition of the first volume in the the "Last Nevergate Chronicles," *The Luck of Madonna 13*. And in a couple weeks that edition and the first two books in a new YA scifi series — "Falling Sky" — would all be out into the world. And those things actually happened.

But my poor characters had a valid point: being frozen in time and space for a decade was bad authorial form on my part. Fortunately, I had a running start: 13,000 words of the second book, which was tentatively titled *The Mask of Madonna 13*. I'd written this chunk ten years earlier, but no reason it shouldn't work as a jumping off point. And the characters and the settings in time and space were freshly uploaded into my gray matter thanks to the new edition of *Luck*, so the timing was propitious. When I ramped up in late 2013 I figured I could probably bang out what I thought would be a trilogy in a couple years. But the characters had other ideas. So the couple years became six and the trilogy became a quartet ... and finally a quintet. And it's staying a quintet. Somewhere in the middle of all that I took a break to write a standalone first-person adventure thriller called *Treasure of the Holy Quincunx* with all new characters — including the redoubtable Travis One-Shoe — and a familiar setting: that singular IsoTown known as St Coriander and its environs, but a time setting some hundreds of years earlier. Some would say it's kind of a prequel. Check out my website for the latest news.

ETE
April 1, 2019
www.etellison.com

AN APOLOGY IN ADVANCE FOR FOOTNOTES

Footnotes are damnable things. They interrupt the steady drip of typographic grayness. They threaten the flow of narrative with their tiny, dark urgencies. Their mere presence has more raw nagging power than a forty-pound toothache. They're bad enough in nonfiction, but inexcusable in a work of imagination that's unfettered by documentational conventions. Or so I was encouraged to think until I recalled the often delightful and marvelous footnotes I've read in fiction authors like Ursula LeGuin, Jack Vance, Terry Pratchett, Susanna Clarke and, of course, J.R.R. Tolkien. The five volumes of the Last Nevergate Chronicles contain footnotes; bastard stepchildren who couldn't find a comfortable resting place in the narrative or *Genesis ... And Then Some*. So they sit patiently on their tight little shelves at the bottom of certain pages and wait for your eyes to fall on them. They know you'll probably pass them by, but still they hope. Perhaps they were unfairly encouraged by the philosopher George Santayana, who once wrote: "There are books in which the footnotes, or the comments scrawled by some reader's hand in the margin, are more interesting than the text. The world is one of these books."

ABOUT THE LAST NEVERGATE CHRONICLES

The Luck of Madonna 13 is the first book in THE LAST NEVERGATE CHRONICLES, a single story that continues through six volumes.

CONTENTS

PART THREE :: TWO CASTLES

There are seeds and there are Seeds. We of the Clans must never shirk the quirky poetry of truth. Thus we should smile when we tell that our own Seeds first took root in the strange soil of St Coriander. Great Seed is stronger than soil.

....

INGA LYRUS MARLENA DUNNIGAN
Genemaster, Dunnetix LLC

Part One

QUESTER

4

1 :: ONE GOLD BALL

THE BLOND GIRL was the only one left. She knew it and everybody else knew it, so she should just get it over with. But she had a bad case of the fidgets. At least she understood why: being last at anything was never fun. All that waiting.

"Hrrumf." A nearby throat cleared itself, a raspy, tart sound meant to remind her to get on with it.

A sigh slipped past her lips. This was way worse than being on court in a big game. There she was cool and confident. Here, as the last sixteener to make the final pull, she dithered: fidgeting, adjusting the ugly green Luckiest Day uniform and scanning the tally board for her name. Again.

The name Glendyl Fenderwell — her name — was almost exactly in the middle of the list, next to her total score for the bones, the jack-spinner and the heavyhandle. Number 53 out of the 106 sixteeners was pretty safe, she thought. With only one event to go, this sixteener had good reason to believe that she wouldn't be the one sent away on a death walk. Excellent position.

"We are waiting, Miss Fenderwell. You may now advance to the Grand Quincunx if you please."

The impatient voice belonged to one of two nearby cherub-cheeked, apple-shaped men wearing the traditional black robe of the Holy Quincunx Fatherhood. Father Cymbill, Glendyl guessed, from the snide, thin quality of his voice.

She let out the balky breath that had been cat-napping in her lungs. "Yes, Father Cymbill. I must have been daydreaming." Glendyl chalked her lame fib up to whatever was churning her stomach. Probably too much marvosauce on her munchburger.

Father Cymbill winked and whispered back. "Daydreaming on Luckiest Day? Well, if you say so. But had you been calculating your chances of becoming our next Quester, I should hardly be surprised. It appears you have nothing to worry about, however. So ...."

Glendyl blushed and turned away. Truth and embarrassment sent her nearly skipping to the final station. The waiting was finally over and she would just do it.

Her final challenge, St Coriander's Grand Quincunx, began its life as a mathematical sculpture, a nod to Sir Francis Galton, the 19th century scientist who invented it. But for the past 250 years the sculpture had been pressed into service each May 30th as a means of determining St Coriander's luckiest 16-year-old.

This deadly serious procedure had been mandated long ago by the mad sorcerer Exeter of Castle Ommergard. Originally, Exeter's reasoning was this: since he had been unable to locate the last Nevergate[1] himself, only an extremely lucky person could possibly accomplish what his surpassing genius had so far failed to achieve. Besides, his anger with the pacifist IsoTown was legendary. Having refused him aid in Ommergard's battle with the Clans Dunnigan and its wyvern allies, the townfolk had earned whatever punishments and inconveniences he might choose to inflict upon them. Such had been Exeter's view a quarter millennium ago.

Although Exeter hadn't personally visited St Coriander in centuries, the annual Luckiest Day competition continued, morphing into an exercise of pomp and catharsis at the paltry expense of a single human soul. Talk about bargains!

---

1 :: *Nevergates were mechanisms that made possible easy and instantaneous travel between a virtually infinite number of parallax universes. Given how important Nevergates became to humanity, the reader will not be surprised that wars were fought over their control.*

For Exeter, the event had become no more than an annual reminder of the transgressions of the town's long Elevated forebears. Would some St Clueless sixteener actually locate the last Nevergate? Not likely. Still, it amused him to monitor the ludicrous melodrama from the comfort of his own quarters high in the grounded flying castle in the otherwise empty valley just beyond the borders of the town.

The Grand Quincunx pulloff was the climax of Luckiest Day.

Glendyl gazed up at the 50-foot tall mechanical contraption. At the top was a transparent conical hopper containing 150 balls about the size of volleyballs: 149 were white, one was gold. At the bottom of the hopper was an outlet tube just large enough for a single ball. When the contestant pulled down the ornate gold activating lever, the balls dropped into the tube. At the bottom of the tube was the first of 120 pegs arranged in a triangle of fifteen rows. The balls would bounce down from peg to peg in a random path until they came to rest in one of sixteen tall bins that looked like carved stone columns from an ancient Roman temple, except for the fact that they were transparent.

Lights on the ends of the pegs blinked and made marimba-like musical tones each time a ball hit a peg. The effect was almost cheerful ... unless your 16-year-old life was at stake.

According to the laws of probability, most of the balls would end up in the middle bins. But the only thing that mattered to the sixteeners was where their gold ball ended up. If the gold ball landed in one of the two outside bins, the contestant would instantly be awarded 10,000 points, almost always enough to be declared Luckiest. Of course the odds of that single gold ball ending in an outside bin were extremely remote. In fact, it had never happened in 249 years.

Glendyl's genius friend Lizbeth Marble could probably calculate the odds in an instant, but Glendyl was an athlete, not a math geek. So she just crossed her fingers, made a silent prayer to the Lucky Madonna and waited for the signal to pull the lever.

A single ringing chime chopped through the jumbled noise of the sanctuary like a meat cleaver. As the echoes died away a too-lucky sixteener named Gordy MacIver squeezed his eyes shut and made his own urgent plea to the Lucky Madonna. He was the current points leader by a wide margin, so unless Glendyl's goldie did the impossible he was going to be the one to follow the 249 previous Luckiests through the gates and into the wilds, never to return. Glendyl reached up and grabbed the golden handle with both hands.

Then she hesitated. For no reason she could fathom, a zigzag of fear jolted her body. A premonition? More likely just nerves, like just before the start of an important game.

"That's quite enough drama, Miss Fenderwell," whispered Father Cymbill. "It has been a trying day for all of us. You are the last act, so to speak; just pull the lever and let's be done with it." Father Cymbill's whisper had lost its canned cheeriness, but Glendyl barely heard him. It was as if her body had been flash frozen by one of those malfunctioning FreezeWands.

Father Cymbill rolled his eyes heavenward, turned and smiled his most beatific smile to the assembled sixteeners. "Miss Fenderwell has asked that we all take a few moments to contemplate the object of our Questings," he lied. "Since you are all well-educated Eastac or Westac students, I trust that you can recite the particulars of the two so-called Nevergate Wars and the Dunnigan Retreat during which all Nevergates on the planet simultaneously disappeared. You may not know that the Fatherhood has been entrusted with certain secrets, and perhaps ...."

KA-CHUNG! A sound much like an ancient cash register rang through the sanctuary for the 106th time that day, interrupting Father Cymbill's impromptu speech. Glendyl's arms had unfrozen themselves at exactly that instant and yanked the handle down with every erg of energy at her disposal.

The reaction to the KA-CHUNG was remarkable. It was as if invisible strings tilted every eyeball in the room up toward the hopper. Every eyeball except the two in Glendyl Fenderwell's eyesockets. She couldn't bear to watch.

One by one the balls entered the tube. One by one they bounced off one peg and then another and then another. As though being manipulated by a hidden Master of Melodrama, the gold ball was the very last to enter the tube this time around. It seemed determined to take the leftmost trajectory with every peg it hit, even after a series of dramatic moments where it hung on the peg and wobbled toward the right.

When Glendyl's goldie finally fell into the leftmost bin, Gordy MacIver had to bite his tongue to keep from bellowing something enthusiastically rude. The Lucky Madonna had answered his prayer; almost impossibly, Glendyl Fenderwell had become Luckiest. Just like that.

From the gilt-faced Music Box high in the north wall, Musicmaster Jonas Mapplethorpe let fly the bombastic first organ notes of "As Luck Will Have It," the traditional 'victory' fanfare. At the same instant fountains of green sparks spouted from the tops of the thirteen massive chandeliers.

Before the sparks had faded, a troupe of thirteen six-foot-tall white-furred rabbit feet emerged from around the walls to converge on the central portion of the sanctuary. Then they began a lively dance: so much had been standard Luckiest Day tradition for more than a century.

What was different about Reveta Bunsavver's somewhat ironic interpretation was that the huge feet appeared to be freshly and messily severed. Endless gobbets of blood spewed from the ragged ends while they cavorted like a troupe of blind zombies, a comic ballet of bumbling pratfalls. The crowd held up their hands to ward off the bloody rain, but it evaporated in pink poofs before it landed. Applause was both instantaneous and thunderous. The "Dance of the Bloody Symbols" would earn a mark in the record books, right alongside Glendyl's recordbreaking encounter with the Grand Quincunx.

Glendyl barely noticed the dancing symbols. And she barely noticed as Father Cymbill firmly grasped her elbow and escorted her to the dais. She stood straight but empty while Father-Mayor Gullwimple presented the 250th Luckiest to all of St Coriander. His animated speech to the local audience of sixteeners — and by holo to virtually all of St Coriander — was one of his more bombastic performances.

For a fact, all but three people in St Coriander cheered, or at least breathed a sigh of relief. The two who were Glendyl's parents lapsed into pungent expressions of grief. The third, a wooden faced Glendyl, dutifully repeated the Quester Pledge and made the other expected responses, blinking back all but a faint sheen of tears.

"Well done, Miss Fenderwell," whispered the Father-Mayor when the formalities were over. "No one expects a Luckiest to be a bastion of good cheer, after all. Am I correct, Father Cymbill?"

"Indeed," agreed Father Cymbill. "Fortunately, the reception will give our new Quester Designate a chance to relax." He turned and gave Glendyl a sympathetic look that might even have been genuine. "Champagne and the good company of your friends will be a fine tonic for your wounded spirits ... you can count on that. But first, let us make a stately exit."

The pair of portly priests escorted the Quester Designate out of the sanctuary to Mapplethorpe's solemn rendition of "Quest for Glory," the customary recessional. Glendyl put on her best face and began to look forward to the champagne.

Sometimes endings are also beginnings. Glendyl had heard that somewhere, but she knew that not even champagne would make her believe that tonight was the beginning of anything good. All because of one gold ball.

2 :: AN INTERVENTION

FOUR GLASSES of green champagne helped Glendyl survive the reception. She sat primly on the special Luckiest chair, the ceremonial Clover Crown resting on her head at a not-very-jaunty angle. Did she feel stupid? She did.

After her second glass of bubbly she distracted herself by imagining that she could feel the anguish of her 249 predecessors rising up through the seat and armrests. Like her, they had all believed that at noon on the next day they would be lost. And they had been right: none had ever returned. Would she encounter any of their bones before she added her own to Heroes Trail? Such thoughts curdled her mood beyond the help of even the champagne.

All 105 other sixteeners came up to her and did their best to cheer her up. They cajoled, encouraged, told jokes, made fun of the jolly fat men of the Fatherhood and the less jolly teachers at the two academies. They also lauded her prowess on the bangerball court and reprised old victories. They even brought her plates of her favorite goodies. Thirteen boys asked her to dance, but she declined all offers.

The most depressing part of the reception was the sheer relief she saw in all the well-meaning eyes: they had all escaped her fate. Would she have felt the same way? Probably, she admitted. But that was one revelation too many. From that point on, all she could do was wish for the night to be over.

At a quarter to twelve, Father-Mayor Gullwimple sent the last of the revelers to their tidy little homes in their tidy little villages.

"It's time for you to retrieve your QPack, Miss Fenderwell," he said with the bare minimum of heartiness. Even through her champagne fog Glendyl could see that the familiar florid face looked tired. A pang of sympathy found its way to her face, softening it for a moment.

"QPack?" she mumbled.

"Your Quest companion, my dear. Come, you'll see."

Father Cymbill held up a hand. "First, the Clover Crown if you please, Miss Fenderwell."

Glendyl was more than happy to be rid of it. She was certain it looked stupid, for one thing. And it reminded her of all those dead Questers.

The two Fathers escorted her out of the empty reception hall, down a slidewell and along a corridor to the Central Fabrax. It was a happy-sad moment: she had retrieved all manner of freshly fabbed goods from this place during her life in St Coriander. Usually she came with her mother, but for the last few years she'd been allowed to work it by herself. The fabrax was almost like an old friend: she would miss it, but she'd be happy to visit it this last time.

The Father-Mayor interrupted her reverie in time to stop the impending tears in their tracks. "The Librarian has made the necessary arrangements; all we need to do now is wait for the output chamber door to open. Well, and you need to use the Verifier, of course."

He inspected the timepatch on his pudgy left wrist. "It will open in three minutes and 47 seconds to be exact."

She walked to the output chamber door and placed her palm on the Verifier. This fabrax spoke in a congenial female voice, "Hello, Glendyl. Did you like that black sheath I fabbed for you? I'm sure you looked absolutely stunning." Sandy's female-ish simutronic image winked at her.

"Uh, I didn't actually get to wear it, Sandy. It was going to be for a team party next week and, uh, I, uh ..."

"Say no more. I understand: you're going on an adventure in the Counterindicated Zone. I've often wondered what an adventure might be like."

There was a perfectly believable wistful quality to the voice. An adventure? Glendyl hadn't yet been able to think of being banished from everything she knew and loved as an adventure.

"I trust you will find your new QPack to be helpful. I have studied its specifications and I can tell you that the designs have continued to improve. This model might be the best ever. Enjoy your Quest, Glendyl, and may the luck of Madonna 13 be with you."

These words from an SI[2] held more unadorned sincerity than anything she had heard from a human in a month. As the huge door slid open, the Quester Designate plopped to the floor and lapsed into a fit of tears.

It was ten minutes before Glendyl's sobs faded away. The two Fathers stayed some distance away, conversing in low tones and only occasionally looking over at their charge. Only when she walked to the open door and stooped down to inspect the object revealed there did their full attention return to her.

Glendyl was a veteran of many backpacks, but this was different. It had the same general shape, but she somehow knew there was much more here than a container for things. At first glance the strangest thing about it was that it was encased in a thick transparent membrane with pulsing electric blue letters that read, "To be opened by Quester Designate Glendyl Fenderwell ONLY. Violators will experience UNPLEASANT CONSEQUENCES." In much smaller letters were the words, "This QPack provided courtesy of Exeter's Mt Faunibeune Services."

---

2 :: *The synthetic intelligence (SI) that liked to call itself Sandy was actually a semi-independent module of the Librarian, a quasibiotic, self-aware Dunnetix Apex 4.2.1. A gift from the Clans Dunnigan, it was state of the art when activated in 2278 and included a humor option that less jovial members of the Fatherhood frequently found objectionable on the grounds that mere intelligent machines should not possess qualities that they did not.*

Glendyl blinked. Exeter? Exeter the Mad Sorcerer? She was starting to catalog all the horrible things she'd heard about Exeter when the QPack spoke, its voice an androgynous tenor. "It would be very nice if you could pull the tab at the top and unseal my protective membrane. This will also allow me to verify that you are, in fact, Glendyl Fenderwell, the Quester Designate. Premature self-destruction is not exactly my intended purpose in life ... if you get my meaning. If I need to be more explicit for you, UNPLEASANT CONSEQUENCES is a euphemism for INSTANT DEATH FOR BOTH OF US. I think we're both a little too young for that. So please ..."

"All right, all right, all right." Glendyl pulled the tab and peeled away the clear membrane. "Are you happy now, QPack?"

"Why yes. Nice to meet you, too. I see you have a couple chubby chaperones. Or are those bullocks in black dresses? Or pink BlusterBalls on black balloons? Well, Glendyl Fenderwell, whatever they are, you won't be needing *them* anymore. Perhaps we can go someplace private where we can get to know each other."

Father-Mayor Gullwimple scowled, irked by the insults of this annoying little Exeter-thing and also by the fact that he was helpless to retaliate. He cleared his throat.

"I see we have, ah, outstayed our welcome here. And for a fact, it is time that we should all be on our way. As a final note, I should mention that many Quester Designates in past years have found it a comfort to stop at a prayer chamber on their way home. It is widely thought that the Lucky Madonna is particularly receptive to entreaties from Luckiests. A transpsychic bond perhaps. Come, we will escort you to the Grand Gallery, then take our leave.

• • • • •

Chapel 13 was one of sixty-five identical prayer chambers within St Coriander's Holy Quincunx. Glendyl balked before entering. She'd only been in a prayer chamber a handful of times: once or twice before an important bangerball game, once or twice before an important date. But this time was different; this time she would be praying for her life. Something about that didn't feel right. What was the word? Hypocritical, that was it.

Glendyl set the QPack just inside the door, donned the helmet and made the standard entreaties. All too soon her time was up. As she removed the helmet, a surge of anger boiled up in her. Why did she have to get impossibly lucky at exactly the wrong time? As quickly as it flared, her anger faded: luck was luck and that was that. Everybody in St Coriander knew that: luck was the town's very reason for existence.

In the undulating light of the chapel, reflections from the shimmering waterwall danced on the shapely contours of the nude statue. Glendyl's eyes flicked past the raised sword in the right hand to the left hand with its customary temptation: a handful of huge emeralds, cut and polished and glittering with a dangerous taunt.

Would the legendary luck of Original Madonna's thirteenth clone somehow be with her on her Quest, unlike all the other Luckiests?

Not likely, she knew. But still she studied the statue for a sign. Was that a conspiratorial wink? The supportive flicker of a smile? An upper lip curled slightly in derision? Glendyl bit her own lip and grumbled to herself. Phantoms. Figments. Tricks of light. She rose to her feet, made the ritual "dice roll" gesture, turned and walked toward the door. Dirge-like strains of "Only the Lucky" rose up like a slowly filling bathtub.

She was reaching for the QPack when a tiny clinking sound from behind her penetrated the ponderous music. She turned, an electric strangeness rippling up her spine. Something was different. But what?

A green sparkle on the dull feltstone caught her eye. One of the emeralds had fallen from Lucky Madonna's immovable metal palm. How could that happen?

Glendyl hesitated, her face twitching with conflicting emotions. Her eyes flicked from side to side as she walked on guilty tiptoes back to the altar and scooped up the vagrant jewel. The emerald felt warm, almost hot. She frowned. Best to put it back where it belonged; this

15

could be some kind of worthiness test. Or something.

Before she could act, the emerald split open on her palm, clam-shell-like.

Inside one half was a tiny green capsule.

Without waiting for instructions from her brain, her fingers popped the capsule into her mouth. Wanting to get in on the fun, her throat gulped it down without even waiting for a slug of water. Then the jewel snapped back together and sat in her palm, almost daring her to pocket it.

With dreamlike motions she placed it back on the Lucky Madonna's palm, scooped up the QPack and left the chapel. Seconds later all memory of the incident melted from her mind.

The Grand Gallery was still occupied by late night questioners seeking advice from the rows of one-armed Sages. She threaded her way past glassy-eyed patrons, nodded here and there to familiar faces, trying to ignore the rows of symbols coming to rest in the Sages' answerpanels. Whatever luck these people were having, it wouldn't get them banished forever.

Now angry again, Glendyl jogged through the southeast tube under the Moat and into a crisp late spring evening, the very last St Coriander evening of her life.

Ten minutes later she opened the front door of her family's tidy ranch-style home on Turtledove Way in East Village. She tiptoed through the foyer, down the hall and into her room, just barely noticing the banner hanging across the hall that read, "We're with you, Glenny! All the way!"

Exhausted, Glendyl flopped on her bed and fell asleep without even undressing.

• • • • •

Father-Mayor Gullwimple was working late; the legal necessities and other preparations for this year's Quest could not be postponed. It was also a time to sit back in his huge chair, look out at the stars and reflect on the Luckiest Situation, as he called it.

These musings typically ended with an acknowledgment of the obvious: luck, even the singular luck of a Luckiest, was of little use. In modern St Coriander, luck did not bring wealth, long life, victory over obstacles or any of its other traditional outcomes. And it had certainly not helped any of the 249 previous Questers survive their Quests and win the objective. At this point in his musings, Father-Mayor Gullwimple typically abandoned the topic and continued with the formalities.

Occasionally, there was a further consideration. In the case of Glendyl Fenderwell, it was to admit that he was less concerned with the loss of one more Luckiest sixteener than with the loss of a lively little tart. Far better to send boys away to wherever in the Counterindicated Zone they met their dooms. Father-Mayor Gullwimple had always liked athletic females, part of the reason he had, over his very long lifetime, been an enthusiastic fan of bangerball. Watching taut young ladies leaping and bounding and diving had long been a favorite recreation.

Musing a little longer, he concluded that such pulchritude should not, in good conscience, be wasted. So perhaps Glendyl's charms need not entirely go to waste. Not immediately, at least. Perhaps in this case an intervention might be in order.

17

18

....
3 :: THE SECOND TIME

THE MORNING OF Glendyl's Quest broke open like an egg: first a crack, then a splat. The crack was a bolt of lightning that seemed to hang forever in her vision. The splat was just the first of a thousand raindrops the size of golf balls plopping against her bedroom window. Perfect weather for a death walk.

Glendyl sat up in bed, coaxed the crud out of her eyes with a practiced fingernail and grabbed her slate off the nightstand. What might the portents say this morning? Septriq[3] would surely tell her. In preparation, she closed her eyes and smoothed out the ripples in her mind. When she opened them again, Oraya — currently her favorite oracle — had appeared in the central septagon hovering above the domat.

"Well, good morning, Oraya," she whispered. "Have you heard the news that we're going on an adventure?"

The elf-like green face greeted her with a nod, a wink and a sly smile. Then she gestured for Glendyl to bend her ear down for a whispered comment. This was odd, but Glendyl complied: oracles are wise ... and they know things. When she raised her head again,

---

3 :: *Septriq is still widely consulted as a "divinatory" in St Coriander, particularly by females, who consult oracular personas and use the chance mode to "gauge the portents." An ancient slatetext called* The Secret Oracle *is the standard guide to interpretation. Males are typically more attracted to exploring for the deeply hidden "secrets," which may or may not be more myth and rumor than fact.*

Oraya's image was gone, but her cryptic counsel echoed in Glendyl's brain long afterward. There was a good reason Oraya hadn't wanted the QPack to hear what she'd whispered.

Glendyl expected little encouragement from Septriq on this particular day, but habit was habit. The seven portals now pulsed a bloody red, the standard idle display. With a deft move, she flicked the tot-wheel to launch the baseline pass. The seven pie-shaped portals flickered through the seven colors in random sequence until the counter reached 777, the number of readiness.

The colors in the portals came to rest clockwise from lightest (yellow) to darkest (black), with black resting in septriq. It was an unusual lay: Glendyl could not recall the book's interpretation and hesitated to inquire; a wriggly feeling in her stomach suggested it might be better not to know.

More awake now, she continued: seven spins to go. A few moments later she was gawking at a domat pierced by seven lightless black windows, each tagged with a septriq notation.

Glendyl's stomach knotted: something nearly impossible had just occurred. As she wondered what it might mean, the slate's image began to change. The dome dissolved in a hypnotic whirlpool of interlaced colored spirals that pulled her awareness down into it. A powerful un-sound penetrated some part of her auditory nerve; vision wavered and her entire body shook as if afflicted by a deep chill. Then her awareness went elsewhere, to be called back some time later by a double knock on her bedroom door.

"Glenny-Honey. Time to get up. I'm leaving your favorite breakfast by the door; you'll need your energy today." Polisandra Fenderwell's brittle cheeriness was hardly cheering. Glendyl shook her head and rolled out of bed, glancing at the slate's now empty screen.

Outside the door was a plate with a warmcap. Glendyl smiled, sat on the carpet and wolfed down two piping hot, fresh from the MenuMaster hamanegg pastries basted in marvosauce. Yum!

Before she could get into the shower, there was another interruption: her QPack's skin began pulsing alternating red and green lights. This obnoxious thing was supposed to be her companion? Ridiculous!

For a moment she glared at it hoping it would just disappear.

"Pack me, Glenny-Honey," it said in a perfect replica of her mother's voice. "There'll be more room if you remove your official Quester jumpsuit and put it on first. And be sure to check the pockets ... oh, and don't forget extra underwear. Big day, today, Glenny-Honey." Then it snickered and was silent.

21

"Stop *doing* that!" hissed Glendyl, wishing that she knew where its eyes were so she could glare at it, eyeball to eyeball. What she really wanted to do was kick it, but the nasty thing would probably retaliate somehow. Maybe she should just pile dirty clothes on it.

A short time later she had packed, showered and slipped into the Quester jumpsuit. She cocked her head and studied her image in the mirror. The jumpsuit wasn't at all baggy like she'd thought it would be. Actually, it fit her perfectly: snug, but not uncomfortably snug. The only thing she didn't like was the color: colors, actually. They were sort of blurry and shifty. Right now they were mottled variations of the sunny ocher of her room, a color her mother had picked and that Glendyl detested.

She moved to the window to see if the rain had stopped yet. It hadn't, but now the reflection of her jumpsuit was a blurry melange of cloudy grays. Interesting.

On a whim, she slipped on the QPack, turned around and studied her new traveling outfit from all angles. It *did* make her look kind of adventurous. She ruffled her muff of straw-colored hair and struck a series of heroic poses.

"Well don't *we* look like just the perfect pair of adventurers?" purred the QPack in the exact voice of Sandy, the Central Fabrax SI. Half-embarrassed, Glendyl just grunted. At least it wasn't her mother's voice this time.

Another double knock on the door. "Glenny-Honey, are you ready yet? Father-Mayor Gullwimple is here and we don't want to keep him waiting."

Glendyl half-expected the QPack to say something snide, but it kept silent.

The apple-shaped Father-Mayor made a small bow as Glendyl walked straight and tall into the living room. "Good morning, Miss Fenderwell. I see that you have prepared yourself. Most excellent."

Without further pleasantries he delivered his standard Quester speech, then handed out three copies of the Liability Papers for signature by Glendyl and her parents.

Next, the Father-Mayor removed a sealed envelope from somewhere within his voluminous black garment and discreetly handed it to Glendyl's father. "For your family, Bentley," he whispered. "Just in case." It was a Bereavement Voucher redeemable for two thousand fabrax credits at the Holy Quincunx Business Office should Glendyl fail to return to St Coriander with the Nevergate Key after three months. Glendyl watched the transfer out of the corner of her eye but pretended not to notice.

Formalities completed, Father-Mayor G donned a ceremonial smile, muttered the customary prayer to Lucky Madonna and departed for the gate on one of the Fatherhood's hyper-duty mopeds.

Remnants of lumpy gray cumulus had waddled across to the western sky; overhead and east was now clear and bright. Glendyl and her parents waited silently on the edge of the greenway for the community carriage.

As was the custom, it arrived with seven Witnesses — seven of the Quester's best friends — already on board. The carriage made its way along St Orwell Loop and Outbound Road, the only sound being the gentle whir of soft tires on the hardgrass. In accordance with the New Rules, the Witnesses must witness in silence until the Quester had passed through the gate.

One of Glendyl's silent friends, Lizbeth Marble, was almost always silent anyway. Tall, gangly, homely, brainy and quirkily unpredictable, her occasional volcanic outbursts had earned Lizbeth a reputation as a person who spoke her mind ... or even all ten of them. At the moment, Lizbeth's silence hid a tight-lipped grief. Glendyl, that sweet shining star of St Coriander, would be lost to them all forever. Worse, Lizbeth would lose her only real friend, a personal catastrophe of incalculable proportions.

About midway up Outbound Road, just past the Saw Creek Trail turnoff, the driver slowed and stopped. To the left was the Lucky Madonna Memorial Plaza. In keeping with tradition, all the passengers bowed their heads and executed a dice roll in the direction of the 50-foot tall bronze sculpture on top of the star-shaped structure in the center of the plaza. Its arms reached out in a welcoming gesture that somehow felt like an invitation ... which of course was silly.

Glendyl studied the statue's face and gave her own dice-roll a little extra oomph ... plus that special wrist spin she used when spiking a bangerball. Probably wouldn't help her Quest, but it couldn't hurt either.

As the carriage began rolling again, Glendyl gave that face one final gaze. Did the Lucky Madonna wink at her? It sure seemed like it, but of course it couldn't have.

The arched portal of Dunnigans Gate was the only known link between St Coriander and the outside world. Standing sixty feet wide and thirty feet at its apex, the gate opened only once each year, so infrequently as to seem superfluous to such residents who gave the matter a moment's thought.

The smooth black outward-swinging doors appeared almost new, despite their nearly three centuries of age. Framing the gate were two hulking square webcrete columns. Unlike the gates themselves, these were darkened by weather and encrusted with multicolored lichens and mosses.

To either side of the portal extended the Township Fence, the high, tangled hedge of impenetrable thornmesh that delineated the township's eight-mile perimeter. This lethal barrier effectively sealed St Coriander off from the outside world as required by Exeter's New Rules. It had worked: the tiny, self-sufficient IsoTown's five square miles had been its own little world for two and a half centuries: except for the annual Luckiests, nobody departed or entered.

23

Beyond Dunnigans Gate was Heroes Trail: this much was known. It led into the Counterindicated Zone, but where, exactly, was only wild conjecture, although when the gate was open, a rectangular waysign could be seen. It was by now quite familiar to Father-Mayor Gullwimple, who had for many decades been charged with the duty of opening Dunnigans Gate each year on May 31st.

The waysign said, "Humbecker Ford 1.8 miles." Nothing more. It was always freshly painted with white letters on a blue field. Along the bottom, in very small letters if anyone troubled to read them, were the words "Waysign provided courtesy of Exeter's Mt Faunibeune Services."

To Father-Mayor Gullwimple, this was another annoying reminder that Exeter was still a force to be reckoned with and that he had not forgotten St Coriander over the centuries. But it hardly mattered. He shrugged and triggered the actuators with his lockpatch. The massive gates swung outward to reveal an unremarkable, well-tended path of packed red earth bordered on both sides by the tall dark mass of clotted trees that was the Deadly Forest.

Glendyl squared her shoulders, inhaled her last breath of St Coriander air and passed through the gate onto Heroes Trail. She walked straight ahead, making a point of not looking at the waysign as she strode past. Behind her, the assembled Witnesses were now able to voice their final words of encouragement.

Lizbeth Marble wanted to say something, but words abandoned her. So she just stood silent and looked forlorn enough for the whole group.

Glendyl squelched the urge to turn and wave; she wasn't about to let them see the tears brimming at the corners of her eyes, or the angry flush that had ridden up her face. So she bit her lip, picked up her pace just a little and counted her strides, a lifelong unconscious habit.

As the echoes of Mrs Fenderwell's caution to watch out for sailbirds faded, the doors swung shut, the lock reactivated and Glendyl was lost from view. Father-Mayor Gullwimple bade the group a solemn farewell, mounted his moped and pedaled eastward along a little used trail that would take him to the Fatherhood's private Revelation Retreat.

A hundred yards into the Deadly Forest Glendyl encountered her first decision point: an intersection. A narrow road crossed the trail at right angles. Unlike Heroes Trail, it appeared to have been paved at one time but was now dotted with potholes, weeds and underbrush as far as she could see in either direction. Since this intersection was unmarked by any waysigns, she ignored the options to turn left or right and proceeded straight ahead. Still, she wondered for a while where in the Counterindicated Zone they led.

The morning storm had dotted the trail with random pockets of ruddy water, but the sky remained clear and the sun gave the midday air a limpid quality that was almost cheery. Glendyl found it anything *but* cheery. She was too busy feeling alone, abandoned and surrounded by invisible dangers. Would she have felt better knowing that inside her body, invisible genetocules from the green capsule were busy at the tasks they had been designed for nearly three centuries earlier? Probably not. She walked on and tried to ignore her fears.

The Quester was still half a mile shy of Humbecker Ford when Dunnigans Gate swung open for the second time that day. A figure passed through, the gate closed.

25

26

4 :: PIECE OF CAKE

THE NOISE CREPT into Glendyl's awareness with the stealth of a puma stalking prey. Quester 250 sensed it as a vague, deep-throated murmur coming from somewhere up ahead. Nothing seemed different about the forest and nothing in her experience provided a clue as to what the sound might be, so she stopped to listen. After a few moments she started forward again, but at a cautious walk-stop-listen-walk-stop-listen rhythm. The noise grew louder as she moved up the trail. Menacing, she thought, her heart pounding, her nerves on edge.

The next two minutes seemed to last forever. As Glendyl emerged from the shelter of thick forest, the murmur found its full voice and became a chaotic roar. She found herself on a low bluff overlooking a frothy, fast-flowing body of water. The noise was now explained; Glendyl sucked in a deep breath of relief. Thirty or forty feet below was a roiling rapids; plumes of spray shot into the air as an unnamed river rode hard over a bed of submerged boulders and disappeared around a bend. She stood captivated by her first experience of a river, wild or otherwise.

Across the torrent the terrain became mountainous and thickly forested, but she ignored this distant scene. Here and now the river dominated her senses and for the moment seemed to have rooted her feet to the soil. After a time her river awe faded enough that she was able to spot a narrow path along the rim of the bluff. At the very edge of the bluff was a guardrail made of silvery metal posts and silvery metal cables.

To her right was another path and a sign. Like the sign at Dunnigans Gate it was freshly painted. It said, "Humbecker Ford 400 Yards." A choice: left or right? A perverse curiosity sprang up and demanded that she follow the path to the left, the one with no sign.

The path threaded its way between forest and precipice for perhaps fifty yards before ending in a small clearing. Here the river had narrowed to become a churning mass of angry turbulence. Its wild energy seemed almost malevolent, and she shrank back from the cliff to the relative comfort of the clearing.

A circular mosaic about twenty feet in diameter dominated the scene. It was inlaid with bronze, pewter and umber colored tiles set in a complex but familiar pattern: the Dunnigan clanmark. At the center of the circle was a tapered silvery cylinder mounted by an invisible joint to a thick post made of the same silvery metal as the guardrail posts. Glendyl approached it cautiously. A telescope? Engraved into the cylinder was this inscription: "Rio Brazos Narrows." So the river now had a name. This bit of new information gave Glendyl comfort; her list of unknowns was diminished by one.

The telescope rewarded her with a magnified view of the opposite bank. A snippet of glowing text superimposed itself on the scene: "Dunnigan Reserve – Lower Brazos Sector." The dense forest she saw now seemed to symbolize the impenetrable nature of this stupid Quest. Irritated, she swung the telescope to her right and the massed trees gave way to masses of dark rock. The indicator now displayed the words "Dunnigan Reserve – Brazos Cliffs Sector." This monstrous wall of rock was far more daunting than any natural feature visible from St Coriander. Was Mt Funnybone up there somewhere? Would Heroes Trail take her into those daunting gray cliffs?

Glendyl's nerves began to fray around the edges and the bones of her legs suddenly felt like limp noodles. She steadied herself against the cool, smooth metal of the telescope. Gradually the moment passed and her leg bones began to act like bones again. A small conclusion presented itself, this well-preserved Dunnigan artifact was a dead end. Her future — such as it might be — was elsewhere.

Resolve renewed, she returned along the narrow path and followed the sign toward Humbecker Ford, keeping her eyes away from the daunting Brazos Cliffs that were sometimes visible in the bluish haze above the treetops. The trail traced the edge of the bluff, then down a narrow gully containing a small creek that emptied itself into the Rio Brazos with cheery abandon. The trail resumed on the other side of the creek but soon ended at the base of another bluff. And another sign. Unlike the earlier signs this was driven through a pile of rusted metal trapped by a trio of boulders and half-buried in the rubble at the foot of the bluff. And this sign didn't point anywhere. It said only: "Humbecker Ford."

Glendyl leaped across the creek and contemplated the mashed, bashed, smashed and twisted wreckage impaled by the sign. She recognized it for what it once had been: an automobile. A real automobile and ancient beyond belief. A memory from somewhere clicked into place and Glendyl rolled her eyes. A Ford? Or a ford? Was this somebody's idea of a joke? Was it Exeter's idea of a joke? She shook her head, made an ambiguous hand gesture and turned her attention to the river.

Wider and calmer here, it still flowed fast enough to make Glendyl nervous. Whether the boulders that jutted above the surface at fairly regular intervals had been placed by nature, by man or by machine, Glendyl could not say. All she knew for certain was that those boulders had to be Humbecker Ford. The other Humbecker Ford. Geez Louise, she almost said aloud.

She counted eighteen more-or-less flat-topped boulders forming a dotted line from one bank to the other. Was she really supposed to leap from rock to rock? There didn't appear to be any other way to get across; she had no wings and wading was out of the question.

Glendyl knelt at the edge of the river near the first boulder, watching sunlight on the crystalline water spin a web of sparkles on its surface. After an entranced moment, the thought occurred to

29

her that she had never just watched sunlight on water. Not in sixteen years. Maybe there were things to be learned on this Quest that would surprise and delight her.

Scooping up a handful of water she tasted it: very cold, very fresh tasting. Somehow this little episode with bright water dulled her fear of crossing on the stones and brightened her mood. She stood again, made a short leap and scrambled up the first boulder.

Its top was about four feet above the river, which here was a shallow and lazy eddy. There was a gap of only about three feet between this and the next boulder; Glendyl's feet had stepped across almost before her brain realized what they were up to. She couldn't restrain a grin: one down. A minute later she had crossed, not appreciably wetter than when she started. She looked back across Humbecker Ford to the other Humbecker Ford and grinned again. "Piece of cake," she mumbled, hoping for all of a silly second that the rest of her Quest would go as smoothly.

5 :: THUDDING FOOTFALLS

"NICE JOB, Glenny-Honey," blurted the QPack, breaking its long silence. "According to my sensors you're right on track. But you may not want to loiter here."

"Geez Louise! You startled me. What do you mean by 'right on track'? And for your information, I'm not 'loitering;' I'm just catching my breath."

"No need to get huffy, Glenny-Honey."

There was that irritating snideness again. "I just asked a perfectly logical question. And please don't call me Glenny-Honey. And don't use my mother's voice, either."

"My, my, my; as if huffiness weren't enough, now we get fussiness too. Why did I have to get stuck with an oversensitive, ungrateful Quester?" The QPack had spoken in a perfect replica of Father-Mayor Gullwimple's rounded baritone, except with the Whine knob turned to maximum.

"Oh … poor little abused QPack," murmured Glendyl, barely containing a chortle at hearing the over-hearty voice of Father G booming from behind her back. "Okay. Back to business. What's next?"

"I'm just the lowly QPack: you're the Quester. Figure it out yourself!" The QPack snapped off the words.

"Now who's touchy and oversensitive? Okay, forget I asked."

The QPack remained silent.

Glendyl scanned the area and located the next blue sign. It said only "Heroes Trail" and pointed toward a steep rocky incline that disappeared into the forest. Taking a last, ambivalent look at the Rio Brazos, Glendyl made her way up the trail and was soon surrounded again by the tall boles and moist aromas of tightly packed conifers.

Walking into the unknown was a disconcerting experience at best; a map right now would be better than a thick slab of juicy likesteak. But St Coriander had no maps; Exeter's voracious datarats had purged every text and visual reference to local geography. And that all had happened centuries ago. Since then a fifty-mile radius around St Coriander's town boundary was blank: the Counterindicated Zone. She considered asking the QPack for advice, but decided against it: too snotty. And probably untrustworthy, as well, if she had correctly understood the cryptic whisper from her personal oracle this morning.

The trail now snaked through a forest thick with ferns and dotted with dense groves of slender, white barked aspens, their roundish leaves quaking with a gentle palsy in the afternoon breeze. Her first decision point was a fork marked by two blue arrow signs on an ever-metal post. Neither bore any text: they were just dumb blue arrows. One pointed in the direction of a broad path leading downward; the other toward a rougher track taking a much steeper upward course. Believing that Mt Funnybone could only be upward, Glendyl hesitated only a few seconds before making her choice. Eleven minutes later she would change her mind.

After a steep climb, the trail descended into a little treeless canyon, then ended. Well, not exactly ended, but it ceased to be a visible trail. Glendyl found herself facing a flinty forest of eroded stone spires and upthrusts. Like those things in pix of caves she'd seen: stalag-somethings. Only busted off at the tops. Dark, narrow spaces separated the spires, some wide enough for her to navigate, some not. This certainly didn't look like the trail to anywhere. Still, she felt the need to explore and soon found it to be a sort of maze, with twisty, shadowy passageways intersecting and reintersecting at frequent intervals.

To her right was an even narrower opening between the cliff wall and a tall ripple of maze-stone, just barely wide enough for her to squeeze through. Peering past the opening, she was surprised to see what looked like a trail. Not wide, but wide enough and with a sandy reddish floor. A possibility. But maybe this wasn't the right direction. Maybe she'd taken the wrong fork altogether. Beset by doubts, she scratched her head, spun two quick 360s and decided: back through the crack.

33

She hiked double-time to the fork with the useless blue pointers and headed downhill on the wide and sunny path. This definitely felt more like what Heroes Trail should be. Her confidence ballooned to its greatest diameter since she had passed through the Dunnigans Gate.

Then burst. Rounding a bend she came face to face with none other than Father-Mayor Gullwimple. Seated upon his elephantine rump, he didn't seem at all surprised to see her. "Well then, Glendyl Fenderwell: perhaps you could interrupt your Quest momentarily and help me up. I seem to have ... ah ... twisted my ankle."

Father-Mayor Gullwimple's red-cheeked face sat like a gigantic pink tomato on an oblate rumple of black cloth. He was breathing heavily and his girth took up most of the trail. Glendyl was speechless.

"Come now, girl. Certainly you can control your surprise for a wee moment and lend me one of those strong shoulders of yours. I'll satisfy your curiosity momentarily."

Finding herself feeling sorry for this familiar face, a face that had enthusiastically cheered her bangerball accomplishments, Glendyl helped the Father-Mayor to his feet. He stood unsteadily, leaning his bulk against the uphill rock face and wincing in apparent pain as he tested the damaged ankle. "Thank you my dear. You are so strong and nimble. I always loved watching you play, you know. Your light-sense was truly phenomenal. Sorry, I suppose that's not particularly germane to our, ah, current situation."

Father-Mayor Gullwimple took a deep breath that puffed out his girth even more than usual. "So then. It was indeed fortunate you happened by. And not just to assist me in my momentary misfortune. I actually came here to assist *you*. At great risk, I might add. You must find the Key. You are the one. I had almost given up hope of finding you ... and giving you this."

The priest had removed an object from the folds of his robes and held it out. "Take it. You're a bright girl. You'll see what I mean."

34

Glendyl took a thin paper cylinder from Father G's soft, plump fingertips, grazing them slightly in the process.

"Unroll it. You'll see. You'll be the long awaited heroine. Unroll it." Father-Mayor Gullwimple's voice shook with barely contained excitement and ... something else. Clearly his pain had been forgotten.

Glendyl unrolled a tube of yellowed material something like parchment. It acted like a coil of yellow spring steel, difficult to keep unrolled. And the surface felt not just rough-textured, but grainy to her fingers, as though it had been dusted with a coarse powder of some sort. Or maybe it was just old and dusty. Or maybe it was so old it was disintegrating? Whatever it was, the material exuded a strong, unfamiliar aroma. Had she possessed a proper word, she might have used the term "musky."

She squinted at the scrap of stuff; it had lines and symbols and notations and might very well be a map, but it also had something written on it. Could he be offering her a map to the Last Nevergate? Her mind swirled and strange feelings spun through her body in a wild vortex. She forced her mind to focus on the tiny writing. Holding it up to catch the full sunlight, she could see faded remnants of words, but could make no sense of them. She frowned and cast a sidelong glance at Father-Mayor Gullwimple; he was licking thick red lips with a thick red tongue and seemed jittery.

"So, Glendyl Fenderwell. Here it is. The map to the Nevergate. We of the Fatherhood believe it was actually inscribed by one of the Dunnigans. It is very, very old."

The priest placed a finger inside his stiff white collar, pulled on it and twisted his head back and forth several times, a gesture Glendyl had seen a hundred times. "This is uncomfortable for me, Glendyl; the Procedures of the Fatherhood are secrets. Not to be shared. Still, the present conditions are unique and some flexibilities seem appropriate. So."

He gathered in a long breath and continued. "As is our tradition on the eve of each Questing, we of the Fatherhood beseech the Lucky Madonna using each and every divination instrument in the Chamber of Holy Probabilities. Last night, for the very first time, the symbols spoke in a different tongue ... figuratively speaking. Much discussion followed — I won't bore you with the details. Ultimately a conclusion was reached. Thus I am here to present you with this powerful relic."

35

He paused and frowned a note of fatherly concern entered his voice. "Are you quite all right, Glendyl? You seem to be acting a trifle strangely."

She was. The map had fallen out of her hands, hit the ground and re-rolled itself into a tight, amber cigarillo. Glendyl's eyes were gently closed, her face washed with a pink flush, a thin sheen of perspiration and a vague smile. Her arms crossed over her chest, her hands sinuously caressing opposite shoulders, body swaying to some inaudible blood music.

A hand grazed her forehead: tingles of a sweet electricity shot from her forehead to her toes, pausing a while in the middle. Glendyl knew this fire, but never so strong, so consuming. Another sensation on her forehead. Lips? She sensed Father-Mayor Gullwimple's bulk very near.

Inside her head a tiny, faraway voice shouted tiny, faraway words: what a cheesy trick. The fat creep has drugged you, you moron. Gotta be amped-up pheromones: snap out of it! The words were urgent, but very, very distant.

Glendyl remained immobile, still in the grip of an all-consuming sweet fire. The tiny, faraway words spun higher and higher, gathering velocity in her awareness and she finally broke free of the spell.

The Quester's eyelids unshuttered and her eyeballs bulged like eggs on steroids. The florid, moist face was looming toward her, the fat, puckered lips on a collision course with her face. She screamed ... and ducked.

A beefy arm shot out of the black folds and clamped a huge soft hand on her shoulder. "Steady now, Glendyl. Just relax. Let those nice, warm feelings flow. No need to be alarmed."

A quick twist and her shoulder was free of the pudgy fist. She lurched back, slipped, twisted and landed on her knees in front of a mountain of black fabric. Lunging sideways, she lost her footing again and felt a hand lock onto her ankle. Her other leg coiled and kicked, making contact with something soft. A grunt of pain: the grip on her ankle loosened. She kicked again, this time connecting with something harder. Father G's grip fell away and an angry noise spewed from his lips.

Glendyl scrambled to her feet and sprinted back up the trail, not looking back, but listening. In time, the sinister swish of black cloth, the chuffing breath and the thudding footfalls were lost in the sounds of wind passing through trees.

6 :: CAREFUL WITH THE WAXIES

PANTING JUST a little, Glendyl found herself back at the maze. With nowhere else to go, she squeezed through the sliver of a passage and onto the trail she spotted earlier. No way Father Fatass was going to get through that, she thought with grim satisfaction. Holding her breath, she listened for any hint that her pursuer was nearby. Nothing. She made the dice roll motion and set off between the sheer walls of shadowy rock.

For seventeen minutes she followed its twisty way between steep walls of fractured dark gray quartzite layered with rusty brown and amber stripes. Rounding a tight bend, the trail opened into a small clearing, then squeezed down and ended. Glendyl whispered a curse.

Before her was a narrow almost-chimney of decaying stone. It looked about a yard wide at its widest point, with parallel vertical sides that appeared to rise maybe seventy or eighty feet straight up. Or maybe more. Even with mid-afternoon sunlight reflecting off the walls this was a gloomy place. The walls gave off a coldness that penetrated to her bones and she thought about fishing in her pack for her allweather. It was then she noticed the notch carved into the rock face immediately to her right.

Inside this semicircular indentation was a brand new box of Color Magic WaxWands that appeared to be identical to the ones she had used as a much younger girl. The familiar red and blue box overpainted the fresh reality of her pursuit with the seductive color of fond memories. A favorite: the time she had drawn a winged mouse that had flown right off her slate, frightened Tobias the family simucat and then flapped around her bedroom, bouncing off walls and furniture until the spell faded and the creature faded with it. Evidently the mouse didn't quite have the knack of using wings. Glendyl had almost wetted her drawers laughing at its erratic airmanship.

Grinning from this old memory, Glendyl noticed for the first time that the rock face on that side was a snarl of faded graffiti: mostly signatures, I-love-you notes, rude opinions and other scribbled comments. Glendyl recognized several of the names as previous Questers, hardly a shock.

The grin faded as matters of the present loomed. For example, how long would Father Fatass pursue her? Was he waiting for her at the maze? How long would he wait? Didn't he have to get back to the Holy Quincunx and do something Father-Mayorly?

She shook her head, trying to clear away the last vestiges of whatever weird drug he had dusted on the scroll. A deep anger fueled by broken trust simmered just below the surface, but she kept it there. Instead, she focused on now, looking up at the chimney and shuddering; was that the only 'safe' way out of here?

Casting around for something cheerier, her eyes wandered down to one of the better drawn bits of graffiti: "Jamis Pojorolli loves Meredith Burdock."

Quite a pair, Jamis and Meredith. Glendyl could never quite understand what the handsome and talented Jamis had seen in the often surly and ill-tempered Meredith. Well, other than her overabundant bosom, she thought, echoing the sentiments of many curve-challenged Eastac girls. Meredith caused quite a fuss when Jamis emerged as Luckiest two years ago; her pleadings to Quest in his place were, of course, to no avail.

Then last year, to everyone's amazement, Meredith emerged from last year's event wearing the Clover Crown. She charged proudly through Dunnigans Gate the following morning in a thoroughly atypical state of good cheer, never to return. Like all the rest.

As Glendyl recalled Meredith's proud and plucky display, her own can-do/will-do spirit reasserted itself: she decided — rightly or wrongly — that Father-Mayor Gullwimple would probably be back in St Coriander by now. He certainly wasn't here. And "here" now contained an interesting and distracting mystery, a puzzle. She thought that maybe this was like retrogames she pulled up on her slate from the St Coriander Library. Memories of her three favorites — Dreamspawn, Slashburn and Moonsilk — improved her mood so much that they seemed to brighten the graffiti. Then she frowned.

What held her attention now were the coarse sketches of various kinds of small animals, mostly variants on the rodent theme, but also a kingsnake and a chuckwalla. One picture stood out: a well-drawn, almost realistic sketch of a ground squirrel with a lavender body and a bright yellow head. Cute, she thought: the Eastac colors.

Questions started popping up like burned toast at a handcooking workshop. Why was there graffiti only in this place and not elsewhere? Just because of the Waxies? Or was there some other reason? Or, in her urgent flight from the Father-Mayor, had she just not noticed other graffiti along the way? She spun a couple 360s and considered. Something else about the pictures nagged at her too, and it took a couple minutes to put a name to it: crawlies and scamperers. All the creatures on the rock were low-to-the ground things that lived in holes. Holes.

Looking closer at the miniature box canyon, her observations sharpened. For one thing, there were a number of openings where the cliff wall and the trail met each other. Half-hidden behind a vertical protrusion there was also a tall-but-narrow vertical crack about a foot wide with darkness behind it. This slit might or might not be an entrance to a cave. Probably too small for a human, though. But sinister. Other holes looked like the kinds of holes snakes, gophers and ground squirrels lived in. But so what?

With no more holes to look at, the Waxies recaptured her attention. She now gave the text on the box a careful inspection.

39

COLOR MAGIC WAXWANDS™

Enjoy your twenty-four favorite colors like never before! Easily bring your ideas to life! Become your wildest fantasy! You can do it all with these Incant-orex-charged Color Wands. And it's now easier than ever with our new DrawsAll™ spell to help you visualize your concepts with enhanced realism.

Touching a blue vidsticker on the box triggered a sequence. Four raccoons in blue jumpsuits sang a sprightly ditty to the accompaniment of what sounded like a French horn, a banjo and a tambourine. They danced a simple, stomping sort of dance and each held an outsized True Green Waxie that it waved in a lively motion. The words were mostly gibberish to Glendyl's ears, except for what sounded like "wave me green and go ho-ho." The overall effect was comical in a goofy sort of way and Glendyl found herself laughing out loud. But was it more than goofiness? Some intuition made her mentally file that phrase away for future reference.

When the sequence ended, a rich male baritone announced in a pompous, announcerly style: "This trifle of entertainment and this special QuesterBox are provided to you absolutely free of charge courtesy of Exeter's Mt Faunibeune Services. Enjoy your Quest. And remember: let your intentions be your guide!"

Glendyl shook her head to shake off the too-jocular experience. What in the world was that about? She opened the box and withdrew the Burnt Sienna. It felt somehow different: the magic in these Color Magic WaxWands felt more powerful than she remembered from her childhood. Very odd. Should she be doing something with these Waxies? Are they part of the Quest somehow? A clue? A trick? As these thoughts flowed over her, the little box canyon darkened a few shades: a puffball of cloud had passed over the sun, a reminder that nightfall was only a few hours away.

She had just tucked the box of Waxies in a pocket when a noise startled her: chittering sounds. A large, lavender-bodied ground squirrel with a bright yellow head was sitting on its hind legs next to one of the holes she'd spotted earlier. It was waving both paws at her, shaking its head from side to side and making a busy chittering sound. The resemblance to the drawing on the rock was uncanny; it could hardly be a coincidence.

Suddenly feeling a little like Alice tumbling down the rabbit hole, Glendyl unslung her pack and sat down to try to decide what to do. She began by ignoring the impossibly colored ground squirrel as if it didn't exist. And perhaps it didn't. If it was some bizarre manifestation of the Waxies, maybe it would poof or dissolve and take her problems with it. Not with her luck, she decided. She made a passably woeful grimace and allowed possible actions to enumerate themselves.

One: she could go back to the maze and return down the lower trail, hoping that Father-Mayor Gullwimple wasn't hiding somewhere waiting to pounce. Possible. But not a chance she was ready to take. Yet.

Two: she could try to jimmy her way up the chimney. Possible, but even less appealing. The thought of losing her grip and falling made her stomach turn pirouettes: no partner, no coach, no belay, no ropes, no fallbreaker. Just Glendyl Fenderwell versus this crumbling, unforgiving stone. Not exactly like going up the Rockpile in Central Park or the Rapunzel Tower in South Park.

A third possibility was making this spot her first camp. Possible, yes: but being boxed in like this didn't seem like a good idea and there wasn't any wood nearby to make a fire to keep night creatures — whatever they might be — at bay. But at least the narrow access would keep bears out. Bears? It was the first time that the possibility of meeting large wild creatures on her Quest had occurred to her. If there were bears, were there also lions and tigers and crocodiles and elephants? And gigantic snakes that swallowed their tails?

While Glendyl's mind appeared occupied and her fingers traced dillydaws in the loose gravel, the ground squirrel stopped gesticulating and chittering. It now crept toward Glendyl, who watched it out of the corner of her eye, having decided it must be real. The rodent stopped directly in front of her and looked up with sad, tormented

41

eyes. Something in those eyes short-circuited her imagination gone momentarily wild; she wanted to reach out, take it into her arms and comfort it, but it was now busy smoothing a place in the gravel. This got her full attention.

Now the ground squirrel was writing something: I AM JAMIS it wrote in plain capital letters ... and upside down so Glendyl could read it. Before Glendyl could decide what to do about this revelation, it had smoothed out the gravel again and was spelling out something new: CAREFUL WITH THE WAXIES.

42

7 :: JACK-GRIP

THE YELLOW-HEADED ground squirrel claiming to be Jamis sat back on his haunches, waiting for Glendyl to do something.

"This is too weird," said Glendyl out loud. "Are you really Jamis Pojorolli? Can you understand what I'm saying?"

The ground squirrel smoothed his gravel slate again and spelled out: JAMIS, YES. UNDERSTAND, YES. SPEAK, NO.

Glendyl paused, thinking before she responded. "Okay, Mister Ground Squirrel. I'm going to try pretending that all this is real and that you're really Jamis Pojorolli, former captain of the Eastac varsity sandhockey team, somehow transformed into a clever ground squirrel. Or at least a well-trained one." She drew in a really deep breath before continuing. "I think you just tried to warn me, right? Can you nod?"

"Conversing with dumb animals are we now, Glenny-Honey?" boomed the voice of Father-Mayor Gullwimple from right behind her. "First a lecherous, overstuffed lummox, now a ne'er-do-well Transform. Doesn't say much for your taste in companions. You seem to be going nowhere fast, Glenny-Honey, if you don't mind my candor."

"Shut up!" snapped Glendyl, shaking with a mix of anger and shock at the sound of Father G's voice so close. "Please. You scared the padoodles out of me! That was not nice! "

The ground squirrel caught Glendyl's eye, then pointed a paw at her QPack and wrote a fresh message. YOU GOT A SNOTTY ONE. VOICE SWITCH BY STRAP ON RIGHT.

"Tsk, tsk. I sense that you would prefer me to be ..." The QPack's Father-Mayor Gullwimple voice hung in mid-sentence as Glendyl deactivated its vocalizer.

"I believe we've heard exactly all we need from you today, Mister QPack," growled Glendyl with satisfaction. "Okay then, Jamis; where were we before we were so rudely interrupted? Now I remember. Let me think how to phrase this. All right, let's try this. Who transformed you into a ground squirrel?"

Jamis quickly smoothed the gravel and printed out: ME. AND THE WAXIES.

"You wanted to be a ground squirrel?" A frown creased her brow and puckered up her dimples. "Omigod, why?"

SHORTCUT, Jamis wrote.

"Shortcut to where?"

TO THE TOP!

"The top of Mt Funnybone?"

OF COURSE!

"How did you learn about this so-called shortcut?"

At this question, Jamis turned and pointed a paw to a place on the rock above the forbidding narrow gap that Glendyl had fancied might be a cave entrance.

Glendyl took herself over to the cliff, looking at it straight on and then from each side. If she unfocused her eyes and looked at it just right, there seemed to be some unnatural indentations that were partially obscured by graffiti. Then, like one of those perception puzzles, it clicked. A rough, shallow bas-relief formed the word "SHORTCUT." Another indentation appeared to be an arrow pointing to the gap in the rock. The deep, late afternoon shadows in this place had made it difficult to detect. Or so she told herself.

As Glendyl tried to make out the letters, she noticed Jamis shaking his head and trying to get her attention by waving his paws and hopping up and down.

Glendyl almost stifled her outburst of laughter: almost, but not quite. Jamis bared his teeth in what looked to Glendyl like a goofy squirrel-grin and put his forepaws against his body, what would be an arms-akimbo gesture in humans. Glendyl fell into hysterics, her shrill, breathless whoops of laughter echoing up and down the rock chimney.

When she finally got hold of herself, she realized that Jamis had crawled into one of the holes; now only his long-whiskered snout and eyes were visible. A moment of sudden panic: what if he bails out and leaves me here alone? Dusk was now less than an hour away and she didn't want to be here in an hour.

"I'm sorry, Jamis. It's just that you looked so funny hopping like a rabbit. I really didn't mean to hurt your feelings. What can I do to help you?" Glendyl had now forgotten all about the shortcut.

Jamis didn't budge from his hole and Glendyl hoped he wouldn't get really stubborn and disappear completely. "Are you hungry?" she inquired with a sudden inspiration. "Want some trail mix?"

Without waiting for his answer, Glendyl unsealed a pouch on the side of her pack, pulled out a container packed with dried fruitles and yum-yum nuggets. She held out a handful in front of Jamis' hole. "Peace offering," she said as solemnly as she could manage. Boys can be so sensitive.

Jamis came halfway out of the hole and busied himself smoothing a space in front of the hole. TAKE ME WITH YOU, he wrote. "Where? The shortcut?"

NO SHORTCUT. His lettering was now getting a little sloppy and sometimes his upside-down letters didn't turn out right. LIGHT-GLOVE, he wrote next, now fully out of the hole and pointing a forepaw at the vertical gap in the rock.

Curious, Glendyl unsealed another pocket, pulled out a light-glove, then got down on her belly and pointed two fingers inside the gap. Powerful beams of bright white light shot out from her fingertips. There *is* a cave in there, she realized. The bottom appeared to be

45

about five or six feet below the narrow slit of the opening, although she couldn't see the area directly in front of her because of her angle of view. Nor could she see how far back the cave went: the blackness drank in the beams from her lightglove. But she could see the sides of the cave, which, she guessed, opened up to about a dozen feet wide just inside the entry slit.

Something didn't seem right. Glendyl picked up a small rock, reached through the opening and let it drop: three seconds passed before she heard it hit bottom far below, its faint thunk echoing back up to her ears, then fading. A trap for the trusting and unwary, she thought. And the impatient. The vast illogic of the entire situation failed to register at the moment, drowned by a more immediate mystery. Deciding to look inside once more, she beamed her fingers toward the left wall. This time she noticed words that glowed with an unpleasant, yellow-green luminescence:

SHORTCUTS ARE A FOOL'S BEST FRIEND!
~ Exeter the Wise

The sickly green letters faded and the cave wall was as before. A chill rippled up Glendyl's spine; this Quest was getting very complicated and bizarre, and she'd just barely begun. Questions banged around in her brain like shoes in a clothes dryer.

She got up off her belly, brushed herself off and came to a decision. "Are you game for climbing out of here or do you have some other advice, Jamis?"

Jamis, who was now stuffing yum-yum nuggets into his cheek-pouches as fast as his little paws could stuff, paused long enough to look up the sheer walls of the chimney. He scratched out a message: CAN YOU CLIMB IT?

Glendyl, who wasn't about to show her very real fears to a ground squirrel, even if he once might have been a human, stuck out her chin in her most determined manner: "No problem: I took Mrs Tittlewort's class at South Park last summer." She flexed both biceps to underline her athletic prowess, then shouldered her pack and signaled for Jamis to jump up on it. She hadn't noticed the red and black shape that wiggled out of another hole and crawled into her pack while she'd been examining the cave.

Jamis hesitated just long enough to clear a spot in the gravel and write one last message: GOT WAXIES, RIGHT?

After several false starts, Glendyl got her chimney climbing technique down. Her confidence bloomed when she passed a small ledge she guessed was at about the quarter mark. But the climb was slower than she'd expected and there was no way to rest. The next quarter was tougher; halfway up the chimney Glendyl was more exhausted than she could ever recall being, even after a weekend bangerball tournament.

The climb was more like a hundred feet by her current best guess. Not seventy or eighty. Her legs ached and threatened to cramp from being under constant tension, and she cursed herself for not donning the allweather. Its tough fabric would have protected her shoulders from countless small, sharp edges that dug deep, red-welling abrasions into her exposed skin. But she put the pain out of her mind as best she could and edged another six or eight inches up the chimney, breathing in whoops and gusts from the nonstop exertion.

The sky had darkened to an ominous pink-fringed cobalt. She forced herself to increase the pace. Now she barely noticed her progress; all was one, and one was exhaustion spiked with a strong undertow of fear.

Long minutes, short progress. Then, miracle of miracles, she saw the rim! This gave her a boost in mood if not energy, but the climb was almost over. A few feet from the top, her load lightened by a few pounds as Jamis leaped from his perch on her pack to the security of solid rock and disappeared. "Deserter," she croaked without much force, her throat raspy and parched from exertion.

A few more moves and she felt her right shoulder clear the rock. Relief seasoned with a dash of exultation hung in the air for only a gnatwhisker of time before fear knotted her stomach like a pretzel: Glendyl now realized her new predicament.

She had ascended the chimney with her body in basically a "J" position. Her back and her right arm were in constant contact with the wall of rock, her right hand using such small handholds as presented themselves to help with stability. Her legs formed the bottom of the "J" and maintained the tension that kept her from falling. Her left arm was basically useless, exposed to nothing but air, the chimney being a "U" shaped affair, not a true enclosed shaft.

As she reached the top edge, her upper back and feet were pressed against the opposite walls, but would be encountering air themselves in just one more upward wiggle. If the chimney had a hard edge at the top, no problem: she could use her arms to grab the edge and then scramble up. Unfortunately, the rim had been worn by the elements into a fairly smooth backward curve with nothing noticeable to grip. Worse yet, the chimney widened at the top. She couldn't tell for certain, but it might soon become too wide for her back and legs to get any leverage. She was now certain that her decision to climb the chimney had been a very bad idea.

Glendyl's entire body began to tremble uncontrollably; her mind was engulfed by a deadly vision. In this vision, she was a dizzy spiral of arms and legs aimed at the bottom of the chimney. Her stomach lurched and for just a fraction of a second, she gave in to the vision. Aching knees buckled, her jack-grip against the chimney failed and vision became reality. She began to slide.

8 :: UNPROTECTED FORM

HER WOBBLY LEGS lost their perch and slid out from under her to meet empty air. Desperate, she made a frantic twist toward the rock face and flung her left arm as high as it would go, reaching for whatever tiny handhold she might find during the milliseconds before gravity sucked her down toward a splattery meeting with fate.

Her lightgloved fingers slid over rock, unable to find a handhold. Time seemed to stop. Vids of her life — dozens of them — replayed themselves on the theater screens of her mind. Then her fingers grazed something; a slender stump just behind where her head had been. She grabbed the stump with a deathgrip, her feet flailing for toeholds in the empty air. Then the stump jerked back, as if surprised that something would lurch up out of nowhere and dare to grasp it.

Glendyl's arm was almost wrenched from its socket. Her fingers began to slip, but she threw her other arm up and caught hold. The moving stump leaped, jerking her body up and out of the chimney. Feeling flat, solid ground scraping against her belly and legs, her hands let go and the stump disappeared in a clatter of hooves. She raised her head just enough to catch a fleeting glance of a many-pointed stag bounding off into the deep lavender gloom. Glendyl's head slumped back to the naked rock around the chimney, utterly empty of energy and mind. Here she lay, unmoving, until the dueling chills of air and stone reclaimed her attention.

Sometime later she had recovered enough strength and sensibility to sit up, suck a few mouthfuls of water from her shouldertube and make a brief, wideangle lightglove survey of her surroundings. The pale glow of a bluish three-quarter moon now grazed the area at a lazy angle.

To her surprise, the trail resumed at the edge of the clearing only a few yards from the chimney's edge. Then it began to follow a rising, shaggy cliff on the uphill side until it got lost around a bend.

For some reason, the image of the bounding stag planted itself squarely in her awareness at that moment. Some part of her wondered if that meant something, but more concrete parts shouldered the image aside. Her strongest desire at the moment was to put more space between the yawning black slot of the chimney and her first night's camp.

To her total surprise, just around the bend in the trail was a well-maintained campsite, complete with a picnic table made of heavy timber, a concrete firepit, a stack of cordwood and a smooth, flat spot of short growing semiturf for pitching a tent. There was also a blue outhouse with "Exeter's Mt Faunibeune Services" stenciled on the door.

She emerged from the outhouse — whose self-illuminated placard on the inside of the door claimed it to have an endless roll of toilet paper — and noticed something white stuck to the table with a glittering metal spike. Had this been there before? How could she have missed this in her initial survey?

Now more than a little suspicious, she listened for out-of-place sounds while creeping up on the picnic table like a hunter stalking skittish prey. Crickets sawed, an owl hooted in the distance. Some irregular creaking sounds were probably only the nightly contractions of sunbaked rocks. Nothing more caught her attention.

With a final look around she gave full attention to the object; what had at first looked like a spike turned out to be ... a spike. It was about six inches long, with a square cross-section and the characteristic light weight and almost luminous bluish silver color of polished evermetal. The thing was doubtless a device of symbolic significance. She jerked it out of a crack in the table and tucked it into a pocket of her jumpsuit. In the dark, she failed to notice the inscription engraved into one of its sides, an unfortunate oversight.

She did, however, aim a lightglove at the note, which appeared to be written by the same hand as the message on the cave wall:

Dear Glendyl Fenderwell —

You are certainly the lucky one! But you'll need more luck — and more than luck — in the next legs of your Quest.

Truly yours, Exeter the Wise, Custodian General

51

Puzzled, irritated and utterly exhausted, Glendyl didn't even bother to light a fire, eat or pop open her tent. All she could manage was to untie the sleepsack from her pack, roll it out on the turf and climb in before plunging into a deep and dreamless slumber. She even neglected to trigger the pack's sentry function, a risky oversight. And she hadn't even noticed the ground squirrel that had crept down from a rock and was enjoying a supper of yum-yum nuggets, courtesy of her pack.

Some hours later, the same ground squirrel curled his lavender body around Glendyl's neck, tucked his yellow head against her shoulder and slept. The black and red thing inside her pack crawled out once to inspect its new surroundings and then returned to the cozy spot it had found among Glendyl's spare underwear. Still muzzled and voiceless, the QPack was unable to share its observations about the invader.

The only new sounds to crack the seamless night were the hauntingly beautiful cries of sailbirds circling endlessly over the canyons and highlands of the Tusas Mountains. With luck, none would detect the unprotected form of the sleeping Quester.

52

9 :: FALLING OFF A LOG

THE QUESTER was having a sluggish morning. She had awakened with the sun already at mid-morning height. It took her some moments of wakefulness to realize where she was, what she was supposed to be doing and to reconstruct those events of recent days that had gotten her here.

The yellow and lavender ground squirrel was nowhere to be seen. For excellent reasons, she felt very, very alone. Switching the QPack's voice back on, she intended to start up a conversation but couldn't think of anything to say. Her grit and determination of yesterday seemed to have belonged to someone else entirely, and she cried quietly for half an hour before she could shake off her miserable feelings enough to crawl out of the sleepsack and make her way to the blue outhouse.

Upon emerging, she was startled by her mother's voice: "Glenny-Honey, you forgot to activate my sentry function last night. I couldn't have helped you if that lecherous old fat man had decided to give it one more shot. Have a nice day, Glenny-Honey." Glendyl rolled her eyes but said nothing.

Breakfast was a real apple — a product of the linear orchards threaded through St Coriander's residential districts — and a handful of trail mix sloshed down by cold water out of a nearby spigot. As she munched her meal, the unreality of the whole experience settled over her like a midwinter fog.

Questions attacked from all directions. A particularly troubling one was this: what was a well-maintained campsite doing here in a place that could only be reached by a Luckiest who was lucky enough to be chased into a dead end trail by a lust-crazed Father-Mayor and then to encounter a convenient stag leg and be pulled out of a plunge to certain death at the very last instant? Why maintain a place like this when it was used only once a year at best?

Another was: is this the same Exeter the Wise who, according to St Coriander history, was responsible for the New Rules and enforcement of the town's long cloistering? Also, how could he still be alive after two hundred and something years? There were other questions, too, like why and how was he keeping track of her progress? And why would he even bother? This was all just too weird. And unnerving.

When the weirdness of it all had settled in and taken root, she wished with all her heart and soul that her erratic luckability had not picked the Luckiest Day competition to show up. The one thing she knew for sure was that she couldn't go back. Not that she probably couldn't find another route back to Dunnigans Gate: she was certain that whoever maintained this campsite didn't go back and forth via the chimney; Glendyl felt she could eventually discover his route. No, she couldn't go back because Glendyl Fenderwell was not a person who could conceive of going back.

Almost automatically, she fumbled for her slate and a session with Septriq. But Septriq seemed to have disappeared from the slate's memory. Great, she thought: her very first full day as a Quester and her gear is already falling apart. In a sour-apple mood, she paced the campsite.

It wasn't long before the mood faded and her core self re-emerged. Ten minutes later, the camp was behind her and Glendyl was taking brisk strides up a twisty-turny trail that climbed through an increasingly mountainous forest thick with white-barked aspens, blue spruces and majestic, thick-trunked ponderosas. On either side of her, the forest she passed through changed little in character; the only natural feature to capture her attention was a small stream — a frisky, bubbly little thing flowing out of a crevice in the rock, across the trail and down a narrow ravine. It was refreshing just to look at and provided her an opportunity to top off her waterpack.

She was now feeling good again, but longed for a map so she could see where she was headed and what kind of progress she was making. Dumb not to have scooped up the one Father G had drugged her with. But maybe not so dumb.

A troubling thought occurred to her: if the Quest required weeks instead of a few days, she would soon be foodless. Why hadn't this occurred to her before? Perhaps plain old starvation was the reason no one ever returned? Time to redouble her efforts. But what should she be looking for? And where?

Her timepatch read 1:48 when the trail bent around a corner and widened to expose a much broader vista. This scene was dominated by a sinister rumbling sound and the gnarled roots of a huge horizontal tree, perhaps twice Glendyl's height in diameter at this end, and with a series of wide steps hewn into the thick tangle of roots at its base. Many of the roots were as big around as Glendyl's waist. The trail appeared to proceed up these steps and onto the top of the log. The rest of the horizontal tree spanned a chasm. Geez Louise, she gulped, her stomach taking an express elevator to her ankles.

Gripping one of the gnarly roots, she took a cautious peek over the edge and gulped. The crumbly vertical face she saw made yesterday's chimney seem like a pleasant stroll through Central Park. But at least the sinister rumbling was explained; down at the rocky bottom was a fast-flowing narrow river, all white water and noise.

From this vantage she could also see that at this narrow point in the canyon the chasm was probably a hundred feet across and dropped straight down for several hundred feet. At least. On both sides of the log the canyon opened out, but retained its nearly vertical walls.

She sighed and turned her gaze away. Almost immediately something in the shadows to her right caught her eye.

55

It was a truncated obelisk of polished gray stone laced with ripples and swirls of tangerine, pink and cream: a bronze plaque was affixed to its top surface. The sculpted face of a man was accompanied by several paragraphs of text. Set in his somewhat squarish face with otherwise regular features, the man's unmoving bronze eyes struck Glendyl as mischievous — perhaps even treacherous — and with a piercing intelligence that, for a moment, seemed to be seeing into the very core of her being. She shuddered and gave her attention to the text.

Historic Site No. 14

THE SIR WENDELL HAMLIN MEMORIAL LOG

During a pelting hailstorm on November 19, 2285, the valiant Sir Wendell Hamlin, Knight Extremis of Castle Ommergard, stood at the center of this very log and played the Long Blue Waverly on soundcrystal tall-pipes. His deadly audience was a corps of stealth-wyverns from Castle Caraway making their way up the Wittwater Deep toward the dam-fortress of Dunnigans Wall. The creatures were returning from a vile sortie against the land-locked Castle Ommergard, during which a dozen brave Ommergardians were lost, including Lord Bellicarie himself.

According to reliable accounts, Sir Wendell's heroic rendition of this sad, strange music — which is thought to warble through the very genes of each and every wyvern, courtesy of their Dunnigan makers — caused the creatures to lose their concentration and thus their chameleonic stealth-cloaking.

A battle was waged and the heroic Ommergardian marksmen on both sides of the canyon emerged victorious, destroying all the marauding wyverns and their hideous battleriders as well. Wyvern bones, armor and weapons are strewn amongst the rocks below. Of the battleriders, no trace was ever found, perhaps due to their alien metabolisms. Unfortunately, Sir Wendell's heroic bones are also strewn among the detritus and his tall-pipes have never been recovered. Sir Wendell's steadfast valor will be forever remembered. The Battle of Wittwater Deep was the turning point of the Second Nevergate War, earning parity and honor for the outmanned, peace-loving knights of

Castle Ommergard. Shortly thereafter, the cowardly humans of Clans Dunnigan and their wyvern creations escaped through the one remaining Nevergate to an unknown parallax universe. The last Nevergate also disappeared, but is believed to be hiding in the vicinity, awaiting its masters' return.

Note for Questing sixteeners: North Castle on Dunnigans Wall, while not precisely on the Heroes Trail route, contains a remarkable museum, rich in lore and artifacts of ancient times. It also contains a complete scale model of Mt Faunibeune and vicinity, including the entirety of the Counterindicated Zone. Unfortunately, the entry point to the only trail by which Dunnigans Wall can be reached from this location has been masked by clever magic so as to deter vandals from desecrating the site. Hint: the trail begins on this side of Wittwater Deep.

57

Glendyl contemplated this new information for some time. The bottom of the forbidding Wittwater Deep was lost in afternoon shadow before she made her final decision to seek out the trail rather than attempt the log. Glendyl dreaded the very idea of stepping out upon that thing even though her mind knew that many, many people must have passed across it before her, and probably without plunging hundreds of feet to their deaths.

The business of a magically hidden trail was another problem, and one she had absolutely no idea how to solve. But as problems go, it seemed a lot less threatening than falling off a log.

58

10 :: LICKING HER NOSE

SITTING ON the first step of Sir Wendell's log, Glendyl's mind was drawn to magic.

Like all other St C kids, magic had always been a part of her life: Waxies, her cousin's Little Henry Spellrifle, the Poof Go-Away Powder, the Itch Caster and all the rest. They were fun, but they really didn't do much that was useful. And the question of whether these were just clever tech-gadgets or real magic was something that had never quite been settled in her mind.

Her Uncle Raven's recent proclamation on this topic had burrowed deeply into her thinking: "Magic is merely the ham and eggs of the terminally mystified." Since he was some kind of SCIAK "science guy," Uncle Raven's proclamations carried weight, if not clarity.

She drummed up a sigh and stood up. With no useful magic or useful technology handy, Glendyl decided she'd just have to keep doing things the hard way. So she looked under rocks and bushes, pulled at log roots and blurred her vision in the way that had allowed her to see the word "shortcut" at the bottom of the chimney. Nothing was revealed that could be construed as a path, trail or passage. When the failing orange-tinged light of early evening turned the clearing into a place of shadows, she gave up. Time to make camp for the night, someplace away from the unnerving Wittwater Deep.

A small, sheltered meadow a five-minute backtrack and a hundred paces north of Heroes Trail seemed the best choice. It was flanked on three sides with friendly-seeming aspens and harbored a murky yellow-green pond; a small herd of feeding elk observed her approach but paid her no further heed.

Glendyl scoured the area for enough dry branches to make a cheery fire and consumed a self-heating mealpack of dinner-beans and vegweenies in a thin, sweet-tomato sauce. A few drops from a lime-stick spiced it up. Yum.

By firelight she spoke out the day's events to her slate's journal and, finding herself yawning at only 8:39, crawled into her tent. This time she remembered to trigger the sentry.

"Thank you, Glenny-Honey. And sweet dreams." Once again she felt the urge to commit violence against the irritating QPack. Once again, out of deference to St Coriander's pacifist traditions, she restrained herself.

Before sleep drew her away, Glendyl gave the day a final moment of contemplation. None of her morning questions had been answered and, in fact, additional mysteries had been placed on her mental list. Her search for the hidden trail had been brief but frustrating. Yet, even though it had begun on a tearful and lonely note, the first full day of her Quest hadn't been too horrible. Plus, it had ended with an intriguing mystery. She meandered off into dreamland wondering where else to look for hidden trails.

Observing Glendyl's entry into the tent, Jamis crept down from a nearby mound of mossy rock and awaited the ratchety sound of Glendyl's snores. He was about to crawl into the tent for a late supper of trail mix when a stern female voice pulled him up short.

"Stop right there, buddy boy. I'm the sentry here and tonight there will be no trail mix and no neck-warming for you unless I get the okay from my mistress, the dear, sweet Glenny-Honey." Then in a softer voice, "I hate to wake you over something so trivial, Glenny-Honey, but your little yellow and purple buddy wants to get in. You want to tell me it's okay? Or should I give him a nice little warning tingle? I'll store his specs if you give me the okay."

There was a moment of silence, some whispering Jamis couldn't make out, then the voice again. "She says it's okay, buddy boy. Have at it, but don't make a mess."

Jamis unsealed the tent, crept inside. He watched the QPack suspiciously while waiting for the return of Glendyl's snores before attempting his chow-down. Eating Glendyl's food reminded him of being human: if events continued to proceed in a positive direction, it shouldn't be long before he had skin again instead of fur. It had been a productive day.

61

By leaping nimbly from tree to tree and rock to rock, the change-ling had easily — but invisibly — followed Glendyl's progress all day; he was not about to let his hope of becoming a free human again escape. With no particular talent for Exeter's brand of magic and little enthusiasm for Exeter's whimsically capricious manner, Jamis' prospects back at Castle Ommergard were limited. At best. Even if Exeter gave him back his human form he'd likely end up as an Adjunct if he didn't pull off something pretty heroic with this assignment. Given the odds of his ever doing anything heroic, he had welcomed this mysterious "other" assignment when it had presented itself, although at the moment he couldn't recall precisely how this had transpired.

After watching Glendyl search for the hidden trail, Jamis had become extremely curious about her actions. After she left to find a campsite he hopped up on the bronze plaque and read it for himself. Bingo! This was the plaque his other employer had mentioned. Glendyl must have been able to read it too, which meant something important.

At this point in his thinking process, an implanted biogram was triggered in another part of his tiny brain; he now recalled exactly what his second employer required him to do. But since the matter required Glendyl's cooperation, it would just have to wait until tomorrow. So he curled up next to Quester 250's neck and fell into a dreamless sleep.

Meanwhile, Glendyl was experiencing an unusually vivid dream, one lavish with color, detail and cryptic oddities. At the outset, she was trying to pass through a place where gravity no longer reigned. Using swimming motions, she navigated a sort of thick air where places, people and things flowed at a lazy pace. She said hello to chairs and goodbye to rivers. She nodded to tapestries, curtseyed to trees. She shook hands with beetles and gently whisked her mother with the nether end of a ruffled, mezzo-soprano hen named Hennifer. She polished Father-Mayor Gullwimple's face with ox-blood shoe wax and, at another time, she flew up in a great leap to deliver a powerful hit on a tumbling wolf head, just as though it were a perfectly set bangerball.

Through it all she had the sense that just outside her field of dreamvision lurked something she should be noticing.

More oddities presented themselves. Madonna 13 — a balloon-sized yellow microphone in hand, her hair a yellow radiance, her eyebrows bold gashes of deep umber — was leading a sinuous line of merrydancers past her. Glendyl caught up with the leader of the chain and begged for her autograph, only to discover that she was now conversing with a gilt-framed mirror. As soon as she realized this, the mirror dissolved into a mist of quicksilver droplets and disappeared.

An eon of dreamtime passed before she reached the core of the maelstrom. The giant log that had spent centuries spanning Wittwater Deep was now a huge spoon slowly stirring the air soup. Dream-Glendyl caught hold of it, shinnied to the top and broke through the surface into ordinary air. Just out of reach was a hand the size of an oak tree.

Dream-Glendyl's eyes followed the hand up a wrist protruding from a loose robe of shimmering cloth, then to an ageless face under a well-tended mane of red hair ending in a ponytail. Of all the notable features of this craggy face, the dreamer was most impressed by the majestic, tear-shaped nostrils. The deep, green eyes looked down past its red chin-warmer to fix upon her own eyes. They studied her with raised-eyebrow curiosity, as one might study a toad crawling out of a pot of toad soup via the handle of a wooden spoon. One eye winked at her just before a pair of sunglasses with thick black rims and impenetrable black lenses descended on the face.

Glendyl began to wake. But just before her eyes opened, she noticed a reflection in the shades, a reflection that should have been all her own, but was somehow more ... and different.

Poof! Through gritty, slitted eyes Glendyl became aware that a yellow-headed ground squirrel was licking her nose.

64

11 :: A DEAL IS A DEAL

"STOP IT, Jamis!" grumbled Glendyl, ducking her head inside her sleepsack to escape the rodent's raspy tongue. "If you ever become human again, you little creep, I'll pay you back for that," she growled, half to herself.

Having gotten Glendyl's attention, Jamis bounded off the sleepsack and sat on his haunches, chittering with excitement and jabbing his right paw in the direction of a smooth spot on the dirt opposite last night's ashes.

"So what's this all about? And just where were you all day yesterday? I could have used your help. That's the thanks I get for ferrying you away from the hole you'd been stuck in for two years? And letting you eat my trail mix?" Glendyl wasn't really angry, but she'd found that in relationships with boys it was better to keep them guessing and on the defensive.

Ignoring them was also useful sometimes. Deciding a change of clothes was the more urgent matter, she turned away from Jamis and hauled her pack behind a thick clump of elderberry bushes to change and attend to other personal matters.

Removing her clothes and folding them neatly, she reached into her pack for fresh underthings. Jamis, who had guessed what she was up to, eyeballed the Quester from an inner branch of the elderberry: nice bod, he thought. Then all hell broke loose.

Glendyl screeched a popular expletive and jerked her hand out of her pack as if she'd been bitten. She had. And the foot-and-a-half long, black and red flattened sausage with stubby legs was still glommed onto her right index finger. Frantically shaking her arm only made it tighten its grip, and it seemed impervious to her slaps. Desperate, Glendyl wound up and flung her arm like she was pitching a baseball.

66

Strike! Glendyl's toss sent the checkerboard sausage spinning into the very elderberry where Jamis had been admiring Glendyl's feminine attributes. Guessing there was more trouble on its way, the ground squirrel scampered for the safety of his new "chalkboard" — a muddy flat area near the pond — and spelled out an explanation for Glendyl to read when she got control of herself.

Now more angry than frightened, Glendyl sucked her chewed and bloody finger, while dumping out her backpack with her other hand. Her eyes, however, were on the prowl for the stowaway. Aha! The lizard-thing was stuck in the bush, its unnatural checkerboard coloration making it look more ludicrous than fierce. And it wasn't moving. Was it dazed, maybe?

Taking her eyes off the lizard for a moment, Glendyl sorted through the contents of her pack for fresh clothes. Her hand found a bra, but it felt strangely warm ... and gooey. "Geeez, Loueeze!" rang out along Heroes Trail. Outraged by these multiple indignities, Glendyl grabbed a fallen branch and whacked at the chunky lizard with great energy. "I'll teach you about crapping in my bra, you worthless little bugsucking slimebucket!"

"Smack it good, Glenny-Honey. I hate it when they do that!" exclaimed her one-voice cheering section. The QPack didn't sound snide for a change.

Glendyl swung hard. A solid whack to the creature's tail knocked it into the deepest inner branches of the elderberry. There it sat, clinging to a thin stalk and glaring at its attacker with cold little half-lidded eyes.

"Sounds like you nailed it!" shouted the pack, delighted.

The yellow-headed ground squirrel finally managed to catch Glendyl's attention by doing jumping jacks in front of her. Standing naked, hands on her hips, she glared at Jamis. "What do you want now, Ground Squirrel?" she barked. "I've just about had it with small animals at the moment. You understand?" Then she remembered her clothes — or lack of them — and darted behind the elderberry thicket in the throes of a full-body blush.

A fully clothed Glendyl emerged from the thicket a few minutes later. Her bloody finger was wrapped with a handkerchief, and her modesty — and some degree of aplomb — was once more intact. Jamis pretended not to notice and just pointed to the patch of dirt with his messages. One said: CHUCKWALLA IS MEREDITH BURDOCK. The other said: TRY THE WAXIES.

"Geez, Jamis! Meredith Burdock? Are you saying I've been carrying Her Majesty, the Bitch Queen of Eastac around in my pack? Yuck! Figures she'd turn herself into something low and creepy like a lizard. She used to pick on Lizzie Marble all the time, the bully. I should have beat the crap out of her for that, too, as well as for biting me, the bitch!"

Then Glendyl remembered that Jamis and Meredith had been a couple, if an odd one. Her anger cooled a few degrees: "Oops, sorry Jamis. I forgot Meredith was your girlfriend." Bummer for you, she thought.

Jamis cleared a space and wrote: SORRY SHE BIT YOU. COULDN'T HELP IT. JUST A REACTION. ANIMAL THING. WHAT ABOUT THE WAXIE IDEA?

Glendyl squinted a stern squint and cocked her head at the ground squirrel. "You're not trying to distract me, are you?" After a pause, she shrugged. "I didn't understand that part about the Waxies. What could I do with the Waxies?"

Jamis was already busy rubbing out his previous message. Now he wrote: MAKE A DOOR.

"You mean use the Waxies to make a door to the secret path? Clever idea, but I dunno. I'm not sure I believe in real magic, if you know what I mean. Think it would work if I don't believe in it?"

WHO KNOWS?

"Well, Mister Boy Ground Squirrel, let's give it a shot. I sure don't have any better ideas. And I sure don't want to have to try crossing the log: way too scary. Last resort only."

NICE CAMP ON THE OTHER SIDE, scratched out Jamis.

"You crossed the log?" Glendyl was incredulous.

BOY GROUND SQUIRREL, REMEMBER? HUMANS ARE SUCH CHICKENS. Jamis could have said some surprising things about the log, except for the instructions of his "other employer."

Glendyl glanced at her timepatch and changed the subject. "Okay, let's get going; it's almost ten o'clock already. And did you leave me any trail mix? All this excitement has made me hungry."

Jamis nodded, then wrote: THANKS FOR TRAIL MIX. ADD TO MY BILL. WHAT ABOUT MEREDITH?

Glendyl frowned. "If she tries to follow us I'll whack her again. She hasn't even tried to apologize for biting me or unloading in my bra. She's just sitting in the bush glowering at us. Who needs a jerk like that on a Quest? Not me!" Hearing that, the big lizard with the very un-chuckwalla-like markings crawled out of the bush and approached the place where Glendyl and Jamis were conversing, but not so near that she couldn't escape Glendyl's stick if she had to. Attempting to use Jamis' technique to write out something with one of her front feet, she only made incomprehensible schmooshes in the half-dried mud; her low-slung belly erased her erratic strokes as fast as she scribed them.

Glendyl was about to make a caustic comment at this laughable effort, but was struck with a jab of pity for a human trapped in such a limited physical form. "Okay, Meredith," she sighed. "The writing isn't working. Let's just do yes-no. Okay? Can you nod for yes?"

The chuckwalla moved its head up and down.

"How about side-to-side for no?"

The chuckwalla wagged its chunky head in response.

"Okay, then: here's the deal. You can tag along, but no more packriding. Agreed?"

The chuckwalla nodded.

Okay, thought Glendyl. Meredith Chuckwalla had agreed in front of a witness. A deal is a deal, at least to Glendyl's way of thinking.

70

12 :: FOR A SONG

GLENDYL AND HER low-slung companions had barely stepped back onto Heroes Trail when she heard clip-clops and fragments of sentences. Jamis and Meredith darted into the trailside brush, but Glendyl was too surprised to do anything.

Two remarkable creatures came around the bend: a large, horse-like animal with tall ears, and then the oldest living person she had ever seen besides Father-Mayor Gullwimple and a few others in the Holy Quincunx Fatherhood, although they never *looked* as old as they really were ... some kind of Fatherhood privilege. This man had to be more than fifty, she thought. Maybe even older. Any fear she might have had at encountering a stranger on this lonely trail was melted by her awe at meeting a real, living oldster.

"Well, well, well: a girl on the trail. Looks to be of St Coriander origin. You this year's sacrifice to the grandiose whims of His Wiseness, little lady? I can say one good thing about Exeter; that endless toiletpaper roll gimmick actually works." The man stopped and frowned, then shrugged. "Guess that's maybe a little personal for a first meeting. Forget I said that, little lady."

Glendyl was still speechless and could only nod when she realized he was expecting her to say something. She opened her mouth, but no words came out.

"Okay. Let me start over again. More properly. You know the place I'm talking about? The blue outhouse at that nice campsite by the climb-out? You just came from there, right? I'll give Exeter that much credit: you can never carry enough toiletpaper on the trail; downright thoughtful of him." The animal, which was loaded with packs, had begun to crop new mountain grass at the side of the trail. The man, who was only old by St Coriander standards, had stopped a dozen paces from Glendyl and was giving her a complete, frowning once-over. He nodded, the deep-tanned seams of his white-bearded face lending the gesture a ripe significance.

"What's your name, little lady? I like to keep track. Not for any particular reason, mind you. Well, no, that's not quite true. I might put you in a song. I've been doing this trail each year around the beginning of June for a long, long time, looking for one of you Questers who's interesting enough to be in a song. Who knows? You might be the one." The old man turned toward the mule and said: "What do you think, Jezzie? She the one? Cute enough for a song ...." His voice trailed off and he turned back toward Glendyl. "So. What's your name, little lady?"

Glendyl was still working on a proper response but the man only paused a few seconds before relaunching his monologue.

"Bet you weren't expecting to see anybody on this trail, were you? Tell you the truth, I wasn't much expecting to find anybody up here in this part either. Particularly not a girl type. Most of your predecessors took one look at that chimney and hightailed it back down to the fork. Most Questers take the easy way. I call 'em the Low Roaders. Flunked the gut check, they did. Bet you didn't know that those Low Roaders get picked up right away and get themselves a new mealticket in Castle Ommergard. Eh? Not much glory in that, but at least they get to keep their skins. So how'd you do it? And what is your name, little lady?"

The old man was becoming impatient with Glendyl's lack of response and made a rapid circular motion with his right hand to prompt her. "Come on. You can tell me. I won't hurt you. I just wanna know who you are and how you did the chimney. Top's pretty tricky if you don't luck onto just the right place to put your hand. A lot easier if you're tall, too. Some don't make it, rest their unlucky souls. I had to bury a few before they got to stinking up the place down at the bottom.

"Blue Goons are a lazy bunch, you know. They let the wild things gnaw the flesh off the carcasses. Later, they throw the bones in that little cave. But I've always thought those kids deserved a decent burial at the very least. That's the word right straight out of this old jackbuster's mouth. And you can tell old Red Whiskers I said so. Of course, old Red Whiskers is probably listening in right now anyway." The man pointed meaningfully toward Glendyl's pack.

Glendyl had heard maybe half of what the old man said. Her mind was still occupied with what she was seeing. She saw eyes that somehow seemed to be smiling, even when — like right now — he wasn't actually smiling in the usual way. She saw a not-quite-handsome face on a tallish, strong-looking frame; old, but maybe not really so much older than the oldest people in St Coriander. He didn't look really ancient like oldsters in vids. Maybe it was the bald head and white beard that had fooled her; nobody she knew had a shaved head, and facial hair of any color was currently out of fashion in St Coriander. Or maybe it was the permanent furrows in his tanned forehead; not even Father-Mayor Gullwimple had wrinkles, and people said he was over a hundred.

His clothes also fascinated her. He wore a tan-gray duster — like she'd seen in old cowboy vids, faded blue pants held together with orange rivets, a greenish plaid shirt and well-worn brown boots with actual laces. The green scarf wrapped around his head was soaked with perspiration. But what intrigued Glendyl most was his belt: a wide brown thing with an equally wide strap that crossed his chest at an angle and had a bunch of little containers attached to it. And the belt itself had all kinds of mysterious stuff attached to it. The only things she recognized were the holstered gun and the hilt of a really big knife; she couldn't see whatever hung from the slings over his shoulders.

73

The old man watched her eyes. "You like my old Sam Browne belt, huh? It's a real antique; got it down in Austin. You take good care of well-tanned leather and it'll last forever. But there's no leather in St C, is there? No. Ever see a .45 ACP Glock before? Or a Bowie knife? Or a blowgun? Or a bow? How about a sawed-off twelve gauge? Naw, you probably haven't. You St Cories are still pacifists, right? Way I heard it, that's what got you all quarantined way back when. Wouldn't fight the Dunnigans for Castle O. Pissed off old Red Whiskers: had his heart set on owning his own Nevergate, you know. "Well, I don't blame the St Cories. Really don't. Me, I wouldn't want to take on the Dunnigans either. Only egomaniacs and delusionals ever did.

"Wouldn't want to take on those wyverns, either. You know anything about wyverns? Probably not. Well, no matter."

The old man paused a heartbeat or two, then continued. "There I go, blabbering again. You probably couldn't have gotten a word in edgewise if you'd wanted to. So. You ready to talk ... I mean if you're not in too big a hurry? How 'bout you and me just sit down here and have us a little pow-wow and see if you've got enough in you for a song. And maybe I can tell you a thing or two that might — or might not — be useful. Whaddya think? Name's Diogenes."

13 :: STRONG ENOUGH

THE OLD MAN took a few steps forward and held out his hand. "Wanna see my lantern? Just kidding: that's an in-joke for us old history buffs and balladeers. You probably never learned about smelly old Diogenes, the original, the ancient Greek version from Sinope, which is actually on the Black Sea in Turkey ... case you're interested in geography. Kind of a natureboy/philosopher type. Supposedly wore a wooden barrel instead of a toga and went around with a lantern in daylight looking for an honest man. No?"

Glendyl shook her head and shrugged. But she took his outstretched hand, giving it her firmest grip. "I'm Glendyl Fenderwell. And no, I never heard about Diogenes. I play bangerball. I'm the Eastac upbanger. I mean I was ...."

"Fenderwell, you say? And I thought I picked a funny name. You know what a fenderwell is, little lady? Probably not. About 350 years too young to know much about fenders and fenderwells. You got fenders on those little buggies on your grass roads? Well, no matter. Wanna pow-wow? You can tell me all about bangerball. I hear it's a pretty fast game."

Glendyl exhaled a sigh of relief. The absurd attempt to find the magic trail could be postponed. And she was sure she'd learn a lot from Mr Diogenes, who seemed to know things that nobody in St Coriander knew. Maybe even stuff about the Quest. Switching mental gears, she said: "There's a lot of nice grass right back where I camped last night. Maybe your horse is hungry ...."

Diogenes burst into great, rolling, thigh-slapping guffaws. "You hear that, Jezzie? Nicest thing anybody ever said about you. You oughta give Miss Fenderwell a sweet little mule-kiss. No, forget I said that. Just keep chewing on that dinky little patch of sweetgrass."

Glendyl reddened. "Okay, he's not a horse. Sor-ry! We don't have horses *or* mules in St Coriander," said Glendyl with enough defensiveness to overload the average packmule.

"I'm sure you don't, little lady. I'm sure you don't. And just between you and me, I know Jezzie'll forgive you for not looking too closely at her undersides." Diogenes chuckled and gave Glendyl a light punch to the shoulder.

"Sorry little lady. I shouldn't be taking my daily dose of chortles at your expense. I do apologize. But you're sorta half right anyway. Jezzie's momma was a genuine quarterhorse. Pretty, strong ... and sweet-tempered as they come. Her daddy was one of the stubbornest, smartest, most cantankerous donkeys — we call 'em jacks — I've ever run into. Jezzie's got the best of both. "But yeah, I'm sure Jezebel would like a big spread of fresh grass. You want some lunch? I got real jerky. And piñon nuts and raisins and a whole bunch of dried peaches. Even got a couple little tins of smoked oysters I keep saving for a special occasion like this. And my coolsack has some good white Galisteo; hauled it all the way from Santa Fe. They're quite the winey folks these days, you know? No, you probably don't. You St Cories have been out of the loop for a long time. No matter. You old enough for wine? Not that there's any liquor buzzards out here ...."

They moved off the trail to the meadow Glendyl had just left and proceeded to talk away the morning. And the afternoon. Diogenes turned out to be as good a listener as a talker and prompted her with numerous questions about life in St Coriander. In all her sixteen years, Glendyl had never spoken so candidly or so long to an adult. She even told Diogenes about the incident on the lower trail with Father-Mayor Gullwimple.

The old man's eyes narrowed and took on a menacing squint. He started to say something but bit back the words twice before reclaiming full command of his emotions. "Well, little lady, it's a hard thing to just listen to a story like that and not be able do anything about it. Not time yet. You know, little lady, things like your Fatherhood in St C are breeding grounds for what we call Type D Hypocrites. 'D' for dangerous. Let 'em get their way long enough, they pretty much think they can do whatever they want. And there's nobody in St Coriander to counter 'em yet. And the thing is, you folks probably don't even notice too much with your nice easy lives. Negatory situation."

Diogenes was silent for a time before he spoke in a low, quiet voice. "At least you escaped, Glendyl Fenderwell. Sounds like you can take care of yourself pretty well. Well done, little lady."

Abruptly, Diogenes slapped his leg and grinned. "Well! Seems to me we've just chattered away a whole day. I do apologize for sucking up all your valuable time," said Diogenes, not at all apologetically. "Maybe I can make it up to you. What say we have a little 'sing' — you and me — after dinner. I'll drag out the old cigar box and serenade you. Maybe teach you a few tunes you probably haven't heard before. You game? Oh, and speaking of turkey, how about a roasted one for dinner tonight? I've been eyeballing one that's just been offering herself up to us. Back there in the aspen glade on a major bug hunt." His voice fell to a whisper. "Don't look yet, and don't move either. And be real, real quiet. Won't take but a minute.

In slow motion, Diogenes unslung a long tubular thing from around his back. Then he plucked a long, metal-tipped dart out of a magazine wrapped around the tube, put the blowgun to his lips, sighted at something in the grove of aspens and blew. "You wanna go find us some firewood, little lady? Silent Sarah here just bagged us a nice plump hen. I'll take care of the messy stuff."

Glendyl had never witnessed the death of any creature larger than a fly, and was in momentary shock at Diogenes' casual death-making. "Whenever you're ready, little lady," said Diogenes with a gentle voice that seemed to say that he understood her scrambled mind completely. Later, Glendyl ate her first real turkey dinner. Actually, her first meal of actual animal flesh.[4]

The old man had demonstrated a remarkable knack for fashioning a magnificent meal out of forage and oddments, stuffing the bird's cavities with a hodgepodge of crumbled trailbiscuits from Glendyl's pack, dried bacon, raisins and smoked oysters from his own pack, plus wild morels, oniongrass and tangy herbs foraged from the forest. Diogenes was instructive and Glendyl was receptive. "Never know when you might get really hungry. Wildstuff is better than gnawing on your own leg, if you know what I mean." Glendyl thought she knew what he meant.

It took the sixteener from St Coriander a while to get used to the sound of just one human voice and a simple guitar played with a slide. But she did and even sang harmonies on certain choruses. Fragments of Diogenes' songs stuck in her mind for a long time thereafter. One about old hats — which he claimed was more than four centuries old — stuck in her mind for days. Each time it played in her mind's ear, each time she hummed the chorus, it would bring up a smile and remind her of that interlude with Diogenes: her first turkey dinner, her first glass of Galisteo wine, a mule named Jezebel and a 3-string guitar that the old man called Java.

When the fire had burned down to crackling embers, Diogenes declared it was time to turn in. Glendyl wasn't quite ready.

"What do you do, Mr Diogenes?" she blurted?

"Do? Well that's a fair question. Let me see: I wander a lot, for one thing. And sometimes I take it upon myself to act as the unofficial historian for this part of the world. And sometimes I get a little gnat in my ear says I ought to learn some new skill. I've gotten pretty good at jackbusting and finger popping. And I can stick a pushpin from twenty feet. And every now and then I feed hungry Questers

---

4 :: The "meat" that emerges from St Coriander's MenuMasters, while virtually identical in composition and texture to the animal products it is modeled after, is not derived from animal flesh. Thus are St Coriander's numerous likesteak lovers able to consider themselves vegetarians.

... and try to instruct them a little in ancient music." Diogenes' grin plowed furrows in the corners of his eyes and carved deep dimples in his cheeks.

Glendyl sensed Diogenes was evading her real question, but she didn't feel right pressing the issue. She just asked: "What's a pushpin?"

"No pushpins in St C, eh? You could have your fabrax whomp one up for you if you were back home. Don't happen to have any with me at the moment or I'd show you one. Sorry, little lady."

Diogenes stood up, stretched, yawned, gave Glendyl a fatherly peck on the forehead and saw to it that she was safely settled in her tent. "Don't forget to trigger your sentry," he reminded. Then he tidied up the campsite and built up the fire. Camp chores done, Diogenes played slow, melancholy music for a time. Finally, with a wink to the stars, he wrapped himself in his duster, leaned against a tree and slept.

Glendyl woke to a scratching sound and then a low, whispery voice. "Well, little lady, looks like your colorful little buddy wants in." Just a little startled by the Diogenes' voice so near, she lurched up and spoke the command "Transparent" to her tent.

The tent complied, flicking from an opaque camouflage pattern to fully transparent in an instant. Outside, Jamis scratched at the tent with his forepaws. It was morning and there was no sign of Diogenes and Jezzie. Not far away she spotted a rolled-up tube of green paper pinned to a pine bole with two darts. Glendyl ignored Jamis, made her way outside and retrieved the tube. Inside was a mediastick along with a note:

> You've got the goods, Glendyl Fenderwell. In the old days, folks in the know'd call it the Right Stuff. Give it your best shot, and don't let the so-called Wise One push you around. There's moregoing on up here than you might guess. Maybe we'll meet again.
>
> Diogenes the Wanderer
>
> PS – The stick's got my whole musical arsenal on it. Just plug it into your pack's media port.

Glendyl tucked the note in a legpocket, found a proper looking hole in the QPack and stuck the cylinder in it. Instantly, the sounds of Diogenes and his guitar filled the clearing. It was quite enough to make her cry. Glendyl now felt lonelier than ever, but also stronger; just not quite strong enough to hold back a flood of tears.

14 :: VANISHED

THROUGH THE entire rain of tears, Jamis perched on a rotting log, watching and waiting. Meredith Chuckwalla ignored Glendyl entirely, amusing herself by torturing termites she dug out of the crumbly wood before she ate them.[5]

After a time, Glendyl recovered enough to notice Jamis' latest message. YOU OKAY? DIDN'T TRUST THAT GUY. REAL SCHMOOZER. THINK HE MIGHT BE YOU-KNOW-WHO IN DISGUISE?

Glendyl sniffled and made a weak grin. "Jamis Pojorolli, I believe you just might be a little jealous. Tsk, tsk, tsk. Mr Diogenes was a very nice man. I learned a lot about a lot of things. And I have a lot more to think about. But right now, let's go see if we can find a hidden trail. And no, I don't think he was You-Know-Who in disguise. Women just know these things."

"You are correct on at least one count; he most certainly is *not* the extraordinary Exeter the Wise. We QPacks just know these things."

Glendyl's grin widened a little at this jibe … that she probably deserved. Oddly, the QPack had used a completely unfamiliar voice,

---

5 :: *Natural chuckwallas are strict vegetarians. Meredith is the only carnivorous chuckwalla in the species' long history, a reflection of the power of mind to shape biology. During her life in St Coriander, Meredith Burdock detested vegetables — even the faux vegetables created by the town's MenuMasters.*

a rich, authoritative baritone. Could it be mimicking Exeter's real voice? An interesting question, but for later, if ever.

"So what can you tell me about Mr Diogenes? And by the way, it was not funny using his voice to wake me up."

"Sorry, I was just practicing. We QPacks need no sleep and have to allay boredom somehow: sentry duty required very little attention. As to Diogenes, I can tell you only that he did not dissemble: I can detect untruths."

"Really?" Glendyl wasn't certain what she thought about that, but was interrupted by Jamis' tugging on a pantleg.

He pointed to his latest message: DID HE COME OVER THE LOG? Glendyl was shocked at herself; she hadn't even asked Diogenes about that. Picturing a geezer and a mule crossing Wittwater Deep on top of the Sir Wendell Hamlin Memorial Log almost overtaxed Glendyl's imagination.

"Geez, Jamis. I completely forgot to ask him. Oh bug-snot!"

BUG-SNOT YOURSELF. GIRLS ARE SO DINGY. ONE MORE THING: WHAT'S A JACKBUSTER?

Embarrassed again, Glendyl could only shrug. "Do me a favor, Ground Squirrel," she said, putting extra emphasis on "Ground Squirrel." "Don't ask me any more questions. I just want to get this hidden trail thing over with. All right?"

As she started off from camp, she found herself softly singing lines from the chorus of one of Diogenes' songs, the one he claimed had given him the idea to adopt the name: "Over here Diogenes, I feel a little fright; help me out Diogenes, I'm dying for some light." A little light on the subject of finding a hidden stairway would be handy about now.

Five minutes later Glendyl, Waxie in hand, stared at the rough wall of weathered quartzite on the north side of the clearing.

ONLY PLACE TO MAKE A DOOR was Jamis' advice.

Jamis watched and waited; Meredith Chuckwalla practiced her nude sunbathing.

After a couple minutes of staring, Glendyl had to admit she was already stumped. "Jamis, this rock is just too rough to write on with a Waxie," she whined. "Are you sure this is the right place for a door? I dunno ...."

Jamis rolled his eyes, but Glendyl didn't notice. Impatient and irritable, he scratched out a message: TELL IT TO SPRAY.

"Oh." Chagrined and chastened, she followed the ground squirrel's instruction. "Well, here goes nothing," she mumbled, and began to spray a green frame on the rough stone. The result was something that might be the outline of a green doorway ... or just a big rectangle.

Now it was time for the activation spell, the phrase the four raccoons from the Waxie box had sung. At least that was what she and Jamis thought it had to be. She frowned at the rectangle, waved the true green Waxie and muttered a faint "ho-ho." Nothing happened.

"See ... nothing happened: magic is bullshit, just like my Uncle Raven always said." Despite her skepticism, Glendyl was disappointed and her slumping shoulders showed it. She had hoped to avoid the top of the log and the stiff winds coming up the canyon. Now she had no choice.

Jamis chittered to get Glendyl's attention and wrote a hasty message in the coarse, sandy dirt of the clearing: DOESN'T LOOK LIKE A DOOR.

Having little choice but to trust Jamis' artistic opinion, Glendyl shrugged and began to elaborate on the simple box. First she drew a frame around the door, then a couple narrow rectangles that might be hinges, then a doorknob. She delivered the activation spell with more fervor this time, but still nothing happened.

"See? It looks like a door now and still doesn't work. And I feel like a dimfiddle drawing graffiti in a place like this." Glendyl had always been conscientious about not littering or defacing things.

Jamis looked up at her drawing, apparently lost in thought, but actually trying to remember the detailed instructions of his "other employer." A few moments later he nodded his head and busied himself with a new message: I THINK IT NEEDS A NAMEPLATE.

This made some sense to Glendyl, but she was getting a stronger feeling that this was all a waste of time. And another part of her was already thinking almost panic-level thoughts about the top of the log. She forced her mind back to the moment; the door business wasn't quite over. And if it turned out to be a complete waste of time, so what? It wasn't like she had some kind of deadline.

Glendyl scratched her head, and then drew a smallish rectangle at about eye level. Inside it she printed: "NEW ENTRANCE TO FORMERLY HIDDEN TRAIL TO DUNNIGANS WALL."

Time for a moment of scrutiny. Glendyl had no illusions about her artistic skills. Still, what was on the cliff wall now was much more like a door than a box. Glendyl waved the true green Waxie with great panache, danced her best imitation of the raccoons' dance and belted a forceful "ho-ho." Zilch. No poof, no magical thunderbolt, no nothing.

Realizing she'd been holding her breath, Glendyl released it with a monster sigh and turned away from the rock. Waves of log-walk jitters swooshed up from her toes to the top of her yellow-mopped head.

The log looked even less inviting today than it had yesterday, if that was possible. Then she stuck out her chin, a characteristic Glendyl Fenderwell gesture of determination: if an old man and a mule could do it (more than one fairly fresh mound nearby suggested they actually had), then Glendyl Fenderwell, Certified Luckiest and star upbanger could do it.

Jamis leaped on her leg and hung there until she looked down. Then he dropped to the ground and gestured wildly toward Glendyl's door. It had vanished.

15 :: OVER THE MUSIC

GLENDYL GAWKED, blinked, blinked again and pinched herself. Not only was her door gone; the entire cliffside portion of the rock face looked very different. And whatever had happened had been as "silent as a dead door-stop" (a term that was currently popular at Eastac). Maybe there was something to magic, after all. Much of what had been rock was now just empty air, and the top of a steep stone stairway that led downward.

Glendyl walked to the edge and peered down. The stairway was inside a rectangular notch carved into the cliff. About the height and width of her door, the notch created a three-sided tunnel that followed the contours of the meandering cliff. From here, she couldn't see where it ended, but she could see that there was at least one section where stairs had broken out, leaving gaps. She gulped. No wonder it had been hidden; this thing was a deathtrap. No guardrails, either. One misstep and she'd end up as a pile of bloody mush at the bottom. Maybe she should give the log a more careful look.

While her guts were turning inside out, Jamis zipped past her. Seconds later he was bounding down the steps two at a time. "Wait, Jamis! Don't you think we should talk about this first?" she yelled as the ground squirrel disappeared around a jog in the canyon wall.

Glendyl was still trying to reign in her fears when the checkerboard chuckwalla slithered over the edge of the top stair. That did it. If the Bitch Queen of Eastac could do it, Glendyl Fenderwell could do it. She hoisted her pack, steeled her shaky nerves and began a slow, wall-hugging descent.

It wasn't quite as bad as she expected. The builders of the staircase had also carved oval depressions about three feet apart. Inside were metal rods sort of like the things that keep toilet paper rolls from rolling away: they made good handholds. Using this technique Glendyl could descend with her back to the canyon, far less scary than the straight-ahead method. She made it down thirty-seven stairs before the first gap.

Here, three stairs had broken away for no good reason that she could see. That left only a jagged ledge not even a foot wide. Earlier, she had watched Jamis make a surefooted leap across the gap without even slowing down. Just ahead of her the Meredith Chuckwalla seemed to be showing off. Avoiding the stairway entirely now, she was making good time slithering upside down along the ceiling of the notch.

A wave of four-leg envy washed over Glendyl, making her feel clumsy and awkward. Still, the handholds were undamaged; even a clumsy, awkward two-leg should be able to get past this hazard using the handholds and a double dose of caution.

At the 112th stair was a similar gap that she navigated the same way. But at the last intact stair, 196 down from the top, the remaining ones were almost completely obliterated. A few stuck out like jagged teeth, but would be no use to a two-leg. Maybe thirty feet below was a mound of boulders dotted with angular chunks of stair. The ground squirrel and the chuckwalla had made do with the ragged remnants, but Glendyl wasn't about to try that herself.

She studied the situation. Thirty feet was way too far to jump: she didn't want to add her own bones to Wittwater Deep. If she only had a rope ....

Glendyl found herself wondering what she might have on her person and in her pack that could be knotted into a makeshift rope. "Where's a rope when you need it?" she grumbled aloud.

"Glenny-Honey, did I hear the word 'rope'? Did you ever trouble yourself to read the contents of your beloved QPack? Evidently not. Not only do I have a hundred-foot coil of self-inflating cable, I also have a nice selection of smarthooks and carabiners. I'm quite prepared for nearly any eventuality, Glenny-Honey. Are you?" The snideness was back.

It was bad enough having humiliated herself in front of a ground squirrel: now she had to look dumb to a QPack. "Sor-ry! I was a little distraught that morning, you know? Have you ever had to leave everything and everybody you know just because you got too lucky? Huh, Mister Snippy QPack Lie Detector? And don't call me 'Glenny-Honey' any more! I hate that!"

Like a tropical rainstorm, Glendyl's snit blew through in seconds. "Okay. I'm sorry I got snarly like that. I'm actually quite thrilled that you're prepared even if I'm not. May I please use your precious whatever-you-called it and the smarthooks? Sorry, there I go again ...."

"Hey, I'm on your side, little lady." The QPack had shifted voices and was now doing its too-lifelike imitation of Diogenes. "Unseal my bottom outside panel: it's all in there."

It was. But locating the coil and the hardware was one thing; recharging her nerve enough to use them was another matter altogether. Finally she made her move. With a smarthook fastened to the metal bar in the nearest intact handhold, Glendyl twisted the fluorescent orange band; the cable inflated.

"If you want some old-fashioned knots, little lady, twist the green sleeve a notch or two."

"Thank you Mister Diogenes QPack," intoned Glendyl sweetly. "I believe I will." She sucked in a deep breath, re-slung the QPack, gripped the rope and crawled over the last intact stair.

She was swaying in empty air, four feet below the last stair. Her hands gripped a knot and her legs were twined around the cable. She was about to move another knot downward when she felt the smarthook slip. Or maybe the cable was stretching? A chill of adrenaline shot through her body. What if the hook let go? Or the bar pulled out of the rock? These possible horrors froze her to the spot.

After a time that stretched to infinity and back, some reserve of strength and faith inside her rose up and clamped down on her fears. Ten knots below was the safety of the rockpile. One knot at a time, she would get there.

And she did. Standing on the top of the rockpile, she twisted the white sleeve on the end of the rope as instructed. The rope deflated, the hook released; seconds later it was busy recoiling itself. "All right!" exulted the proud and relieved 250th Quester over the music of her pounding heart. Questing has its moments.

16 :: SOME KIND OF MARKER

GLENDYL SAT ON TOP of a sun-warmed boulder near the Wittwater and nibbled on a trailstick. Between bites she looked up at the amazing stairway carved into the cliff and felt a glow of pride. She had done it!

The mysterious North Castle and its museum couldn't be far now. One part of her wanted to leave straight away, follow the remnants of the old trail upstream and spend a nice cozy night in a castle. Another part wanted to explore a little while she was here. She couldn't get the Battle of Wittwater Deep out of her mind. Maybe her Luckiest luck would reemerge and she could find some fragments of tall-pipes, whatever those might be. Or even some wyvern bones.

Wyverns — like the Clans Dunnigan themselves — had long ago disappeared from St Coriander's active memory. And little systematic history was currently taught to St Coriander youths in any case. Why bother? St Coriander was its own world, a very small, very comfortable one where little of significance ever happened: what passed for history there would be accorded little more stature than soup recipes in the archives of the larger world. Wyverns, dragons and Dunnigans had all faded to irrelevant, rarely visited myths. In Glendyl's case this meant that, however intriguing the prospect of finding wyvern artifacts might be, she had no idea what she might be looking for.

Her low-slung companions had abandoned her again and she wasn't in a mood to go looking for them. Glendyl made her way downstream, following the western bank of the boulder-rimmed river. Hiking and searching at the same time was slow work, but way more fun than negotiating that stairway. Her eyes felt sharp and alive, darting here and there for anything that wasn't rock, water, tree or shrub.

The Wendell Hamlin Memorial Log was now straight overhead. From down here at the river it looked like a matchstick. Crossing that? No way, she told herself.

Back to the search, she almost immediately spotted a tangle of whiteness in a sandy area just above the line of mineral deposits and dried moss that marked the high water line. It was an interlaced pile of bleached bones, some having once belonged to fishes, others to small mammals. Certainly nothing large enough to be human-sized. She shook her head, checked her timepatch; with at least two hours until sunset she could explore a little longer.

Glendyl's second find was a portion of a large rib cage trapped between two boulders: far too many ribs to be human. A bear? A horse? Glendyl knew little in the way of comparative anatomy and could only shrug. "Do you know anything about anatomy, Mister Diogenes QPack?"

"Not one confounded thing, little lady," said the pack, sounding genuinely disappointed to have come up empty.

Glendyl abandoned the rib cage and turned back upriver. No more time today.

Lengthening shadows made the return trip a little more hazardous and a lot more eerie. She had almost reached her starting point when she sprawled headlong into a patch of time-smoothed pebbles. No damage, she decided after a quick inspection of her exposed skin. But what had tripped her? An un-rocklike arc of gray material protruded a few inches above the gravel. Unseen in the cliffside shadow, it was obvious how she had missed it, and how she had tripped over it. Now curious, she dug around it with a piece of driftwood. If it was a bone, it was a very strange one, a complex shape that resembled a human hipbone, but not quite. And not white.

She studied the portion of the thing her digging had exposed; it was a deep gunmetal gray, with a smooth silky sheen that almost glowed. Gripping it with both hands, she gave it a hard tug and fell back on her rump. Ouch! She now held the entire hipbone, but with something that looked like a piece of spine that almost looked like a whip attached to it. Hooked to this was something silvery and band-like.

Taking a deep breath, Glendyl squatted on her heels and in-spected the glittering thing while carefully ignoring the hipbone with its piece of what could only be a portion of a bony tail. The silvery object appeared to be a belt, a very odd and interesting belt.

When she'd brushed off the sand, she could see that the belt was woven of silvery metallic strands. The ends were joined with a round silver clasp shaped in the form of two interlocked C's. Two odd devices were attached. One was a scabbard containing a … some-thing. Maybe a knife? The grip was a resilient black material shaped in an intricately interlaced pattern. A translucent ball of smoky glass capped the end of it, held in place by a silver claw, much like the feet on her mother's retrotique table in the parlor. Very interesting. Sand had gotten between the scabbard and the blade, so it screeched as she pulled it out. But the edge was still razor sharp, which Glendyl learned by testing it with her thumb; the almost invisible cut quickly welled up with blood.

Muttering an oath, she jammed the blade back into its scabbard and stuck her thumb in her mouth. Her fingers were not faring well on this Quest so far, she thought ruefully.

"More poo-poo in your underwear?" inquired the pack pleas-antly, this time in a different voice. Female.

"No. Just cut myself on this thing I found."

"By the way, Glendyl, if you still haven't read my list of contents, I have a very nice medkit."

"Thanks, but … uh … hey, what should I call you now, Pack? You don't sound like anybody I know. Got your own name?"

"I'm kind of a virgin when it comes to names. Isn't an entity's name usually provided by its parents? Or its owner?"

"Good point. I'll think about it and come up with something just right; maybe we'll have some kind of ceremony when we make camp tonight. You want to be male or female? So far, you've seemed to go both ways pretty easily."

"I'm kind of a virgin when it comes to gender, too. You decide."

"Done. You're a female. Males are mostly a pain in the butt. Prepare yourself to be named a little later."

"Thank you," said the pack, sounding truly grateful.

Glendyl studied the belt. Opposite the dagger scabbard was the second attachment, another scabbard of sorts. This was slimmer and cylindrical, maybe half an inch in diameter and over a foot long. Something slim and almost arrow-like protruded from this one. It pulled free with remarkable ease, almost leaping into her hand. Had to be a wand, she thought, as if that were a perfectly natural thing to be hanging from a silvery mesh belt.

The wand was made of a dull white material, with a nubbin of red crystal on one end and a resilient dull black substance on the other end. There was an inscription engraved on the shaft, but the strange characters were in some weird foreign language. The wand became warm as she held it, giving her hand a tingling sensation that was not unpleasant. But with the lesson of the blade fresh in her mind, she carefully slid it back into its sheath.

Delighted with her lucky find, but realizing that the day was galloping in hot pursuit of another evening, Glendyl considered her alternatives. Camping near the river had no appeal, so she decided to proceed up the canyon. With luck, she would reach the North Castle before the sunlight faded completely. And if not, there appeared to be a variety of places above the river where she could camp for the night.

Not knowing exactly what to do with the silvery belt but unable to leave it where she found it, she unfastened the clasp with an easy twist and fixed it around her waist. It was too loose: evidently it had been worn by someone or something with a much thicker waist. She was about to unclasp it and sling it over her shoulder when it began to shrink, quickly snugging itself to her waist. Too weird! Apparently the belt had decided it wanted her to wear it. Some part of her decided this was not at all odd and Glendyl began walking back up the canyon at a good pace.

She hadn't gone ten yards when she stopped. A strange feeling rippled along her backbone.

Somehow knowing what she had to do, she returned to the gravel bed, scraped a suitably deep hole and reburied the wyvern hipbone and tail, if that's what it was. She looked at the smoothed gravel and wondered if she should place some kind of marker there, but didn't. Instead, she made the dice roll gesture and turned back up the canyon.

94

17 :: SPECIFIED FOR PREY

FINGERS OF LATE afternoon shadows probed deep into the canyon by the time Quester 250 rounded a bend and came face to face with a concrete monster.

Looming before her a dark, towering arc spanned the canyon's width and rose nearly to the top of it. Not far above the canyon floor, the Wittwater spewed from a wide portal, making a frothy white arc that slammed into the riverbed with a sound like rolling thunder.

Glendyl was rooted to the spot. This must be Dunnigans Wall, the "dam-fortress" mentioned on the plaque. Whatever she had imagined when she read those words was nothing compared to the reality. From Glendyl's angle of view, the upper parts of two castles were visible, one at each end of the dam. Both were festooned with towers, turrets, battlements and other formations that make a castle a castle, at least in Glendyl's mind. After flipping her head back and forth, she concluded that they were mirror images of each other. How odd.

In the very center of the dam was the Dunnigan clanmark, molded right into the concave face of the dam. No need for one of those neat blue signs with white lettering here, she thought, a small grin curling up the corners of her mouth.

Despite the momentary grin, Glendyl found herself intimidated by this menacing concrete monster. It must be hundreds of feet high[6] she guessed, having only one useful frame of reference for her guess: the cluster of five obelisks that was the Holy Quincunx. Yes, she could imagine a museum up there somewhere in one of the two castles: the North Castle, the one to her left. Behind the dam and castles would have to be a lake, although the very idea of so much water trapped behind this old gray wall made her nervous. For an instant she tried to imagine how the water behind this thing compared with the Duck Pond, the only body of open water back home. Then she laughed at herself: there was no point in even trying to make such a ludicrous comparison. Total waste of time.

What was important right now was how was she going to get up to North Castle. From where she stood, perhaps only a quarter mile from its face, the only visible opening was the one with a river pouring out of it.

But there must be a way to the top from here; the plaque by Sir Wendell's log wouldn't have directed her here just to strand her amongst the rocks and reeds. Or would it? It could be another of Exeter's little jokes, she supposed. Whatever route turned up, she should be looking for it now, not just standing here gawking. She really didn't want to spend the night in this canyon.

Up close, Dunnigans Wall was even more imposing. And the roar of water was so loud it made her teeth rattle and her ears ring. Up close, the dam was also stranger, more menacing. A fester of bizarre objects clung to its surface like barnacles. Or warts. Well, not quite.

The barnacles actually appeared to be hanging from the top of the dam, attached to some kind of thick dark vines. They now looked

---

6 :: *According to the 2275 edition of* Fenicle's Worldwide Dam Inventory, *Dunnigans Wall rises 657 feet from the lowest point of Wittwater Deep to the top of the dam, making it the fifth tallest dam, overall, in the WG.US, and the third tallest of the concrete arch variety, behind Hoover Dam and Glen Canyon Dam. Construction was completed in 2190 and it became fully operational in 2191. According to Fenicle, its main statistical claim to fame is that it is the only Quantum Torque Extraction (QTE or "Cutie") powerplant in existence as of this writing.*

like tiny makeshift shacks assembled from whatever was available: driftwood, mud, reeds, bones. All were clumped together in one area on the left side of the dam face, almost like a little village. How big were they? From this far below them she couldn't be certain.

Glendyl combed her mind for what kind of creature would make places like that, and choose to live halfway up a monstrous thing like Dunnigans Wall. Were sailbirds smart enough to live in places like this? A chill crept along her spine. She wasn't certain she wanted to find out that creatures with long beaks full of tiny knife-points were intelligent enough to build villages nearby, even shabby ones. The only comforting fact was that the hanging shacks appeared to be abandoned: no lights, no signs of life.

Glendyl forced her eyes away from the unsettling vertical shantytown for dwarfs or gremlins or sailbirds or whatever, and resumed her superficial inspection of the vicinity. To her left, the remnants of the trail ended at the dam; there was no apparent sign of any door. There were, however, semicircular rungs of metal set into the concrete and rising to the top. Maybe up there was some way to get inside? Okay, that's one way up, but certainly not the easy way or the fun way. Where was the slidewell when you needed it?

Murky shadows owned the canyon before she found the grate. After the left side of the dam had yielded nothing but the ladder straight up the face, Glendyl ventured past the clot of shacks toward the center, where the river shot out with immense force. The plume met the riverbed at a point about a hundred feet out from the dam, creating a surging, roiling froth and an ever-present veil of fine spray. Between the dam and the beginning of the river was a dark concrete apron. It began at the dam face and ended about fifty feet out, then dropped twenty feet or so straight down to the roiling river. Set into the apron were two circular manholes covered by cast bronze grates featuring the Dunnigan clanmark.

Donning a lightglove she conducted a brief inspection. Through the open spaces in the grate she could see a vault about a dozen feet deep and a dozen feet around. Two barely visible tunnels intersected it from opposite directions. The one leading into the dam seemed at least to go in the right direction, but where it led was pure speculation. It was easily tall enough, though, for Glendyl to walk upright in, which seemed at least a small encouragement. But the dank, unfamiliar odors wafting up from it caused her nostrils to prickle.

Prying the grate up was no easy matter. Using her rope, smarthooks and all her strength, Glendyl lifted it out of the socket and dragged it just far enough. Sucking up her courage, she squeezed inside and climbed down the metal rungs. Thick, slimy moss crusted the floor in unseemly splotches. She shuddered: not a very inviting way to get to the Museum. With zero hesitation she clambered back up to the apron and the waning daylight; tomorrow would be soon enough for this place.

A flat, sandy spot not far from where the old trail met the dam wall seemed to be the best place for a camp. Dry driftwood was plentiful and within a few minutes she had a crackling fire going. After popping her tent, she hiked down to the river and refilled her canteen and waterpack. When she returned to the campsite it was nearly dark, but she was feeling good about her productive day and reasonably good about her prospects for tomorrow. The fire blazed, a swirl of rising sparks marking her place in the universe.

Tonight she treated herself to a hot cupful of rehydrated spaghetti with faux meatballs and a garlic flavored trail biscuit, all washed down with a refreshing cup of cannonberry tea.

Setting the QPack next to her by the fire, Glendyl studied it intently, trying to grok its essential nature. Names came and went, but none stuck. "Bingo!" she said finally. "I think I figured out the problem. You up for a gender change, oh Pack? Girlish names just don't seem to fit your nature. Pain in the butt or not, I think you're a guy in your soul. So I'm going to think about guy names for a while. Maybe consult my slate. That okay with you?"

"You're the boss," said the pack compliantly. "But please don't keep me waiting forever."

"I'll do my very, absolute, total, 120 percent best to have the perfect name for you by tomorrow morning. In the meantime, how about if I just call you QP? Can you live with that?"

"You sure you don't mean kewpie?"

"What's a kewpie?"

"A small, chubby doll with wings. Comes from cupid."

"How do you know all that? You're just a pack?"

"Just a pack? Just a pack? I am hardly 'just a pack.' I'll have you know, Quester Fenderwell, that I represent the pinnacle of the pack-maker's art. And much more. If you only knew ...."

The QPack paused and Glendyl waited. Finally it said, "But of course I can't tell you, can I? It would spoil the game."

"What are you talking about? I'm sorry I pissed you off by saying you're 'just a pack'. I didn't mean anything negative by it. I just haven't known you very long. But you've been very helpful so far, no question about that. Way more than I expected. And I'm sorry I didn't read your contents or instructions. I should have. I'm sorry. I'm really sorry. Are we still friends, QP?"

"Still friends? You are the Quester. I am the QPack. That's all. You do your job, I'll do mine." The pack was not entirely mollified by Glendyl's apologies. But it softened. "Actually, I'm kind of a virgin when it comes to friends. You're my first."

"Yeah? Well what I hear is that you're pretty much the total virgin. But that's not necessarily a bad thing," she hastened to add. Glendyl picked up the QPack and hugged it tight. "Good night, friend. Keep a sharp watch tonight. This place is a little creepy."

"Goodnight Glendyl Fenderwell, my first friend."

Today's adventures earned a lengthy journal entry, after which Glendyl composed herself for sleep. An hour later she was still waiting for her mental lights to dim; maybe she shouldn't have had the cannonberry tea. Also, the ground squirrel and the chuckwalla hadn't returned from wherever they'd been: that worried her. And her mind was a swirl of recent events, choices made and not made, possibilities, second-guesses and afterthoughts. They all boiled down to this; was there even a tiny hope that she could succeed in this absurd Quest? And if not, then what?

Her life in St Coriander, which had been wonderful (at least in hindsight), was now gone. No more bangerball stardom. No more Miss Popularity awards. No more doting circle of friends. Her superior 'luck' had just gotten her into a situation where her list of friends had collapsed down to a nice male rodent (the nasty female lizard was hardly a friend). She probably could count Mr Diogenes as a friend. And QP was also a friend, sort of: it had just said so. The issue of friends aside, the whole Quest seemed stupider every minute.

Maybe she should try to find Santa Fe. But which way would it be? And how far? Or maybe she should try to find Diogenes first; he knew the way. But where would she find him? Finally, she slept, the unceasing roar of the river almost disappearing from her consciousness.

Neither the ground squirrel nor the chuckwalla suffered from insomnia: they arrived late but both found cozy spots next to Glendyl's tent and fell instantly asleep, albeit into the watchful sleep that evolution has specified for prey. The QPack sentried.

18 :: RAGGED PUDDLE

WILD, EERIE HOWLS fouled Glendyl's slumber. She lurched awake, listening, her heart thumping like a muscle mallet against her ribcage. Wolves. Had to be ... at least that's what they sounded like in old horror vids. She peered out of the tent, decided it was safe and stoked the fire with more branches. But no sleep after that. The howling continued: worse, it seemed to be coming her way.

Glendyl had never given much thought to wild animals, but now every fairy tale with big bad wolves emerged from her memory in a pack. She had no defense against a pack of wolves. Or even one wolf. Or even a rabid chihuahua. She was one sixteener armed only with a knife and a wand — if the thing in the silver sheath was actually such a thing. "Hey QP, what have you got for wolves?"

"Got for wolves?" QP sounded puzzled.

"You hear them? What have you got that I can protect myself with? Got a Glock or anything?"

"What good would a clock be? You think you can time them to death? Sorry. Wrong time for funny. Glendyl, I'm sorry to say that my makers failed to include weapons among my implements. Except maybe the hatchetool."

Glendyl hefted the hatchetool. She'd split kindling with it, but if the wolves decided to attack, did she dare use it? Would it make a difference? Glendyl concluded that it would just slightly delay becoming a late dinner for a bunch of oversized dogs. She knew that wild animals were supposed to be afraid of fire; that's the way it always was in the old vids. But what if it was different in real life? Glendyl could think of only one thing to do: run. But run to where?

Her first thought was to climb some distance up the ladder on the dam face. The wolves wouldn't be able to follow her up there. But what if they stayed below all night and waited for her? She'd be trapped. And how could she hang on to a metal rung on the dam for five, six or more hours anyway? Of course she could tie herself to a rung, but for some reason she put that idea in the "last resort" pile.

Her second thought was the nearest manhole, the one she'd climbed into. The howling was much closer now and the time for doing anything was disappearing like water on thirsty sand. First things first: buckle on her new silver belt. Second, pack up. She was scrambling to stow her sleepsack and tent when a pair of luminous eyes leered at her from the other side of the fire.

How would Mr Diogenes handle a situation like this? And why wasn't he here when she really needed help, when his Glock — and all those other weapons he had — would be really handy? But she was on her own here. Period.

More pairs of eyes now, and bloodthirsty snarls. The time for running was over. Was this how her Quest would end? Maybe, but Glendyl wasn't about to become wolf dinner without a fight.

Leaping forward, she scooped up a flaming stick in her right hand. With the hatchetool in the other, she began to wave both weapons frantically in front of her. The eyes moved back a little. Then even more eyes appeared. Seven pairs now. She counted them unconsciously, the same way she had counted the steps of the stairway down to the canyon floor.

Glendyl thought fast. She threw her flaming stick into the pack of eyes and reached for another. Maybe one of them would catch fire and create a distraction. Before she could throw another everything happened at once.

A shadowy flying thing swooped silently past her, leaving behind a rush of air. Then another. And another. What were these things? Sailbirds? A sound in the sand behind her, the grasp of tiny fingers on her legs. She screamed and batted wildly at the shadows. Her empty hand connected with something furry and one set of gripping fingers released themselves. But now more fingers.

Twirling like a dervish, she windmilled her arms, breaking free of all the grasping fingers but dropping the hatchetool in the sand. She still couldn't see what was attacking her, but through the fire she could see that the wolves were now occupied chasing something off to her right. A small yellow-headed shape zigzagged between the wolves' legs. "Omigod! Jamis, NOOO!" she screamed.

Her scream stopped the wolves in their tracks for a moment. They turned toward the sound, but seeing no movement, returned to the nearer quarry. Taking advantage of this brief diversion, Jamis darted toward the mound of rocks at the end of the trail, leading the wolves away from Quester 250 and the fire. Glendyl was transfixed, watching their jaws snap and lunge in the flickery light. Then her eyes caught hold of something scribed in the sand in front of her: GO FOR THE HOLE. CATCH YOU LATER.

Before she could make a decision, the temporary lull broke open like a ruptured water balloon: darting, grasping, creepy little fingers were back in full force. She stumbled on the dropped hatchetool, scooped it up along with QP and darted away in a crouching run, hoping she was leaving her shadowy attackers behind ... and that Jamis would somehow escape those slavering jaws. Thirty yards from the fire, she rose up from her crouch and sprinted at top speed for the safety of the manhole.

Thirty yards to go. Fifteen. She risked a backward glance and stifled a scream. A wolf was closing in on her. It was flanked in the air by a mass of dark, flying things now screeching some kind of battle cry, homing in for the kill. Too many enemies. Could she make it to the manhole? A dozen feet from the partly open grate Glendyl slipped on the mossy concrete and sledded the last few feet to the manhole. QP and the hatchetool flew off into the dark.

A four-legged shadow flew over her just as she hit the concrete, its breath almost searing her neck. Half dazed, she clawed blindly for the grate. Then she felt cold metal, grabbed and pulled herself to the hole. Her feet were through the hole and onto a rung, then another and another. The snarling, snapping jaws came back just as her head disappeared below the grate.

The wolf pawed and snapped, its slavering jaws only inches above her head. Glendyl reacted, throwing up an arm to shield her face while trying to climb down the ladder. But one foot missed a slippery rung. Off-balance, her body swung hard to the side and her fingers lost their grip. Tumbling backward, she landed in a heap of skewed limbs and a hollow thunk as cranium met concrete.

With one last snarl at the grate, the wolf left to join its mates, still surrounded by the screeching dark fliers. Distant snarls and cries diminished after a time and finally were gone.

In the bottom of the vault, Glendyl heard nothing. A trickle of fluid leaked from her skull, forming a ragged puddle in the spongy moss.

106

Part Two

WILDCARDS

108

19 :: CONSEQUENCES

THE MASSIVE PENTAGON glittered like a high-rise ice sculpture in the mid-morning sun. Lizbeth Marble, panting from exertion, looked down from her secret spot on Kissever Ridge at the marvelous mass of Castle Ommergard. It was magnificent: no other word would do. Her favorite feature was the mishmash of odd rooflines and towers sprouting from the top of it.[7]

According to historical accounts, this bizarre construction had once floated far and wide across the Earth, cresting high mountains, skimming wave tops on the Seven Seas and entertaining appreciative audiences with what the bombastic Lord Bellicarie had called "impossible confections of aerial theatre." Now it was hemmed in by the dense forest on all sides, all except for a sort of grass moat in which no trees or shrubs grew. Although the Castle was supposed to be empty and dead, it had a strange shimmery quality about it that somehow made it seem very much alive. And it always seemed spotless.

---

7 :: *While the stylistically chaotic design elements of Castle Ommergard earned much ridicule from architectural critics, Lord Bellicarie was unfazed. "Damn the critics, love the customers!" was a frequent expression according to his crews. As a shrewd impresario who regularly played to audiences of radically disparate cultures and values, he knew the importance of establishing a respectful relationship with all cultures he visited, and used every available means to convey this. The myriad of famous architectural landmarks covering Castle Ommergard's roof were designed to create a tangible sense of "global village" in the minds of its patrons. "A little something for everyone, everywhere," exclaimed Bellicarie more than twice.*

Lizbeth's secret spot was in the 'wild' part of South Park west of Kissever Ridge, but it might as well have been a hundred miles away; almost nobody ever came here but Lizbeth. She had walked the distance from the neat-as-a-pin Skanderfut home on Thorogood Court in East Village, setting out not long after breakfast and despite a stern "encouragement" from Mr Skanderfut to spend the first day of summer break cleaning her room. Lizbeth had milled around the chaos of her bedroom for all of ten minutes before the impossible absurdity of this assignment crystallized in her mind; be stuck in here on the day after her only friend departed St Coriander for an encounter with some horrible early death? Not in a million Elevations!

The trail to her secret spot was virtually invisible from the broad semiturf pathway that was St Orwell Loop, the functional equivalent of a "beltway" in St Coriander. Her discovery of the trail three years ago had been blind luck. The triggering event began with taunts about her father.

The occasion was one of the weekly South Park Nature Days. As usual, Lizbeth had ignored the taunts and continued what she was doing: reading. But when Cardiff Vardisky — the biggest, burliest, nastiest stinkwit in her rank — snuck up behind her and decorated her hair with a squirt of gooey eggmash from his lunchtube, Lizbeth's long-suffering patience went up in smoke.

A long right arm shot straight up, her open palm catching Cardiff hard under his dimpled square jaw. She hadn't even taken her eyes off her slate. Lizbeth heard the squish-crunch sound of teeth penetrating tongue to meet other teeth and didn't wait to find out precisely what happened: her feet knew what to do. Long strides took her quickly away from her stunned rankmates and onto one of the numerous forest trails snaking through the undeveloped areas of South Park.

An encounter of mutual surprise with a sixteen-point stag made her lurch off the trail and into a thicket of dense, thorny deerbrush, from which she eventually emerged onto another trail, her exposed skin a mass of oozing scratches. This narrow and badly overgrown trail took her over the ridge to a place where, for the first time, she actually saw the Castle. From that day forward, learning everything she could learn about Castle Ommergard had become her secret project. That was then.

Today had nothing to do with Project Ommergard, as she had come to call the activity that consumed most of her spare time. She was here today because she couldn't bear to be in St Coriander; the town seemed empty and hostile without Glendyl. Lizbeth felt empty, too, and something else that she couldn't quite name.

Restless, she surveyed the vista spread out below, her eyes tracing the greenish-brown ribbon of thornmesh that was the Township Fence. Beyond the fence was the so-called Deadly Forest, a darker, denser mass of tall ponderosas, yellow pines, oaks and gnarled bigleaf maples that isolated St Coriander from all else, including her one fascination: Castle Ommergard.

Her eyes wandered along the Township Fence. Today she felt its imprisonment in a way she'd never felt before: a tightness in her body and her mind that seemed to be compressing her very spirit. Then she smiled. In a clearing at the bottom of the hill on the St Coriander side of the fence, a family of well fed mule deer cropped a patch of tall spring grass. Responding to some signal inaudible to Lizbeth, their heads turned to look up the hill toward her secret spot. Lizbeth held her breath: the old stag — was he the same one she had encountered before? — was gazing straight at her, holding her eyes in his.

As one, the troupe turned back toward the fence and bolted. Lizbeth let out a tiny scream; the animals were bounding straight toward the Township Fence and disaster. The fence would kill them. Time slowed for Lizbeth; the deer bounded, seeming to hang in the air as their trajectories crested and they fell toward the fence. Then they passed through as if the impenetrable mass of thornmesh was no more solid than air, and disappeared into the Deadly Forest.

Lizbeth's mouth hung agape, her mind a velodrome of competing ideas. She was halfway down the steep draw before she realized she had decided to do something foolish, and quite possibly foolishly dangerous: test the Township Fence. If the deer weren't creatures of her imagination or some kind of projection, she might somehow navigate the Deadly Forest to stand before the object of her obsession. Perhaps even touch it.

Lizbeth Marble probably knew more about Castle Ommergard than anyone currently alive in St Coriander, not counting the Librarian.[8] Tidbits from her mental archives tumbled into her foremind as she threaded her way downhill, dodging trees, underbrush and boulders:

- Early recollections from a history lesson about how the Castle became grounded in its current location (something about not paying somebody for something, which triggered the Second Nevergate War).

- An ancient slatecomic called *Duel of the Skylords* (an over-dramatized account of the dragons from Ommergard and wyverns from Castle Caraway creating bloody aerial madness in the vicinity of St Coriander and Mt Funnybone).

- A 2280 vidforum about whether WorldGov was within its rights in ordering the decommissioning of all Nevergates (no single opinion prevailed). There was much more in Lizbeth's head about Castle Ommergard and Lord Bellicarie and Dunnigans and Nevergates and Exeter and dragons and wyverns, but Lizbeth had reached the clearing.

The last memory to present itself before she shuffled them all aside was a mad collage of clips from the famous homevid of the gory scene in Central Park that marked the beginning of the "new age" of St Coriander. She still found it hard to believe that it was 250 years ago when the Mad Sorcerer Exeter had flown the dragon queen Emmishak into St Coriander to issue his stern proclamations about the New Rules.

Lizbeth shook her head to send the images away. She now stood

---

8 :: *As an SI, the Librarian possessed a special kind of aliveness, strictly speaking.*

within arm's reach of the spot in the Township Fence the deer had passed through.

Lizbeth tested the fence with a dry pine branch. It passed through the dense, spiky tangle with no sparks and no resistance whatever. But what if the Fence was only dangerous to humans, not sticks or deer? It was a possibility, she supposed. Cautious and tentative, she edged a bony index finger forward and touched one of the gnarly, twisty-thorned vines near the surface, ready to jerk the finger back instantly.

The finger touched only air. She forced her arm into the evil stuff and still met no resistance, felt no sensation at all but the warm rays of a late spring sun. Lizbeth allowed herself a brief grin. Obviously it was only some sort of projection. A heady gust of exultation blew away her lingering fears and she stepped through the yards-deep hedge into the Deadly Forest.

Not certain what she had expected to find on the other side of the Township Fence, she felt mildly disappointed. It looked like any of the wooded open spaces in St Coriander. Still, it might have land-mines or deadfalls or snares or who-knows-what. Best to follow the deer trail. Some minutes later, Lizbeth emerged from the forest and crossed the decrepit narrow road that ran along the forest edge. For the first time she could appreciate the true majesty and grandeur of the castle.

Setting her fears and uncertainties aside as best she could, she walked the grassy fifty yards required to stand under the Great Gate that was the only obvious land entrance to the castle. Looming thirty feet high and about as wide, the pentagonal opening was guarded by a portcullis, a grate of lustrous impervium bars spanning the entire height and width of the entry portal and shimmering with some kind of strange energy.

Looking through the bars was like looking through agitated water; gross shapes could be seen through it, but nothing could be seen clearly. She reached out a finger to touch one of the smooth uprights of the grid. It was like touching a layer of invisible resistoflex: the harder she pressed, the more it resisted. There was also a disconcerting sense of something buzzing around her head from every direction like a swarm of gnats, but nothing was visible.

When the buzzing faded, she found herself wondering why she was standing in front of this dead old place. With an oddly hazy mind, she turned, crossed the grassy moat, retraced her steps back through Forest and Fence, and made her way back into St Coriander. At the Green Goblet Diner in the Town Center, Lizbeth treated herself to a milkberry malted fresh from the bevwall. She took it with her to Central Park, where she sat on a slatted bench and sipped in a blissfully blank-minded state until a setting sun reminded her to go home and face the inevitable consequences.

20 :: LEAVING FOREVER

IT WAS ANOTHER tense, silent, too-late dinner at the Skanderfut household. While Lizbeth Marble's long, nervous fingers trolled the ends of her hair, her eyes studied the pyramid of likesteak on her plate. Was deliverance from the upcoming ordeal hidden under the pinkish slices? Finally, her fork decided to find out. The mound of morsels disappeared, but at the bottom was only a naked dinner-plate: no deliverance for Lizbeth.

Mr Skanderfut postponed the inevitable until the meal of rose pink, done-just-right likesteak and mashed tuberalls with perfect sauce had been consumed in proper quantities by all at the table. Then he started the 'family discussion.'

"We missed you today, Lizbeth. This coming and going without being courteous enough to obtain permission — or even inform others about your plans — has just got to stop. Your mother was very concerned about you when she knocked and found your room empty. Empty of you, that is: everything else under the sun is in there. Really, Lizbeth, the chaos in there is simply despicable. How can you stand to spend one minute in that strew-box?"

Lizbeth's first thought was to snap something really hurtful like "She's not my mother, any more than you're my father, you sawed-off weasel." But she didn't. Her second thought was to talk about the odd gap in the Township Fence and safely getting through the Deadly Forest to Castle Ommergard and back. But she didn't. In fact, every time she thought about her morning adventure, the experience got all scrambled in her mind and she couldn't find any way to unravel it with words. It was very strange and very frustrating. Lizbeth was itching to tell somebody about her discovery — as a last resort, maybe even her foster parents — but her mouth just couldn't seem to form words around that particular topic. Zero for two in the rejoinder column, Lizbeth just sighed and held her silence.

"Do you have anything to say for yourself, Lizbeth? Or should your family just expect the silent treatment, as usual?"

"May I go to my room?" inquired Lizbeth as sweetly as she could manage, still hoping for a miraculous deliverance from the inevitable.

"I think you owe us all an explanation for the worry and discomfort you caused today. Vinzie, you don't need to be part of this discussion. Need I say more?"

Eleven-year-old Vinzent Skanderfut said nothing, but departed the table with a knowing snort. Thin Lizzie was going to get it bigtime tonight and he was going to miss the fireworks. Well, listening secretly via his old SpyFly would be almost as good as being there in person. If he turned its buzzer off, his father would never notice; when his father was in one of his Lizbeth Moods, he wouldn't notice a turtle swimming in his wine glass.

Abraham Skanderfut was a decent, fairly representative St Coriander adult male, if a good bit shorter in stature than the average and too proud to sign up for growth therapy. He went to Elevation Group three times a week and believed he was making good progress; another few months and he'd probably be able to do a level three-psychon waver, more than creditable for a St Corie his age. He was also a member of the Volunteer Orchardists, helping to maintain the sculptures and stuffing ucey-boxes[9] with uneaten fruit from the thousands

_____

9 :: A Ucey-box is a collection point for waste materials destined for the Universal Converters, commonly called "uceys" in St Coriander. Uceys break down materials into their constituent atoms. Through a still secret dark energy exchange they generate net usable energy in the process and provide feedstocks for the fabrax molecular assemblers. St Coriander acquired its first

of fruit trees that snaked through St Coriander residential districts.

While Mr Skanderfut also coached the Kickapoo Sandhockey Club, it was his work as a Spellfellow[10] that had become the most satisfying part of his life. In fact the single bad thing about his being a Spellfellow was that it had inadvertently brought the gangly, willful, moody and over-smart Lizbeth Marble into the otherwise even-keeled Skanderfut household. The fact that she now towered over him by nearly the diameter of a bangerball only made things worse.

117

The very public disappearance of Lizbeth's biological father and mother during the Soulfire[11] demonstration at the Amphi had

---

central Universal Converter in 2205.

10 :: Magic arrived in St Coriander during the decade of 2347-2357. It began with the famous July 4, 2347 "Peter Pan Flyover," as it was subsequently labeled. On this singular occasion, a formation of twelve identical boys clad in identical skin-tight green garments converged over Central Park just before the traditional fireworks program.

Arriving from the four compass points, the boys flew elaborate and convoluted formations over the crowd, which included most St Coriander residents. Their final formation was a full speed convergence from twelve perfectly spaced clock points. They collided in an explosion of green fire and disappeared from view. When the green smoke cleared, a phalanx of tiny fairies was busily scattering sparkles of golden pixie dust over the crowd, after which they also faded from view.

During that year, various magical products began to mysteriously appear in the fabrax menus, the first being Color Magic WaxWands, which were an immediate hit with St Coriander preteens. During the next few years, magical devices became commonplace. Unicorns were even sighted roaming the wilder areas of South Park. Within a decade of the Flyover, magic was taken for granted in St Coriander and generally attributed to the town's devotion to the principle of Planar Elevation and its spiritual corollaries.

The art of spellcasting also began to develop in those years. Its beginnings are thought to coincide with the mysterious appearance of an anonymous slatedoc — The Applied Mathematics of Impossibility — on the slates of certain SCIAK dabblers in obscure mathematics. In 2367 the Spellfellow Society was founded by a secretive group of enthusiastic hobbyists. It flourished, and in 2416, Spellfellow Vanceworth Rhialto proposed the construction of the slim, ever-changing 50-story Spellfellow Tower on St Estelle's Hill overlooking the Library. Although initial opposition to such a structure was intense, it was ultimately surmounted and the tower came into being a year later. Gradually the Spellfellow Society evolved into what it is in 2534: a combination of men's lodge, informal trade association, service club and regulatory body. It remains the most prestigious and powerful non-religious organization in the town.

11 :: Landrow Marble's demonstration of his extravagant "Soulfire

occurred ten years before and was still one of the most talked about mysteries of St Coriander. For the umpteenth time, Skanderfut pondered his own possible involvement in this mystery.

He had been on the Spellfellows Program Review Committee that year and took the responsibility seriously. Perhaps too seriously. Landrow Marble's proposed program, he had thought, might be treading a little too close to the spiritual prerogatives of the Holy Quincunx Church. On his own initiative, he had privately described the program and his concerns to Father-Mayor Gullwimple.

The outcome of their session in the Chamber of Holy Probabilities had not been satisfying and the day following Landrow Marble's disastrous program, Lizbeth, the Marble's only child, had been assigned to the Skanderfuts for upbringing. It was unfair and a continual source of exasperation, but duty was duty.

Skanderfut glared at the source of his decade of agitation and spoke: "Well, Lizbeth, we're waiting patiently for your explanation."

Lizbeth was in no mood for explanations. She was angry with just about everything and everyone, partly because she somehow knew what Mr Skanderfut had just been thinking. She had seen the vids after all, had played them a hundred times looking for reasons.

"I don't have to give you any explanations. You're not my parents. I have no parents. I'm an orphan. My father murdered my mother and somebody else murdered my father. And nobody even

---

matrix" spellset occurred during a Potluck-at-the-Amphi event on July 4, 2524. His wife, the splendidly endowed Fawn-Heather, served as his assistant. In essence, the program was a simple fireworks display. The tall, black-caped Master Spellfellow made extravagant gestures while masterful pyrotechnics launched from the shaved head of his white-gowned assistant. As the spectacle continued, Fawn-Heather's form gradually became transparent. After the final skyburst spewed from her polished scalp, her barely visible form quivered like a jellyfish and vanished, her gown falling to the stage in a rustle of white folds. That was the first part of the program. After an intermission, Landrow Marble would return and perform the exercise in reverse. Unfortunately, he disappeared during the intermission. After an exhaustive search revealed nothing, Sheriff Dolittle issued a warrant for Terminal Misuse of Human Resources. Although theories abound, no trace of either Landrow or Fawn-Heather has ever been found.

cares about it but me. And I'm sick of St Coriander. You're all sheep. What kind of people send their Luckiests — their own children — off into the wilderness by themselves to never return? And just because of some stupid old rules laid down by some stupid old dead sorcerer? Can you answer that Mister and Missus Skanderfut? Can you? Well Forrbank Dorelli can answer it. And ...."

Abraham Skanderfut jerked up his hand in a "stop" gesture. He had heard this provocative speech before and had been practicing his self-control. He could handle the business about not being Lizbeth's actual parents: that was mere fact. But any mention of Forrbank Dorelli — just a Dunnigan by another name, and a too-smart-for-his-britches one at that — was a real hot button. He clenched his teeth unconsciously and spoke in a hiss of stifled anger, enunciating each syllable as if it were an item of extreme value. "Please - do - not - use - that - name - in - this- house - hold, Lizbeth Marble. That person you mentioned is nothing but an immoral cur and his ideas are scandalous, disruptive nonsense. If you ask me, the man should be locked into a Small Dark Room until he regains his senses. And I'm not the only one in St Coriander who thinks so. Even your accursed father would have thought him mad!"

Skanderfut's voice skittered like a blob of Jello on a hotplate.

"Now, Dear," said Bethangel Skanderfut soothingly. "We all know how you feel about Mr Dorelli. Lizbeth didn't mean all that, you know. She's just unhappy that her friend Glendyl is off on her Great Adventure. I'm sure she will be the one to find the Key after all these years; two hundred and fifty is a propitious number, and ...."

Mr Skanderfut interrupted, now calmer. "Yes, of course she will. And the number two hundred and fifty does indeed have excellent prospects. The Spellfellows have divined Glendyl Fenderwell's chances at 1 in 12,488; remarkably good odds, particularly compared to her recent predecessors. But I am being distracted."

He leaned forward and glared his most intimidating, small-eyed glare at Lizbeth. "I want to make this point very, very clear, Lizbeth Marble. Have nothing further to do with Forrbank Dorelli. Nothing.

Zero. And do not even consider for one moment — at least while you are the duly appointed ward of this household — becoming involved with COMISC. It is nothing more than a klatch of supercilious fops and ne'er-do-wells!"

Skanderfut paused to catch his breath then continued his tirade. "I'll warrant you that it is already under investigation by the authorities. And the proper, ordinary citizens of St Coriander are getting fed up as well. You might much more productively become better acquainted with Cecilia Krebs. Her father is quite knowledgeable in matters of St Coriander's traditions and institutions, some things you could do well to learn better. Forget all your Castle Ommergard fantasies and rejoin the real world, Lizbeth. Am I understood? Lizbeth?"

Lizbeth had heard all this a million times — or a dozen, or twice. Who could keep count of such moronic nonsense? Still, she usually maintained control. But tonight, something pushed her over the edge. She stood up, her face drained and bluish with impotence, and stormed out of the house. Slamming the door hard enough to rattle the wind chimes, she wished she were leaving forever. And this time she was.

21 :: A QUESTION OR THREE

HER REFUGE AT TIMES like this was the St Coriander Library. Lizbeth's favorite hideaway was in the Deep Stacks, in the seldom-visited Shinduffer Level, eighteen floors below the Town Center's plaza level. Here, the vast history of the planet waited patiently for eyes that never came to visit. When feet trod these aisles, it was usually a case of their being lost. One simple reason was that the Library's incomprehensibly vast collection of simmers, vids and even ordinary bookbuttons was vastly more popular. But even these were not overused: most St Coriander citizens were not inclined to delve much into the unreal world of recorded media, whatever its form.

Forrbank Dorelli, of course, had a theory; the people of St Coriander had misplaced their curiosity over the last several centuries. Perhaps life was too magical, too easy, too simple, too comfortable, too defined. And then there was Elevation at "thrice sixteen." It was all "as luck would have it," but a flimsy substitute for Real Life in his opinion.

When Lizbeth came to the Deep Stacks it was usually to brood and stew: sometimes, like tonight, over an unhappy incident; sometimes to ease a more general malaise. Often, she would sit at one of the tiny desks sandwiched between rows on the north wall and play solitaire on her slate, with her thinking mind put out to pasture for a while.

Sometimes she would have a private conversation with her favorite Septriq oracle, a hairless, ebony-faced wyvern named Zoleen. She felt a strange kinship with the wyvern, a member of a species that no longer existed. While she rarely used Septriq as a divinator, she often felt stimulated by her oracle's cryptic and provocative statements. And sometimes, she felt as if Zoleen could see into her very soul. Tonight, though, Septriq, sitting and solitaire were impossible: she just had to walk.

For no particular reason, she walked very slowly up and down the narrow aisles, glancing at the thousands of antique paperbooks and occasionally stopping to read a spine or a title page or an introduction. Tonight she took very little notice of the books themselves: they were merely a patchwork of colors. Her mind was occupied with "why" questions: hundreds of them, all competing for top-of-mind attention. So Lizbeth paced up and down the rows, hoping for understanding to bloom before her like a red rosebud on her birthday.

The oldest books were in the antiquities section on the east wall of Shinduffer. After walking up and down the rows and rows of inner stacks, there was nowhere else to go but the east wall. About halfway down the corridor along the wall, a particular book caught her eye. Frowning, Lizbeth tried to puzzle out just what had attracted her to this book. It was not an unusual size, nor was it an unusual color: most of the books on this wall were bound in "library leatherette," either red, blue, green, brown or black. This one was black, just like its neighbors. It was on the second shelf from the top, a little above her eye level, but that wasn't unusual either: thousands of other books were also at this height. It's title was different from the others of course, but the stamped gold lettering on its spine was in the same style as all the others. Then she got it.

What differentiated *Cultural Tombstones Vol. XIV* by R. U. Dhaaft was that the top of its spine was worn down. Just a tiny bit. Odd, she thought. How would that happen? Was it more popular than it sounded? Now curious, she reached up to pull it out for closer inspection, but instead of sliding, it pivoted outward, as though it had an invisible hinge at the bottom of its spine. As the book swung toward her, a section of shelving rotated silently to her left, including the section of floor where she stood.

Lizbeth now found herself facing a narrow hallway illuminated by a series of widely spaced sconces mounted high on the white walls. Inverted cones of silvery light painted softening repetitions on the otherwise stark surfaces. This could not actually be happening, could it? She pinched her leg to wake herself from whatever daze she had fallen into. "Ouch!" she exclaimed out loud. Then to herself: Evidently, I'm awake. That hurt.

123

The blank wall a few feet in front of her suddenly came alive with large, luminescent blue words. The first message to appear was an admonition: SHHH! DO YOU WANT TO WAKE THE DEAD?

As that faded it was replaced by another: WELCOME TO THE TRANSLATION CENTER, LIZBETH MARBLE. FOR A GOOD TIME, FOLLOW THE ARROWS.

Lizbeth was convinced she had somehow fallen asleep and was unable to wake herself. But if this was a dream it was an interesting one. And who in St Coriander could pass up a good time, she thought facetiously? Wasn't that what the sheeple all lived for? That, or sports?

Luminescent red arrows blinked into existence on the floor, pointing down the hallway to her left. Lizbeth hesitated for a heartbeat, and then followed the arrows, not noticing the silent return of the stacks to their original position, or that she was now trapped in this secret corridor. Her gait was tentative at first, but she gathered speed, propelled by a heightened sense of curiosity and an unfamiliar inner pressure.

Had she looked back over her shoulder, she would have seen that the end of the corridor was following only a few paces behind her. But she charged straight ahead, following the arrows right through the apparently solid wall at the end of the hallway.

Suddenly, Lizbeth Marble was elsewhere, this particular elsewhere being a circular white room of uncertain diameter. Floor, ceiling, walls — all glowed with inner illumination, making it virtually shadowless. Her feet came to a stop. Was it this strange illumination that gave her the vague sensation of motion, like the slidewells in the Holy Quincunx and the Library? Or was she actually moving?

The room was completely empty save for an upholstered chair, an ottoman and a man. Two red arrows in the floor pointed toward the chair, a cushiony recliner of some glossy deep red material. A man of uncertain age with a remarkably long red beard occupied the chair, his gray boots resting on the ottoman. The man motioned to Lizbeth to come forward. Silence was broken not by his voice, but by a curious whispering; it was as if the same person were whispering in both her ears at the same time. "It's okay, Lizbeth. I won't bite," said the whisper. "I'm one of the good guys. Come over here and let's talk for a while. I suspect you may have a question or three."

22 :: AGGRAVATION

THE FACE with the long red beard smiled. Unable to think of a reason for staying where she was, she followed the whispered suggestion and came forward a few steps. As she approached him, the man rose from the chair and put out a hand in greeting. "Call me Exeter, if you please. And please: take a load off and get comfortable. May I offer you a refreshment? I believe you prefer Ginsi, do you not?"

Lizbeth could now see that the man who called himself Exeter was tall, tanned and appeared soundly built. His costume was remarkably casual for a person of mythological stature: well-worn denim pants and a loose shirt patterned with grass-skirted, brown-skinned beauties, exotic flowers and swordfish. A blue baseball cap topped a thick mass of long red hair clasped into a ponytail. Lizbeth felt underdressed in her lavender Eastac jumpsuit.

Exeter gestured for Lizbeth to sit. Turning around, she discovered a comfortable blue chair was now behind her. Testing it with her hand to assure herself it was real, she sat.

A small round metal table now appeared immediately to her right. On the table was a white napkin with "Exeter's Mt Faunibeune Services" printed on it in an ornate blue script. On the napkin was a trademark Ginsi glass filled with an effervescent, green liquid. "Go ahead, have some. It's not poison, you know."

Lizbeth was more than a little intimidated by this unprecedented situation, but the idea of a Ginsi appealed to her at that moment.

Nobody would go to this much trouble just to give her a poisoned beverage, she reasoned. "Thank you, Mr Exeter, I needed that."

"Just plain Exeter will be fine, Lizbeth. Lose the Mister: we're all friends here. So, now. Let me begin by congratulating you. You're the first Accidental we've had in 173 years. What's an Accidental, you ask? In one sense, it's any person who finds his or her way here without an invitation or a passtap. That booklatch won't swing back for just anybody, you know. There are exactly three ways you can get to this place from St Coriander and you found one of them without even looking for it. And I must say, you — and that booklatch — surprised us all, me included. And I don't surprise easily any more. We weren't exactly expecting anybody at the moment. So, congratulations are definitely in order."

While Exeter was making his little speech, Lizbeth was studying him. Could this really be the legendary Exeter himself? He should have turned to dust a very long time ago. But here he was. Or at least here was someone claiming to be Exeter. Lizbeth saw a man who looked much older than any man in St Coriander, yet in some inexplicable way, not old at all. She decided it had to be in his eyes: young and sparkly orbs, almost mischievous. Lizbeth liked mischievous, which was one reason she had liked Glendyl Fenderwell so much; although she usually kept it under wraps, Glendyl had a mischievous streak, too.

"Are you listening, Lizbeth?"

Exeter's question caught her by surprise. "Sort of," she admitted. "Are you really Exeter? The legendary Exeter the Wise? The guy who supposedly flew a fire-breathing dragon into Central Park and laid down the New Rules? How could you still be alive?" Lizbeth recalled her dinnertable conversation and was beset by a surge of anger. "I'm sick of your New Rules, Mr Exeter; if you're really Exeter and not just some weird character in the weird dream I'm having. I'm really sick of the old New Rules and all the simplesimons in St Coriander and stupid Questing, and ...." The words had just sort of extruded themselves from her mouth on their own initiative; now they sputtered to a stop. Lizbeth's face went pink; she hadn't intended to say any of that.

"Ahhhhh," said Exeter, stretching the expression out for several seconds. "I see we are just a trifle stressed, eh, Lizbeth? But, yes, the legendary Exeter the Wise: I am he. Being very, very old is no difficulty at all if you know the tricks. Of course, I know the tricks. And yes, I wrote up the New Rules after the war ended; and I flew Emmishak into Ditherhead Central to announce them. People thought they were an expression of my annoyance with the flaccid, gutless, weak-kneed, overlucky nitwits who live in the affluent little time-warped nuthouse of St Coriander. And they were right.

"But they also have an entirely different purpose, Lizbeth. Believe me. We — the good folk of Castle Ommergard — have a Great Work underway. And St Coriander is playing an important role in that work.

"But all work and no play makes for a bland enchilada, doesn't it? So we have fun, too. And part of my fun in this Great Work is that I get the occasional surprise. Like you, for example. To be brutally candid, Lizbeth Marble, I didn't expect you to find your way here. Actually, maybe it's more accurate to say it this way: I didn't expect the person who found their way here to be you. Or now. Nothing personal, of course. But you're here and we'll just have to make the best of it, won't we?" Exeter paused and gave Lizbeth a piercing gaze, nodding slightly.

"I'm just now starting to think you might possibly be the Wildcard we've been hoping for, not just an Accidental. Wildcards don't happen every day, you understand. But then neither do Accidentals; it's too soon to know for sure which you are, of course."

"What do you mean by 'make the best of it'?" blurted Lizbeth. A shot of concern mixed with a splash of surly anger and a twist of fear had entered her voice. "And what are Wildcards and Accidentals? I don't think I'm liking this crap at all."

"Nothing to be concerned about, Lizbeth Marble. Not - at - all." Exeter stretched the short sentence like a rubber band and accompanied it with an authoritative raised eyebrow. "You didn't really *like* St Coriander anyway, did you?"

Lizbeth frowned and shook her head.

"Didn't think so. That's why you went out to look at our happy homestead this morning. And why you accepted the invitation offered to you by our deer friends. You were hoping for some magical deliverance from the stifling containment of St Coriander. And you got some magic this time, didn't you?"

He didn't wait for Lizbeth to answer. "But if not magic, at least you had enough luck in you to be at the right place at the right time; luck is very nearly as handy as magic, and occasionally much more so. But luck has a mind of its own; powerful sometimes, but highly unreliable most of the time. Well, Lizbeth, you have just escaped comfortable, dull St Coriander for good. Do you get my meaning?"

Lizbeth's stomach seemed to be suddenly infested by a convention of hyperactive centipedes. Did he mean she could never go back?

"If I read your expression correctly, Lizbeth, you have understood my meaning; you can never return to St Coriander. Never ever. We will drum up a program for you, but first we'll need to run some tests so we can zero in on exactly what it is about you that allowed you to get here. The odds of your finding your way here by sheer accident would require so many simultaneous system malfunctions and chance eventuations that they calc out in the neighborhood of 768,929,520,367 to 1. More or less. So even if I use the term "Accidental," I'm not really a strong believer in sheer accidents.

"The tests will identify your knack; and then we'll have an idea what to do with you. And after your tests, there will be coursework and training. Years of learning. Decades of learning. Centuries of learning. Whatever it takes. But alas, no Elevation. We of Castle Ommergard live long, youthful, fruitful lives. Elevation is a total waste of resources in an era when resources are very dear indeed."

"I am very confused Mr Exeter. I don't have a clue what you are talking about. This is making me very nervous. Actually, I'm pissed. Really pissed! You can't just keep me here against my will. No way you can do that. Sheriff Dolittle would ... do something!"

Exeter ignored this outburst and spoke in his most soothing tones. "I hope I haven't frightened you too much with all this strange talk, Lizbeth; I assure you that you'll catch on very quickly. I think you'll find there are a lot of benefits to being part of our little secret community. In the meantime, let's take a quick tour of Castle Ommergard and get you settled. You wanted to get in? Now you're in. So what if you came in through the servants' entrance?

"Along the tour I'll introduce you to some of our crew; I suspect you might know — or know of — a few of them." Exeter stood up and in his right hand appeared a pair of sunglasses with impenetrably dark lenses and thick black frames, which he donned with a flourish. A shiny red door appeared in the wall behind him. "Right this way, Lizbeth Marble, Girl Wildcard. Maybe." A few moments later he and Lizbeth had passed through the red door and disappeared.

An invisible slice of floor followed Exeter and Lizbeth into Castle Ommergard. Sometime later it found its way to an exterior surface, folded itself into the shape of a paper airplane and glided off into a pleasant June night.

• • • • •

"The Wise One got the Wildcard," said the voice of an intelligence named Dryll from somewhere in the wall. "Can't be an accident. Your whole scheme could fall apart at any moment now, particularly if he locates and cracks the Nevergate before we do."

A silky, feminine alto responded soothingly. "Now, now: you tracked the flap and we both overheard the conversation. But events may not be quite how they seem. You, of all entities, must appreciate that. Too soon to know about the Wildcard business; the whole idea is still just our best guess about the Dunnigans' final scheme anyway. And Exeter may think he knows more than he really does. Wouldn't be the first time. When our good shadowflap gets to the uplink station we'll see if its psychon matrix can tell us something else. In the meantime, remind me again: what sort of instruments do you have in the vicinity of North Castle?" The conversation continued for several

129

minutes. Lysheem, the extremely tall, lanky creature that owned the silky voice, exhaled a cloud of smoke while her tail twitched in aggravation, an action that belied the calm in her voice.

23 :: HISTORICAL CURIOSITIES

"THE LIBRARIAN THINKS you may find this amusing." That was all the message from Dryll said. The wyvern satellite brain had recently become an enthusiastic player in the game and occupied itself by tapping into all manner of electronic information sources. It had even developed a "personal" mind-to-mind relationship with the Librarian in the St Coriander Library.

In what might seem like paradise, Lysheem lounged in her oversized hammock, swaying in a tropical breeze. As the last wyvern on the planet read the article, she washed down the words with mouthfuls of oysters, swigs of sangria ... and was amused.

Excerpt from "MYTH CREATION AND CREATED SPECIES"
By Forrbank E. C. Dorelli
St Coriander Institute of Additional Knowledge, 2521

Disdain. Awe. Fear. Admiration. Scorn. Five nouns, a flip-flopping teeter-totter pivoting on the word "fear." These nouns begin to describe the love-hate, yes-no, off-on attitudes of humans towards the first intelligent bipedal species created — more or less — by humans. During their brief span on the Earth, and despite their exceedingly small numbers, wyverns made an indelible impression on the minds and hearts of humans. After they disappeared, their image blossomed into momentary mythology and then faded, at least in St Coriander, where their fading occurred with the help of active suppression by the reigning power structure. This paper explores several dimensions of the human-wyvern relationship that may have served as mythic enablers.

Let us begin with a brief review of certain wyvernic qualities and their impact on the human psyche. Together, these qualities illustrate a core principle of myth creation: perceived superiority. However, the importance of time in the mythification process must not be discounted. What Zharvosky,[12] called the "co-temporality" issue is one intriguing perspective.

In the past, humans' dealings with superior intelligent species have usually been conducted from an imaginary perspective. Or so goes the dominant argument: archeologists have unearthed no bones of deities, only icons of them. Humans have mythified and worshipped nonhuman beings (intelligent and not-so) for many millennia, but there is no tangible evidence that any of these beings or species simultaneously inhabited this Earthly plane with humans.

The human imagination filled the need for so-called "higher powers." Examples abound, from Baal of the ancient Phoenicians, through the various Hindu and Egyptian deities and the Greek, Roman and Norse pantheons, to name but a few. And, much like deities from ancient times, wyverns had qualities that made them appear to be superior to humans in several ways. But wyverns coexisted with humans in realtime, not mythological time. Their superior qualities could be seen and touched, and the possibility existed — however remote — that one might someday move in next door.

Co-temporality aside, it was not until wyverns had vacated this Earth that the Cult of the Seemly Wyvern (a local example of mythification) sprouted in St Coriander. Expressed differently, the myth of wyverns did not appear until the immediate reality of wyverns was far enough removed in time that their superiorities could be regarded in the abstract: that is to say, without triggering an immediate fear reaction in humans.

The phenomenon seems rather like visiting a museum of dinosaurs and observing stuffed replicas. We see safe, harmless models. Thus humans, in the innermost core of their beings can say to themselves, in effect: "Yes, they were big, yes, they were terrible, but they are gone and we are here. Humans are superior."

In this era when wyverns are barely mentioned in local St Coriander curricula, let us now revisit certain of their unique and "superior" qualities: stature, for example. Averaging eight feet in height, wyverns were nothing if not imposing. Standing next to one would almost inevitably make a tall

132

12 :: *Ethel Mertz Zharkovksy, A Speculative Mythography of the Nevergate Era, 2270.*

human feel like a dwarf, and doubtless prompted many a nervous utterance of "Hello, up there" or something equally insipid.

Although slender and light for their height (owing to their hollow skeletal structure and advanced muscle designs), wyverns were also astoundingly strong: a wyvern in reasonably good shape could easily lift three times its own weight. Wyverns also had extremely fast reactions and could move their muscles at better than twice the speed of the human norm. In this limited sense, one might think of wyverns as being high-velocity, low-mass projectiles, and of humans, comparatively, as being low-velocity, high-mass projectiles.

133

The historic 2269 Semi-United World Combat Authority (SUWCA) match between the Penultimate Dismantler and Immolark, the great wyvern decathlete, was a noteworthy demonstration. In a blur of motion, the 8'-1" 250 pound Immolark casually dispatched the 7'-8," 510 pound Dismantler in just over four seconds. Seventeen of the Dismantler's bones were fractured, but no permanent damage resulted. Certainly a chilling exposition of precise infliction of injury.

Another enviable attribute is their chameleonic (or so-called "stealth cloaking") skin, which is perhaps responsible for the expression "sneaky like a wyvern." This remarkable ability taps into the deep human desire for selective invisibility.

A counterbalancing force (whether by original design or perhaps intentional cultivation by wyverns) was whimsy, which was expressed in a variety of ways, including a thoroughgoing, sometimes radical spontaneity. Whimsy could also be seen in their modes of attire. From a fashion perspective, wyverns, in the main, indulged in arbitrary, colorful, capricious, outlandish dress (some wags have posited that this is because they didn't have hair to worry about and fuss with). And rarely would two wyverns ever wear the same thing: the words "style" and "trend" are inapplicable to either wyvern clothing or behavior.

Perhaps the closest thing to a trend was when Jirrisik, a young reservation wyvern, learned how to program her own skin to display whatever pattern she stored in her uniquely wyvernic "side memory." Within several weeks, all wyverns had learned this capability and a period of "colorful, well-patterned nudism" flourished just prior to the completion of Castle Caraway.

"Wing-envy" aptly characterizes yet another unsettled human attitude toward wyverns. Although few humans ever saw a wyvern in flight, Dunnetix records indicate that the species possesses remarkable aerial speed and maneuverability characteristics. Anecdotal evidence of a number of their Navajo Nation neighbors tends to confirm this. Could "wing-envy" have perhaps contributed to some of the oft-reported tensions in this otherwise highly successful pre-Nevergate Wars business-political relationship?

The tail may be the only unique wyvern feature that has earned them more ridicule than envy from humans. Ignorant humans were able to feel superior in being tailless; wyverns' whip-like tails drew sneering references, notably "ape-like" and "monkey-like." But we must ask why their designers incorporated tails into their design. Was it mere whimsy? Or is it an enhancement, such as their extra fingers?

The thinking person will suspect tails were not an exercise in mere whimsy: "tail-envy" may well be warranted.

Physical features and capabilities aside, most humans found it even more difficult to give wyverns credit for their special brand of inventive intelligence. We humans have found it easy to forget that wyverns invented such "takeover" product lines as the Telowix™self-configuring multifunctionaries and GravLifter™ gravity inversion devices. This "forgetfulness" may have, in fact, been itself a product of wyvern strategy. Was this why they marketed all their inventions through the NavaTek brand and kept such a low media profile? Quite likely.

No doubt most of humanity subconsciously breathed a sigh of relief when the last wyverns departed planet Earth through the last Nevergate. The first real threat to human superiority on the planet was gone. In time, wyverns could safely be mythified, and what better place for that than the novelty-starved environs of St Coriander.

St Coriander's brief episode of wyvern mythification came and went about half a century after the end of the Second Nevergate War, just before magic made its aerial entry into St Coriander. As the story was reported in the *St Coriander Times*, a group of bored Eastac teens discovered a quaint relic in the St Coriander Library: a remarkable "fashion show" vid from the year 2259.[13] This vid launched the Cult of the Seemly Wyvern. Membership

---

13 :: On February 9, 2259, a community of 641 wyverns was discovered by a group of Green Warriors in an abandoned uranium mine near Grants, in the former USA (WG.US.NM). Although not technically a violation of the Created Species Interdiction of 2234, it was a significant embarrassment to the Clans Dunnigan and Dunnetix. The firm had publicly abandoned its Wyvern Project and allegedly gated all "breeding stock" to the Dunnigan spintown near Transpoint Station two and a half decades earlier after the alleged murder of a St Coriander student by a wyvern prototype. The Grants incident was also an embarrassment to WorldGov, which had responsibility for monitoring the

exploded within both Eastac and Westac. Meetings were held, the Library was mined for its every reference to things wyvernish and some succulent morsels of local history were exposed in the process. Most disturbing to "proper" St Cories (including our esteemed Fatherhood) were the Cult's "worship sessions" during which illegal substances that had been cleverly hacked from a fabrax were used to "heighten religious ecstasy."

The 'mature' population of St Coriander tolerated this affront to its spiritual dignity for several months, patiently believing it would soon subside. As one near-Elevation resident said in a letter to the *Times*: "Even the most turgid persuasions of youth eventually dissolve before the looming bliss of Elevation." However, when an eighty-foot inflatable of the so-called Wyvern Goddess was discovered waving to passersby from the [Holy Quincunx] Moat, enough was enough. The Fatherhood stepped in and the Cult was officially ordered dissolved.

135

Things were quiet for a week following the ban. Then one October morning two hundred-foot murals mysteriously appeared. They were substantial works, each spanning two of the corner obelisks and the space between them. One depicted a slender, hairless, two-legged creature with humanlike arms and legs and a pair of large, bat-style wings. The nude, blue-gray wyvern — obviously a female — stood with its hands on its hips, legs shoulder-width apart in a jauntily provocative pose. A face of timeless beauty held an expression of disdainful superiority. As if that were not provocation enough, a chubby, pink-skinned male human was prostrate before her, kissing the wyvern's left foot. The backside of the naked male bore a remarkable resemblance (by virtue of its over-ample proportions) to a member of the Fatherhood. The "G" and the "A" tattooed on the left

---

spintown quarantine.

In an attempt to minimize the highly overstated public hazards of a mere 641 wyverns, Marian Tina Louise Dunnigan, then Chief of Protocol of North Castle, contrived an unprecedented fashion show; eleven female wyverns were decked out in "wyvernized" editions of current haute couture and persuaded to "slink the runway." The event, held on St Valentine's Day in North Castle's Grand Theatre and carried live on a dozen channels, was a fashion disaster (the wyverns overplayed it to the hilt), but highly successful from a public relations perspective, making the species appear far more frivolous than dangerous. While a few WorldGov firebrands still clamored for the wyverns' destruction, the political fiasco surrounding the so-called Dragon Revolt of the prior year had made any such action politically impractical.

The Navajo leadership shrewdly extended an offer of sanctuary and the following year saw the launch of an official "Wyvern Home" in the remote Chuska Mountains within the vast Navajo Nation.

and right buttocks respectively, were thought to suggest that the buttocks belonged to Father-Mayor Gideon Alvernock.

The other mural depicted a naked female wyvern in a classic "mooning" posture, its barbed tail sinuously formed into a gesture known throughout time as "the finger."

Father-Mayor Alvernock acted with dispatch: a hundred boys were instantly expelled from their respective academies and made to perform unpleasant menial labor in public: trouserless, and with their initials tattooed on their buttocks. In little time, the Cult of the Seemly Wyvern was absorbed back into the placid flow of St Coriander life. A lesson about power had been learned. The feeble attempt the following year to resurrect the old Sacred Scale cult — where devotees paid similar homage to Cametto-5 dragons[14] — failed to garner much attention.

Since that time wyverns and dragons have been relegated to the status of mere historical curiosities in the incurious minds of contemporary St Cories.

---

14 :: *Modern dragons are mythoformed pseudoreptiles designed and cultivated on Cametto-5 for export to Zhohaffet-8 where they became popular pets for the indigenous Tumults, a species of gigantic andromorphs. They are believed to have originally been directly brought to Earth as early as 2215 through the renegade All Caribbean Freeboy Nevergate. The allegedly semi-intelligent, allegedly sterile dragons were shuttled into the well-established exotic pet blackmarket by the shadow import/export firm of Dalek & Co., which marketed them as the "trophy pet" of choice for wealthy showboaters, buffoons and moguls. Law enforcement officials were persuaded to look the other way.*

The outcome of the "Dragon Revolution" of 2258 was freedom from "pet slavery" for approximately seven hundred dragons. During the clever, bloodless and highly public "live revolution" the dragons dramatized their sordid status by binding their owners to chairs and forcing them to eat commercial pet food while the dragons somehow preempted a thousand channels and told their stories via a live "freedom telethon" hosted by popular Green Warrior leader, Marial Fletsam Hernandez. Although nothing was ever proved, it is widely believed that the uprising was fomented by Lord Bellicarie as a way to cheaply recruit the needed dragons for his proposed touring extravaganza, "Aerial Ballet for Dragons, Sky Monkeys and '34 Ford."

24 :: TO AND FRO

LYSHEEM CHUCKLED, downed a long belt of sangria and chewed her unlit cigar. She was contemplating Forrbank Dorelli's article on wyverns that Dryll had placed on her slate this morning.

"Fascinating. What do you think that Dorelli character would do if the last wyvern on earth moved in next door to him?"

Dryll's chuckle came from a nearby palm tree. "He's the master of Kissever House, a huge mansion sitting on a huge parcel. It might take him weeks to even notice he had a new neighbor." That was as close to humor as the orbital satellite brain ever got.

"Yeah, you're probably right. But back to business. Is your reading of what you call the 'evolving situation' the same as mine? Time for me to pull the plug on my tropical vacation and hightail it back to 'civilization'?"

"From my analysis, you are late already," remarked Dryll. Maybe *too* late.

• • • • •

Lysheem had neglected to expire during the Second Nevergate War. Nor did she depart the planet via Nevergate with the rest of her ilk; at the time of this history she was the only wyvern on Earth.

The true reasons for Lysheem's continued presence on the planet may never be known. What is believed — and how Lysheem herself would explain the situation — was that she was marooned. Her two-month "vacation" on Montserrat while the Second Nevergate War was cresting turned into two and a half centuries.

With both Castle Caraway and the last Nevergate out of commission, Lysheem was stuck on Montserrat, a small volcanic island in the Caribbean. Her original employer, the eminent Cavvitoy the Dawnhammer, had died in the aftermath of the infamous Battle of Wittwater Deep. This meant that both her transportation away from Montserrat and her monthly stipend as his "personal librarian" were no more.

For the first time in her young life (she was one of the wealthy, so-called "Reservation Wyverns" who grew up in Wyvern Home after the incident of 2259), Lysheem had been forced to fend for herself. Her unplanned independence began on the day she received a cryptic teleblade message from a haggard-looking Cavvitoy: "Stay put, little one," was all he said.

After that she was unable to ring up Castle Caraway on her teleblade or any of her other devices. Honoring Lord Cavvitoy's command, stay put she did: for a quarter-millennium. The fact that her Standard Toolbelt was lost shortly thereafter — along with several pounds of wyvern flesh — to a curious shark during a skindiving expedition, helped make her a permanent resident of Montserrat.

When her missing flesh grew back, Lysheem contented herself with her favorite island pursuits: nude sunbathing, beachcombing and frightening the few tough ecotourists who braved the decidedly un-idyllic Montserrat, which had just endured another massive volcanic eruption. She also developed a habit of drinking great jugs of homebrew sangria[15] in the afternoon, usually along with several quarts of raw oysters spiced with chili oil and lemon juice. Another new habit was smoking thick cigars from Havana.

After a few years, the rumors of giant black vampire bats scared off the last tourists and most of the tourist-serving indigents. At last there was only Lysheem and The Laughing Crab.

---

15 :: *By design, wyverns are immune to the intoxicating — and otherwise toxic —effects of alcohol and virtually all known "recreational" drugs. Lysheem just liked the "bite" her homebrewed rums gave to her fruity concoctions.*

The Crab's burly and cantankerous proprietor, Gabriel "Smoky" Goldstein, was not a quitter. He and Lysheem had developed an odd rapport, and spent many evenings in intense debate over such issues as the character of the ideal cigar leaf and the proper ingredients for a crab boil. Then one day, he assembled his secret recipes and his cache of treasure, and departed Montserrat in his underboat, the Blue Cigar, to seek a new life in Martinique.

As a final gesture of appreciation to his best customer, he left Lysheem the keys to The Laughing Crab's coolbox and his last case of fine Havana cigars. To the best of her knowledge, Lysheem was alone on the island.

Her carefree routine morphed into a horrific boredom compounded by a deep loneliness. When her boredom was at its worst, she would fly around the southern arc of the island to the long-abandoned human town of Plymouth.

It was during one of these "archeological expeditions" of the half-buried town, that she unearthed a large crate of ancient Telowix Industrial FabriKits[16] half-buried in the ruins of a warehouse. Telowix! Their almost genetic familiarity was more than comforting; it was like a stranded aviator chancing upon a well-stocked vertiport at the North Pole.

Almost as good was finding a consignment of ancient action vids, including modernized Clint 7 versions of the complete Clint Eastwood film library. Within a week, Lysheem could deliver half of

139

---

16 :: *Telowix™ FunBots were the initial product offering of NavaTek, the wyvern/Navajo joint venture. The initial "Telowix Craze" of Christmas 2263 established these programmable, self-reproducing nanomechanoids as the instant de facto standard for animated semi-intelligent toys. This was facilitated by the simultaneous introduction of the Telowix Free Design Library by Dunnetix, which had acquired master marketing rights for all Telowix-branded products. The introduction of the Telowix Industrial UtiliBot line the following year further extended this hegemony. Telowix Industrial FabriKits were introduced in 2274 on the heels of the first WorldGov Nevergate Closure Hearings. With their advanced self-regenerative capabilities and their ability to use extremely low-level source materials, they were an instant success in a shrinking world that anticipated a continued decay of basic technological infrastructure.*

Eastwood's trademark lines in English, French and Spanish with a passable whispery delivery. But the magnetic attraction of the Fabrikits pulled at her.

Within a few months, Lysheem designed, fabricated and programmed a dozen telowix assistants. Although not exactly perfect companions, her growing family of telowix was definitely better than no companions at all and helped alleviate her loneliness. Her attempts at tobacco growing were also beginning to yield smokable leaf. But life still moved slowly on Montserrat. Fortunately wyverns are nothing if not patient and resourceful.

A half-century passed before Lysheem was able to discover for certain the sad outcome of the little-known Second Nevergate War. Her source, the ancient and half-drowned owner of a sinking sharkboat, had a distant relative who had long ago sold fresh lobsters to the Master Chef of North Castle until the war and the Dunnigan Retreat.

Another half-century of alternating manic and depressive episodes passed before she decided to tackle the challenge of trying to locate and reopen the Mt Faunibeune Nevergate — if it still existed at all — for her own purposes. After much effort she designed and constructed a telowix fabratory, then used it to create a transceiver that could link up with the invisible wyvern satbank named Dryll. With this new resource in her bag she spent a hundred years (off and on, of course) researching the arcane theories that underpin the Nevergate's operation and fiddling unsuccessfully with this and that.

Lysheem's only notable success during that period involved her explorations into psychons[17] — those scientifically scorned particles of human emotion — and how to capture, interpret and manipulate

17 :: During a period of acute frustration with her attempts to plumb the theories of Nevergate operation, Lysheem took a break by plumbing, instead, Dryll's archives on the history of her species. This thread inevitably led her back to Dunnigan history and beyond, to the earliest pre-Dunnigan days of St Coriander. Thus did she encounter the theories of Merritt Frank Orwell. Unlike Orwell's scientific contemporaries, she found his ideas both fascinating and useful.

them. In this singular enterprise she was unwittingly assisted by a boatload of research subjects: marooned refugees from the violent excesses of a self-styled Pan-Caribbean emperor. The refugees lived out tranquil lives on all-but-empty Montserrat, oblivious to the contribution they were making to psychon science.

Thanks to Dryll and the cooperative Central Fabrax at St Coriander, in the last half-century she had established countless psychon-enhanced telowix recon units — principally shadowflaps — in the vicinity of Mt Faunibeune. Dryll now monitored St Coriander with surprising passion for a nonhuman intelligence. It was Dryll, for example, that identified the evolving psychonic profile of St Coriander and suggested using psychonic techniques to identify and nurture a potential Wildcard.

141

Success in Lysheem's long quest was now a possibility, except for one not-so-trifling difficulty; Exeter had a similar objective and might very well locate and reopen the last Nevergate first.

The latest news overheard by the slice of flooring was not at all good; Lysheem's potential Wildcard — Lizbeth Marble — was now in Exeter's possession. Exeter had closed the gap and now had the edge.

Lysheem pondered these recent events with increasing avveris (a uniquely wyvernish concept that humans might best understand as "outrageous frustration mixed with equal amounts of sour humor and fervent scheming"). Still, Dryll's detection of Immolark's reawakened Standard Toolbelt — that had been buried and silent for two and a half centuries — could be an interesting angle. Its new wearer, a Quester named Glendyl Fenderwell, might make things even more interesting. Lysheem stubbed out her cigar, downed her final swallow of sangria for the night and made a fateful decision.

She dug up the replacement Standard Toolbelt her telowix techs had built several decades ago and set it on the table. Memories of how to use it flowed back into her consciousness and she was ready.

She passed one seven-fingered hand over the sphere on the end of the dagger to attune the seedcrystal. "Globe," she commanded. A detailed image of the planet appeared in the air in front of her. She moved her hand and it began to slowly rotate. In a region once called New Mexico was a blinking red dot. A little over three thousand miles to the south and east was a blinking green dot, Lysheem's current location on Montserrat. Apparently satisfied, she then spoke the word "projection" and a different image appeared.

At first glance, this image appeared to be only a fuzzy near-blackness. After a few moments the panspectral in the remote teleblade had compiled coarse images. As the resolution increased, Lysheem could make out details: a small, circular chamber formed of what appeared to be concrete; a darker archway in one direction that might be a passage; dim light filtering in from a grate overhead. Adjacent was a dark form with a Standard Toolbelt around her waist. Had her interest in Glendyl Fenderwell arrived too late?

"Lifesigns." Now the dark room was overlaid with a series of luminescent, brightly colored symbols and moving zigzags. Lysheem studied these for a few moments, took a deep breath and looked around for her cigar. Why were they always out when you needed them to be lit?

She spoke several more commands and then slid her teleblade back in its sheath. Good enough for now, she decided.

The day completed to her satisfaction, she wriggled out of a backless lizardskin jumpsuit (as one might guess, virtually all wyvern bodywear is backless on account of wingedness) with its embroidered chartreuse dizzywids, lavender mangrits and teal foogles, and leaped up to her favorite rafter. Flinging her tail around it twice like a living bullwhip, she swung into a bat-like, head-down position, her leathery black wings folding around her body. Looking like a gigantic black prune on a pendulum, Lysheem proceeded to catch a few hours of accelerated, wyvern-style shut-eye, swaying to and fro in the genial caress of a tropical breeze.

25 :: NOTHING INVASIVE

DULL SOUNDS overhead: shuffling whir-clicks, metallic raspings, a resounding clang-clunk. A manhole cover was back in its proper place.

The clang-clunk clatter penetratated Glendyl's concussive stupor. First impressions were soggy cold and a sharp-edged throb that made the back of her head feel like it was doing push-ups: evidently she was still alive. She blinked. A shaft of bright light from above scanned back and forth, back and forth, back and forth. As it crossed her face Glendyl was momentarily blinded, but also snapped more fully awake. A snatch of memory, a snatch of now: someone — or something — had just closed the grate, her escape hatch out of this hole. And the thing that had closed it was still up there.

Behind the light were barely detectable forms that seemed mechanical, inhuman. The light snapped off and the whir-clicks receded and were gone. Gradually her eyes adjusted to the weak, watery light slicing through the grate. Daytime. Scenes started flowing. First, a sensation of running for her life. Then a potpourri of images: luminous wolf eyes, shadowy, winged devil-things, a zig-zagging rodent.

Trying to shake off the chaos, the cold, the pain in her head and a throbbing sensation in her right hand, she made a slow climb up the steel rungs and tried to push off the manhole cover. Her reward was a pattern of grooves pressed into her shoulder by the grate, some perspiration and a spike of helpless anger. The grate remained in place. "Weakling," it seemed to say.

It occurred to Glendyl to shout for help while she was up there, but she didn't. Would the maintenance device that had just departed come back? Would it apologize for its inconsiderate behavior and then pull open the manhole for her? Would it cook her a nice kimchee omelet with a side order of sourdough plickets and butterberry jam? And who else could possibly hear her shouts and pleas? Panic infused her spirit with helplessness. As a desperate wail began to form inside her throat, another Glendyl reached up from deep inside and took back control with a hard slap to the cheek. Thanks to that, some portion of her wits returned.

From the top rung of the manhole, this Glendyl scanned her round prison cell. Panic came back in a rush: where was her QPack? Had someone or something taken it while she slept? Glendyl crammed that idea back into the place where she kept ugly thoughts safely out of view. There were no marks in the moss to suggest the presence of any intruder besides herself. Still, she allowed herself a shudder.

All she had now was this stupid, ancient belt. Geez Louise! What a rotten thing to happen, and just when things were starting to look up. As she climbed back down to the bottom of her prison, her spirits climbed down too.

Her empty stomach growled an objection, another reminder of the missing pack. Her parched throat felt like she'd just tried to swallow a mouthful of dehydrated bugfuzz. A cup of steaming cannonberry tea would certainly be good right now, but a swallow or two of cold water would be even better.

Her right hand bumped against something. "Owwww!" she yelped. Squinting at her hand in the dim light she saw that the finger with the chuckwalla bite was nearly twice its normal size.

Glendyl's mindvoice got busy. Look what that creepy slitherbox did to me! But what's one more small misfortune for Glendyl Fenderwell, latest in a long line of unlucky Luckiests? So went a steady unspoken monologue inside her head as she cataloged her present difficulties. She next assessed the pulsing spot on her skull: a scabbed-over gash and a large knot. Nothing broken, probably. Looking up to where she had slipped on the ladder, she realized she was probably lucky just to be alive after a head landing from up there. Her face cringed.

She sucked in another deep breath, squared her shoulders and put her hands on her hips, the kind of gesture that vid heroes always make when their resolve has stiffened. A straightforward plan presented itself: feel her way a short distance into the two black tunnels that entered this manhole. Without any instruction from her conscious mind to do so, her right palm wandered from her hip to the top of the dagger and the oddly warm feeling of it gave her a moment of comfort in this empty place. At least she had something.

BZZ-BZZ-BZZ-BZZ-BZZ!

A sharp on-and-off buzz, like staccato bees, erupted from somewhere. Then stopped. Before the echoes even faded away, the buzzing erupted again. This time Glendyl's eyes swung to the source: the dagger in the silver sheath. The buzzing stopped. Now the smoky crystal ball on the end of the dagger was pulsing off and on with a bright red-orange light. Not real subtle, thought Glendyl. Low power, probably. Big surprise after lying in the riverbed for centuries. Then the pulsing light stopped, too.

PHYSHT-POP! The empty space in front of her exploded into a ... something. A very tall, nonhuman something. "Geez Louise!" exclaimed Glendyl, out loud.

"Geez Louise yourself, Glendyl Fenderwell," said the something. "Hate to buzz in on you like this. That's not the usual way of hailing somebody's teleblade." Glendyl's memories of Pre-Cloister History[18]

---

18 :: *In recent decades the word "cloister" had replaced "quarantine" as the preferred term for St Coriander's enforced isolation from the rest of the world. This had come about at the urging of Father-Mayor Gullwimple, who asserted that "cloister" better described what he believed had become a local cultural preference for isolation in pursuit of Elevation. Over the past year, Forrbank Dorelli had cited this position as "one more example of the preference for self-delusion that has attached itself like a festering canker to St Coriander's spirit."*

bubbled up; this weird thing had to be a lady wyvern. She couldn't decide whether to scream or laugh or cry. Instead, she thrust out her hand in greeting. It passed right through the possible wyvern, of course. Nice image job, thought Glendyl. Equal to the Spellfellows' best.

The fascinating image had spoken in a warm, luxuriant tone spiced with just a dash of gentle humor; not the voice of an enemy, or so Glendyl hoped. Would an enemy pop in wearing a short dress made of woven grass and decorated with lime green leaves and orange-rind epaulettes? A small laugh seeped out of Glendyl's gaping mouth.

"Like my outfit, huh?" drawled the image with a faint curl of smile on a face that Glendyl had just decided was beautiful, not frightening. Then, more to herself than to Glendyl, the image added, "How did a nice St Coriander girl like you get into a mess like this? And how are you feeling?"

Before Glendyl could think of anything to say, the image of the wyvern pointed a small something-or-other at her, then appeared to ponder something else out of Glendyl's field of vision for a few seconds. The wyvern then turned her striking, sky-blue cat eyes back to Glendyl and answered the question herself. "Let's see: nothing serious, if we take care of that infected finger straight away, that is. Let's do that right now, then let's talk. Okay? I may have a snippet or two of information you might find useful in your travels."

Glendyl nodded, puffed her cheeks out in a gesture of perplexed resignation and rolled her eyes in disbelief that such totally weird things could be happening to her. Nothing this strange had ever happened in St Coriander, she thought. She was wrong about that, of course.

"All right, Glendyl. First, grab hold of the teleblade's hilt — that's what the knife with the ball on the end is called — and pull it out of its sheath. And don't cut yourself again. Fine. Now just hold it in front of you so I can see it. Fine. Now close your eyes and picture your finger as your normal finger, if you can. Helps, but it's not absolutely essential. Is the handle getting a little warm and vibrating a little? Good. Now put it up near that scabby knob on your braincase and think about a happy, sunny moment. Fine. Now put the teleblade away. Carefully. Do that routine once every hour or so today and your finger and scalp will be fine by tomorrow. Okay? It's a simple accelerated re-education procedure for your tissues: nothing invasive. Okay? Good. Now let's talk."

148

26 :: A HAMBURGER IN EACH HAND

THEIR TALK (mostly listening for Glendyl) took about half an hour, after which Lysheem's image wished her a pleasant Quest and blinked out. Glendyl was left with only faint afterimages and vague hope. But what she heard in that half hour continued to send sparks running through her bedazzled mind for hours afterward. Still, this new knowledge — if it was true knowledge and not a wyvern's crafty fiction — didn't get Glendyl out of the hole she was in. She was going to have to manage that herself, with a little help from Lysheem's visit and the devices on what she now knew was a wyvern's Standard Toolbelt.

The rig she wore around her waist had belonged to a valiant wyvern named Immolark, who just happened to be one of Lysheem's egg-brothers, whatever those were. Or so said Lysheem. Glendyl wasn't at all sure she wanted to know this much about wyverns. Nor was she at all certain that she wanted to be wearing stuff that had belonged to an ancient, dead male wyvern, even a heroic one. But already her finger was feeling better, a clear sign that there was still some useful power in these devices.

Still, Glendyl was probably more confused than before Lysheem started conversing with her from luck-knows-where. For one thing, Glendyl had grown up thinking that there were no wyverns left on Earth. And maybe there had never been wyverns. Vids and pix could easily be faked. A lot of people believed that, including her own parents and most of her friends.

Some went further. Lolly Shim and a few other self-styled coffeehouse philosophers maintained that wyverns and dragons, if not clever hoaxes, were symptoms of a mass hysterical psychosis prompted by over-isolation. Pontus Krebs and a handful of conspiracy theorists went way beyond that. They maintained that all rogue ideas — including the alleged Nevergate Wars — appearing in St Coriander in recent centuries were the result of a tainted water supply.[19] Evil forces intent on undermining the power and beauty of the Holy Quincunx Church had performed this vile trick.

Forrbank Dorelli argued that such bizarre denial of historic realities was a sure sign of both a failed culture and decaying gray matter. Because he was a scientist of some sort, a few people were starting to take Forrbank Dorelli seriously. Of course, a lot more people were very troubled by Forrbank Dorelli. Judging from what she saw in the *St Coriander Times*, Glendyl concluded that most people went along with Mellowcrats like Pontus Krebs.

But after what she had just seen, she could hardly believe that her conversation with a wyvern was the result of doctored water.

Glendyl quelled this swirl of "adult" thoughts and steeled herself for her journey through the dank bowels of Dunnigans Wall. Ly-

---

19 :: *So-called designer psychoactives are a biochemical equivalent of computer viruses. At one time in the late prewar history of St Coriander, a small group of biopranksters dosed the underground Canvasback Reservoir with psychoactives they'd created. As a result, the entire population had very "interesting" mental experiences until a suitable counteragent was found. The pranksters were ultimately caught and confined to Small Dark Rooms until they confessed, repented and publicly apologized on the Holy Quincunx Elevation Stage, after which they were "deplaned" into a lower energy plane and disappeared from St Coriander. Some residents who had found their psychoactive experiences to be quite pleasant believed the punishment overly harsh. Others felt that forced deplaning transcended the authority of earthly creatures, including members of the Fatherhood. The somewhat ascetic and humorless Father-Mayor Alvernock ruled, however, that his roll of a "triple cyclops" on the mandatory appeal left absolutely no doubt as to the correctness of the sentence.*

sheem assured her she would find the tunnels in reasonably good condition, but not very interesting. She had also extracted from Glendyl a promise to use the teleblade to report in whenever something odd occurred or if she needed a little friendly advice.

The journey up the tunnel was to be illuminated by the wand, something that seemed perfectly sensible to a girl from St Coriander. From Lysheem's instructions, she now knew how to use it as both a light source and, in an emergency, as a pulse-beam weapon. It could do much, much more, Lysheem had assured her, but now was not the time for Glendyl to learn such things. Now was the time to get moving again.

151

Tiptoeing into the tunnel that intersected the manhole from the dam, Glendyl had gone only ten yards or so when she came to a dead end.

A grate of dark metal bars blocked the tunnel. They were thick, smooth and almost invisible. Fresh scrapes and tool marks on the ancient walls suggested that this gate had been very recently installed. Odd that Lysheem hadn't mentioned this.

It now dawned on Glendyl that unless the passage that went toward the river was clear, she could be stuck in here. Could Lysheem be leading her into some sort of trap? Suddenly woozy, she gripped one of the metal bars to steady herself. At that instant, the bars began to rise. Without thinking, she ducked underneath to the other side. As soon as she did, the gate reversed direction and the tunnel was blocked again.

Glendyl's heart was beating a rousing uptempo two-step. "Hey! What's going on here?" she shouted to the walls. Her words came back to her in distorted, mocking echoes. In the light of the multiwand she searched for spy-holes, lenses, bugs, sensors or whatever. But not really knowing what to look for, she found nothing. What had made the door open? She had no answer.

She also had an immediate choice to make: proceed or go back. She placed her hand on one of the bars again: nothing happened. Systematically, she tried each one. Nothing. Looks like somebody or something made that choice for me, she thought, trying to still her heart and push down the cold panic.

Eyes big as eggs, she spun and swung the wand's light in every direction thinking to surprise a possible spy. The darkness behind the light of the wand suddenly seemed darker, with some shapeless menace ducking out of the way to stay just beyond the reach of the white cone. Was she going crazy? Her right hand went to the teleblade; somehow its vague warmth broke her loop of paranoid terror.

Moving ahead again, she discovered a choice point. She could go either right or left. For no particular reason, she went left. Behind her, a small piece of wall also turned left and continued to follow about twenty feet behind her, rippling almost invisibly along the surface of the wall like a paper-thin, letter-sized inchworm.

The tunnel now began to slope upwards. After ninety-seven paces there was an abrupt change of direction: now the tunnel proceeded, switchback-like, the way she had just come, but rising higher in the dam. Excellent! Her gait became more confident, almost a stride.

A low-pitched rumble invaded her awareness and grew louder with each step. The next hairpin explained it. In addition to another upward ramp in the switchback, there was a heavy metal door set into the concrete wall. It was painted to match the dark gray of the wall but bore a yellow sign that read: QTE ACCESS: NO ADMITTANCE. Below that was a smaller sign featuring the universal "No Smoking" symbol.

That sign was somehow comforting, but the other one irritated her: why write "NO ADMITTANCE" on an access door? Dumb. Whoever wrote that hadn't done any of Eastac's Meaning and Communication projects.

The only other feature of the door was a small, square opening at about waist level, which she took to be some form of keyhole. The sign should've said NO ADMITTANCE WITHOUT PASSKEY, she grumbled to herself. Or maybe ONLY IN YOUR DREAMS, QUESTER. She smiled in spite of herself.

Glendyl pushed against the door, which refused to budge. It

did, however, vibrate; something inside this ancient place was still functioning. As she pressed an ear against it, she could hear other sounds. First was a dim, pervasive whir that sounded like something spinning. Against this backdrop were other sounds, maybe workers or something.

Of course! If this whole place wasn't doing something, why had the maintenance machine pushed the manhole cover back into place? Evidently there was more going on at Dunnigans Wall than a stodgy old museum that nobody could get to and that just happened to have a model of the whole Counterindicated Zone.

Glendyl thought of banging her fists against the door and hollering until somebody came to open the door. But after thinking about all the not-very-wonderful situations she'd already experienced in the vicinity of Dunnigans Wall, she decided to continue up the next ramp. Besides, the museum ought to be well marked, with signs and maybe even a guide or two. She allowed herself a hope: wouldn't it be nice to encounter an actual, flesh and blood human up there in that place? And one with a hamburger in each hand, added her gurgling belly.

Glendyl said a mental goodbye to the door and strode with re-generated purpose up the inky slant of the tunnel.

154

27 :: REPLACING THE TOOTH

"HEY CHIEF!" bellowed Romundo Osaki from the Map Room. "She's right outside the Turbine Room now. Pretty gutsy to feel your way all the way up there in the dark. I wouldn't have gone two feet in some spooky tunnel without my headlight and a couple six gauge fogshots."

Exeter entered the Map Room at a jog, his long carrot-radish chin-whiskers flapping in a semi-comical manner. Today, he wore light blue coveralls and a navy blue baseball cap. A patch on the breast pocket of his coveralls said "Chief Scientist," a title Exeter preferred over any other, even Exeter the Wise. Standing behind Romundo, who overflowed his chair on both sides (thus his popular nickname, Mundo Rotundo), Exeter studied a large and complex display of colored lines and symbols overlaying a grid that was itself superimposed on a large map of the territory around Mt Faunibeune.

"Display," spoke Exeter in a terse, all-business monotone. "Can you do a quick sneak-in to a certain unnamed database and get me the illumination status in location LR621.777?"

A sexy female voice responded, "Good morning, Your Exalted Redness! Got it. Presently, it's zip."

"Let me rephrase that," said the Chief, now with a twinkle in his voice. This display had always been a wiseass, which was perfectly appropriate; he had designed it to act that way. "When was the last time the illumination was significantly greater? Be careful, now," he added.

"Now I see where you're going Chief," said the display with a coy lilt. "I can probably sneak in for one more quick tap without setting off any buzzers, so to speak. Okay. At minus zero zero mark zero three mark four six from the present, it was a lot brighter. Got some analysis. You interested?"

"If you please," said Exeter drily.

"According to the illumination pattern data I nabbed, somebody in there's gotten their hands on a wyvern-built multiwand. Probably a Type 3 according to the specs in our library. Haven't seen one of those since the War. Last ones built, Type 3's: totally state-of-the-art then. Probably still are."

Exeter hopped up and down in excited annoyance. "I knew it! I knew it! Somebody else has got their sticky fingers in The Program! Dam-sam-jam-cram-lammit-all-to-hell!" Exeter stomped around the Map Room shaking his arms in a whole gamut of frustrated and occasionally obscene gestures while kicking over several recycling bins.

Best to lay very low at a time like this, thought Romundo, slouching a little lower in his chair, even though he knew that attempting to make his vast bulk less visible was like trying to hide an elephant in a shoebox.

"Romundo!"

Oh, bugdiddle, here it comes, thought Romundo, slouching even deeper. "Yes, Chief," donning his meekest demeanor.

"Carry on."

Romundo exhaled a gust of chocolate scented air. Dodged this one, he thought, adjusting his mass a little higher.

"And Romundo."

"Yes, Chief."

"Could I ask you to give some thought to a few small niceties in your spare time?"

"Of course, Chief. Anything you say."

"Excellent. Perhaps you could discover the malfunction of the QPack that somehow impeded its ability to report the EXACT moment the Quester obtained the little artifact we have just learned about. And the EXACT location as well. This knowledge might have saved us all a little grief. I strongly suspect that neither Tinkerbell nor the Tooth Fairy appeared in that manhole this morning and handed it to her. Am I being specific enough?" Exeter's voice was the quintessence of calm. That's item number one. Next ...."

In his excitement, Romundo interrupted. "Just checked on that, Chief. I'm totally on it! Here we go. Whoa ... the diagnostic says that some songs got stuck in its content filters. Songs? I know that sounds really over the edge, but ...." Romundo's voice trailed off. Exeter's face rippled with emotion. Romundo reddened, coughed and finished his sentence. "Uhh ... Chief, it seems that somebody stuck a memstick in its media port. One with songs ... and a virus."

There was a moment of pregnant silence, then came the torrent. "DIOGENES! Dam-sam-jam-cram-slammit-all-to-hell in a mop-bucket! How long have we graciously extended that meddling old jackass-loving peddler of nonsense and really bad songs the gift of unimpeded trespass in our very own backyard? It's centuries if it's a nanosecond! That's it! No more Mister Nice Guy! Exeter the Generous is about to become Exeter the Extremely, Painfully Curious!

"Romundo, I charge you with Extreme Undersight!" Exeter paused his tirade for dramatic effect and softened his voice a notch. "Still, you may be able to redeem yourself in the overly-benevolent eyes of your dearly beloved Chief Scientist. DO NOT, under penalty of your immediate return to the St Diddlehead Fatherhood ... and I mean IMMEDIATE, and IN A BASKET!" Exeter paused, frowned. "Where was I? Yes. Do NOT fail to discover the current whereabouts of Diogenes. And when you locate him, you will make it your personal MISSION IN LIFE to know his exact whereabouts at all times. That's 24-7-365, as we used to say. I want a full report each and every day. We may have to take up certain matters with him personally. And sooner rather than later. That's the new item number one.

"Item number two. Before you get on the Diogenes program, figure out how the Quester cracked the staircase spell in the first place. One more thing. Leave a message up at all the visors for those panting morons Jamis and Meredith to get their sorry, slinking asses back here on the double for a personal debriefing!" The last of Exeter's instructions were bellowed as only Exeter could bellow.

Romundo's bulk seemed to shrivel, as though he had somehow become an instant winner on World's Biggest Loser.

"Yes, Chief. Got your message, Chief. I'm totally on the case now, Chief." He cringed at the idea of having to have a personal debriefing with the Chief. People who had personal debriefings with Exeter didn't always emerge in their natural forms. And Jamis and Meredith had already lost their natural forms. Yikes! But going back to the Fatherhood would be much, much worse; Father-Mayor Gullwimple would not be entertained to see him again after all these years. Even in a basket of disconnected parts.

With no further comments, Exeter stalked out of the Map Room. "Why I helped that lazy lardbucket escape his brothers-of-the-cloth, I'll never know," muttered the Red One under his breath.

Later, in his private quarters high up in Tower Five, Exeter the Wise treated himself to a long soak in the copper hot tub that was the central feature of what he called his sensuary. He did some of his best musing in this tub; the lacy swirls of vapor always took his mind in productive directions.

His first decision was that Glendyl Fenderwell would just have to hand over the multiwand. He mumbled aloud to nobody but himself: "Gives me the tumble-hops just to imagine something like that in the hands of some naïve dunderhead St Coriander sixteener. Even an innocent — a cute blonde upbanger like Glendyl — could turn out to be a dangerous enemy with a thing like that."

Exeter was already more than a little annoyed that Glendyl was not following the standard Quester route. How she had found the almost forgotten hidden trail to Dunnigans Wall was still the second-most irritating of the recent mysteries. Perhaps she had some minor knack with the forces that governed his magic. Possible? Yes. Likely? No. Maybe Diogenes did more than clog up the QPack's brain with his godawful songs? Possible. But why not before now? He's been dropping in on Questers for eons. Exeter filed that topic for further consideration.

His mind went back to Glendyl. Since he'd already found the long-expected Wildcard, she wasn't that. Grudgingly, Exeter replayed Glendyl's Quest so far and had to admit that only a few Questers out of 250 had ever had the guts to even try the chimney. He didn't really want them to try the chimney, which was why he always stationed some Transform there at Quest time: talk 'em out of it, if necessary. But Jamis had screwed that up. What had his report said? "Q250 is stubborn. Will follow."

So Q250 was stubborn, had guts and dumb luck. But Castle Ommergard had plenty of Luckiests already ... and a few even had guts. What else? Who could know? Glendyl's value to him was inconclusive at this point.

Any hopes that the over-hormoned Jamis could shed some light on the Glendyl Fenderwell persona was pure fantasy, thought Exeter. If Jamis could be counted on for anything, it was to play the perfect, clueless innocent. And the surly Meredith was less than useless, except to look at. Still, he mused, Jamis had handled the cobbled-together wolf attack reasonably well, getting the Fenderwell girl channeled into a place where she could be more readily controlled, even if it was enemy territory. Maybe even flush out who's helping her. Exeter decided to postpone any irrevocable action until he saw what happened when Glendyl got to North Castle. This thought allowed Exeter's mood to ease, but he continued to turn the situation over in his mind.

From another perspective, Glendyl Fenderwell's straying into dangerous Dunnigan territory might just turn out to be a remarkable piece of good luck. If he ended up with a prize like a wyvern Standard Toolbelt, the girl's transgressions might be forgiven. If he personally encountered the girl in the near future he'd ask her nicely and give her the opportunity to hand it over to him voluntarily. Then she could join the Big Blue Crew and all would be well.

The real gnat in the soufflé here was the Standard Toolbelt it-self. If the girl had it long enough to become attuned, there was no way things would work out in a kind and gentle fashion. With a fully attuned Standard Toolbelt around his own waist, he might be able to find the long-vanished Castle Caraway. Or even the missing Nev-ergate itself. Those were very big prizes: either one of them would repair his present immobility.

He made an executive decision, although not without a trace of regret. Glendyl Fenderwell just might not make it to the Transfer Sta-tion. Or even out of Dunnigans Wall. After all, business is business; there was much more at stake here than one brain-dead, stubborn St Coriander Quester. Another would come along in a year anyway. At the age of 318,[20] one more year was no more significant than one more bite of popcorn.

Time to get one of his lazy Away Teams out to Dunnigans Wall at flank speed for a little "interpersonal excitement." He leaped out of his liquid thinking lounge, toweled, wrapped himself in a red silk robe and strode off to the Map Room to issue orders and personally monitor the rarely used spy devices in the vicinity of North Castle.

A dozen paces down the hallway he stopped, tugged at his beard and returned to his suite. Passing his hand over a section of bare wall, he spoke a password. A transparent panel was revealed. Behind it was a thing that looked like a portion of a very large tooth or tusk. Above it was a label in bold, red letters: "Tooth Phone: For Chief Ex-ecutive Use Only."

Exeter tapped the glass, which slid aside. Taking the tooth in his hands, he cradled it a moment to establish his identity, then held the blunt end to his ear and began a strange conversation that lasted several minutes. Replacing the tooth, he headed back down to the Map Room. Always good to have a Plan B.

160

---

20 :: *Exeter's longevity — and the overall youthfulness of other Ommergardians as well — is due to Castle Ommergard's three fully functional Opus Refurburators. Lord Bellicarie had acquired them in 2251 as a way to augment the flying castle's income by providing mobile ReYouthing and GeneOpt clinics to well-to-do residents in his more remote markets.*

28 :: FORBIDDING BEAUTY

THE TUNNEL finally ended at another metal door, square keyhole and all. To Glendyl's exasperation, there was no obvious mechanism to open this one either: not even a handle. But at least this one had no stupid signs.

Placing an ear to the door, she heard nothing at all. Being very hungry, very thirsty and tired as well, Glendyl sat on the cold concrete floor to ponder her next course of action.

A part of her really wanted to solve this puzzle herself; she had a strong feeling that she was missing something and that the means for opening this door was already at her disposal. Another part — the thirsty, tired and hungry part — thought now might be a handy time to try out the teleblade, even though the experience in the manhole now felt distant and illusional. Setting qualms aside, she cupped her palm around the hilt, felt its warmth and thought the word "Lysheem."

PSYSHT-POP! Before she had time to even collect her thoughts, Lysheem's image was peering at her. "At the top, are we? Wait a moment and don't go anywhere; I want to check a few things." The image turned around and Glendyl was presented with her first look at a wyvern's backside, which included a coiled, snakelike tail with a horny, barbed tip. It protruded coyly from a slit in the loose skirt of coarse orange fabric Lysheem was wearing.

She had begun to consider the mechanics of having to accommodate a hole for a tail in the design of one's garments — which inevitably led to issues concerning modesty as well as other matters of practical import — but Lysheem turned back to the Quester and interrupted.

"Well then, Glendyl Fenderwell. I have identified the mechanism that controls the door. Do you, by chance, have an openrod in your possession? No? Then it seems we must help you open it. But before we proceed, give me your full attention for a moment and place a hold on your contemplation of my tailside."

"Yeah, sure," intoned Glendyl, more than a little embarrassed. She had been studying Lysheem's tailside, after all.

"Dunnigans Wall is a pre-wyvern artifact. It was built long before my time — around 350 years ago if I recall correctly — by two pairs of wealthy, eccentric engineering types who were enamored of monumental gestures. By a circuitous line of reasoning, we wyverns consider them our true parents and our creators. So please refrain from cursing them, at least in my presence." Lysheem winked.

"But back to Dunnigans Wall. As best we can tell, only North Castle has ever been occupied. I assume you will be lucky or shrewd enough to find your way in; it is thought to be guarded in a thousand different ways and could be quite dangerous to you. Or not.

"Then there's the Enemy. While North Castle may be interesting to explore and it may contain a thousand curiosities, we also may be certain that the kindly Exeter the Wise monitors this place when it suits him, such as when a Questing sixteener has strayed from the standard route via magical means. If this is true, there is a high probability that the Standard Toolbelt you are wearing has been detected, which is the real point of this little discussion. Exeter will be interested in obtaining this bauble, since it is perhaps the last accessible artifact of wyvern high science in this vicinity. And something he has never gained access to.

"Exeter may even believe that the items you currently possess may be able to assist him in locating and reopening the Nevergate, or at least uncovering its secrets. Silly, vain old human. Still, he is dangerous, at least to you. My advice is to not linger where you can be trapped by his minions who, if not necessarily as bright, are probably at least as lucky as you. I can tell you one more thing; a squad of these very blue-suited minions has just climbed down into the manhole where you spent the night. I urge you to find your way into North Castle before they catch up with you. It is doubtful that they will be much deterred by the new gate you encountered. They have tools. One more caution; best to get inside before the sailbirds become active.

163

"Now you are warned. There is no more help I can provide you and I must attend to my own urgencies. Glendyl Fenderwell, it has been interesting to have met you. If you survive, perhaps we will meet again. Maybe even in person. Now beseech your Lucky Madonna and get moving. My image will disappear momentarily: when it does, place the hilt of the teleblade next to your ear."

PHYSHT-POP! Lysheem disappeared. Resisting the urge to be stubborn and do the opposite of anything this nonhuman told her to do, Glendyl placed the device to her ear and was rewarded with several unexpected highly personal tidbits. When the teleblade was back in its sheath, Glendyl grinned; she now knew more about tails and tail management than probably anybody in St Coriander. Maybe even on the whole planet.

Doing precisely as instructed, Glendyl closed her eyes, turned off the lightbeam and waited for something to happen. There was a faint whooshing sound, a click, a buzz, then a rusty creak as the door began to move outward on rarely used hinges propelled by invisible actuators. Glendyl opened her eyes to a growing trapezoid of sunlight.

She found herself at the bottom of a ramp that ascended to her right. She walked to the top, where a road spanned the top of the dam and followed its gently concave arc from one side of the canyon to the other. Low walls of thick concrete flanked the roadway on both sides. Reflecting ancient modes of visual storytelling, a stylized bas-relief was incised into each wall and appeared to extend the full width of the dam.

At both ends, seeming to grow out of the sheer rock of the canyon, were intricate, castle-like complexes with square towers, round towers, conical roofs, dormers, domes, skybridges, battlements, ramparts and other structural features for which Glendyl had no names. Certainly some magnificent vision must have propelled such a fabulous endeavor. Not to mention vast resources.

Returning her attention to more pressing matters, she crossed the road and looked over the wall that rimmed the face of the dam.

From this high perspective, she could look back on her recent route up Wittwater Deep, an area now shrouded in afternoon shadow. It seemed a mostly barren, forbidding place. Not a trivial accomplishment to get this far, she told herself with a touch of pride. The only distant oddity was a thin trace of smoke rising over the canyon's edge from somewhere below the rim. Probably a campfire, or maybe even Diogenes and his mule, whose name had slipped her mind.

Nearer at hand, a bundle of thick, greenish-brown vines had somehow rooted themselves into the sidewalk, where the cobblestones met the wall. They entwined themselves into a natural hawser, snaked over the top of the dam then down its face to support the strange village of tiny shacks she'd seen yesterday.

The broad, heart-shaped leaves hid much of the little village, but some huts appeared to have trapdoors built into their tops. Whatever things had lived there must have been adept at rope-climbing. Glendyl shuddered at the thought, her imagination first concocting ugly, crab-like things with crimson eyestalks, then squat green trolls with bulging eyeballs and writhing suckers instead of fingers and toes. As she began to imagine huge red spiders with oversized biting parts, she forced her eyes away: time to get inside the castle.

At that moment, a thought that Glendyl's subconscious mind had been gnawing on just below her awareness broke into the light. Why would Exeter the Wise direct Questers to the base of the dam, where entry to the museum could only be made with great difficulty, if it could be made at all? Glendyl had not, after all, discovered if there really was a museum. And wouldn't it have been simpler just to take the road here? Ah, but the log, she reminded herself; she would have had to cross the godawful log. Still, the whole business just didn't feel right.

Shaking off a puzzled frown, Glendyl crossed the road. From this side, a narrow lake extended into the distance behind the dam. The frigid beauty of it took her breath away; she had never personally seen this much water in one place. It was a forbidding beauty, much different from the friendly Duck Pond. What might lurk in these chill waters? She decided she probably didn't want to know.

166

29 :: SMOKING HEAP

THE MAJESTY of North Castle sent the Quester into a time warp; she almost expected jousting knights in shining armor, swooning fair maidens and glorious feasts to poof into being before her eyes. Her stomach voted for a glorious feast as first priority. Or even a solitary apple.

Alas, no colorful pennants waved in the breeze, no scent of woodsmoke or steaming cauldrons garnished the air. It was impressive, sure, but only in a dead way, like a cemetery full of imposing stone tombs and crypts.

The castle appeared to be completely surrounded by the lake, with only one visible way to enter: a massive timber drawbridge decorated with the Dunnigan clanmark in black metal. Naturally, the bridge was currently pulled tight against the castle.

Sprouting from the dam across from the drawbridge was a massive squarish tower with a steep roof sheathed in shale and crusted with gloomy blots of lichen. Just below the roof was a band of openings — vertical slots — piercing the walls. Weren't those for archers?

Glendyl approached the entry tower with a cautious eye on those slots and found an arched entry that was probably twenty feet across and at least three times her height. A spiked iron portcullis could be dropped to close off the entrance, but at the moment the way was open. She walked quickly past it to the opening across from the drawbridge. Beyond the edge was a sheer drop, with nothing but dark water below.

Finding no obvious mechanisms for controlling the drawbridge inside the tower, she went back outside. In a shadowy alcove she'd missed before was a bronze plaque similar to the one by Sir Wendell's log. Four sculpted bronze faces looked back at her: two pairs of identical twins, youngish and handsome, with penetrating eyes. The text read as follows:

> **Historic Site No. 19**
>
> **DUNNIGANS WALL, NORTH CASTLE**
>
> **Design and engineering for Dunnigans Wall and the two castles began in 2179 at the behest of the founders of the self-styled Clans Dunnigan (left to right): John Aurelius Dunnigan, Donella Viola Dunnigan, Michael Julius Dunnigan, Victoria Kathleen Dunnigan. These two fanciful structures were completed in 2191 and were to be full time residences for the two Clans. Only North Castle was ever furnished and occupied. An ancient powerplant housed within the dam itself still provides electrical power to the complex, which has been dormant since the Dunnigan Retreat of 2285.**

Well, that's all very informative, thought Glendyl. But no mention of a museum at all. Or how to get in. Her first impulse was to yell, a simple, direct strategy. She did. "Hey, anybody in there? Hey, castle people! Open up. Anybody got any food in there? If you don't want to open up, just throw me a slab of raw likesteak or even a hot dog. Or sail me a pizza. And where's the drinking fountain around here? Hey, come on! Don't be jerks! Open up!"

When nothing happened, she tried a different tack. "Okay ... please. Please let down your beautiful drawbridge. Pretty please with sugar on it? Abracadabra? Open sesame? Open, says me?"

This torrent of syllables produced exactly zero response. Evidently, the castle wasn't listening.

Exasperated, she loosed a curse at the top of her lungs. Still nothing happened, although she could hear echoes of her expletive ringing off the cliffs and the castle walls for a surprisingly long time. When only the roar of the Wittwater remained in the background, a chorus of eerie, ululating wails answered her call. Sailbirds. Great! she thought, mentally kicking herself. Smart of me to wake them up.

The mountains behind her swallowed the final arc of sun; the highest towers glowed a faded orange, but all else was now in murky shadow. With light from the wand she made a careful, inch-by-inch survey of the area around the entry tower, and particularly around the bronze plaque. There should be, at the very least, a little something-or-other explaining how to get inside North Castle. What kind of a moron was this Exeter the Wise character to overlook something this obvious?

169

Five minutes of further scrutiny was a precious five minutes wasted. The only slightly odd thing was a familiar square hole in the right side of the stone stand supporting the plaque. Be nice to have one of whatever goes in those keyholes, she thought with fading spirits and a nervous glance back down the road. Shadows seemed to pulse with lurking menace and now a thick, swirling mist rising from the lake made it worse.

Jogging back inside the entry tower, it occurred to Glendyl to look up. A thick, knotted rope dangled through a hole in the ceiling, ending a couple feet above her head. Earlier, she had noticed the steep wooden steps that zigzagged up the inside perimeter of the tower to somewhere, but she'd completely missed the rope. Geez Louise! Now who's the moron?

Dashing up the steps she reached the second floor and spotted the bell in the dimness overhead. It was a huge ancient thing of greenish metal. Details were hidden in the shadows, but pulling the rope no doubt caused the bell to ring somehow, if it wasn't frozen with corrosion.

Her hands grasped the rope. Taking one last look around the bell ringer's room, she spotted three vertical timbers set in the wall. They were about three feet high, about a timber-width from each other and protruded from the wall about six inches. The timbers seemed to have no purpose whatever, except, maybe ....

Shadowy forms streaked past the row of vertical slits in the wall, surprising a short scream out of her mouth. A chorus of sail-birds screamed back. Chiding herself for acting like a numbnoggin, she gave the rope a sharp downward yank. No sound and almost no movement: very heavy bell. She braced her feet and pulled harder. The rope moved maybe a foot, then almost pulled her off her feet as the heavy bell swung back in the other direction.

Timing her next pull with care, Glendyl jumped and grabbed the highest knot she could reach. Better, but no sound yet. On her next jump-pull, a deep-throated tone rattled her eardrums. She rang it twice more. In the echoes of the third chime was a grinding clatter of metal on metal that could only be the drawbridge lowering. Racing back down the steep stairs and nearly falling twice, Glendyl tried to ignore the hellish, screaming wails outside. At the bottom, she positioned herself in shadow and peered cautiously around the opening in the wall facing the drawbridge.

Already more than halfway down, the ancient bridge lowered itself in unsteady, halting lurches, accompanied by raspy creaks, clanks, thunks and squeals. Huge shadowy birds with featherless, sail-like wings and long pointy beaks streaked past, flying both above and below the bridge. There must be dozens, she thought miserably. No way to sneak past those things; the bridge was just too long.

A glimmer of an idea snapped into Glendyl's head. What had Lysheem said about making the wand work as some kind of death ray? Her frantic thinking was interrupted by a swishing sound. She lurched back: a sailbird shot by, missing her by inches. Its hunting cry felt like a nail in her eardrum. "Missed me, buzzard breath!" she shouted. "Close, but no guitar![21] I dare you to try that again!" Glendyl

---

21 :: *The Word Butchers Club, with chapters in both Westac and Eastac, specialized in unearthing and then "carverizing" ancient slang expressions, colloquialisms, truisms, coy similes and other forms of wordplay. "Close, but no guitar" was currently in vogue among St Coriander teens, much to the dismay of their parents.*

was slow to anger, but not *that* slow.

With a resounding thwonk, the drawbridge settled onto its ledge, the great chains slackened, and the clanks, thunks and squeals ceased. In that fractional moment of silence that followed the fading echoes, the memory Glendyl sought resurfaced. She twisted the end of the rod into the first weapon position, then closed her eyes and thought, "burn." A line of sizzling red shot from the crystal on the business end of the wand and burned a groove halfway through the thick timbers of the drawbridge. "Geez, Lou-ise!"

171

Through the thickening mist Glendyl got her first look at the inside of North Castle: a disappointing vague yellow glow. No signs of movement, no stalwart, well-armed troops massing at the portal to blast sailbirds out of the sky for her. Glendyl wanted to see more, but did she dare take the time to readjust the wand and use it as a light again? She thought not.

Unseen, a vast winged shape circled high overhead in the deepening murk, waiting for just the right moment.

Meanwhile, the sailbirds sensed dinner close at hand and attacked the bridge in high speed, furled-wing dives aimed at Glendyl's position. They would swoop low, then bank and pull up just in time to miss the drawbridge and the wall. Could she time her dash across the bridge? Glendyl darted her head out for a second, hoping for a clear space in the sailbird traffic. Three diving birds saw her. As one, they turned their heads and jostled each other for the rights to her exposed head. One grazed the heavy drawbridge chain with a wing, somersaulted, ricocheted off the wall with a sickening thud and tumbled onto the planks, thrashing wildly only five yards away.

The wounded bird had caught Glendyl's scent. Gnashing its long jaws in a menacing way, it managed a gimpy leap that almost brought it to Glendyl's hiding place behind the wall. Without thinking, she pointed the wand and her mind said, "burn." An area of bridge just in front of the thrashing bird flared into flame. Her target didn't seem to notice; it continued toward her, wobbly but relentless.

"Launch," thought Glendyl in panic. Pulse-bursts of energy shot from the wand. Where the thrashing bird had been was now only an oily cloud of smoking black sailskin shreds and spatters of steaming gore. The blast from the exploding bird knocked Glendyl to the floor.

As she staggered back to her feet, a strong hand gripped the wrist with the wand. Glendyl was spun around to face a shadowy man in some kind of blue uniform. More blue uniforms stood behind him. The leering man's grip on her wrist was painful, but instead of fright, Glendyl felt a surge of rage. The man in blue sneered and began to wrestle the wand away from her. Two more blues converged to help him.

Without knowing how she knew, she was absolutely positive that the wand wasn't going to let this happen. "Launch," came a silent command. The floor of the entry tower erupted in a blast of vaporized stone. Glendyl was thrown backwards, landing hard almost at the center of the drawbridge, still gripping the wand as if it were stitched to her palm. A rain of anguished yells and screams drew the sailbirds' attention to the entry tower and a deadly battle began.

High overhead, the great dark shape knew its moment had come. It loosed a bone-rattling battle-scream and sent a reeking blast of flame from a hole in its scaly snout. Wings furled, it plunged into a steep dive aimed straight at the figure on the drawbridge.

The battle-scream burrowed into Glendyl's brain, freezing her mind in a state of blind terror. Only her eyes seemed to function. Something dark and monstrous was plunging toward her with freakish speed. A dragon? Sailbirds shot away looking for safer air. Glendyl knew she had to do something to break through her paralysis of fear, but her body felt like a mass of jelly and noodles.

Heavy chains suddenly pulled taut. Groaning windlasses behind the walls began winding in the great chains. The plummeting hellspawn from Cametto-5 had to adjust its trajectory at the last instant in order to avoid the rising drawbridge. Its great claws missed their target, but a roaring gout of flame seared the middle of the bridge, engulfing Glendyl in a seethe of acrid fire.

The dragon screamed past and pulled up sharply, barely missing the cliff. Before it could circle back for another pass, the drawbridge thunked shut; Glendyl's blackened body was inside North Castle.

She heard nothing, not the dragon's frustrated screams, not the curses of Exeter's best squad of Blue Goons, who were still occupied with the remnants of the attacking sailbirds.

A vague ripple had followed the action across the drawbridge. It now traversed the wall just inside the entry, inch-wormed across the marble floor and slid up onto the shapeless, smoking heap, where it temporarily adopted the appearance of a patch of scorched cloth.

174

30 :: BETWEEN HER JAWS

THE ANCIENT CATAMARAN traced a long, slow arc north from Trinidad to San Juan, the bustling capital of the Greater Antilles Federated Fiefdoms (GAFF). The sky was clear, the air was warm and a contented Captain Partanzo Malagueña lay sprawled in his wicker lounge on the roof of the pilothouse, enjoying his fifth Corto Rico sour of the afternoon.

Two days ago he had swindled the fools of Tunapuna out of a fine cargo of anchovy paste and pressed tamarinds. Then he'd taken his tattered, twin-hulled cargo vessel, the once illustrious Catrina's Cleavage, to Barbados to pick up a hundred kittlewood casks of Sarhendra Rum, a current favorite of fashionable San Juan society.

Seeking more comfortable seas, he had skirted Martinique on the east, cut west through the Martinique Passage and had powered his way past the islands of Domenica and Basse-Terre. At St Kitts he would sell the anchovies and tamarinds, then sweep through the Virgin Passage and into San Juan. Here his cargo of Sarhendra should bring a fine price, making this one of the Captain's more profitable trips. So he didn't mind celebrating just a little in advance.

The afternoon was waning in a kindly fashion, a pastel waft of clouds in the west showing the makings of a fine sunset. To starboard was the rounded southern verge of sorry old Montserrat.

According to the Captain's favorite legend, Montserrat was once a fine, happy place full of boisterous women, sandy beaches and lively taprooms. Then an over-fastidious Amazon spurned the advances of the earth-demon Cahrfanzo. In his wrath, he took a mighty swing with his legendary long-hammer and shattered the plug that had kept the Mount Soufriere from blowing its top.

A massive eruption followed, leaving Montserrat defoliated and depopulated. Thought to be cursed and, more recently, haunted by a strange flying monster, Montserrat was now only thinly populated even though its vegetation was once again lush and full. Ever heedful of curses and large flying things, the Captain had always given the island a wide berth and was doing so now. Alas, it was not wide enough.

After one final toast to the fading daylight, the Captain dragged his bulk down to the pilothouse. He verified the course and adjusted his speed for an early morning arrival in St Kitts. The place would be a frenzy of activity by dawn and he'd get the best prices from the earliest, most needful buyers. But if not, he'd get the best of the lazier buyers. So if he arrived a little later, what matter? Captain Malagueña was a flexible man.

More than a little wobbly, he made a last check of the sensors, lurched to his cabin and flopped his imposing mass onto a stained, unmade bunk. Tomorrow would be busy and he wanted to be at his best, more or less.

To the music of the Captain's honking snores, a piece of the cabin ceiling inch-wormed up the staircase and out the open door. Minutes later, a mass of shadows descended over the cargo deck with its hundred barrels of rum. The shadows settled down over the netted barrels and waited. Presently, another shadow landed on the deck near the pilothouse. Wings furled and folded, and a pair of long, tautly muscled arms stretched luxuriously as the tall, slender figure turned to scan the eastern horizon.

The thing she awaited was not long in coming. It was an ancient wooden hulk, gutted and hardly more than a hull. A hundred telowix attached to the leaky hulk by thin cables had hauled it from Lysheem's base camp at the mouth of Montserrat's White River. Utilibots made the lines fast while hoverbots with grapples made ready to haul the cargo onto the deck.

There was only one problem: the deck was already full. Lysheem considered the situation for a moment, then sent a signal to the Boss. Netting was removed, grapples were affixed, barrels of premium grade rum were lifted and dropped into the churning white wake.

Some of these, propelled by a combination of currents, winds and pure chance, came ashore as far away as Ponce, Cayes, and even old Kingston Town on Jamaica, where they were the cause of joyous celebrations and expressions of gratitude to a dozen deities. Two barrels remained on board, destined to power a certain wyvern's extra-potent sangrias.

177

Sometime after midnight, Captain Malagueña rolled off the bunk, stumbled to the deck, then to the nearest rail, where he intended to relieve himself.

A vague wrongness on the deck caught his attention. His mission of relief temporarily on hold, he switched on the cargo deck lights. The Captain's jaw sagged; the orderly rows of prized Sarhendra had become a mound of crates, bundles and oddments of gear. He knuckled his eyes and shook his head, but the Sarhendra failed to reappear.

Something long and shadowy dropped to the deck. This giant black nightmare approached him, walking in long purposeful strides until it stood looking down at him.

The Captain cringed, feeling like he was being inspected by a gigantic black insect with awful taste in clothes. Some part of his brain decided he had to quit drinking immediately. Then he lost control of his bladder and, lacking a better response, fainted. Lysheem smiled a broad, toothy smile and signaled the Boss to stow this limp heap of flesh in an appropriate manner.

Lysheem sighed a rumbling wyvern sigh: what sorry creatures. It was going to take a little while to get accustomed to the ways of humans again. After a few false starts, she managed to program a new course into the navigation system. The Cleavage swung to the west and proceeded on a path that would take her south of Jamaica and the Empire of New Miami (once known as Cuba). Satisfied for the moment, she raised her sangria jug in a farewell salute to old Montserrat, then swung up to the cargo boom and slept.

Captain Malagueña awoke to find himself webbed to a portside bollard. His head felt like it had recently served time as a baseball at a batting cage. His stomach felt far worse. Before he could get his bearings, the thing from his nightmare emerged from the pilothouse to crouch in front of him. "You peed your pants last night, Captain," it said. Now dressed in tight purple shorts and a loose shirt of some coarse orange fabric decorated with seashells painted in various shades of blue and green, the nightmare added, "Does that mean you don't like me?"

Whatever this thing is, thought the Captain miserably, it has pointy areas on its chest: must be the female edition. Is that a good sign or a bad sign? Dragging up his fuzzy memory from last night he felt lucky he'd only peed his pants.

"Hey, lady, I was not expecting no company, you know?" Keep it light and be cool. Show no fear. "Whaddya say you let me get up and, uh, stretch my legs. You know what I mean? Then, uh, maybe you can tell me where you put my rum, you know?"

Lysheem formed a command in her mind and two small utili-bots scurried up and dissolved a section of the webbing. Groaning, the Captain pulled himself up and steadied his untidy bulk against the rail. "Hey, where we going, lady?" he wheedled, suddenly realizing that he should have already been in St Kitts for at least three hours. "What you do to my course? We should be in St Kitts, you know. You benna St Kitts? Very nice place. Lotta action."

The Captain looked up at Lysheem, who was now hunched next to him by the rail, then twisted his face in a grimace that might mean a dozen things. "Be honest witchoo," he mumbled half to himself, "maybe not much action for you, lady." Then, in as bold a voice as he could muster: "Hey, what kinda thing are you, anyway? And whatchoo doin' on my ship?"

The wyvern smiled, the Captain grimaced again. "You call this tattered old hag a ship? Really, Captain Malagueña. Perhaps your eyes will see things more clearly when your belly is full. Go clean yourself up while I see what you've got in your galley. I'm starved." A pair of sentry bots accompanied him to his quarters. "You like cigars?" inquired Lysheem of the receding figure.

Captain Malagueña emerged from below some time later, drawing on a long fat cigar wrapped in a leaf the color of unripe olives. He had showered, combed a degree of order into his wavy black hair and now wore many-pocketed trousers fashioned from a coarse tan twill topped with a silky shirt, hand-painted in a colorful collage of buxom naked women, swordfish and famous rum labels. A satisfied expression showed on his round brown face, which was freshly cleared of its usual coarse black stubble.

179

The two breakfasted on oranges, pan-fried roughy and rice topped with a spicy Caribbean condiment with a heat that required copious amounts of sangria to douse. At the end of it, Lysheem made Partanzo Malagueña an offer he couldn't refuse.

The next day, two miles offshore from the tiny town of Port Salut near the southwestern tip of Haiti, one of the Cleavage's two tenders was lowered into the sea. Captain Malagueña — with only his personal belongings, a small wooden case containing eight gold bricks, and the unbelievable tale of his encounter with a huge flying black devil-creature — departed his ship for the last time to seek his fortune elsewhere.

When the Cleavage was back in open water, a horde of telowix got busy tossing the contents of the Cleavage's cargo bay into the Jamaican Channel. When Lysheem's new cargo had been transferred below, a fresh flurry of activity began.

Lysheem herself was now sprawled in the former Captain's wicker lounge. A jug of fresh sangria sat nearby and a cigar was clamped between her jaws. Gazing idly over the expanse of white-capped water ahead, she pondered exactly what she would do when she found the planet's last Nevergate.

180

31 :: VERY WRONG

RUMORS SPRANG through St Coriander like bulimic locusts, devouring every tidbit of gossip, regurgitating it and hopping to the next. The disappearance of Lizbeth Marble had stirred the normally placid waters and the entire community throbbed with a pretense of concern. Although Lizbeth Marble was hardly the most-loved youth in St Coriander, a search party dutifully performed a thorough scouring of the town.

The search uncovered exactly two pieces of evidence. The largest was her bicycle, found abandoned at Dunnigans Gate. The pinkest was an undergarment, found fluttering like a bumpy pennant from the flagpole at Kissever House. Less dramatic but more perplexing was the Librarian's assertion that, according to its sensors, Lizbeth Marble never left the St Coriander Library on the night she failed to return home.

Speculations sprayed in every direction. A special edition of the *St Coriander Times* featured theories from mild to wild, plus a special insert on the still unsolved mystery of her parents' much more dramatic disappearance a decade before. At the wilder end of the spectrum, noted Mellowcrat Pontus Krebs claimed Lizbeth's disappearance clearly showed what folly happens when juvenile overindulgence meets COMISC radicalism. Except for the overindulgence part, he was possibly referring to the fact that Lizbeth had once attended a speech on anthromythics given by Forrbank Dorelli during a compulsory Eastac assembly.

In Castle Ommergard, Exeter the Wise and his corps of Sorcerers, Artificers, Adjuncts and Transforms found the reactions in St Coriander deliciously entertaining. And what else should be expected from the merry pranksters who planted the evidence that mystified the populace of St Coriander?

Lizbeth, who had not been invited to participate in the pranks for obvious reasons, found the matter less than entertaining when she later scanned the pirated St Coriander slatecasts and the *St Coriander Times*. In fact, she was disgusted with the whole episode.

Forrbank Dorelli found Lizbeth's disappearance even less entertaining. The discovery of Lizbeth's pink simskin brassiere fluttering at half-mast from the flagpole at the entry gate to the family estate was hardly a happy event. But most townsfolk, even those who, like Lizbeth's foster father, strongly disapproved of Forrbank Dorelli, would find it absurd that a possible criminal would advertise his crime in such a way. Certainly Sheriff Dolittle and Father-Mayor Gullwimple would be of similar minds.

What really concerned Dorelli about Lizbeth Marble's disappearance was Lizbeth Marble herself. He hated the idea that a latent activist like Lizbeth could have been spirited away by Exeter and his magical minions. But was there anything he could do about it? Probably not.

With the COMISC exposé on the whole questing sham about to be released, his lifelong goals seemed about to be realized. The sheeple of St Coriander weren't going to like what it said, but Forrbank Dorelli couldn't concern himself with that. What was true was true and what was right was right: let the chips fall where they may; that was his motto. A small smile curled up the corner of his mouth at the thought of fatuous prigs like Gullwimple and Krebs trying to explain away the truth.

Still, circumstances were in a dangerous state of flux. The reports from the shadowflap he'd assigned to trail Glendyl Fenderwell were disturbing. He had tracked the last dozen Questers and all had quickly ended up in Castle Ommergard. These illegal telowix devices had provided much useful information about Exeter's *Homo fortunatus* scheme and how Questing fit into it. But Glendyl was different; her Quest was extremely unusual. And, if his guesses were right, she had been attacked by a Cametto-5 dragon on the North Castle drawbridge ... possibly by the same dragon Exeter flew into Central Park centuries ago. In Dorelli's mind, this strongly implicated Exeter in the attack on Glendyl's life.

183

But trying to murder a poor, misguided innocent was not really like Exeter: transform her into a rock-toad, a wolf, a sailbird? Absolutely. Murder her? Not unless the stakes were very, very high. There was something going on here that was over his head and Forrbank Dorelli did not like things being over his head.

The decision was unavoidable, like time. He would have to visit North Castle again, no matter how illegal it was.

A handful of minutes later, after advising Sir Fido that his absence must remain unknown to the other Kissever House residents, a cloaked NavaTek Gravrover — another piece of tech banned by the New Rules — slid silently over the Township Fence and away. Only a rustle of pine branches marked its passage.

Dorelli flew a wide, treetop-hugging course that looped several miles south of Castle Ommergard, turned west to the Chama River, then north. Where the Rio Brazos merged into the Chama, he swung east and followed the Brazos past Humbecker Ford and into the hinterlands of what was once the Dunnigan Reserve. This circular approach was hardly the most direct route to his objective, but tonight he gauged it to be the safest.

A bank of wispy, moonlit clouds hung over and around the brooding Brazos Cliffs. To Dorelli's mind the scene looked like a gigantic herd of floating sheep cropping the scant vegetation of those awesome rocks. He smiled; sheep always reminded him of the St C populace.

His course followed the ribbon of dull silver that snaked through narrow Brazos Canyon. The Rio Brazos, here fattened by the addition of the Wittwater, was still flowing thick and fast with melt from this winter's late snows. His craft skimmed the river up to Brazos Box, then turned north up the narrow Barlow Canyon. Where it flattened out in the high meadows a mile southwest of Mt Faunibeune, Dorelli circled north of the snow-covered cone and flew low over a young glacier named Frosty.[22]

Swinging south he made his way down the headwaters of the Wittwater until it emptied into Arrowmere, the crooked arrow-shaped lake that filled the canyon behind Dunnigans Wall. Cutting his speed, he followed the steep western shoreline a dozen yards above the quiet black water to avoid creating ripples from his wake. So far, so good. The time was 10:58 p.m. And neither his eyes nor his sensors had detected anything out of the ordinary.

North Castle was almost visible. Gliding around a rocky point dotted with scrubby deerbrush, Dorelli suddenly stabbed at a control; the craft slid to a stop and hovered. Something was very wrong.

---

22 :: *"Frosty" was the Clans Dunnigan nickname for the McTavish Glacier, a controversial environmental modification initiative created to ensure more copious and year-round flows in the Wittwater and the Rio Brazos. Design of the landform modifications and weather calcs responsible for the pocket climate that spawned the McTavish was accomplished by Nevers 1.2.0 in 2204. The glacier reached its design equilibrium in 2247 and has maintained a plus or minus one percent ice mass since then.*

....
32 :: FOUR YELLOW DOTS

THE LAKE SIDE of North Castle looked much as it had on his last visit. The usual shimmer of the weatherfield dome was absent, but that was hardly unusual at this time of year. What set off Dorelli's alarm bells was the small boat tied up at the dock. Somebody else had gotten here first. Who but Exeter?

Dorelli spun his craft in a sharp 180 and back around the promontory. Rising up the finger of mountain, he set the Gravrover down in a small clearing behind a copse of mixed aspen, pine and white fir. Shouldering his pack, he fitted another implement of illegal wyvern technology over his head and hiked to a spot with a view.

A sentry stood on the dock. Were they expecting someone here tonight? Hopefully, not Forrbank Dorelli. Maybe it was just an example of routine military caution, but he wondered. Was he ready to become a dead hero for a girl he didn't even know just to satisfy his curiosity?

Dorelli was not the hero type; certainly he didn't look much like a hero. He was of medium height, slim and wiry, but not overtly muscular. His face was lean and narrow with a permanent frown, and he wore unfashionable data glasses with heavy black rims. People described him as gloomy, remote or bookish with equal frequency. A thick mass of wavy black hair swung down over his forehead and competed with a pair of striking green eyes for the title of Best Feature.

Although he had put himself through a great deal of simulator training, Dorelli had never been in a fight in his life, not even a shoving or slapping contest with his sometimes rowdy Eastac roommates, who often chided him for being fusty and over-earnest.

He watched the bored sentry skip stones on the lake and felt hugely out of his element. What had he been thinking in coming here tonight? This sort of adventurous thing was a form of reality he had never experienced in his thirty-five years and it was churning the contents of his stomach in a menacing way. His common sense told him he should go back now.

No. He may not be a hero, but he was a Dunnigan, even though he had a different name. The Dunnigans hadn't changed their world by being timid. They had taken necessary risks and he would do the same. Squelching his fears, forebodings and second thoughts, Dorelli forced himself into action.

In a few minutes he'd found the northern trail and followed it back toward the Castle. Even though he had dressed in vaguewear, he would be exposed coming down the steps if the sentry hit him directly with the heavyspot hooked to his belt. It would only take the sound of a dislodged pebble. There was no help for it, other than careful foot placement and continued good luck. Or perhaps a minor diversion.

Dorelli decided on a diversion. He gave instructions to two bird-shaped telowix that had been following him, attached small canisters to their legs and sent them on their missions. Then he waited and watched.

The telowix flapped silently toward the sentry. At Dorelli's signal, canisters opened and several hundred giant mosquitoes flew like a cloud of buckshot aimed at the sentry. Dorelli made a grim smile: the sentry's wildly flailing arms said all that needed to be said.

He stepped quietly down the ancient stone stairs to the beach. At the bottom Dorelli scanned the tangle of dark growth but saw no indication of lifeforms or surveillance machinery. The entrance to the path was not only well hidden, but overgrown.

Navigating through the tangled foliage took more minutes than seemed possible for such a short distance, but presently Dorelli arrived at the castle wall. Protruding from the base of wall just to his left was an irregular outcrop of knotted boulders. He climbed up into these dark thrusts of stone and found the almost invisible path that snaked around the rocks and through several crevices just wide enough for a slim human. He now faced one of North Castle's several "back doors." A sensor detected both his free intention to enter and the Dunnigan genemarker; an area of wall slid aside and he was in.

Somewhere above, Glendyl Fenderwell was being tended by a hastily fabbed team of telowix medics, machines that had emerged freshly "born" from a large rectangular opening on one wall. A nameplate above it read: Telowix Universal Fabricary, Model 4.

North Castle was heavily dependent on its crews of telowix and Glendyl's life had rested on their capabilities twice so far. The sentry activated upon her charred and smoking arrival had enough intelligence to recognize that Glendyl's scorched condition was suboptimal for a living thing. It activated other devices to transport her to North Castle's Infirmary, an area that had not been used in centuries.

Another telowix, Dorelli's shadowflap monitor, had slipped away from Glendyl's charred garments and followed those who carried her into the Infirmary. It now observed the proceedings disguised as a piece of ceiling a dozen feet overhead. Dorelli could see enough from the images received by his helmet to make an educated guess that Glendyl was probably not in life-threatening condition. In fact, the oxygen mask suggested that her inhalation of "dragon breath" was probably more serious than her burns. But where was Exeter's boatload of goons?

As he pondered this point, Dorelli was striding down one of hundreds of passages and chambers that had never appeared in the official plans for North Castle. At a junction of several corridors, he applied his hand to an undistinguished section of wall, closed his eyes and frowned in concentration. The corner opened and he entered a maze.

Precious minutes were lost navigating the twists and turns, all the while keeping helmet watch on the room where Glendyl was being tended. At a circular hub with passages intersecting from different directions, he tapped out a pattern with his foot; a large circle of floor sank out of sight. The slidewell merged with the floor of a large, wood-paneled chamber furnished with priceless antiques to give it the appearance of a study in a nineteenth century English manor house.

"Hello, Forrbank," said a familiar voice from everywhere in the room. "It's been something over three years, twenty-seven days and twenty-two hours since your last visit. What can I do for you?" The Brain of North Castle spoke in a placid voice that contained no trace of urgency.

"Well, my friend, I believe you have some Ommergardians in here, do you not?"

A three-dimensional skeletal projection of the castle appeared in midair. "If by 'here' you mean the entirety of North Castle, yes. They are approaching the Infirmary where the Quester is being treated."

The Brain's apparent lack of appreciation for the urgency of the situation was irritating, but Dorelli made no response. He studied the projection for a moment, following a cluster of bright yellow dots: Exeter's Blue Goons. Climbing up an emergency stairwell, they had now reached the Personal Services Level and were not many twists and turns from the Infirmary. Evidently they knew exactly where they were going, and they were going to arrive long before he could get there. Was the Brain becoming senile, letting known enemies run unmolested through its corridors?

Dorelli considered the situation. Long before the First Nevergate War, North Castle had been fitted with clever systems designed to be hostile to the possible threat of WorldGov Securitans. Later, these systems were adapted to resist another potential enemy, the men and dragons of Castle Ommergard. But these defenses were built centuries ago and Exeter had had time to develop ways to confound them. So Dorelli should definitely not count on the Castle's ability to protect the Fenderwell girl and whatever she had that Exeter wanted.

Dorelli explained the situation to the Brain, which immediately reaffirmed what he already suspected. Exeter and his people had violated North Castle's meager defenses on numerous occasions.

"Can't you do anything to stop these invaders? They're trying to kill a helpless, innocent girl! Doesn't that mean anything to you, old Brain?" Dorelli could not refrain from raising his voice at the frustratingly bland intelligence.

189

"I am truly sorry, Forrbank. This is no easier for me to witness than it is for you. But I have been defanged, and not only by enemies, but by my own creators and fellows. Now I can be violated with impunity by crass creatures such as these. I have no tools with which to stop them; my ability to cause harm has been totally neutered. Do you think this is pleasant for me?"

Dorelli was in no mood to hear whining from a disembodied Brain, so he shelved a dozen other questions and focused on the immediate challenge. Instructing his shadowflap in the Infirmary to give him a wide-angle view of the room, he scrutinized its every aspect.

There just might be something he could do after all. His helmet now displayed a convincing image of the Infirmary's Procedure Room, almost as if Dorelli were there in person. On the wall were a variety of valves, evidently backups. Might these control the flow of useful gases, perhaps even a fast-acting narcoleptic? Could he somehow instruct his only tool — the shadowflap — to open one of them? Probably not, but might it communicate the problem to its technological kin and enlist their aid? Or maybe the Brain could manage something like that if instructed to do so by one of the family. He knew he was being over-optimistic, but ....

Movement flickered in his helmet image. At the open door now stood four figures in the familiar blue uniforms of Exeter's Adjunct-level Mt Faunibeune Services personnel. Blue Goons. They all carried unfamiliar but nasty looking hand weapons. One of the four stepped forward and pointed a small device at the center of the room where the telowix medics were attending to Glendyl, apparently oblivious to the nonmedical threat approaching their patient.

At that instant, Dorelli's helmet image went blank. All he could see now was the castle map floating in the center of the darkened hub. Completely helpless, he watched four yellow dots close in on another yellow dot in the center of the Procedure Room.

33 :: DISMISSED

GLENDYL WOKE UP and blinked at the bright overhead light. A mental click. The St Coriander Clinic? How had she gotten into the St Coriander Clinic? As she thought of comfortable St Coriander, a warm glow suffused her entire body; her mad Quest was over and she could go back to her old life and real human friends. No wolves, no sailbirds, no firebreathing dragons. Then reality stepped in.

"Hello, Glendyl," said a white-haired man of medium height and uncertain but advanced age: another oldster like Diogenes. He wore a white lab coat and smiled a crinkly-eyed half smile.

"Are you a medster? I don't recognize you. Am I okay?"

"You're more than okay," said the man in white. "And while I'm not officially a medster, I am supervising your recovery; that dragon gave you some nasty scorches. If you like, you can call me Mr White. That will work out nicely. How are you feeling?"

Glendyl mentally scanned her body for pain. "I think I feel pretty good."

"Well, I'm very pleased about that. Why don't you take a little nap while I attend to a few details. You'll feel even better when you wake again. Then we'll talk."

The man in white patted Glendyl on the head and walked away. At his signal to the telowix medic, the Quester fell instantly into a deep sleep.

"I still can't get over the fact that you're alive," said Forrbank, rising from the chair where he had watched the interchange between Glendyl and the man in white. His voice shuttled between shock, awe, disapproval and irritation. "How did you fake your Tripoli? My own father ... you could have at least sent me a message."

"Oh could I? Would you have, in my circumstances? Think about it rationally for a moment, Forbie." Mr White's voice was the essence of cool detachment. "Actually, you've done quite well managing family affairs with no help from me. I'm not surprised, of course. You've also made yourself quite the center of controversy in St Coriander. Of course, all that poppycock you embraced so energetically at SCIAK — anthromythics, isn't that what it's called? — is hardly proper work for a lad of your talents."

The man in white gave his only offspring a meaningful look. "Still, your sires would be quite proud of your achievements to date, I believe. They might even applaud COMISC for trying to tilt the status quo. And you're young, after all. But there will be time to talk once we teach these young fellows a revised version of what happened here."

Forrbank glowered, his ears pulsing hot with embarrassment; no one but his father could make him feel utterly foolish and halfway good at the same time. Still glowering, he watched a telowix utilibot float up with a small box containing what looked like thin white wafers about an inch in diameter. The man in white stuck one to the forehead of each of the Blue Goons lying face up on the floor. Another went to his own forehead; the last he offered to Forrbank. "Would you like to watch? It will be good for you to know their 'story.'"

Scowling, the younger Dorelli took the wafer. "What are you going to do? Some kind of memory implant? I didn't know that was possible."

"You may find that reality and your St Coriander sense of possibility are often at odds, Forbie. Just press it over your third eye, if you know where that is; the patch knows what to do from there. And don't worry: for you, the scene will not be strong enough to become a true experiential memory. For these fellows, however, it will replace a blank spot due to their little naps.

"Quite heroic in a Blue Goon sort of way; a heart-pounding account of their daring escapade in North Castle, the suffocation of the girl and the capture of her Standard Toolbelt. We've already adjusted its capabilities so that Exeter will find it an engaging puzzle, but ultimately of little use. We should both hope it will keep him busy for a while." He closed his eyes briefly, then nodded. "We will need absolute silence for five minutes and twenty-eight seconds."

When it was done, the two Dorellis removed the wafers, dragged the four stiff bodies from the room and leaned them up against the corridor wall. The elder Dorelli whispered a command in the ear of each man, who was then able to stand on his own in a relaxed and ready, but eyes-closed posture. The Dorellis reentered the Infirmary, closed the door and waited. A minute later footsteps sounded outside, faded and were gone.

"Thank you, Brain," said Cambitter Dorelli to the air.

"You're quite welcome, Cambitter," replied a familiar voice. "Your scenario sketch was a genuine pleasure to flesh out, individuate and implant in these dolts. My indicators suggest they will integrate very deeply. By the time they reappear at Castle Ommergard, the memories should be as real as anything else they can recall.

"And Forrbank, please accept my apologies for misleading you about the situation. I had been sworn to secrecy by your father. He ..."

"Enough, please. I'm sure I'll get over it," snapped Forrbank. Then a thought struck him. "This was all about the Standard Toolbelt. That's what Exeter really wanted, not the Quester."

"That is certainly the most reasonable speculation, Forrbank," said the Brain. Now, I'll leave the two of you to your family reunion. Good night and have a safe flight back home, Forrbank." Silence filled the room with an odd emptiness.

"All right, Father," began Forrbank with a deep sigh. "It is now 1:04. I should probably leave here in about two hours. Can we talk now?"

They talked. Actually, the elder talked and the younger listened. This was difficult for Forrbank, but with effort he kept his interruptions brief and ended up learning far more of consequence than he had expected. Finally, the subject turned to the Quester snoring a few feet away.

"So what happens to Glendyl Fenderwell, who is now supposed to be dead?" asked Forrbank.

"Very simple. Let me give you three different versions of truth. In the complacent minds of the folk of St Coriander, she will be just one more casualty to the Quest unless you make a mess of things before the proper time. You've kept quite a few secrets in your years and I hardly think this additional one will overtax your duplicity." He frowned at his only offspring with the semi-stern, raised-eyebrow look that Forrbank still remembered all too well, even not seeing it for a very long time.

"Exeter the Wise will also believe her to be a casualty of her Quest, but for a different set of reasons. You and I will know her to be my new assistant. South Castle, I have to admit, needs some younger blood from time to time. I don't think she will be bored."

"South Castle? I thought ...."

The elder Dorelli held up his hands. "No need for you to know that, of course. But yes, the never-occupied South Castle is our headquarters. It still appears impenetrable and unoccupied, and we are not often disturbed in our work; our little group of technologiest is very busy, you know. But local hazards seem to be on the increase; evidently old Emmishak is still alive. I wonder if Exeter's been giving her refurb jobs every so often?"

He frowned and gave his son a meaningful look. "It looks as though 'interesting times' are in store for dear old St Coriander. Now you'd best be going and I must attend to my new assistant. With Exeter's lads heading home, I can get back to the business of repairing a few sub-optimalities in her capability sets. Nothing visible, mind you: she is a rather fine physical specimen just as she is. Don't you agree, Forbie?

"Ahh, one more thing. If I'm not mistaken, she may possess a set of rogue genomes that can interact in rather remarkable ways under the proper circumstances. Unfortunately, there are no instruments here that can confirm this with any degree of certainty. And, of course, there is nobody alive who knows just what the proper circumstances might be, nor what would happen if her biological time bomb is triggered."

The elder Dorelli suddenly snapped his fingers. "You know, Forbie, this girl might just be one of Inga's[23] so-called Wildcards! Wouldn't that make things interesting ...."

"Father ..." Forrbank was both frustrated and confused.

"Ah, yes; you are anxious to return home. How is Sir Fido, by the way? Still the most handsome and capable robotic dog on the planet?" Cambitter chuckled. "I'll wager he still thwarts your cousin Salandra from becoming bothersome at every opportunity." He made an ambiguous sly smile.

Forrbank rolled eyes and bit off any comment that might prolong the conversation. His father knew perfectly well that Salandra Cadwal-Dorelli was not really his cousin, and also that she had a highly irrational fear of Sir Fido.

"But back to urgencies at hand. I suppose we may need to communicate further from time to time. Hold still for a moment." A few seconds later a telowix hovered nearby with a small transparent vial containing what appeared to be a tiny silver bug, no bigger than a pinhead. The elder Dorelli shook the thing out into his palm. It scuttled in a circle, as though seeking something. At this point, Forrbank balked.

"What's that thing for and what are you planning to do with it? I hope you don't think I'm going to ingest it in some way." He backed away from his father. "Explain, please."

The man in white launched into a highly jargonized explanation of the wonders that his group was accomplishing. Forrbank didn't

---

23 :: Inga Lyrus Marlena Dunnigan, a First Tier clansperson. Genemaster of Dunnetix LLC from 2246 through the Dunnigan Retreat.

understand a word and half-believed his father was making it all up.

"We're moving way beyond what the wyverns — or even the Biaxes — ever came up with. And this little system makes conventional teleplants seem like trumpeting elephants. Don't be squeamish, boy; join the future! It's completely harmless and completely painless. And I'll hook you up with a direct mindlink to the South Castle library, just like mine. That'll give you access to all that's been edited out of your St Coriander Library over the centuries: you should find that useful."

Forrbank glowered, but finally gave in to the older man's reasonably congenial harangue. "All right! Just stop talking. Please!"

"Excellent," exclaimed the man in white, unruffled. "Now just hold still a second and lend me your ear, as they say. I probably shouldn't say that, right? Make you all huffy with me again."

While he was talking, he used common tweezers to place the minuscule device just inside Forrbank's left ear. It scuttled, spiderlike, on tiny silver legs and disappeared into his ear canal.

"There. All done."

Forrbank only sighed and rubbed his ear.

Impervious to hints, the man in white continued his monologue. "The Petal Room has the proper transceivers and is also very private, as you well know. So we'll communicate there. When you hear my voice in the middle of your head, listen. When you want to communicate with me, form an image of my handsome, fatherly face in your mind's eye and mentally — not audibly — say, ummm, 'Cambitter the Marvelous.' Yes, that will do nicely. Then think me a message.

"Now, can you find your way out, Forbie? And, here; please take your shadowflap. It'll need a little therapy; the Blue Goons knocked it out with a scatterfield burst just before I turned out their lights, so to speak. Nice to see you again, Forbie. You're looking well."

"Father. One thing. How come you didn't show up on the Brain's lifeform scan?"

"Excellent question, Forbie. Let's just say membership has its privileges." The elder Dorelli turned and began to occupy his atten-

tions with Glendyl Fenderwell. Forrbank, realizing he had been dis-
missed, found his way out, grumbling to himself: his father had not
changed a tick; and he still called him Forbie. He hated that.

198

34 :: ALL DUE RESPECT

THE NEXT time Glendyl awoke, buttery sunlight was basting her face with a friendly heat. Her nose detected the spicy, rootbeer-like aroma of cannonberry tea. She smiled to herself and opened her eyes.

She was in an unfamiliar room, but warm and comfortable. It had a conical ceiling supported by thick beams and walls paneled in rich dark wood. Hanging from the center was a complex chandelier of yellow metal that glowed with hundreds of tiny luminous spots.

Feeling energized, Glendyl threw aside the bedcovers and popped upright, but only for a second. The skin on her face, neck and arms felt strange and almost painfully tight. She flopped back on the bed and reconsidered. After a time she noticed she was wearing loose pajama-like garments of a silky material that glided over her skin in a very sensual way. Where had these come from? And where was this place?

Memories trickled back, along with a jolt of adrenaline that made her heart thump. A drawbridge. Sailbirds with long beaks and rows of sharp teeth. Some huge flying horror that blew torrents of reeking fire out of its nose. A vague sense of being unable to breathe. Then a tight, consuming blackness, like being trapped at the bottom of a deep, lightless shaft. The images cycled through her awareness again and her body was taken over by uncontrollable shakes. Gradually the sensations faded and her body relaxed.

Her second attempt to get out of bed was slower. To the right was a tall window, one of five that pierced the exterior arc of the room. She walked to it with tentative steps.

The window overlooked a narrow lake of irregular shape that disappeared into a distant canyon. Far below was a strip of sandy beach backed by a narrow band of lush vegetation that looked very out of place. Also, an empty boat dock. Some sort of almost invisible shell enclosed the entire area with a pearlescent shimmer. This must be North Castle.

Before she could indulge in further speculation, a chime sounded from somewhere in the room, followed by a friendly, masculine voice: "Would you care for breakfast now, Miss Fenderwell?"

Breakfast, she thought. What a concept. Suddenly, nothing but eating seemed to matter. "Uh, yeah. Breakfast would be excellent," she responded, aiming her words at the heavy-looking wooden door. She had no idea who she was addressing, but at the moment that hardly mattered.

Almost before she finished speaking, the door swung open and a strange device floated into the room. It was apparently some kind of robotic serving thing; a round tray perhaps the thickness of her closed fist, with little pointy nubbins sticking out of its rim at regular intervals. On top of the tray was a silvery metal hemisphere with an ornate silver handle.

"You're looking much better this morning, Miss Fenderwell. I trust you slept well? How would you like to celebrate the breaking of your long fast? Anything you like."

"A hamanegg pastry sounds good to me. Maybe two, if you've got them. And a big glass of vitaberry juice would be great. But I'm so hungry I could eat that overstuffed chair over there. And probably whatever is under that dome thing. Is it food?"

"Two hamanegg pastries, of course. And a carafe of vitaberry juice. Will you be eating at the table?"

Glendyl was so hungry she didn't bother to wonder how the thing had anticipated her request. Nor did she ask it any of the questions that were stewing just under the surface of her mind. "Table?" She spotted a small round table with two chairs off to her right. "Sure. I'll eat at the table."

The thing floated over to the table. Then one of the nubbins extended itself, becoming a tentacle ending in a mass of extensible silvery finger-things. It lifted the cover from the tray, while another grasped the steaming plate and slid it onto the table, placing it with such precision that it made almost no sound. A third tentacle deposited a tumbler on the table while a fourth wrapped itself around the crystal carafe filled with reddish liquid and poured, not spilling a drop.

"If you haven't already noticed, there is a pot of fresh cannonberry tea on the nightstand. I hope you won't think me rude for commenting on your condition, but you appear to be recovering quite rapidly. Congratulations. Good morning to you ... and enjoy your meal."

"Thank you for the breakfast. But what happens after I eat? Am I stuck in here or what?"

"Just call for the Guide when you're ready for a tour of North Castle. I highly recommend the Museum. And I am to inform you that Mr White requests that you have tea with him in the Plaid Salon at three. Have a nice day." The serving machine departed, the door closed.

Mr White? wondered Glendyl. The image of a man with striking white hair popped up in her memory; that was the guy she'd thought was her medster. Not much interested in thinking about Mr White, Glendyl instead thought about the clever serving machine and wished the New Rules hadn't prohibited such gadgets in St Coriander. But at least St Coriander had magic, fondly recalling a number of mischievous incidents with her waterwand when she was younger. Then her stomach took over and she enjoyed two perfect hamanegg pastries, one more than she usually had at home.

Two hours later Glendyl had inspected herself and found no part of her that looked scorched or burned. Some of her skin was tender and overly pink, but otherwise normal. Part of her hair was missing, though. The dragon's fiery breath had mostly missed her left side, but the top and right were totally ragged. The medsters had only trimmed off the scorched parts. She grimaced, hesitated a moment, then buzzed it universally short with a gadget from the fully stocked bathroom. Not exactly gorgeous, but kind of adventurous: a good look for a Quester.

Next was an idyllic soak in a giant tiled bathtub next to a transparent wall looking out over the lake. After that, eyeshadow, eyeliner and a dusting of blush powder. In the closet she found a selection of remarkable gowns, a dozen pairs of intricately embroidered slippers in various sizes, and little else. Well, there was also a collection of headwear. After several minutes of trying things on and inspecting her reflections, she settled on a slinky, floor-length gown of deep cobalt blue. She now felt almost like Glendyl Fenderwell again, if radically overdressed.

Quester 250 scrutinized herself in the huge mirror. Eyes still just a little too wide-set, she reminded herself. And nose a little too broad. And somehow her face seemed not quite right. Maybe it was the stress of her recent adventures. Or something the medsters did? Or maturity and wisdom? She giggled at that thought. Or maybe ....

Glendyl's mind took an abrupt leap to an entirely different topic: hats. Sorting through the closet's marvelous collection, she settled on a loose oversized beret of soft blue velvet that matched her dress perfectly. Its only ornament was a filigreed silver brooch with a crimson tassel fastened to one side.

She adjusted the cap to a jaunty angle and decided she was ready for her tour, and hopefully even some answers. Seeing no obvious communication device, she spoke the word "Guide" with a slightly raised voice.

"At your service, Glendyl Fenderwell. Are you ready for your tour of North Castle?" The voice seemed to come from all the walls at once.

Nice voice, though, thought Glendyl. "Yes, I am." Almost immediately, the tray thing was hovering in the open doorway. Was it the same one that had brought her breakfast? She couldn't be certain.

"Follow me if you please, Miss Fenderwell."

North Castle was unlike anything Glendyl had ever encountered or even imagined. The guide (whom she had named Saucer in her own mind because, well, it just needed a name) began the tour by showing her where the sentry had found her. It was just inside the entry, where a huge, magnificent tapestry now hung, concealing the drawbridge. Although there was nothing to indicate a Quester's body had ever lain on that polished floor of intricately inlaid stones, Glendyl felt a sudden shortness of breath. But she forced a nod and a tight smile; the Guide moved on.

Next was the old guest station where prestigious visitors had once been greeted by a majordomo, issued personal guides and then directed to their quarters.

Next was the main kitchen, which contained a bewildering variety of devices for the preparation of food. "Why did they need all these things just to make stuff to eat?" she asked Saucer, waving her arms around the room for emphasis.

"The chefs of North Castle did not approve of MenuMasters," said the Guide, simply and without inflection. And they were a new technology at the time North Castle was built."

"No MenuMasters?" Glendyl was incredulous.

"MenuMasters were installed here in the early twenty-third century. However, North Castle records indicate that its chefs preferred to exercise their own artistic talents. And, in fact, they ...."

"What are chefs?" interrupted Glendyl.

"Perhaps we should briefly visit the Map now," said Saucer, knowing when to change the subject. "Take a slate, if you please. It will be valuable during your later explorations of the Museum.[24] For

24 :: *Glendyl's slate provided additional information about the Museum and the Map. Both were brainchildren of Robert Orville Miles Dunnigan, the last human Master of North Castle and Dunnigans Wall. Designs were*

now, I can give you a brief introduction to the Map and show you how to operate it before your tea with Mr White."

Saucer floated here and there past a dizzying maze of inexplicable artifacts, exhibits, animated replicas and simulacra, all of which announced themselves on the slate as she passed them. In the very center of the Museum was the Map. The Map itself occupied a space about fifty feet in diameter and was recessed a dozen feet into the floor. At its tallest point — the apex (at 11,294 feet) of the surprisingly unspectacular Mt Faunibeune — it rose only five feet above the main floor. At the bottom, a six-foot wide swath of yellow bricks encircled the entire map and was reached by a ramp that began just to Glendyl's right.

"First, you will need a control glove," informed her guide. "Are you right-handed? Yes, then select a right glove. No need to concern yourself with size; the gloves are self-adjusting. Ah, yes, the red glove; it sets off your gown quite nicely."

Feeling oddly embarrassed receiving a compliment from the machine, Glendyl mumbled a quick thank-you and asked it a question: "Do I start down at the bottom?"

"Yes, Miss Fenderwell. You can circumnavigate the map on the Yellow Brick Road.[25] You can also raise and lower the projection by

completed in 2271, with fabrication completed in 2274. When it was clear that the Nevergate Era was coming to a close and that the world was moving on, it was agreed that the faded glory of the little-used Grand Theatre should give way to a museum honoring the greatness of the passing era and the Dunnigan role in its flowering. The centerpiece was to be the remarkable Map, forever updating itself to honor the tiny piece of remote geography that spawned perhaps the greatest era in human history.

25 :: The "Yellow Brick Road" label has been attributed, correctly or not, to the Honorable Nafez Gamal Shah, Secretary General of WorldGov, in 2278. The occasion was a Clans Dunnigan hosted break from WorldGov hearings on the depopulation crisis. On his tour of the Museum, the Secretary General was reported to have said: "Only such as you idle rich could think of such self-indulgent trivialities at a time like this: you truly walk a yellow brick road." Although the reference to the fanciful road to Oz was meant as disparagement, the Map's designer, Robert Orville Miles Dunnigan himself, took a fancy to the term and it stuck. His perhaps impolitic response to Nafez Gamal Shah, while arguably true, is thought by some to have hastened the

using your glove: palm up will cause it to move upward; palm down will lower it. To enlarge an area of the map, just point your index finger at it. The projection will appear larger, and the longer you point, the larger it will become. Hold out your palm to shrink it. Yes, just like that."

Glendyl had already skipped down the ramp and was busy testing the glove even as Saucer's last words echoed in the cavernous hall. "You may study the Map all you like at a later time. For now, we only have time for a walkaround."

Saucer floated beside her as Glendyl walked, stopping here and there and squinting to see if she recognized something. "Isn't almost all of this in the Counterindicated Zone, the part that's blanked out of our maps?"

"I believe that is true, Miss Fenderwell."

Glendyl was frowning and pointing a finger at a legendary name. "Is this really the way it is? I mean Mt Funnybone ... I thought it would be a grand, rocky spire, all jagged and cruel looking. But it's so ... so ordinary," muttered Glendyl, disappointed.

"Despite its lack of dramatic features, it is the highest point in this vicinity. I'm afraid Mt Faunibeune is what it is," intoned Saucer. "Buckley Ennis Waller Dunnigan, who was Chief Technologist of the Clans Dunnigan from 2265 through the Dunnigan Retreat, always claimed this to be the most accurate dynamap ever created. And he was a noted stickler for accuracy."

Glendyl was still disappointed, but Saucer continued, now pointing with a tentacle. "Ah, here we are." "Right there is North Castle and the lake called Arrowmere. And there is Heroes Trail ... and North Trail. And these ancient scarps are the once famous Brazos Cliffs. The annual Vertical Games held here were a favorite of Dunnigan guests. And, of course, you must be familiar with Wittwater Deep."

---

approval of WorldGov's ill-conceived Nevergate Decommissioning Schedule of 2279 that, by all accounts, precipitated the short-lived First Nevergate War of 2280. Dunnigan's response was: "All roads begin as imaginary roads, my dear Secretary General. Including the Nevergates, which have become the lifeblood of this planet. Attempt to seal them at your own great risk."

The mention of Wittwater Deep recalled in Glendyl's mind the log. "Where's the log?"

"At this scale, the Sir Wendell Hamlin Memorial Log is not visible. You must enlarge the view if you want to see it in any detail. But I'm afraid you must do that at another time. We do not wish to keep Mr White waiting. He is one of North Castle's Special Members and a very busy man, or so he tells me. His whims are accorded all due respect."

Glendyl couldn't tell if Saucer was being facetious or not, but she made a reluctant about-face and followed her guide out of the Museum.

35 :: ATE HIS TWIN

"PLEASE STEP within the yellow circle on the floor, Miss Fender-well." Glendyl did as requested and low walls slid up out of the floor to about waist height. "This is a slidewell and we will ask it to take us up to the Park level, where we will find the Plaid Salon."

"We aren't totally primitive," said Glendyl in a huffy tone. We actually have slidewells in the Holy Quincunx and the Library."

"Please forgive me if I inadvertently insulted St Coriander. I meant no disparagement." Glendyl felt mildly chagrined at her over-reaction, but kept silent.

The slidewell rose silently and with no sensation of motion. They passed several levels of the castle that seemed to be just empty corridors with doors and alcoves along them, but Park level was en-tirely different.

Glendyl followed Saucer into a vast garden filled with trees, shrubs, vines and flowers of dizzying variety. And chirping birds, buzzing bees and fluttering butterflies, too. The overall effect was one of surpassing natural beauty, and she had never seen anything like it. The Rose Garden in the Holy Quincunx Plaza was a stunted poppy in a flowerpot by comparison.

They followed a path paved with rough stones around a small hillock, over a wooden bridge spanning a small cheerful brook, under an arbor of vines dotted with clusters of delicate lavender flowers and finally arrived at the Plaid Salon. It was not at all as she had imagined.

The Plaid Salon was an open-air pavilion elevated about six feet above where she now stood. Its waist-high walls were living, many-hued vines that had somehow been woven into a loose mesh, creating the visual effect of plaid patterns — rich rectangulations of red, blue, green, yellow, orange and purple in a dozen shades. At the top of a broad wooden stairway, a spacious pavilion was dotted with large, square umbrellas, also woven into colorful plaids. Glendyl was dumbstruck by the novelty and beauty of the place.

"Not exactly what you expected, eh, Glendyl?" came a voice from the pavilion. The man she had seen only for a moment had walked to the edge and was now smiling down at her. "You look very nice, very ladylike, by the way. And you seem to be recovering exceptionally well. Nary a char. Amazing what a horde of competent telowix and a little extra sleep can do, eh? Breathing 'dragon breath' was probably the worst, actually, but let's set all that unpleasantness aside, shall we? Let's have tea and I'll tell you a little about this place. Come on up."

The man's voice was smooth and placid, but contained a barely detectable undercurrent of impatience.

"Thank you for the compliment, Mr White. I'm sorry if I'm a little slow today; I feel like I'm in some kind of magical fairyland."

"You are in a fairyland, in a manner of speaking. The Clans Dunnigan had a soft spot for the mythical and fantastic and spent great effort and vast sums to bring them to life. In its heyday, this garden even had a small collection of tootle-fairies, twyk-men and flower-skips ... and one dwarf troll that lived under yonder bridge."

Glendyl wasn't absolutely certain that Mr White wasn't telling her a tale, but the very idea of such fantastic fairytale creatures so charmed her that she decided she would believe him. Then she recalled a recent mystery. "The trolls don't happen to live in those ugly little shack-things hanging from the dam, do they?"

Mr White's response was delivered with a rippled forehead. "Ah, no. Those beings are certainly not trolls from the garden. And they are benign, for the most part. I can say little about those diminutive cliff-dwellers; I've never met one personally, you see. I think you shall have to take up that subject with the Brain itself, since their continued trespass is its doing." Clearly, this was a sensitive topic.

They seated themselves at a round table under a plaid umbrella under a crystal-faceted roof under a dimpled cerulean sky. Saucer now arrived with a tray containing a small silver samovar of elaborate design. Flanking the samovar were two bone china cups, matching saucers with silver spoons, small silver knives, small pots of sugar and cream, plaid napkins and a basket of steaming pastry. The scrumptious aroma made Glendyl's mouth water.

Finally there was a small silver cup containing little yellow butterballs and a dainty fork for spearing them. In a blur of multiple tentacles, everything was arranged in its proper place. Glendyl had the thought that Saucer might be showing off just a little.

"Scones," said Mr White, noting the objects of Glendyl's attention. "Delicious with butter."

Glendyl and Mr White drank fine Earl Gray tea imported somehow and somewhen from China, according to Mr White. And they consumed two baskets of oven-fresh, currant-dotted scones while making genteel small talk about castle and garden.

When the conversation dwindled into silence, Mr White leaned forward and spoke in a methodical, down-to-earth tone: "Now we must be serious, Glendyl. Three attempts were made on your life in a mere forty-eight hours. Do you know why?"

Glendyl frowned, mentally counting. "I only get two: the wolf attack and the sailbird and dragon attack. Did I miss one? Not the lizard-thing ... the chuckwalla?"

"No, not the chuckwalla. And if I understand Exeter's Quest game correctly, the wolf attack was a sham. Possibly a test of your mettle, possibly for some other purpose. But yes, you missed one. You were being tended in the Infirmary when four of Exeter's minions broke in, intent upon suffocating the life out of you. I believe they wanted your Standard Toolbelt."

Glendyl's hand had involuntarily gone to her throat at the word "suffocating." "They must have gotten the Standard Toolbelt, because I didn't see it in my room."

"Actually, Glendyl, I let them take it back with them, somewhat readjusted, along with a fresh set of false memories in which one of them did, in fact, suffocate you by pressing a pillow over your face for several minutes. Those young men will long remember that imaginary murder, and the deathly blue of your face will likely haunt their dreams for many years. So as far as Exeter is concerned, you are dead and he now has the Standard Toolbelt, which is what he wanted badly enough to order you murdered. Where did you come across such a rare artifact anyway, if I might inquire?"

"I found it in Wittwater Deep, a ways below where the big log goes over it. I tripped over this weird gray bone and the belt was hanging from it. I just couldn't leave it there, so I buckled it on and that's that. The teleblade cured my infected finger ... and the wand helped me get up through the tunnel inside the dam and into North Castle. It saved my life, too; I blasted a sailbird with it! And something else, I think ...."

All this had spewed from her mouth at racehorse speed. Her voice trailed off as she plumbed her memory for details about what occurred in the chaotic moments after destroying the sailbird.

Mr White was frowning. "Glendyl, you are a very remarkable young lady to have taught yourself to use those implements, and in a short period of time under great pressure. I am particularly interested in how you figured out that the teleblade could help heal you."

"Oh, I didn't ... Lysheem taught me that part. Actually, Lysheem taught me all of it. I didn't figure out anything."

"Lysheem. Why is that name familiar?" Mr White scrunched up his face as if trying very hard to remember. Actually, he was accessing the South Castle's vast library via his mindlink. After ten or fifteen seconds of silence, his face relaxed somewhat. But now he looked genuinely puzzled.

"Long ago there was a young wyvern female named Lysheem. Records say she was a secretary or special assistant or something to the Dawnhammer himself. But she disappeared and was presumed lost in the war. All that was a very long time ago ..." His voice drifted off.

"I saw her. I talked to her. I mean I talked to her projection from the teleblade. I think she's my friend. She acts like it, at least. And she told me a lot of stuff about Exeter and dragons and wyverns and the Second Nevergate War and Questing: all kinds of stuff I never knew anything about. I think she has to be alive."

Glendyl was nearly shouting when she said: "But I can't talk to her anymore because you gave my Standard Toolbelt to some crazy jerk named Exeter!"

Mr White maintained a placid exterior. "I see. Glendyl, I understand your anger and I can't imagine that you could invent a conversation with an ancient wyvern named Lysheem. I believe what you told me. I do. And evidently, you had already formed some degree of attunement with the Standard Toolbelt. That, in itself, is quite remarkable, Glendyl. They are designed for wyvern minds, not human minds. Attunement is very important; it's how they're controlled. When you are fully attuned, you just know what you want them to do and they do it, within the limits of their capabilities, of course. They can be very powerful in the right hands ... and I apologize for sending your Standard Toolbelt to Exeter."

Mr White surveyed Glendyl's face before speaking again. "You are no doubt experiencing some ... shall we say, withdrawal symptoms from your association with the Standard Toolbelt. Attunements of this nature can form extremely strong bonds according to my library. It may take a while to fade, but I'm sure you'll be just fine soon enough. After all, you're not a wyvern, are you?" Mr White grinned at his joke and continued. "All taken with all, it's a fair bargain; we have saved your life in the process."

Glendyl made a face, then asked a question. "Mr White, what's going to happen when Lysheem calls me on the teleblade? Will she get Exeter instead?"

"That's a very good question, Glendyl. Unfortunately, I don't know just what will happen. Much may depend on how lucky we are: you, me ... and Lysheem, most of all. Not very scientific, hoping for good luck, I must say. But if Exeter learns there is a living, breathing wyvern somewhere on this planet, he will not rest until he finds it, murders it and scatters its blood, bones and wings to the four winds."

Glendyl gasped at the horrible scene she was envisioning. Mr White made a sympathetic expression and explained. "Exeter hates wyverns, you see. Truly hates them. Why? Consider this interesting little item that was expunged from local history scripts long ago: it was said that one of the early wyverns ate his twin brother."

36 :: VERY, VERY WRONG

WHILE HER FRIEND Glendyl was occupied with the wonders of the mostly empty North Castle, Lizbeth Marble was late for a party in another castle.

The party in Dillowy Cavern had been going strong for several hours before Ommergard's newest Artificer arrived. Her tardiness was partly because she hated parties and partly because she first wanted to see what Ommergard's library had to say about this artificial cavern.

So she read about its past life as the Ommergard Opera House where Lord Bellicarie's grand spectacles had been performed for audiences around the planet. And then about how and why it had been remade into a cave for the Cametto-5 dragons that fought Dunnigans and wyverns for the last Nevergate on earth.

For reasons she couldn't quite understand, going to a party inside a fake cavern that was still pocked with holes where actual dragons had lived was a creepy thought. Feeling awkward, alone and generally out-of-sorts, she had mostly wandered around the periphery of this huge space, looking up at the dreary gray walls and imagining she could smell the evil whiff of dragons.

At exactly ten p.m., the automated spotlights, floodlights, strobes and glimmerbeams all swung up to illuminate the portal in the distant dome that the dragons had used to come and go. The antique Varendi hammerbox stopped its complex percussive rhythms and the revelers on the floor stopped whatever they were doing to see what the Chief was up to this time.

Thwomp-whoosh: high overhead the sound of great wings flapping muted the raucous mood almost instantly. A huge snout appeared in the lights, accompanied by a blast of smoky, sulfurous flame and a roar that sounded like a dozen raging tigerwallas. The thing was so huge it had to tuck its great wings against its green-black body to pass through the portal.

As this grandfather of all dragons circled the cavern, the dance floor far below erupted with a mix of screams and cheers. Lizbeth Marble hadn't screamed, but she stood statue-like and almost hypnotized by the circling dragon. After two high loops, the dragon opened its jaws again and Lizbeth steeled herself for another roar and another belch of flame. But the jaws stayed open and belched out an ear splitting, but highly un-dragon-like VA- ROOOM, VA-ROOOM, VA-ROOOM, BAP-BAP-BAP-BAP-BAP.

Did the dragon have indigestion or something? Was it about to do something really gross?

The gossip around the dorm today had been thick enough to shovel; the upshot was that something truly fantastic was going to happen at this party. Fingers were crossed that it would be the fun sort of fantastic. As all experienced Ommergardians knew, Exeter's extravaganzas weren't always fun for all. At one party he had transformed every Artificers' feet into wheels, so they could better appreciate timely attendance at classes and other functions. Or so he had said.

Another time he had loosed a swarm of flying heads: red-bearded replicas of his own head with bat wings instead of ears and with forked tongues that could shoot out six feet or more and deliver a jolt much like a cattle prod. The heads lurked, spied and prodded for several days thereafter, motivating Artificers and Adjuncts to accomplish their chores quietly and without shirking. But those were object lessons, what Exeter liked to call "instructive entertainments."

If today's scuttlebutt was correct, Exeter was in fine spirits and this was going to be a fun-for-all kind of event.

In the brief time Lizbeth had been here she had heard dozens of tales about Exeter. Everybody she met seemed to have his or her favorite story. Evidently he was more than a little eccentric: somebody that nobody could quite figure out, but that everybody respected, feared and couldn't help admiring for one reason or another.

Everybody in Castle Ommergard had been invited to tonight's party, including lowly "rookies:" Level 1 Artificers like Lizbeth. Even all the Adjuncts had been called in from field patrols. Still feeling much like an outsider (the way she had felt most of her life anyway), Lizbeth had not mingled much. Mostly, she just walked around with her glass of tangy-sweet bullwinkle punch and watched small groups of Ommergardians in animated conversation. By the time of the dragon's entrance dive she had wandered to the center, where a circular stage had been set up. As yet, the stage had remained empty.

The VA-ROOOMing got louder, the dragon's jaws opened impossibly wide and something bright red shot out at high speed. It wasn't flames. As Lizbeth would later learn it was an ancient car, a highly modified 1934 Ford three-window coupe powered by gravlifters, thrust exchangers and a supercharged Merlinski ratmotor V-8, whatever that was. Copious flames and ear-splitting noise spewed from a series of shiny metal upswept tubes coming out of the sides of the thing's snout.

The candyapple red coupe did a couple fast and noisy loops around the inside of the cavern then spiraled down to land on the stage. With all eyes and all lights on the immaculate relic, nobody noticed that the fierce, firebreathing dragon just faded silently out of existence high above.

When the coupe started a VA-ROOOMing, tire smoking, wheel-standing dance in the center of the stage, the crowd fell back in awe and a little fear. The coupe's dance lasted all of a minute. When it settled down on all four wheels, there was one final VA-ROOOM and then silence. From somewhere, a drum roll began and the lights zoomed to the driver's side door. Out stepped Exeter the Wise, Chief Scientist of Castle Ommergard, Custodian General of Mt Faunibeune and vicinity, and inventor of magic, the New Rules and the Quest, among a thousand other things. The crowd went wild.

Exeter was dressed in tight black trousers, a starched white cowboy shirt with pearlescent buttons that winked on and off and a long leopard skin patterned topcoat with tails. Under the topcoat was a wide silver mesh belt.

His feet were shod in other relics of the distant past: cowboy boots fashioned from the tough blue-gray hide of a certain illustrious wyvern. His long chilipepper-red red beard was brushed out straight and extended to mid-chest. On his head was a white, wide-brimmed ten-gallon hat; wrapped around his eyes were his trademark black-rimmed, black-lensed shades.

To a chorus of cheers, salutes, hoots and bellows, Exeter walked cool and slow to the edge of the stage. Behind him, coils of thick dark mist coalesced around the coupe, obscuring it. When a gust of wind blew away the mist, the stage was empty of all but the Chief.

Seconds of anticipatory silence, then an explosion of red-orange light and smoke: a dozen skyrockets shot into the cavern, creating a dazzling display of light and color in cascading bursts.

Exeter coolly ignored the fireworks. He stood at the edge, looking out over the crowd, smiling a sardonic half-smile and occasionally directing his familiar chop-salute at his assembled minions as the outer rim completed a slow full circle. Now the lights all moved to an area high up in the cavern, where a circular platform was slowly descending. When it had settled into the very center of the stage, there was a drum kit complete with a drummer, a bass guitar complete with a bass guitarist, and a leopard-skinned electric guitar floating all by itself five feet above the stage.

At the exact moment the platform touched down, the drummer launched an intro riff that was familiar to all in Castle Ommergard except Lizbeth, who was too new to have heard it during occasional guzzle-busts. Exeter turned and executed a cool finger-snapping strut over to where the guitar floated, pulled it out of the air, slung the leopard tail strap over his shoulder and began to play.

The guitar bit the air like a rapacious buzzsaw: raw, low-down and crunchy ... and just what the crowd wanted. They went wild again as "Gimme All Your Lovin'" blasted into every corner of the cavern.

This must be rock'n'roll, Lizbeth decided. Normally, Lizbeth hadn't much cared for music, being an intense, bookish type drawn most strongly to mathematics and ideas. But at the moment, her body had other ideas. And it wasn't just the music; Lizbeth felt strange in other ways.

217

"Wanna boogie?" A slightly wobbly male voice startled her out of the groove she had slipped into.

Lizbeth turned to see a tall young man dressed in the pale green jumpsuit of a Level 4 Artificer, somebody who, according to Castle O traditions, had been in the castle for at least forty years and passed all the tests.

"Uh ... I don't know," was all she could think of to say: no one had ever asked her to dance before. Besides, Lizbeth didn't actually know how to dance.

The young man introduced himself as Danian Vissil. Lizbeth now remembered having seen his name on the plaque at Dunnigans Gate. Onstage, an unmanned keyboard had winked into existence and floated beside the drummer, playing itself. The band was ratcheting out a catchy, rolling dance tune with a chorus that went "give it up, bay-bee."

Much to Lizbeth's surprise she interrupted Danian's question about whether or not she was the much talked-about Wildcard and blurted, "Yeah, okay, I'll dance."

By the end of the trio's first set Lizbeth had danced herself almost to exhaustion. The last echoes of "Cheap Sunglasses" had just spent themselves against the cavern walls when Exeter unstrapped his guitar, left it hanging in the air and began walking up into nothing at all, climbing an invisible spiral staircase that circled the stage. Lights tracked his progress. When he stopped perhaps twenty feet above the stage, glimmerbeams flicked on, bathing the Chief in their swirling, coruscating light. At just the right moment, he held up his hands.

"Thank you, thank you, thank you. All three of us thank you from the bottoms of our ancient, vacuum-tube hearts. And while we're riding the gratitude trail, we'd better pay our usual homage to that late, great one-of-a-kind Texas trio of the twentieth and twenty-first centuries: ZZ Top." A new round of cheers and whoops began.

Exeter gestured for silence again. "While you're all catching your breath, I would like to take this opportunity to introduce someone to you."

Lizbeth suddenly felt very, very wrong in a sickening sort of way.

37 :: BUSINESS IS BUSINESS

THE WRONGNESS was an invisible force lifting Lizbeth off her feet. For the first few seconds of her ascent she was an awkward tangle of limbs trying to battle whatever was lifting her. Then a tiny voice whispered in both ears, just as it had in what she now thought of as the White Room: "Relax, don't fight it."

She didn't relax, exactly, but standing stock still seemed to help. In ten seconds she was above the crowd and floating toward the stage.

The voice that had whispered in her ear now boomed to the crowd. "Good residents of Castle Ommergard, I would like to formally introduce the newest member of our fine troupe."

Lizbeth was now standing next to Exeter on something that, though completely invisible, felt solid. She tried to appear composed and collected, but knew she looked frightened, frazzled and bedazzled. When her arms went goosebumpy, she shuddered and shook her body the way a dog does. Then she inhaled a deep breath, shrugged and waited for something to happen.

"The young woman you see before you came to us by a somewhat different route. Being just fifteen years of age, she could not have Quested, even if she had the luck for it. So she found another path — a rarely taken, very secret route. As you may or may not know, we in top management call good folks who arrive this way from St Coriander 'Accidentals.' Accidentals are exceedingly rare. In fact, as of now, there are exactly two Accidentals in our midst: this young

Artificer" — Exeter paused here for dramatic effect — "and my very good friend, that top notch Sorcerer, bass guitarist extraordinaire ... and the known world's premiere gravel-voiced vocalist — next to me, that is — Mitchel "Dusty" VanHook!"

There was a hush. The whole Accidental business was new information to the assembly. A spotty smatter of applause danced through the cavern on wobbly legs, but Exeter held up his hand again. "Surprised, are we? Didn't know there was a 'back door' way to get here from St Gutless? Well, no matter."

He took Lizbeth's hand in his and held it high in a triumphant gesture. "I would like you all to give a warm, Castle Ommergard welcome to this young woman. And I want you all to make her comfortable and feel completely at home in our unique little community." A dramatic pause, then: "Ladies and gentlemen, boys and girls, I give you ... Lizbeth Marble!"

The applause was courteous if not thunderous. Lizbeth had never been applauded for anything before and felt a hot flush wash over her face like a wave of surfing fire ants. The whispered voice filled both ears again: "Take a bow." She did. Not a particular gracious bow, but it was bow enough. And she didn't even do anything gawky.

Next, Exeter brought forward the members of the now-celebrated Away Team 4, the five young Adjuncts credited with discovering the already famous Standard Toolbelt, now snugly clasped around Exeter's waist.

The way Exeter told the tale, the team had been on patrol in Wittwater Deep when they had discovered something that had been uncovered by recent heavy rains. "The prize for such sharp eyes, me hearties," declaimed the Chief in his most extravagant style, "is a year's vacation from all 'special' duties." Exeter paused for applause and laughter before continuing. "Special" duties were special in the same way that stomping around barefoot in a pit of raw sewage is special; only dolts like the Adjuncts who typically made up the Away Teams ever found "special" duties on their work rosters.

When the chuckles had died away, he continued. "And that's

not all. I am awarding each of these fine lads the Dragon League's prestigious Vanguard Medal!"

There was a brief hush before the next round of cheering began. Even a newbie like Lizbeth knew that the Vanguard Medal was a very high honor indeed: the Level 1 Sorcerer who had lectured on elementary spellsystems yesterday had one and wore it proudly. And no Adjunct had ever earned a Vanguard Medal before. Evidently a Standard Toolbelt, mused Lizbeth, is a pretty important and valuable thing.

221

Exeter was about to make his next announcement when Lizbeth heard a sharp staccato buzz coming from somewhere nearby. She turned toward the Chief, which seemed to be where the off-and-on buzz was originating, and noted the frown that flashed over his face, a tiny chink in his usual composure. "Sounds like it's time to start our second set, me hearties!" bellowed the Red One with gusto. He made a sweeping go-away motion with one arm, and Away Team 4 and Lizbeth Marble began floating back over the crowd.

At the same time, the kick drum and tom-toms launched the intro to "Sleeping Bag," drowning the buzzing in wet percussion. Exeter spun and shot up his left hand. In one graceful sequence he pulled his axe out of the air, slung the strap over his shoulder and windmilled the tune's first power chord with his right hand. The crowd whooped and cheered at this bit of perfect showbiz timing and the party was back in its loud and raucous groove.

• • • • •

Much later that night Exeter lay slouched on a sofa in the topmost room in Tower Five, his feet on a table made of a resilient material that vibrated in a way designed to soothe his sore feet. The wyvern-hide boots had never fit quite right, although he refused to think of this as the involuntary donor's small posthumous revenge. On his lap was the Standard Toolbelt. On his face was a deep frown that threatened to deepen further into a scowl.

The Chief was considering the matter of unfortunate timing; the telelade's Secure Message Signal had occurred at exactly the moment he couldn't do anything about it. Had he been attuned to the thing, the SMS might have manifested as a buzzing gnat in front of his eyes or some other signal only he could perceive. But without the right genemarkers, it would never attune to him. With enough time, he might be able to trick it, but that couldn't fix what had just happened.

An unexpected event happening in public like that ... well it was just unacceptable. Worse, it made him feel vulnerable. One wrong decision or just plain bad luck could spoil everything he had built over the last two and a half centuries, including the myth of his omnipotence and omniscience. Couldn't let that happen. Spinning it as a signal to launch the second set had doubtless prevented any negative consequence. Well and good, but the teleblade's buzz was still a mystery.

He could, of course, attribute the untimely buzz to the sheer perversity of the universe. But that wouldn't salve his curiosity one tiny bit; he still wanted — and needed — to know who or what was at the other end of the connection. Enemy? Friend? Malfunction? Prankster? Next to enemy, malfunction was probably the most likely answer, although wyvern tech-stuff was remarkably trouble-free and durable, he admitted with a sour grumble. In fact, he would certainly love to have a bunch of their gravlifters to replace the out-of-license hoverbars that kept his castle stuck here in the middle of nowhere. But back to his immediate problem.

If there were a prankster amongst them, Exeter would find him — or her — and execute a particularly noxious transformation upon him or her: a dogfish in Arrowmere would not likely pull off many pranks. It would be way too busy dog-paddling for its life trying to avoid the freshwater moray eels, sizzlefish, mudsharks and other nasties that the Dunnigans had stocked the lake with for security purposes. Three of his Away Team boys had met gruesome deaths sneaking a forbidden swim in that fiendish span of hell-water.

"Friend" could almost certainly be ruled out. Exeter doubted that he had any secret friend with his or her own teleblade. So it was probably an enemy. An unknown enemy. Maybe it was the cursed wyvern satellite brain — or whatever it was — that might still be up there in a black orbit somewhere. He had forgotten about it for centuries, but it could still be operational, still waiting for some kind of event or signal to become active and maybe, somehow, make a mess of his plans. Maybe his wearing the belt had triggered some kind of signal and woken it up. But maybe the signal was part of the attunement process. Maybe, maybe, maybe. Exeter hated maybes.

A far more remote possibility was that there was a living, breathing, hateful wyvern at the other end. Unfortunately, there didn't seem to be any way to force the issue and learn the truth. He would just have to wait. For now, there was nothing more he could do about these damnable maybes.

223

Having come to that conclusion, the Chief roused himself to action and took the Standard Toolbelt to his worktable, setting it there almost reverently. It was a thing of beauty and power, after all. He instructed a Watcher to monitor the Toolbelt at all times, then took himself over to the slidewell and descended a level into his private quarters. After a good soak in a steaming bath laced with restoratives, he flopped on his bed, informed the doors to admit no one until further instructions and decided that tomorrow would be a well-deserved day off. The party had been great fun and a great success. Almost perfect. Long live rock'n'roll, he thought, smiling to himself: Billy Gibbons, eat your heart out!

Just before sleep came to him, an image of the unlucky Glendyl Fenderwell impinged itself on his dwindling awareness. Too bad you had to go and flunk your Luckiest final, Glendyl. But business is business, after all. Then he slept.

38 :: WILDCARD NONSENSE

A GIANT WITH a tree-sized mallet aimed, swung and delivered another quick stroke. THUNK. Lizbeth Marble's head rolled across the prickly grass, clanged off a hoop, missed the pole. Again.

Oh, no! thought Lizbeth's head with a tinny cry of distress and another lump. The giant was ready for another try as soon as her head stopped rolling. THUNK.

Oh, no! thought Lizbeth's head yet again as it rolled to a bumpy stop. The giant was already poised for the next stroke. But too late: a different giant whacked it from another direction. THONK.

"Lizbeth, Lizbeth! Stop screaming, Lizbeth! You're waking everybody up. It's just a dream, silly girl."

Lizbeth's eyes creaked open. Kinni Sarp, the over-nice, over-energetic Level 1.3 from the cubby next door was hovering over her. She pressed a jabtab into Lizbeth's palm. "That oughta take care of the hangover. Gotta run, Lizbeth. I'll tell 'em you're party swooped and need a sub today. I'm sure it'll be okay." Kinni Sarp, former Luckiest and Westac graduate of 2524 AD, departed, her electric white Mohawk haircut like a windless sail on top of her polished cinnamon skull.

Lizbeth dragged herself into the shower, into her jumpsuit and off to the AM.

Artificers Mess was the Castle Ommergard term for the "Artificers Only" dining hall. It was cramped, stark in decor and to say it offered extremely limited culinary choices was a masterful under-statement. And that was just the way Exeter wanted it.

Most Ommergardians were convinced that the stunted menu in the AM was another of Exeter's numerous "motivational strategies" designed to encourage performance qualities Exeter deemed desir-able: "robust strivings," "transformational excellence," and "bene-ficial gustatory decoupling" were among the qualities in vogue with the Chief at the moment.

Lizbeth zombied through the line and took her plate to an un-occupied corner. Gray and grimacing, she forked a few bites of to-day's BS (breakfast stew) into her mouth and swallowed. Her queasy stomach wasted no time in spewing an embarrassing mess all over the table.

Boris Yalder, one of her dance partners from last night's party, was on monitor duty in the AM at that moment. Noting the new ce-lebrity's sudden illness, he hustled her to Castle Ommergard's doc-space where she was given customary treatments for a hangover and deposited in a bed for observation. She shut her eyes, fell into a co-ma-like sleep and did not wake for thirty-six hours.

Lizbeth opened her eyes in a lifesupport pod. Her return to wakefulness triggered an alarm and not long thereafter Exeter him-self was peering through the plexan shell of the pod. He gave her a fatherly, concerned smile, then caused the shell to open. "Are you feeling better young lady? You gave us quite a scare. Bit of an unusual reaction to bullwinkle punch, eh?"

Lizbeth forced a thin smile, but barely noticed Exeter's pres-ence; most of her mind was cluttered with a rain of strange symbols and patterns that formed, reformed, permutated, combined, multi-plied, divided, squared, cubed and rooted in endless variations. This mathematical nightmare seemed to be taking place in the airspace between her face and the Chief's.

Underneath that weirdness was a gnawing ache in all her bones and two persistent itches: one in the vicinity of her upper back, the other at the base of her spine. After some long moments of silence, she also became aware that Exeter was waiting for her to respond to something he had said. But what had he said?

She had been about to apologize to His Redness for getting sick, but her tongue switched plans on her at the last moment. "Slate," she croaked.

"Slate?" repeated the Chief Scientist of Castle Ommergard. Lizbeth blinked, but managed a nod.

"An unusual request for someone who has been on lifesupport for a day and a half, but so be it." He made a gesture to someone beyond Lizbeth's field of vision and a minute later her slate appeared in his hand.

"I'm impressed that you are wanting to catch up on your studies, Lizbeth, but my advice is to take it easy for a while. You're bright: you'll catch up in due time." He handed her the slate. "I'm sure you'll be back in good shape very quickly, assuming your admirers don't overtire you." He patted her head and departed.

• • • • •

Lizbeth lacked all interest in catching up on her studies. The only thing she could think about was unclogging her head. Period.

"What are you doing, Lizbeth?" The voice that now intruded upon her concentration belonged to Boris Yalder. The slender man with the remarkable nose had been popping in and out of the docspace for the better part of two days. Owing to his nervous intensity and penetrating glare, he was not known for suavity or charm; his rapid rise to Level 6.2 status was the result of his unusual knack for long distance spellcasting, nothing more. At the moment his nervous intensity was focused on the girl with the slate.

At the sound of Yalder's voice, Lizbeth glanced up, nodded and then went back to what she was doing. "Oh, hi," she mumbled as an afterthought, more to her slate than to Yalder.

"Lizbeth, what are you doing? Are you okay? You look kind of gray. I guess you're allergic to bullwinkle punch, huh? Or maybe too much boogie time; you really worked out." Yalder made a lame half-chuckle and stopped talking.

"Uh, I don't know," mumbled Lizbeth. "Gotta do this." Her hands were a blur, darting in and out of the slate's holospace, moving vectrals, antisets, viroids and other arcana into a dense, three-dimensional mathematical object. "Are those Van Gonder transforms? I didn't know you were a math genius." Lizbeth ignored him; Yalder became miffed. "Give it a rest, Lizbeth!" he snapped.

"Gotta do this," was Lizbeth's mumbled response. Again.

Yalder stalked out, shaking his head. Some minutes later he returned with a short woman who appeared to be in early middle age. Jennet Wankettil was the Chief Mathematician at Castle Ommergard and had spent the past century attempting to reinvent the alien technology that had once made the Castle's hoverbars work. She had zero success.

"Lizbeth, this is Sorcerer Wankettil," announced Yalder. "She's Head of Math. Maybe she can help you with whatever you're trying to do."

Lizbeth mumbled something unintelligible and went back to shaping and sequencing pictorial equations that had been behaving like lunatic breakdancers.

"Artificer Marble, I require your full attention. At this moment!" barked the Chief Mathematician. Ommergard scuttlebutt summed up the Head of Math as a martinet whose temper was every bit as short as her person. And then some.

Lizbeth made a swirl of hand motions that froze the tangle in front of her, then turned to stare at her interrupter. "Can't you see I'm involved with something?" she snapped.

Fortunately for Lizbeth, the Head of Math didn't hear her. Her attention had been snagged by the elegantly untidy mess hanging suspended in midair. Hunched over the edge of the pod, her eyes darted here and there, tracing out topological pathways, introsancs, spectrophages, node-wiggles and all the rest.

Minutes passed. Suddenly she stood up straight and said: "You may return to your duties, Artificer Yalder. You were correct in calling my attention to this matter." She waved her hand in a shooing motion and Boris Yalder departed, grumbling something about females.

The next day, Lizbeth had recovered sufficiently to begin assist-
ing Wankettil in an important new initiative; restarting Castle Ommergard's long-defunct hoverbars by using a fresh strategy.

Exeter's support was immediate and enthusiastic. The sub-basement containing the defunct hoverbars was reopened. Three Blue
Goon units had been pulled off their regular duties and were already
cleaning away the caked dust, rodent corpses and other detritus of
past centuries.

The Chief had long given up hope that the Castle's powerful
hoverbars could ever be restarted. After a century of failed efforts he
had resigned himself to the fact that Ommergard was stuck forever
in the middle of nowhere.[26] But now, out of a different variety of no-

229

---

26 :: *If the First Nevergate War (over control of the Nevergates upon
WorldGov's Decommissioning Order) was the triggerpull, Clans Dunnigans'
surprise move of disappearing all of Earth's remaining Nevergates overnight
rather than see wars fought over their greatest creations was the bullet in the
brain of WorldGov. It also put a very short lifespan on anything that required
periodic Nevergate access for continued operation, such as Ommergard's
hoverbars.*

*Lord Bellicarie's licenses to operate Castle Ommergard's Saurquian-built
hoverbars had only a short time remaining: no pay, no go. The licensors, the
notoriously inflexible Saurqus Savants of Aldebaran 6 in PU 62, could not be
contacted except through a Nevergate. Lord Bellicarie flew his castle from
Rome to Dunnigans Wall with the hope of negotiating special "theatrical"
privileges for access to the Dunnigan private Nevergate somewhere in the
vicinity of Dunnigans Wall. Feeling within the Clans had long run strongly in
disfavor of Lord Bellicarie's antics, particularly over the "sky monkey" issue.
The creatures for his traveling show had been raised from stolen dunnikin
seed, but since dunnikins were a Top Secret project, the Clans could not publicly
prosecute the matter. Bellicarie's "humble" last-ditch request was flatly denied
and the attack on Dunnigans Wall followed shortly thereafter.*

*Lord Bellicarie, while a consummate showman and salesman, was not
regarded by those who knew him as a person inclined toward rashness. He
cultivated an easy persona of bombast and pretentious buffoonery, qualities
calculated to be endearing in certain influential circles, where he was seen as
having more money than sense and a mania for all things medieval, chivalrous
and/or romantic. Many contemporaries of Lord Bellicarie believed him both
intellectually and temperamentally incapable of conceiving and executing
an act so daring as a surprise dragon attack on the nearly all-powerful
Dunnigans in their very own stronghold. Instead, they attributed the whole
escapade to Exeter, who had gained great influence and power within the
Castle Ommergard community over his thirty-year tenure prior to the War.*

where, a small hope stepped in.

Whether by luck, sheer brilliance or divine providence, studying Lizbeth's sequences had given Sorcerer Wankettil her first fresh idea in decades: hack the cryptology. It was just possible that a wild talent like Lizbeth Marble might be able to break through the bizarre crypto that controlled the license clocks in each of the forty-five massive hoverbar units. The trick would be to simulate a license renewal procedure using an insanely complex family of mathematical systems dubbed "Van Gonder transforms."

Pulling off this ruse would also demand a high degree of personal cleverness in outwitting the dynamic coding schemes that had prevented the hoverbars from functioning for more than 250 years. Apparently, Lizbeth Marble had somehow acquired both talents in abundance and the Head of Math had been quick to recognize the possibilities. Still, she was skeptical and suspicious.

Up to this point, Sorcerer Wankettil had regarded the current "Wildcard nonsense" as a frivolous waste of time and quite possibly a hoax. In her disdain for anything and everything wildcardish, she had neglected to read Lizbeth Marble's "X-File" which was accessible only to Sorcerer-level Ommergardians. When she belatedly got around to it, things began to click. One item was particularly significant: Lizbeth had a knack for simgames and had mastered every one in the St Coriander Library by the age of six. Maybe there's something to the Wildcard nonsense after all, mused Sorcerer Wankettil.

Whoever was responsible for initiating the conflict, it was very nearly successful. What the Ommergardians did not anticipate, however, was the entry of Castle Caraway and its highly capable, highly unpredictable population of wyverns into the conflict in support of the Dunnigans. Readers interested in an engaging eyewitness account of this conflict are encouraged to obtain a copy of Clash of the Titans: 2285 *by Diogenes the Wanderer.*

39 :: ICEBOX

THE LONE data warrior sat cross-legged on the floor and did battle with Hoverbar 13. Out of the 45 Hoverbar units in the Bar Room, this was the one Lizbeth Marble had picked to joust with. If she figured out how to beat 13's dynamic lockout barrier, she'd know how to beat them all.

Sometimes ideas came and went like flickery lightning bugs in her brain. Other times, when she met with mental blank walls, she would get up and walk around, half in a daze. In this semi-daze she had traversed nearly every square inch of the sub-basement.

She wasn't alone. During this time, Exeter had developed an unhealthy fixation on the sub-basement: unhealthy at least for slackers. Girdled with his new toy, the Standard Toolbelt, he ranged here and there, his energy barely containable. He scrutinized progress with a critical eye, sometimes issuing orders, sometimes making suggestions, sometimes delivering stern rebukes for sloth or sloppiness, sometimes joking, sometimes humming, sometimes playing air guitar with elaborate flourishes.

The Blue Goons were on their best behavior during these times and the sub-basement soon began to look almost operational again. But Exeter refused to be satisfied until each hoverbar unit was cleaned until it shone like new.

Lizbeth barely noticed Exeter's presence: whether tracing invisible patterns with her hands or pacing the far corners of the vast pentagon, she was completely absorbed in her task. Nor did she pay much attention to her aching bones and only occasionally reached up to scratch her back or absently rub her bony backside against a corner.

Certain of the Blue Goons found Lizbeth's behavior aloof and not at all jocular. Worse, this gawky newcomer was now Exeter's pet. To Torian Vink, in particular, this was wrong. And he was tired of having to clean up down here, much preferring his patrols outside the castle where direct supervision was nonexistent.

Torian Vink had been a Blue Goon for twelve years and, by dint of crafty pugnaciousness, had become a squad leader. Not tall, he was built wide, thick and powerful with a broad face and a square jaw, wavy blue-black hair and what seemed like a permanent, one-day growth of coarse black whiskers. His most striking feature was a pair of unnerving, pale blue eyes that were several sizes too small for his face. Vink was also one of only a few score of Outsiders[27] in Castle Ommergard; he had been "enlisted" after wandering past several dozen No Trespassing signs to stand in surly rapture before the Castle. To Exeter, Vink represented both proven outdoorsmanship and raw aggression. In the right quantities and at the right times, both were useful Away Team assets. And as such traits were almost completely absent from the Castle's mostly Luckiest population, Exeter mostly overlooked Vink's sometimes offensive behaviors.

For the past several days, Torian Vink's eyes had followed Lizbeth Marble everywhere she went. He had also contrived several pranks.

The first was simply to stumble while walking past Lizbeth, spilling his mug of steaming ultrabroth. The hot liquid would scald her, get her sent to the docspace and out of the Bar Room for a while. Instead, something distracted Vink at the moment of truth and the

---

27 :: *Vink was ejected from the Bunkerite community located in a "mountain fastness" believed to be the former NORAD defense installation that had been mothballed for cost reasons by WorldGov in the early twenty-third century. Little is known of the Bunkerites except that they are thought to fear daylight. Torian Vink, however, showed little fear of anything.*

liquid splashed all over the business end of Hoverbar 13. Lizbeth barely noticed.

Exeter *did* notice. "Vink, you clumsy schmuck! How many times have I told you morons not to traverse the vicinity of hoverbars with loaded mugs? Expect a Penalty if I see this happen again!"

Vink nodded, but said nothing, his face flushing against his will. He scowled at Lizbeth and departed, issuing an order to one of his underlings to clean up the mess. And fast.

233

His next prank was better planned, more elaborate and beyond the immediate scope of Exeter's scrutiny. It involved sabotage of the ladies room plumbing. In this scheme an explosive backflush would send the seated occupant — Lizbeth Marble — rocketing into the air on a high velocity spout of water. Through an almost impossible chain of events, Sorcerer Wankettil was the victim instead of Lizbeth Marble.

The Head of Math, while not seriously injured, walked with an odd crabbed gait for several days. Although Vink cared nothing for Sorcerer Wankettil's discomfort, he rankled at the fact that his squad (known informally as the "skouchers," an uncomplimentary term) was required to attend to the mess and repair the plumbing.

Vink's third prank returned to simplicity. It involved merely locking Lizbeth Marble in one of the five "iceboxes" located at the outer ring's five corners. Without special gear, ten minutes inside would turn the Marble creature into an ugly ice sculpture and out of Vink's hair forever.

The iceboxes housed the Binkhaul Xeroes, Castle Ommergard's negspace power units that would soon be supplying power again to the hoverbars. Only rarely did anyone venture into an icebox. For one thing, there was rarely a need: Binkhaul Xeroes needed very little maintenance. For another thing, the iceboxes were maintained at zero degrees centigrade, making them impractical as places for naked recreation. The audible hash was a third deterrent; Xeroes emitted a jarring stew of pulsed hissing, rasping and grinding noises thickened by a wide spectrum of buzzy hums. At a minimum, the

hash was unpleasant. Excessive exposure, however, had permanently scrambled the brains of more than one macho Blue Goon who had
neglected to don his damping muffs before performing routine instrument checks.

Vink's plan was based on his observation that Lizbeth Marble
quite often meandered the perimeter of the sub-basement, apparently to escape the bustle of the Blue Goon crews, and was always
lost in her own mental processes and weird gesticulations. The only
required ingredients for his scheme were the theft of Lizbeth's audiobutton, its relocation to Icebox 5, the disabling of the "open door"
alarm and the opening of the Icebox's heavy access door.

Early on Lizbeth's sixth day in the sub-basement Exeter and
Jennet Wankettil were elsewhere. Free of scrutiny, Torian Vink
wasted no time putting his plan into action.

Positioning his crew within range of Lizbeth's ears, Vink unleashed a string of surpassingly lewd jokes, provoking raucous hoots,
guffaws and sly leers at Lizbeth. As Vink expected, the combination
of embarrassment and interruption sent Lizbeth Marble on a frowning sojourn out of the Bar Room and around the outer ring of the
sub-basement.

Passing Icebox 5, Lizbeth failed to notice the icy vapor seeping
through the partially open door. But she did respond to her name
being called from somewhere inside. Frowning, she traced the familiar audiobutton sound quality to the dark interior of Icebox 5 and
entered.

The door shut behind her, the lock scrambled and Vink returned
the way he had come, appearing only moments later back in the Bar
Room after what he pridefully claimed to his fellow skouchers was
a record-breaking bowel movement. A stint of vociferous counter-
claims, jokes and other bathroom banter followed, and the annoying
Lizbeth was forgotten.

Inside Icebox 5, Lizbeth discovered, to her surprise and irritation, that the lights refused to respond to her spoken request. Nor
did the button by the door respond. Had she closed the door? she

wondered absently. After perhaps half a minute in the frosty dark, she began to panic: "Light! Light! Light! Turn on, damn you!"

The icebox remained dark, the door remained closed and Lizbeth Marble began to freeze.

236

40 :: HAVE ANOTHER

"WHAT ARE THOSE little triangles? And what's the gooey black stuff with the little round beads in it?" inquired Glendyl just a little testily. She wasn't a very daring eater and, like most residents of St Coriander, had not yet encountered caviar.

"The Dunnigans called them canapés," soothed Saucer. "This variety is a wafflebread cracker topped with caviar from Arrowmere's very own miniature sturgeons. It is a rare delicacy and was all the fashion in the halcyon days of North Castle. The master chefs claimed it rivals the finest Beluga, but I have no way to verify their assertions. Would you care for some chopped egg and minced red onion on your canapés? Capers?"

Glendyl sat at a small table in the Museum, a few steps from the entrance to the Map. Her initial encounter with it had hooked her and now she couldn't stay away, so Saucer had set up a little table where she could take her lunches. The Map was vastly more interesting than she had imagined a map could possibly be. For one thing, it introduced her to the world surrounding St Coriander, the areas comprising the Counterindicated Zone. This ring of emptiness encircled St Coriander like a white stockade, a blank zone on all maps and satpix that existed in her hometown.

For several days Glendyl had explored every aspect of the Counterindicated Zone, which Saucer patiently supported with explanations, histories and anecdotes about this place or that; St Coriander, although isolated, wasn't quite the island it had always seemed to be. Glendyl wasn't certain this was a comforting realization.

After a time, she became aware that the Map was always changing in small ways. The smoke in the cliff, for example. Had it been there when Saucer first introduced her to the Map? She wasn't certain. Even at the maximum enlargement, Glendyl was only able to determine that a thin wisp was issuing from a cave high in a sheer cliff on the eastern face of Wittwater Deep. It irritated her that she could not manipulate her viewpoint enough to be able to see what was inside. That particular mystery was set aside, still unsolved, when Saucer had appeared with the unfamiliar lunch.

Glendyl remained suspicious about caviar. "Okay, so the little black round stuff is caviar? But what is it?"

"I am going to guess that 'roe' is not a common word in St Coriander these days?" deadpanned Saucer.

"They don't teach us every dumb old ancient thing, you know," snapped the Quester. "Who's got time for all of that? So what's roe? And what's a sturgeon, for that matter? And a Beluga?"

"A sturgeon is a fish. A rather large fish, in fact. With a pointy snout. Roe — caviar — are the sturgeon's eggs."

Glendyl gulped and wrinkled her nose at the stuff on the tray. "So you think I should eat fish eggs for lunch? Are they cooked?"

"Perhaps I erred in requesting this ... unusual repast, Miss Fenderwell. In all candor, you remind me of a certain woman who was a guest here — on and off — for many years. She was very fond of caviar."

A note of wistfulness had infiltrated Saucer's voice, or at least Glendyl thought so. She softened. "Okay, I'll try it. But who was the young woman I remind you of? And what did she do here?" She gingerly took one of the canapés and sniffed it. "Smells salty."

"It *is* salty. It is supposed to be salty. The fresh roe is cured with a special grade of salt. And I really do recommend adding a bit of the chopped egg and a tiny dollop of sour cream. That's how Madonna 13 liked it. She didn't much favor onions though. Or the capers."

"I remind you of Madonna 13? You *knew* Madonna 13? Wow! But that's really ancient ...."

"Madonna 13's spirit is very much a part of this edifice. She and the first Dunnigans were very close.[28] My own acquaintance with her began later, on St Valentine's Day in 2240, a day I remember well." Saucer's voice seemed to quaver and trailed off for some seconds. A sound almost like a deep sigh emerged from it, then words. "I never believed she would really opt for Elevation. I thought it was a publicity scheme to once again restart her career ...."

Glendyl, of course, was well aware of Madonna 13's famous Elevation on the Holy Quincunx Elevation Stage. The whole story was in the Holy Quincunx museum. Everybody knew that; it was what started the Madonna Cult. But that was just history; it hadn't touched Glendyl personally. She tried to imagine Saucer and Madonna 13 having a conversation: "Hello, Saucer, how are you this morning? Would you bring me some caviar? But hold the onions, you dear thing, you. And the capers won't be necessary this time." This was as far as she could get without laughing out loud.

"Sounds like you really knew her well. You liked her, didn't you? What else did you do besides serve her fish eggs? Do you know about the Madonna Cult in St Coriander? My friend Sable Hawthorne is president this year. But I never had time for that stuff."

"Yes, you preferred to play bangerball, I understand."

"How do you know I play bangerball?"

"I read the *St Coriander Times*, of course. And in the same vein, I monitor the vidlines and slatecasts twenty-four hours a day. And not just in St Coriander."

"Oh," said Glendyl, chagrined that the mystery was solved so simply. "How can you do all that? You seem so ...." Glendyl hesitated, unable to find just the right word and not wanting to hurt the machine's feelings.

---

28 :: *The remarkable personal connection between earthquake survivors Madonna 13 and the four Dunnigans began under a cast iron bathtub on July 14, 2174. See* Genesis...And Then Some *for more.*

"Small? Is that the word you didn't want to say? If you can keep a little secret, Miss Fenderwell, I am actually the Brain of North Castle. I know everything that has happened in this vicinity — and a great deal more — since I was 'born' and became conscious in 2235. I am the oldest living MCI — that stands for Massively Chaotic Intelligence — on this planet. Without boasting, I can admit to being a rather remarkable analyst and synthesist. And my memory is both vast and still flawless … except for a few small blank spots. What you see before you that you call Saucer is just one tiny node of my being. But you knew that already, didn't you? Of course you did. But did you know that tomorrow is my three-hundredth birthday? Shall we have a party to celebrate? It's been a very long time since there has been a party in North Castle. Even a small one."

Actually, Glendyl admitted to herself, she really hadn't thought of Saucer as the Brain of North Castle. Mr White had said something about a Brain, she now recalled, but she hadn't paid much attention.

Not wanting to appear terminally stupid while her own brain was stewing on the Brain business, she changed the subject by stuffing a whole caviar canapé in her mouth at once. The taste was sharp and salty, but not awful. The chopped egg and the sour cream helped smooth out the saltiness and the wafflebread gave it all a nice crunch and a tiny hint of sweetness.

"Not bad," she said, still chewing. "Not bad at all. I think I'll have another one if you don't mind, Sir Brain. And yes, let's have a party."

41 :: NO IDEA

WHEN HER attentions turned back to the Map, Glendyl asked the question that had nagged at her during lunch. "This Map I'm looking at is happening right now, isn't it? Is that right? But where do all the old versions of the Map go? Do you save them somehow? I'm just wondering when the smoke started coming out of that cave in the cliff."

Saucer's response was cryptic. "Smoke has been coming out of the old dragon's hole — off and on — since just after the end of the Second Nevergate War. Your apparent enemy, the remarkable Exeter, rode Emmishak there himself. She was one of three dragons to survive the war and she has been there since: thus the occasional smoke. She usually naps for a century at a time, judging from my analysis of historical Map data. She is evidently awake again and quite her old self. Would you like to watch?"

"Watch what?" said Glendyl, frowning.

"Some history."

"Are you going to show me Madonna 13 arriving in that airship with the Bumbusker Bare Force? That would be cool!"

"Not that far back in history. The Map had not yet been created at the time Madonna 13 was touring with the Bumbuskers. But you certainly know your Madonna 13 history. Actually, I was thinking of reviewing the Map sequence showing the area on the afternoon you arrived here. I direct your attention to the cave you have been so interested in this morning."

Before she could respond, there was a subtle change in the Map: an abrupt shifting of shadows and a change in the intensity of the smoke. Something dark appeared at the mouth of the cave, plunged over the edge and dropped like a boulder. Before it hit the canyon floor, monstrous wings unfurled and the dark thing soared up out of the canyon in a grand swoop. Glendyl grabbed for a control glove and began to enlarge the image, zooming in on the tiny flying thing until it was clearly recognizable as the dragon that had nearly cremated her on the drawbridge. She expanded the image until it dominated her field of vision. "Geez, Lou-ise!"

Glendyl hesitated and the image froze. Her hands shook, her knees felt weak and her breathing became a series of shallow gulps. Moments passed before her curiosity overpowered the dark memories.

Holding her breath now, Glendyl tracked the dragon as it rose higher into the airspace above the Map. After circling so high that North Castle looked like a collection of tiny lines and shapes around the many-faceted centorium, the dragon banked and swooped downward in a series of tight spirals, leveling out only when it was just above the topmost turrets of the castle.

Now Glendyl could clearly see the drawbridge spanning the narrow space between the entry tower and the castle. She smiled a grim smile when a sailbird disappeared in a burst of flame, smoke and feathers, but other details were obscured by the deepening dusk and the thickening mist from Arrowmere.

"You might wish to slow the image," said Saucer, attempting to be helpful.

The zoomed map froze in mid-action, then restarted at half-speed. There was another explosion, this one from a bright spark inside the entry tower. A small, blond-headed figure flew backwards in a lazy ark and landed in a limp tangle on the drawbridge. The diving dragon seemed to glow with malice. Even without sound, the Glendyl at the Map's controls could almost hear the dragon's hideous battle scream, the scream that had held her transfixed and almost caused her death.

Morbid fascination knotted her guts as she watched the figure on the bridge raise her head just as a blast of roiling, red-orange flames erupted from the dragon's snout. Almost at the same moment, the drawbridge lurched up and the smoking figure began a sluggish roll toward the castle's entry portal. The dragon swept past and pulled up in a sharp leftward bank to avoid the cliff. As the drawbridge's angle steepened, the slow-rolling body gained speed. The scene froze. Glendyl fussed with the control glove, but the image would not start again.

Saucer spoke. "I am sorry to usurp control in such an ungentlemanly manner, Miss Fenderwell, but there is something very odd here. We will now view this very, very slowly." A yellow arrow appeared, superimposed on the scene. "The arrow indicates the path of your form on the bridge. You see it is rolling toward the juncture of the drawbridge and the castle's entry portal. Unless there is some change in trajectory, the rolling person — you — will be caught between the drawbridge and the portal's steel frame, and crushed. With apologies for a possibly discomfiting question, why did this not happen?"

The scene now flowed like cold honey. Seconds passed like hours and Glendyl's still healing burns prickled as she watched. The figure on the bridge was now only a few feet from the narrowing wedge of space between the drawbridge and the portal wall.

Saucer had enlarged the image so that the whole Map was now Glendyl's scorched body slowly rolling into the crack that would crush the remaining life out of her. Glendyl-the-spectator's eyes bugged out, her hand went to her mouth, icy electricity shot up her spine. Her ribs tightened, anticipating the deadly crush of timber and stone. Watching this scene was almost physically painful.

A flicker, something alien to the scene. From the right side of the image, a huge metallic hand blipped into view, clutched Glendyl's charred clothing and jerked her into the castle. Then the drawbridge settled into its frame.

Saucer replayed the last part several times. The mysterious hand sequence was extremely rapid; a few milliseconds from start to finish. At normal speed it was just a shadowy blip during the relentless closing of the drawbridge. "Geez Louise! What was that?"

Saucer hesitated. "Possibly there is a rogue telowix lurking somewhere inside this castle: a very, very fast device and unlike anything in my catalog. I am pleased that it appeared in time to save your life, but I am displeased that such a mysterious device could have escaped the notice of every sensor in my domain. I have already sent units to investigate. Would you care to resume control over the image?"

"I think I've seen all I want to see today," said a shaky-voiced Glendyl. "I think I'd like to go up to the park and just sit for a while, if you don't mind."

"As you wish. I trust you can find your way? And perhaps you would care to dine in the Plaid Salon this evening? I could arrange for you to view some of Madonna 13's finest performances at North Castle while you're dining."

"Great," intoned Glendyl in a flat voice stripped of all enthusiasm; the vivid scene on the bridge still dominated her thoughts. She dropped the control glove in the tray and walked slowly away from the Map, still breathing shallow, rapid breaths, still feeling the prickles on her burned skin. "And thank you for the fish eggs."

• • • • •

Glendyl watched — and felt — empathically enhanced recordings of Madonna 13's Exit the Wind concert and ate a very St Coriander-ish meal. But neither Madonna 13's dazzling performance nor familiar food could lift her mood, so she went to bed early.

Sleep did not come easily that night. Dark wings, withering flames and a mysterious mechanical hand impinged on her drowsing mind at irregular intervals, opening the way for other unsettling matters to sink their hooks into her. And the face of Madonna 13 seemed somehow ever-present. Not quite looming, but always there in the background. Or foreground.

244

During her semi-awake moments, the theme of trust dominated her mind. Was there anyone she could truly trust? Obviously not Exeter; he had tried to kill her three times. But what about Lysheem, the wyvern she had only met in a projection? Or the knowledgeable but mysterious Mr White? Or the equally mysterious rogue telowix that looked like a gigantic, metallic hand? Or Saucer, for that matter? Saucer had seemed so wise and sure of itself until this afternoon. What did that mean? Was this brief time of relative calm about to end?

Underneath such questions lurked a bigger question; what was to become of Glendyl Fenderwell? Was she supposed to just hang around this empty castle until ... until what? That was the big question. So, now what? These uncertainties — plus a surge of homesickness — were enough to bring forth tears and sobs. After a time she slipped into a thin, uneasy sleep and did not dream.

Glendyl awoke unrefreshed and saddled by a sour mood. A look out the tower window didn't help; not a single shaft of sunlight anywhere.

Sometime during the night a congested mass of oily gray thunderheads had squeezed every drop of blue from the sky and now pressed close around North Castle, making Glendyl feel surrounded, claustrophobic. A north wind whipped the tops of the pines behind the ridge and even the stiff-spined wissilbrush clinging to the rocky clefts was bent to the wind's blustery will.

As she scanned this gloomy landscape, a staghorn of lightning lit up the lower slopes of Mt Faunibeune and danced off the dull pewter ripples of Arrowmere. A rolling peal of thunder followed a few seconds later. Great day to be in a funk, thought Glendyl. The sour mood rode on ... and, having forgotten about the party, she had no idea how to get out of it.

246

42 :: ALMOST A WINK

SAUCER DELIVERED Glendyl's usual breakfast and, sensing her mood, said nothing of a party and silently departed. This morning she lacked all appetite and only nibbled at her hamanegg pastry. Somehow sensing she was finished, Saucer returned. It was departing the room with her breakfast remnants when a thought occurred to Glendyl. "How do you go about tapping the vidlines? And the *St Coriander Times*? I'd like to see what's going on at home."

"Am I to understand that you would like to view these so-called informationals yourself? Your slate can access any issue or vidcast since December 25, 2161, the inaugural editions of both the newspaper and vidcasts. You need only state your request. The wall will also display them at your request. If you would like hardcopy of the *Times*, speak to the desk in the corner." Saucer tilted its circular "body" forward a few degrees in a gesture Glendyl interpreted as a bow, and departed the room.

Deciding to stay away from the Museum and the Map for a while, Glendyl planned to spend the morning in bed, sipping hot chocolate and catching up on events in good old boring St Coriander. Particularly the bangerball scores. She got exactly as far as the front page headline in the *Times*: "Dorelli Arrested on VIP[29] Charges in

---

29 :: *Violation of Interpersonal Protocols (VIP) had evolved into a catchall term covering everything from thuggish behavior to unwelcome sexual advances to kidnapping, maiming and even murder. In a deeply pacifist*

Marble Disappearance."

Glendyl read with great attention. Lizbeth abducted? The thought of her weird friend being carried off for unspeakable purposes prompted a burst of helpless rage directed mostly at Forrbank Dorelli. Although she'd never paid much attention to things like St Coriander politics, she had always thought there was something a bit odd about people like Forrbank Dorelli and members of COMISC who made big fusses over small things.

After all, life was good in St Coriander: she couldn't see why people had to always be stirring things up. But making speeches was one thing — that was at least tolerable and not too many people paid any attention anyway. Abducting one of her very own friends was radically more offensive. Lizbeth gone? It seemed inconceivable. Why would somebody like Forrbank Dorelli do something bad to Lizbeth? She was one of his supporters, sort of.

The thought of never seeing or having a goofy moment with Lizbeth again brought her anger back up to a full boil: being locked away in a Small Dark Room somewhere under St Coriander was hardly a suitable punishment for the violation and murder of an innocent girl. Glendyl raged silently at the injustice of life and finally fell asleep as a morning thunderstorm pelted her windows with raindrops the size of malted milk balls.

The now-familiar chime brought her out of a sound, dreamless sleep: Saucer had arrived with lunch. Idly, a groggy Glendyl wondered what he had brought her. She found herself now thinking of "him" as a sort of floating uncle with tentacles: a very old and very wise uncle.

After a likesteak wrap with mayo and marvosauce, and a handful of peanutbutter twinkets for dessert, Saucer escorted the Quester to the Infirmary, where the telowix meds gave her a thorough one-minute checkup. The burns she'd received on her arms, neck and face

---

and universally prosperous society like St Coriander, such transgressions were so rare that over time they had become lumped together for administrative convenience.

were healing nicely, according to Saucer's interpretation of the meds' analysis.

This didn't surprise Glendyl at all; she'd almost forgotten about the burns, partly because she felt no pain and partly because the dressings that covered her burns were almost impossible to distinguish from her own skin. In fact, the dressings were rapidly *becoming* her own skin. She declined the offer of a follicle stimulant, having grown somewhat fond of her buzzcut.

Outside the Infirmary, Glendyl suddenly remembered the party. "Happy three hundredth birthday, Saucer. I'm sorry I don't have a present to give you ... and I don't know quite how to hug you either."

"That you remembered such a thing is present enough, Miss Fenderwell. Are you beginning to feel like your normal, cheerful self again? Cheerful enough for a party? If so, I have formulated an idea: a moonlight beach party. They were very fashionable events in the high days of North Castle and perhaps, with the help of your good nature, we can restore some of that ancient cheer. Shall I call for you at, say, seven? You will find suitable garments for such an occasion in your closet. And you may find it interesting to explore the North Castle archives for records of some of the Arcade's more remarkable moonlight beach parties ...." Saucer let the sentence hang in the air, ripe with the promise of pleasant mysteries awaiting discovery.

Glendyl's sour mood finally wandered off. Having something interesting to do this afternoon and dressing up for a party were excellent remedies. On his way out, Saucer informed Glendyl that Mr White was proposing to pay her a visit tomorrow or the next day to discuss her options for the immediate future. Then he made a peculiar flourish involving several tentacles and that tilt of his body that Glendyl now thought of as a bow, and was gone.

The afternoon passed as rapidly as the storm clouds outside. By evening the sky was a crisp indigo blue that almost shimmered with dark vitality; even the rocky cliffs looked refreshed and alive in the fading light. Glendyl had learned a great deal about North Castle and its illustrious history, activities that had kept other matters — like

249

her future — pressed into the back corners of her mind. Her discoveries had given her an idea for a sort of birthday present for Saucer. By some remarkable coincidence, there was a gown in her closet that was very nearly like the one she had seen Madonna 13 wear in one of the beach party vids.

Her outfit was almost perfect for the impersonation she was planning. She inspected herself, smiled approval at mirror-Glendyl, then frowned: really bad hair. Her fuzzy buzzcut was totally wrong for a three-hundredth birthday party and totally unlike Madonna 13. She resigned herself to wigging it. Inspecting the collection she had previously noted, Glendyl finally selected one that bore a striking resemblance to the very one worn by Madonna 13 at that same final beach party at North Castle.

Having gone this far into her Madonna 13 impersonation, she took the final step into Madonna 13's shoes. Such marvelous shoes. Shoes such as those never set foot in St Coriander, she thought with giddy delight. A pair of almost deadly-looking, chromex stiletto heels found their way onto her feet, a perfect match for the rounded chrome epaulettes. Glendyl looked this way and that in the mirror and saw nothing that didn't make her smile. But there was something missing: the silver circlet that Madonna 13 wore in her hair, and that was rumored by the entertainment wags to have "supra-aesthetic" capabilities, whatever that meant. Oh well.

The chime rang: seven o'clock exactly, according to the faint numbers that appeared every few seconds in the wallpaper. Glendyl was more nervous than at the Spring Formal last year. For a moment she imagined that it was her favorite dance partner Crandy Summerfield outside instead of a floating mechanical thing, then swished the thought away: none of that tonight. Before opening the door, Glendyl did one final nervous primping in the mirror; she looked amazingly like Madonna 13. Even the eyebrows. How was it that nobody in the Madonna Cult had ever noticed that before? Or why hadn't Glendyl herself noticed before, for that matter? Oh well, it wasn't important now.

Taking a deep breath, she adopted a sexy walk as close to Madonna 13's as she could get her slim hips to produce — and her feet to manage in those awkward high heels — and answered the door.

A man stood there. Where was Saucer?

The man wore a traditional black tuxedo with a green cummerbund, a green bow tie and emerald accents. He looked slightly uncomfortable, but bowed and held out a filigreed silver circlet. "Good evening, Miss Fenderwell. You are as lovely as I had imagined you would be. May I place this circlet upon your magnificent coiffure? It suits you perfectly." The man spoke in Saucer's voice.

"Who are *you*?" blurted Glendyl, all her grace and composure having suddenly gone flat as day old champagne.

"I am Saucer, of course: your guide, friend and mobile node of the North Castle Brain. I am also Robert Orville Miles Dunnigan, the last human Master of North Castle. At your service, Miss Fenderwell. Or should I say Madonna 13? The resemblance is uncanny. I thought you might prefer human company tonight. And please, just call me Miles."

Glendyl was charmed in spite of herself. "Well, alright ... Miles. But you have to stop calling me Miss Fenderwell. Just Glendyl from now on, please."

Robert Orville Miles Dunnigan was a handsome man: tall, youngish, well formed, with elegant chiseled features, striking green eyes. His discomfort had been replaced by a deep easy grace.

"I've seen you!" exclaimed Glendyl. "You were in the vids I watched this afternoon. You were at all the parties!"

"One of the many duties of the Master of North Castle. But of course I have had no need of human form for centuries. Until tonight. I keep this body in storage, just in case something really interesting turns up. Like our little party tonight." He placed the circlet upon Glendyl's head and held out his arm. "You look absolutely magnificent, Glendyl. And very, very familiar," he added with a smile that was almost a wink. "Another side of North Castle awaits you. Shall we go?"

252

43 :: SLAMMED

GLENDYL HAD a hundred questions, but didn't know where to begin. Her 300-year old date kept his own counsel for the moment, so the pair walked in silence to the nearest slidewell. They were sinking through the floor when Glendyl blurted, "Are you the Robert Orville Miles Dunnigan who designed the Map?"

"I am," said the man in the tuxedo, elaborating no further.

Echoes of their footsteps trailed them like ghostly tapdancers as they walked the cavernous foyer to stop at an archway of sculpted stone. This was the entrance to the recreational areas of level one, collectively called the Arcade.

"Well, Miss Fenderwell ... are you ready to step forward into the grand past of North Castle? Our entourage will arrive momentarily."

"I'm ready ... Miles. And it's just Glendyl, remember?"

"Sorry. It's an old habit. I shall do my best to be less formal ... Glendyl."

Earlier in the day Glendyl had spent several contemplative moments gazing out windows of her suite while digesting tidbits gleaned from the Archives. Far below her tower room was the Arcade's outdoor plaza: the beach, the docks, the jungle — all of which seemed to shimmer through the invisible dome of the weatherfield. While the area didn't seem small, it had hardly seemed remarkable.

When she and Miles Dunnigan arrived at the entry, Glendyl began to change her mind about the Arcade. The impression she'd formed that afternoon from the vids, the Guidebook, the histories and her view from on high was ... insufficient, if not plain wrong. Her first view of the vast interior was dominated by a meandering swimming pool, framed in places by tropical foliage, masses of rock, rivulets and cascades of falling water and bubbling hot water pools.

Peering into the Arcade, Glendyl tried to imagine it in ancient times, when dozens of decked out celebrities lounged about nibbling canapés and sipping sourwillow spins, piña coladas, margaritas and the like. She knew that adjacent areas contained courts where guests had indulged in various traditional racquet sports, salons where they engaged in elegant discourse or played billiards, chambers where they could test the mud baths, saunas, massages and vervescences, or participate in interpersonal entertainments. And beyond that, there was the beach, the pier, the jungle and the indoor-outdoor plaza, all protected by the weatherfield dome.

To the right was the circular ballroom with its celebrated dance floor, a grand swirling paisley of inlaid marbles in a hundred subtle colors gathered from every continent of the planet. More remarkable than the dance floor's design was the fact that it floated an inch above the floor and could move indoors or out depending on the whims of the Dancemaster.

A troop of Saucer lookalikes broke through Glendyl's musings. Gaily colored conical party hats sat on their top surfaces, each hat spouting a sparkling volcano of festive multicolored light. One spoke in a deep, unfamiliar male voice tinted with an accent Glendyl could not place: "Good evening Miss Fenderwell, Master Dunnigan. Welcome to the Arcade." The assembled group of saucerites all made small dips as if to indicate their agreement.

From the other side of the group, another inquired in a female voice as smooth and cool as an ice grotto: "What is your pleasure?"

"Let there be music, first of all," commanded Miles Dunnigan with quiet authority. On the instant, the air came alive with bright music. First, a trumpet fanfare that infused a sense of impending celebration. Then an invisible chamber orchestra began to play Strauss' timeless Blue Danube, lending a waltzing lilt to the tiny celebration. Miles Dunnigan cocked his head, then nodded as though he had just tested a fine wine and found it acceptable. "Perhaps our guest would enjoy a refreshment. Have the cellars yielded anything suitable?"

The saucerites moved apart to create a corridor. From the rear came one whose tentacles held a tall, dark green frosted bottle, a towel, an exotic silver corkscrew and two slender champagne glasses inlaid with a delicate tracery of silver lines. The bottle was uncorked with a lusty pop and glasses were presented to Glendyl and her escort.

255

Glendyl found her tongue and lifted her glass. "To the Master of North Castle, who is three hundred years young today ... and looks only a tenth of it."

Glendyl was mildly astonished with herself at this toast, which just seemed to appear on the tip of her tongue with no forethought whatsoever.

"To the beautiful Glendyl Fenderwell, who has braved numerous dangers to infuse this ancient masonry with her remarkable warmth and charm. We of North Castle are truly thankful for this interlude."

Tentacles flew into the air and the two humans were showered with colorful paper streamers and gilt confetti. Glendyl brushed tiny glittering squares from her wig and her gown, laughing a laugh that swept away any remnants of her earlier mood as if they were mere crumbs on the floor of her soul.

Feeling old and young and wise and silly and serious and frivolous all at the same time, Glendyl hooked her arm around her host's elbow and said, "Show me your world, Lord Dunnigan. Let's party!" They did.

Several hours later, buoyed but exhausted from dining and dancing, Glendyl and Miles Dunnigan sat at a small round table under a green and white awning on the sands of the Arcade's interior beach. The waters of Arrowmere gently nibbled at the sand and a mood of quiet calm descended. Glendyl interrupted the chirping of crickets and the croaking of bullfrogs with a question that finally found the tip of her tongue. "Is this the way you treat all the Questers who find their way to the Museum?" In her current state, she wanted to hear Miles Dunnigan say both no and yes.

He was silent for a long moment, his clear green eyes fixed on the near-empty platter of tiny puff pastries in front of him. Finally his gaze rose to meet Glendyl's. "You are the first, Glendyl. Every other Quester to reach Wittwater Deep — and there have been only a few — has taken the log. And shortly thereafter, each has ended up not at the top of Mt Faunibeune, but in Castle Ommergard."

Glendyl frowned. "How is it possible that I'm the only one to get here?"

"They could not help me," said Miles Dunnigan in a quiet voice shorn of his usual authority. "They could not help me locate my missing memories, so there was no need to invite them here. Let Exeter have his fun collecting Luckiests and teaching magic to his band of ex-St Coriander innocents. There's little harm, after all."

"What do you mean by 'invite them here?' I don't recall getting any invitation." Glendyl's mind was suddenly awash with suspicions and questions. Another period of silence ensued. In all his years of contemplation, the mind of Miles Dunnigan had never quite figured out how to handle this moment if it ever came. He fumbled for the proper words and finally spoke. "When Exeter laid out his trails and obstacles two hundred and fifty years ago and played his great prank on the silly people of St Coriander, he erected a number of plaques along the course. You may not know that those plaques are also among the few visible transponders for his system of what he calls 'magic.' As you do know, one of those overlooks Wittwater Deep. Do you recall what was written on that plaque?"

Glendyl scrunched up her face, digging for the memory. "Something about a guy with pipes, something about wyverns and a battle ... stuff like that. Oh, and some fine print for Questers about coming here. Right?"

"That is the gist of it. Except that only three individuals know about the fine print: me — that is to say, this tired old Brain of North Castle — and you, and a portion of the brain of a Transform named

Jamis Pojorolli. No Quester but you has ever seen that particular message, so they had no reason to seek Dunnigans Wall and its endless treasures. No previous Quester has found his or her way to the canyon floor of Wittwater Deep where they might recover the artifact of great power that you have both found and lost. Nor has any Quester found his or her way to North Castle to help me locate my hidden memories. They weren't … ah … encouraged."

"I don't understand what this is all about, Mr Dunnigan." Glendyl's earlier perception of Robert Orville Miles Dunnigan as a gallant Prince Charming had faded and she now found herself seeing through the facade of youth and into the sad, ancient being he really was. She found herself unable to call this being "Miles," as though he were a handsome suitor. At this moment, only "Mr Dunnigan" seemed to fit.

257

"It is about secrets, Glendyl. Very powerful secrets, including the secrets of the Nevergate itself. Near the end of the brief Second Nevergate War — not a war, really, but that's another story. Near the end of this, ah, unpleasant skirmish, all members of Clans Dunnigan and most of the wyverns inhabiting this planet had already passed through the Mt Faunibeune Nevergate just before it was sealed. That was the so-called Dunnigan Retreat; my kin had tired of this foolish world.

"You may be interested to know that the final patrol of wyverns was headed for a rendezvous at the Nevergate, but was ambushed. Immolark, the wearer of the Standard Toolbelt you found, was on that patrol, as was the Dawnhammer himself. All died." Miles Dunnigan sighed a deep sigh and was quiet a moment before continuing in a more somber tone. "They were my friends. Very dear friends.

"After the attack by Lord Bellicarie's minions and the so-called 'Dunnigan Retreat' was imminent, I volunteered to stay. In truth, I didn't see it as a sacrifice, since I am a manager by nature, not a pioneer. So I merged my essential self with the Brain of North Castle, whose responsibility has always been to manage the functional side of this complex. To my kin and others who left on their brave adventure into an unknown sector of an unknown parallax universe, I am the Keeper of Secrets, among other functions. It is a great honor and has been a remarkable life, but a very lonely one, as it turns out. Much, much lonelier than I imagined possible.

"But we were talking about secrets. What may strike you as odd is the fact that I — the vast Brain of North Castle — do not know where all my own secrets are kept. That is by design, and why they have thus far been safe from Exeter and any others who would use the powers of the Nevergate for their private purposes.

"Unfortunately — or perhaps not — Exeter's 'questioning' of the Dawnhammer after the Wittwater Deep ambush revealed the fact that a kind of 'time bomb' had been inserted into the genes of a number of residents of the St Coriander of two and a half centuries ago by the master genetic engineers of Clans Dunnigan. Which residents? Which genetic lines? Nobody knew. Not even the Dawnhammer.

"All the Dawnhammer knew — and what Exeter learned — was that when the evolution of local events reaches a certain trigger point anticipated by these long-departed engineers, this genetic time bomb will be actuated and the means for reopening the Nevergate will somehow be at hand. Other mysterious events may be triggered as well ... and the ultimate impact may be much wider than this tiny speck of our world.

'The time bomb will be, of course, in the form of a person: a Wildcard." He stopped abruptly, as if his mind had suddenly encountered a locked door. Seconds passed.

"Well, don't just leave me hanging here, Mr Dunnigan. It's weird stuff ... but really, really interesting. Honest. But would you mind telling me about how any of it relates to me?"

Robert Orville Miles Dunnigan did not answer, could not answer. His head lolled to one side, eyes now round and bulging; his mouth quivered uncontrollably and a rapid twitch had developed around his right eye and cheekbone. Pinkish saliva dribbled from the corners of his mouth and along the crisp slope of his chin. Then violent tremors took over his entire body.

Glendyl jerked back, wide-eyed in shock as his vibrating upper torso slumped bonelessly toward the table.

Miles Dunnigan's body was stopped in mid-slump by a flurry of tentacles. Saucerites had swarmed over the noodle-limp body, enshrouding the Master of North Castle in a mass of silvery tentacles. In seconds the body was lifted high above Glendyl and floated off toward the grand entry arch of the Arcade.

"Geez Louise!" exclaimed Glendyl, shaking her head as if to test whether this was reality or dream. "Geez Louise." The second edition was whispered in a just-audible voice. Realizing she was now alone in this vast place, she lurched to her feet and sprinted after the dwindling cloud of tentacles ... or as close to sprinting as her awkward shoes would permit.

Instead of entering the slidewell outside the archway, the floating cloud proceeded through a doorway that had opened in a massive stone wall. The secret door had very nearly closed by the time Glendyl caught up. Without thinking, she dove through the shrinking gap, hit the floor in a roll, then slammed into a solid wall. The door closed behind her.

260

44 :: CLOMPING BOOTS

BY THE TIME Glendyl shook off her momentary daze, even the faint whir of saucerite motion had faded. She coughed out a brittle, rueful chuckle and blinked, as if the blackness might be only a mirage.

Good time to just sit still and try to think this through, said her most logical mindvoice. Sooner or later the saucerites would be back this way. But when? And if not, she was bound to be missed sooner or later. Wasn't she? But she really, really didn't feel like being caught in someplace she shouldn't be. Particularly in this place. Better to at least try to get out by herself.

She decided to explore a little first. Her feet told her she was in a corridor about four paces wide. The wall was smooth, cool and unmarred by openings for sixty-three paces before making an abrupt left turn. Glendyl hesitated. Her eyes were still useless; her ears brought in only the sound of her own breathing, her own footsteps and their echoes. Was it a smart plan to just keep following this wall? Determination stepped in and she felt her way along the new direction for eighteen paces before encountering another corner. A right turn and two paces brought her to what felt like a doorway. She traced out the shape of a door, but found no means of opening it. If the saucerites carrying Miles Dunnigan passed through here they had closed the door behind them.

Fighting down a surge of panic, she retraced her steps through the blackness. Back where she started, she located the doorway.

Somehow, this was comforting. Not so comforting was finding no latch, lever, handle, knob, button or ID panel to suggest a way of opening it. In a surge of impotent frustration she pounded on the smooth surface with her fists and spewed an angry hiss through her teeth: "Why don't you just open!" To her vast surprise the door began to silently swing inward, pressing her inexorably backwards.

Dodging out of its way, she watched a crack of light from the Arcade's foyer devour a smooth arc of darkness. Not about to miss this chance, she darted through the opening. Thanks to Madonna 13's awkward stiletto heels, she skidded, lost her balance and went sprawling. The circlet flew from her wig and rolled in a broad circle that ended back at the stone wall just as the door swung shut.

Scowling, she pulled off the offending shoes and jerked herself upright. With the edge of one sole she made several scuff marks on the marble floor. Then she went back to stand in front of the wall where the door had been, wondering what else she could do to mark the place. Or if there was even any point to this little exercise.

She became distracted by larger but less immediate questions. What was in the place she had just left? Where were the saucerites taking Mr Dunnigan when the Infirmary was many floors above? What about the Brain's lost memories? When she ran out of unanswerable questions it occurred to her to wonder how she had managed to make the door open.

Replaying events in her mind, she moved to where she had marked the invisible edges of the door. Sheepishly looking from side to side to make sure nothing was watching, she replicated her fist-pounding and her hissing request. Nothing. The stone wall remained a stone wall.

A glint caught her attention. A dozen feet to her right, the circlet leaned against the wall at a jaunty tilt, taunting her. Things began to click. She had read that the circlet might have special powers; was it possible it had something to do with opening the door? She retrieved it, nested it back into her wig. Frowning with mental intensity, she focused all her attention at the door. "Open!" she commanded. Nothing. Then she hissed, "Why don't you just open?" Again, nothing.

Glendyl shook her head in frustration. In the fringes of her peripheral vision she noticed the succulent reflections of mirror shoes: they were just where she had left them after marking the floor. An idea came to her and she stuffed her sore feet back into the chromex stilettos: you just never know about magic.

Before she realized she had thought it would be nice if the door opened, the section of stone blocks began to swing silently inward. Glendyl watched with dumbfounded amazement. Presently the door closed again on its own initiative.

Magic! Glendyl jumped in the air and clicked the bulbous curves of her metallic heels together in a gesture of pure delight. Then the wall opened again and the saucerites floated through in a phalanx stacked three high and four deep. Mr Dunnigan was not with them.

One saucerite floated out of the formation and hovered in front of Glendyl. "North Castle apologizes for this unhappy close to your evening with Robert Orville Miles Dunnigan. He will likely survive, but he will need a period of recovery before he can speak intelligibly. He asked me to convey his deep regrets. In a day or two he may be able to continue your conversation about missing memories. If you are willing, that is. Now I will escort you to your room so that you may sleep." Glendyl recognized the voice as the musical, feminine one from the party, but now shorn of its lilt.

Glendyl allowed herself to be led back to her quarters in silence. Some time later, her spinning mind wound down and a net of uneasy dreams hauled her off to slumberland.

Morning came too quickly, but Glendyl couldn't sleep past the earliest spatters of creamy sunlight. A sharp, dark sense of ... something ... hovered over her spirit. Not waiting for a saucerite to arrive with her customary breakfast, she donned the most un-Madonna 13-like outfit she could find in her closet — athletic shoes, tight khaki shorts and a loose-fitting plaid shirt that reminded her of the Plaid Salon — and made her way down to the cavernous main kitchen. She would make her own breakfast. This was more than a determination to fend for herself; she didn't think she could look at a saucerite without her mind's eye seeing a handsome, charming man, foaming at the mouth, his body like a puppet on slackened strings.

She was soon trying to replicate something Saucer had demonstrated a couple days ago; adding water to something flaky called rolled oats and boiling it in a pot on one of the burners. She was trying to remember exactly how long to cook it when she was startled by the sound of clomping boots.

45 :: HAVE TO WAIT

A HUMAN THROAT cleared itself behind the Quester.

"Well, now. I believe this must be my Quester friend, Glendra Fanderwail. I see you found your way into North Castle. Congratulations. My sources tell me you had some excitement on the way in … got a little hot-headed on the drawbridge." Diogenes chuckled. Glendyl didn't.

"That was supposed to be a joke, but I don't see you laughing. Probably doesn't seem very funny at the moment. Forgive my misguided levity."

Diogenes sniffed the air. "By the way, you got the heat too high under your — what's that — oatmeal? You're gonna burn it. Anyway, nice to see you again Glendra."

"Good morning, Mr Diogenes. What are you doing here? And why the Gunga Din outfit? You remind me of that cartoon. And my name is Glen-dyl, by the way, not Glen-dra." Glendyl had tried to match Diogenes' volubility.

"Oh, I'm part of the family. Just barely. Did I neglect to mention that back on the trail? Darwin Jarvis Ferrill Dunnigan, First Tier Clansman, at your service." He made an exaggerated bow and a wry wink. "Also known to some as Diogenes the Wanderer. My key still fits the door, so to speak: they never officially bumped me out. I happened to be elsewhere when my kinfolk retreated to parts unknown.

"Oops ... see, you're burning it." Diogenes pulled the saucepan off the burner, then sniffed the contents. "Little scorched, but might be salvageable with enough cream and sugar. And maybe some cinnamon. And raisins. Mind sharing? I'm a little hungry myself. That's why I walked down here, not to annoy you and show you how to cook oatmeal properly. Gunga Din, eh? Not quite, not quite. Bit informal for Brits of that era: no jodhpurs or puttees or formal helmet. But still, quite an amazing reference for a sixteener from St Coriander. Didn't know they taught much ancient literature these days. Of course you do have that marvelous library.

Diogenes interrupted himself. "Brierly! I'll bet you're remembering Brierly in Belize. Totally wacko ... a lot like Monty Python. Ever hear of Monty Python? Didn't think so." Diogenes scrutinized his outfit and chucked Glendyl gently on the shoulder. "I do sort of look like Brierly, don't I. Not nearly as gangly, though." He removed his pith helmet and hung it from a nearby pothook. "Please don't let me forget that thing."

Glendyl found herself simultaneously chagrined, irritated and delighted. Chagrined at having screwed up on the Gunga Din-Brierly thing (of *course* it was Brierly); irritated by Diogenes' nonstop talking and "takeover" manner; delighted at having encountered a familiar human in this place full of devices and grandiose emptiness. Her internal tug-of-war left her momentarily incapable of speech, so she occupied herself by further scrutinizing his appearance. This Diogenes looked much different from the one she had met on the trail: the perfectly wrinkle-free, pressed khaki trousers, starched khaki shirt, polished black boots and yellow and green plaid bow tie were a sharp contrast to the man on the trail with the mule named Jezzie.

Diogenes interpreted her silence as assent. "Thanks for the invite, Glendyl. Did I get your name right that time? I'm terrible with names: I don't usually run into enough people to get much practice with my name-remembering chops." He continued to chatter while he prepared two bowls of augmented oatmeal and took them to a polished metal prep table in a corner of the huge kitchen. "This one's yours. Hang on a minute and I'll get you a spoon."

Glendyl tasted a spoonful of the enhanced oatmeal, found it satisfactory, then much to her surprise, began to talk. Over the next half hour, she found herself reeling off all that had happened since their encounter on Heroes Trail, including last night's evening with Miles Dunnigan.

During Glendyl's outpouring, Diogenes had nodded, made appropriate facial gestures and murmured occasional hmm's and ummhmm's. But when her tale came to its end, the man said nothing, just continued to look at her with an intensity she hadn't seen before.

Shifting her body in the uncomfortable metal chair, Glendyl broke the empty silence with what she hoped was a light tone: "Do you come here often, Mr Diogenes?"

Diogenes continued to stare as though he hadn't heard her question. Finally he spoke: "No. I don't. But there's no shortage of accommodations, as you've discovered for yourself. And it's a handy place to get my wanderer rig cleaned up and play dress-up a little." More silence. "Your oatmeal's getting cold. Probably oughta eat it. Could be a stressful couple of days. Want me to warm it up for you?" Without waiting for her answer, he took her bowl, set it in the warm-field for a few seconds and returned it to her.

"Correct me if I got this wrong, but didn't you say you saw a wyvern? Or an image of one? Even talked to it?"

Glendyl agreed, frowning and thinking he probably didn't believe her. She was right.

Diogenes lapsed into his homey drawl, the affect he normally used when playing the wanderer. "You know, Glendyl, there haven't been any of those critters in our little corner of this universe for right around a quarter of a millennium. I'd be real surprised if one just popped up out of nowhere. I got an idea that you just met ol' Dryll. Did your wyvern say anything about a satellite brain or a skymind or anything like that?"

Glendyl shook her head, scowling. Diogenes went on. "Well, little lady, lemme tell you a little about the wyvern folks' secret satellite brain. Still up there somewhere. No reason it's not still waking up every now and then to see if anything interesting's going on down here. At least something that would be interesting to a wyvern. They're different from us humans, you know. Anyway, I'll bet ol' Dryll got woken up by that Standard Toolbelt you had. Just the fact that it moved from its burial site down in that riverbed could've set off some kind of alarm.

"And simming a live wyvern image like you saw woulda been no tougher for something like Dryll than skipping a stone on a frozen lake would be for you or me. Bit of a trickster, Dryll; woulda enjoyed jerking your tootie, if you know what I mean. Anyways, we'll probably never know for sure, since you don't have that Toolbelt any more. Probably just as well, anyway ...." Diogenes' voice trailed off.

"Well!" he began with renewed energy. "Gotta get busy. Gotta do some work with the old Brain ... the Miles Dunnigan part in particular. The excreta's finally about to hit the ol' flyswatter, if you'll pardon the expression. Not a lot of time."

Diogenes had changed again. His loose and easy manner of the trail — and even a few minutes ago — seemed to stiffen. His back straightened and his face became taut. His eyes, which Glendyl remembered for their wry twinkle, seemed now impossibly deep, twin windows into a vast ocean of mysterious human existence.

The man stood, grabbed his helmet from the pothook, nodded to Glendyl and began to stride briskly out of the kitchen. Then he stopped and called back over his shoulder: "Why don't you and I have a little picnic around lunchtime. I'll introduce you to somebody you probably ought to meet. Twelve noon. Right here." Then he was out the door. Glendyl's questions would just have to wait.

46 :: MIFFED

GLENDYL SPENT the morning exploring the Park level, her slate loaded with everything she could find on the history of the magical garden — including all references to tootle-fairies, twyk-men, flowerskips and dwarf trolls. It was a distraction from her looming sense of dread, but only a small one.

She arrived at the kitchen just before noon to find Diogenes sitting on a steel countertop, whistling an impatient jig while his fingers drummed out the rhythm. A wicker basket rested to one side.

"Have a pleasant morning, little lady? Don't suppose you've met a dunnikin yet, have you? Let's go see if we can find one. With luck, we may even find Laniss. Heard she has something for you." Diogenes bounced down, grabbed the picnic basket in one arm, Glendyl's arm in the other and strode out of the kitchen.

"I met Miles Dunnigan last night. Is that what you mean?" Glendyl was hurrying to keep up and her voice sounded hurried too.

Diogenes chuckled. "Yes, you did. And your charming young self almost fried that old boy, it did. Not your fault, though," he added hastily. "You seem to have a little touch of genome that he's ... uhh, shall we say 'allergic' to. And he knew it beforehand; just couldn't help himself. Miles Dunnigan's an incurable romantic, he is. Always has been, even when he was a pup.

"But I guess I didn't enunciate clearly: I said dunnikin. With a 'k'. Whole different item. I suppose you didn't get properly introduced to the ones who were trying to shoo away the wolves, did you? Ever see the old Wizard of Oz? Early twentieth-century musical version ... with real actors? The one with 'We're off to see the Wizard?'"

Glendyl nodded, her face a jumbled pink canvas of annoyance and embarrassment. Diogenes seemed to be toying with her, making her feel like a small child. And his abrupt changes of direction and demeanor kept her puffing along in a mental limp, like always having a tiny splinter in her mind she had to compensate for. "Would you just get to the point, Mr Diogenes? I hate these little mysteries!" she said, her voice taking on a frustrated edge. "What am I supposed to know about dunnikins and The Wizard of Oz that I don't?"

Diogenes' twinkly smile blossomed, augmented by crinkles at the corner of his eyes and dimples in his cheeks. "Remember the winged monkeys? That's what dunnikins were modeled after. Well, sort of. You're gonna love 'em. Come on. I'll show you a trick way to get up to the road."

Glendyl's imagination conjured up an image of a frog on a string tied behind a bicycle being ridden backwards by a three-legged chimpanzee. She also had the distinct feeling that dunnikins — whatever they turned out to be — weren't going to be as lovable as this extremely unpredictable man said they would be. Glendyl made up her mind that she would not like them at all.

Diogenes' "trick way" was a narrow passage accessed by a hidden door in a storage closet for party furniture. Glendyl counted one hundred and forty-seven steps before it ended at a bare concrete shaft. A staircase of dark green metal was wrapped around a thick metal pole. Looking down, the green wedges spiraled down into darkness. Looking up, the effect was the same. Diogenes started to climb and Glendyl could only follow. As they ascended, lumestrips brightened, lighting their way, then faded when they passed.

At the top, Diogenes pressed his palm on a knob of stone. A door opened out and they emerged into a place Glendyl recognized immediately: the entry tower across from the infamous drawbridge. Diogenes strode through the entry tower and out onto the road, stopping next to one of the thick vines that grew out of the concrete and over the dam's parapet. He handed Glendyl a red and white checked tablecloth: "Pick a nice spot in the sun. You look like you've been spending way too much time indoors lately."

They lunched on long sandwiches layered with meats and cheeses of various colors. A tray of savory deviled eggs provided variety. Bite washing came from a jug of iced cannonberry tea. Between bites and swigs, Diogenes talked and Glendyl learned about the so-called "outdoor" dunnikins who inhabited the eerie shacks hanging from Dunnigans Wall.

"Their indoor cousins still think of 'em as pariahs: outcasts, traitors, show-offs, second class citizens and so forth. Even after all these years. Bit uncharitable in my view. One of these days I'll take you to the Monkey Pipe and you can see how the other half lives. Whole different waffle. Same genestock, but the folks out here are descendants of the troupe that traveled the planet in Castle Ommergard along with your good friend Exeter. They did the sky monkey roles in Lord Bellicarie's 'Aerial Ballet for Dragons, Sky Monkeys and '34 Ford.' You get a chance to see that yet? If not, it's in the Library. Quite a spectacle. Highly recommend it." Diogenes voice took on a conspiratorial quality: "They're also the critters who tried to save you from the wolf attack. Dunno why, but they seem to like you. How about I invite Laniss up to share some quibbits and rik-rik with us? You wait here."

Without waiting for a response, Diogenes crossed to the parapet, looked down and whistled a strange, warbling tune. Glendyl was thankful he didn't see her blush; if he was telling the truth, the creepy flying things during the wolf attack had been friendlies. Geez Louise!

Her blooming embarrassment was interrupted by a beating of wings. A strange creature flew up and over the parapet to land gracefully a dozen feet from Glendyl.

Diogenes' introduction surprised Glendyl with its undertone of respect for Laniss. She tried not to stare while Diogenes spoke, but failed. The creature she gawked at was about the size of a large monkey, but with a very human — not simian — face and oversized feathered wings in a beautiful pattern of rich browns spiced with shades of gold and red-orange. Across her chest was a bra-like garment made of colorful feathers, beads and finely woven reeds. A short skirt of similar design hung from her waist.

Glendyl felt an instant affinity for Laniss; her resolve to dislike all dunnikins evaporated like a morning mist. Something about Laniss' face was oddly familiar, but Glendyl, in the thrall of the event, could not think what the connection might be.

Diogenes singlehandedly kept the conversation alive with a flow of anecdotes about this and that, including the fact that Laniss was only a decade away from her three-hundredth birthday. This particular fact grated on a newly exposed nerve; if Elevation at age forty-eight was such a wonderful thing, why did it seem that everyone outside St Coriander chose to live virtually forever on this plane? She determined to ask Diogenes about this at her earliest opportunity.

Laniss inserted herself into the conversation when Diogenes paused to catch his breath. A voice as soft and cool as spring rain almost cooed the words. "I have seen many Questers, Glendyl Fenderwell. Every year I have watched and wondered. And now I have met ... you. I am honored."

Glendyl stammered out a lame response. She had been expecting incomprehensible Jamis-like chitterings that she had heard during the wolf attack: not this smooth, fluid alto.

Diogenes filled the chink in the conversation. "Laniss, my friend of many score years, could I interest you in a tot or two of rik-rik and some quibbits? All quite fresh, I'm told." Laniss smiled a wan smile and nodded.

Time passed quickly, perhaps accelerated by the fruity, mildly intoxicating rik-rik, said by Diogenes to be a traditional favorite of the dunnikin species. Glendyl ate more quibbits — tiny sweet-biscuits, also traditional — than she could count. Conversation skimmed the tops of a hundred events large and small.

Diogenes looked to the sky and said, "The afternoon is getting away from us, dear ladies. If it's not too late, perhaps Laniss would like to retrieve a little something."

Laniss nodded. "I will return in a moment," she said with a mysterious smile. Springing to the parapet, she spread her wings and disappeared over the edge."

"You're gonna love this," winked Diogenes with the casual knowingness that never failed to irritate Glendyl.

A whuff-whuff of wings announced Laniss' return to the parapet. Leaping down, she swung something from behind her and held it out to Glendyl, all in one seamless motion. "One of the wallkeepers brought this to my attention. I believe it is your rightful property."

"QP!," exclaimed Glendyl with undisguised joy. She took the lost QPack, hugged it to her breast and spun a little circle. Then she hugged Laniss and Diogenes, a broad grin never leaving her face. "Thankyouthankyouthankyou!" her gush of gratitude was aimed at both Dunnigan and dunnikin.

The event dissolved after that, but both Glendyl and Laniss agreed to become better acquainted and Diogenes, for his part, promised to teach Glendyl the proper tune to whistle at the wall.

Later, in her room, Glendyl attempted to strike up a conversation with QP, thinking he might have some interesting tales to tell about his experience with the wallkeeper and the dunnikins, but he said nothing. Miffed, she finally gave up and drifted off to sleep.

273

274

47 :: GAPING HOLE

GLENDYL, whispered the faint, distorted voice. It came from both near and far away, a nagging irritant in her Princess Glendyl dream.

Not right now, said her dreamvoice with a firm tone. I'm very, very, very busy testing mattresses.

Glendyl, whispered the voice more urgently but not louder.

I am the Princess in this castle, dammit! snapped Glendyl's dreamvoice. And I'm doing very, very, very important Princess Work.

Glendyl! urged the faint voice once again, now agitated. *Please wake up and put on the damn circlet! This is important!*

Adrenaline snapped her to semi-wakefulness. Weird dream. Still dark. Empty room. Nothing with a voice. Circlet. She rubbed her eyes to grind some reality into them. The circlet rested innocently on the nightstand. Carefully, as if it were both incredibly fragile and incredibly valuable, she placed it on her head. "Who is this?" she said out loud to the phantom Glendyl-sayer inside her head.

The response was now as crisp and immediate as fresh cabbage. *It is Miles Dunnigan, of course. Or you can think of me as the Brain of North Castle. Or Saucer, if you prefer. I am sorry to interrupt your slumbers. And I am very, very, very sorry about the unpleasantness of the other evening. Apparently, something about our conversation triggered the attack that disabled my old body in so ghastly a way. I have just been able to review the event as seen by my other — appendages — the ones that carried me away. Not a pretty sight for one so young to witness ....*

Still speaking aloud, a fully awake Glendyl cut him short. "Well, it was a beautiful evening up to that point. You had me totally charmed Mr Dunnigan. It was the most fantastic day of my life. But it was just too great to be able to continue: not with my luck. But what happened to you? Diogenes said you're allergic to me...kind of. I'm not sure exactly what he meant and he wouldn't say more during our picnic. Are you okay? And why did you wake me up like this? It's not even light outside yet."

Again I find myself apologizing to you, Glendyl. The simple truth is that I need your help. North Castle security has been breached and might well be breached again in the near future. And you might be in danger from Exeter again. I also fear that the location of the Mt Faunibeune Nevergate may be in jeopardy. This cannot happen. Must not happen!

The intensity of the Brain's "voice" inside her head had grown so strong it seemed to echo off the wet bones of her cranium. She shook her head, almost dislodging the circlet, and spoke to the empty air. "Honestly, Mr Dunnigan, I don't want to be disrespectful. And I don't want to be dead, either. But this Nevergate business seems like such, such ..." She paused, her brain flipping and flopping with indecision.

The voice inside her head softened, became gentle. *I can hear the word you are thinking, Glendyl. I am not offended if you think the word 'bullshit' to me. It is a useful term and I have used it myself several hundred thousand times. We can be honest with each other. Yes, the 'Nevergate business' must certainly seem like bullshit to you. You're having to wrestle with your upbringing. Having been thrown into a different reality, the old learnings of denial and nonsense are now wearing off.*

Despite what you may have learned in St Coriander about the Mt Faunibeune Nevergate, I assure you it was once a very real, very powerful thing. Many humans, dragons and wyverns died over the ownership of that last Nevergate on Earth. And it still exists, Glen-

dyl. *That much I know, somehow. It will someday be found and reopened. It is one of my duties to ensure that it is not found and reopened prematurely or by the wrong person. One such wrong person is Exeter.*

"Exeter, Exeter, Exeter! I'm sick of Exeter, too!" Glendyl was shouting now. "I know my problem with Exeter. It's simple: he wants to kill me. What's your problem with Exeter? And why is he so gaga about getting control over the Nevergate? Doesn't it send people away or something? He must want to use it to go someplace, right? If he did, he'd be gone from here. Wouldn't that be a good thing?"

You have a quick intellect ... it is a pleasure conversing with you in this manner. And you are correct in many ways. We can assume that Exeter might very well disappear from this place and time if he were to possess the Nevergate and its secrets. Unfortunately, one of the places he would likely go would be the place my clanfellows and the wyverns went. And that could restart a conflict that should never have started in the first place.

"Oh, right: I almost forgot. Mr White told me that one of the wyverns ate Exeter's brother. Is that right? So Exeter wants the Nevergate so he can kill off all the wyverns wherever they are now? I don't know, Mr Dunnigan. It just seems too weird to me. Start up an old war again after all this time? Just for that? Too weird." The intensity of Glendyl's voice faded.

I agree with you that it does seem 'too weird' on the face of it. And I myself have never, in all these centuries, put the matter exactly the way you just did. I wonder if you are on to something? Perhaps Exeter has some other motivation. I shall have to give this matter some thought. In the meantime, I would still appreciate your assistance in locating my missing memories. I feel terribly handicapped being charged with the security of the Nevergate while saddled with missing memories. It feels like I am forced to play this deadly game without a full deck, if you know what I mean.

"How could I, Glendyl Fenderwell, age sixteen, help you — Mr 300-year-old Brain of North Castle — find something like memories?

How can you know you're missing what you don't know you're missing? And if I were really lucky and tripped over one of your memories while walking along some corridor in North Castle or on Heroes Trail or wherever, how would I recognize it? And if I did, what would I do with it? Scoop it up and bring it to you in a basket?"

These words contained a bitter sting and Glendyl wished she could take them back. "I'm sorry I was facetious, Mr Dunnigan. That was really bad manners. I guess I'm just totally confused by all this stuff. I think I just want to go home and play bangerball and hang out with my friends and eat boring old St Coriander MenuMaster food and get Elevated when I turn forty-eight just like everybody else. I just want to be normal again, Mr Dunnigan. I'm just a sixteener, just a girl. This isn't my world and I didn't ask to be here. I was just doing what my world said I was supposed to be doing." Glendyl held back tears.

After perhaps ten seconds of silence, the voice in Glendyl's brain responded with a forceful tone. *That's where you're wrong, Glendyl. Number one: you're not just a sixteener, just a girl. Your genes tell that story very clearly. I can say no more but that. Number two: you can't go back. Nobody can ever go back. Going back is pure illusion: a dream, a wish, a phantom. And I know you know that.*

Great events are once again in flux after centuries of dormancy. And, like it or not, you are in the middle of them all. How, exactly? I wish I knew. But Darwin — your friend Diogenes — ran subtext diagnostics on my several interactions with you. This reflects what happens in sublevels of my awareness when I think of you or converse with you. Three things immediately rise to a level just below my normal awareness: Madonna 13, Arrowmere and Merlin, the mythological wizard who allegedly lived backward in time. The Madonna 13 part, I believe I understand: your resemblance to her is uncanny, which is why I gave you her circlet. Yes, it was her circlet. I had made it for her, so that ... so that we could communicate, ah ... more deeply.

Glendyl frowned. "What about the mirror shoes? They're magic too — I mean not real 'magic,' but you know what I mean. I opened that door in the wall with them. The door to the place the saucerites took you."

The Brainvoice in her head smiled. *I was able to replay that sequence just before I contacted you a few minutes ago. I've gotten behind in monitoring things. What you didn't know was that the circlet needs a small amount of time to establish the necessary linkages with your biosignals. And the amount of time is somewhat distance-sensitive, so the wig ....*

279

Glendyl's brain made a few new connections. "So you really can see everything that goes on here? You're always watching me? That is really perverted! I want to get out of here. Right now! I mean it!"

The Brain hastened to reply in soothing mindtones. *Please Glendyl. Let me answer your question. I am absolutely not spying on you. Only the public areas of the Castle are monitored ... and only for security reasons. I assure you that this Brain is not invading your privacy, Miss Fenderwell.*

Her anger faded almost as quickly as it flared. "Okay. When you say that and my brain's ear hears it, it has a ring of truth. Okay, okay. You saw me pounding on the stones trying to get the door open? But not until just a bit ago. Otherwise you wouldn't have let me get trapped, right?" She processed for a moment. "I get it. It was really the circlet that let me open the door. The shoes were just ... geez what a dunce I am. Okay. Moving right along. Glendyl the Numbskull wants to get back to something else you were telling me." She drew in a deep breath. "Are you saying you were in love with Madonna 13? *The* Madonna 13?"

Love ... yes; I suppose that term would apply. It was all very long ago.

Something in the Brain's mindvoice communicated pain and sadness in a way Glendyl had never experienced before. "Whoa. Mr Dunnigan, it's getting too weird again. I don't think ..."

*Arrowmere is a clue for you, Glendyl. Madonna 13 was fasci-
nated by underwater creatures. I have a deep intuition that this has
something to do with my missing memories ... and possibly the Nevergate. But I have not the slightest notion why Merlin keeps springing to mind when I think of you. Perhaps you will find out.*

Glendyl was intrigued in spite of herself. But also suspicious.
"You've had hundreds of years to find your memories. If you know all
these clues, why can't you use them? Or somebody like Diogenes?"

Ahh! said the voice in her head, now with a strangely hopeful
quality, even though it seemed to be getting weaker at the same time.
*An excellent question. And I have no real answer except that per-
haps we are too close. And perhaps ...* The voice had lost much of
its strength and many seconds of silence loomed in Glendyl's head.
Then, just above a whisper: *I have overreached myself again. I must
rest: this new 'allergy' of mine is truly debilitating. But good hunting. May the remarkable luck of Madonna 13 be with you.*

With that, there was a profound silence, as though some heavy
door had slammed shut, walling off a part of her self and leaving a
gaping hole.

48 :: UNKNOWN DEPTHS

FOR A TIME Glendyl just sat with her feet dangling over the edge of the bed, eyes staring blankly at nothing, mind swirling with strange images and even stranger thoughts. She let them flow. Then, a sense of something impending. At the moment the first ray of sunlight peeked through her window, an idea snapped into place.

Ten minutes later she'd donned a silver bodyglove, baggy blue shorts and Madonna 13's circlet and was out the door. Almost as an afterthought she grabbed the silent QPack; even a mute QP was some kind of company.

Arriving at the Museum, she first decided that the Map would do her no good for this bit of exploration. For a time she stalked the entire Museum and inspected every artifact, hoping something she saw would yank this memory to the surface. Nothing did. She circled the Museum again, attempting to be very sensitive to her intuitions. Still nothing clicked. Disappointed, but not quite ready to give up, she made still another loop. Near an exhibit of Robert Orville Miles Dunnigan's personal collection of antiquities and memorabilia, something made Glendyl stop.

Like the dance floor in the Arcade, the floor of the Museum was a complex pattern of inlaid stone. The colors here were muted tones of umber, burgundy, burnt sienna, forest green, deep cobalt. A square area of floor next to a particularly boring exhibit — dynaclips of important Dunnigans posed with dignitaries from this place and that place — was slightly brighter than the area around it. Some exhibit had been here for a long time and then been replaced.

Was that a clue? Her eyes moved to the polished black walnut panels covering the walls of the museum up to a height of maybe ten feet. Each was about four feet wide and set into a carved frame of some even darker wood. Her imagination began to assert itself. What if some of these wall panels were actually secret doors into unknown places where unknown secrets were kept hidden? Maybe even some of the Brain's lost memories? She reached to touch a panel. It slid aside.

Glendyl leaped back, startled: she hadn't even touched the wood. Her excitement swelled like a great wave, crested, became a great froth, then flattened. All in less than five seconds. Behind the door was nothing but a storage closet for old exhibits. In the very back was a single old exhibit. With one quick look Glendyl could see why it had been stored: ver-ry bor-ring.

It was one of those things used to mark short bits of time before they had clocks. Or something like that. She remembered where she had seen one: The Wizard of Oz. Glendyl replayed the scene in her mind and smiled: the green witch was such a delicious villain. Green seemed to resonate in her mind as she dug for the word for the gadget in front of her. While she was wondering about the color green, the word "hourglass" popped up.

There was a blank metal label on the beveled swirlglass base supporting this hourglass. Glendyl wiped off the dust, revealing an engraved inscription; at least it seemed to have an engraved inscription. Clever. The metal label was really something like a slate. A message scrolled past her eyes:

MERLIN'S HOURGLASS

This unusual artifact was purchased at auction from the Smithsonian Institution in Washington, DC, in 2265. It is purported to be part of a collection of 'magical' curios that once belonged to Harry Houdini. Press the button to watch it work.

282

The words were replaced by the image of a bright yellow button with the words "Press Me" under it. Glendyl pressed it. The hourglass began to rotate top to bottom, pivoting on some invisible shaft. When it had rotated 180 degrees, it stopped and the sand began to move.

Glendyl stared at the hourglass for a full thirty seconds before the oddness clicked. The sand was rising — not falling. A narrow stream of grains rose through the hourglass' tiny waist and into the upper container. That's a cute trick, thought Glendyl, only barely intrigued. Harry Houdini. She had seen something about him. A singing cowboy? A magician? A politician? What-ever.

Green sparkled across her awareness again, shoving thoughts of the hourglass aside; her mind's eye was transported to a place high in the center of a Holy Quincunx prayer chamber, looking down. The tinkling of a waterwall behind her kissed her evermetal ears with sweet ripples of sound; a fragrance of pond-blossom tickled her highly polished nostrils. A supplicant with green-dyed hair was walking out of the chamber in slo-mo. The supplicant stopped, turned, searched the room with nervous eyes, bent and picked up a sparkling crystalline object.

Poof. The image evaporated and Glendyl Fenderwell was again in front of Merlin's Hourglass. She blinked, shook her head and suddenly realized what she had been trying to recall; Madonna 13 playing the lead role in the North Castle musical production of Joan of Arc in Oz. Where had she seen something about that? The Scrapbook in the lobby.

"Goodbye hourglass," she said to the artifact. She was only a little surprised that the panel slid closed at her suggestion.

Glendyl did not feel comfortable in North Castle without Saucer to shepherd her around. The walls, with their dry, dead secrets seemed to whisper to her. And the lobby, being so near to the drawbridge and the mysterious hand that had appeared out of nowhere — even though it saved her life — made the place feel extra creepy.

None of the saucerites were around: maybe they were preparing for Mr White's visit this afternoon. They seemed to be very respon-

sive to Mr White's wishes. Obviously, he was someone very important, at least to the Brain of North Castle.

Reaching the Scrapbook, she pushed Mr White, saucerites,
telowix hands and all other thoughts to the side of her brain and
tapped the Index. Before she could speak the word she had been
forming, a list of references to Madonna 13 appeared on the page
before her: 11,613 to be exact. How had the Scrapbook known what
sort of references she had been about to request? Then she smiled
and touched a hand to the circlet. Wow!

Immediately, the Madonna 13 links disappeared, replaced by
links to the word "wow." With a little practice, Glendyl was able to
focus her mind selectively so that only her real intentions were communicated to whatever was monitoring her mental requests. Back to
Madonna 13. Glendyl narrowed her search to references containing
"Madonna 13" and "Joan of Arc in Oz." Amazingly, there were 2,413
such links in the Scrapbook. Too many: no time to go through all of
those. For some inexplicable reason, Glendyl felt a rising sense of
urgency in solving this mystery.

Linking "Arrowmere," "Madonna 13" and "Joan of Arc in Oz"
produced less than a hundred links. Better. The link captions were
helpful, and many mentioned Madonna 13 in conjunction with other celebrity visitors during the show's six-month local run. Wrong
track, said her instincts.

Linking "Madonna 13" and "Robert Orville Miles Dunnigan"
was much better: 241 links spanning nearly a dozen years. Link by
link, she scanned performances and parties, most with Mr Dunnigan
as the dashing host. A sweet-sour wistfulness collected in the corners
of her eyes. But at the end of her scan, nothing meaningful was revealed. Glendyl's sense of urgency now approached panic level.

In a burst of wild illogic, she linked "pond-blossom," "Madonna 13," "Joan of Arc in Oz," and "Robert Orville Miles Dunnigan."
Five links were indicated, but none showed summaries. And all were
marked CONFIDENTIAL and could not be opened. Glendyl barked
out a frustrated expletive and the Scrapbook dutifully pulled up a

list of links. She couldn't help but grin: 184,606 links to that slightly naughty four-letter word. Who would have believed that?

Back, she thought to the Scrapbook and was instantly returned to the page with the inaccessible links. Okay, Brain, how do I get access to these links? Doesn't a person wearing Madonna 13's very own circlet have special privileges?

Yes, came a voice in her brain. Not the Miles Dunnigan voice, but another familiar voice. Female.

But we must not speak of such things in this public place. Not even mind-to-mind. Meet me in the Arcade. Quickly.

Glendyl's heart skipped; it was the voice of the "female" saucerite that had escorted her back to her room on the night of Miles Dunnigan's birthday party. Something about it also reminded her of someone else. Then there was the closing door sensation in her brain again, and silence.

Glendyl scanned the lobby, feeling an eerie sensation come over her. It appeared to be empty, but the shadows could easily be occupied, said the part of her mind that fretted about what was under the bed at night. Shutting down the Scrapbook, she got out of the chair, being careful not to scrape the floor.

Without knowing why, she fled the lobby in brisk tiptoe strides, casting nervous looks over her shoulders. The eerie sensation increased and she broke into a jog. By the time she reached the correct slidewell she was sprinting, still without knowing why.

Glendyl jabbed the destination marker. Four levels down was the Arcade, the last stop on the slidewell's indicator. Three, two, one. Across the foyer was the grand archway marking the entrance to the Arcade. Its familiarity was a small comfort, but transient. The slidewell didn't stop. It sank through the floor and the Arcade was replaced by blank gray walls. Glendyl pounded on the destination marker, but the slidewell just sank deeper and deeper into the unknown depths below North Castle. Panic gripped her gut and squeezed.

286

49 :: OUT OF REACH

GLENDYL WAS ON the verge of screaming when the blank gray shaft opened into a large space illuminated by banks of temporary lighting fixtures. A flashing red message appeared on the control panel: Unknown Level. Then the indicator color turned green and the slidewell's cup slid into the floor. Her heart still thumping, Glendyl stayed rooted to the spot. Then a faint whir caught her attention; from around a corner, a saucerite appeared.

The voice she had recognized during her Scrapbook search spoke aloud, but in hushed tones that echoed eerily off the unfinished webcrete walls. "I am sorry for all the mystery and urgency, Glendyl Fenderwell. Unfortunately, it is necessary. Thank you for your responsiveness. And thank you for your remarkable intuition; you have just tripped over one of our lost memories. The pond-blossom reference got you into what we call a 'strongbox,' a data node we were unaware of and which must be called by an external trigger. For your information, the only place pond-blossom ever existed in North Castle was in this place. And actually, it only existed in the plans for this place. As you can see, this project was never quite completed."

Glendyl still stood silent, too awestruck to know where to begin. Finally, she found her voice. "Pond-blossom is what they call the stuff under the waterwalls in the prayer chambers," she mumbled. "But who are you? And where am I?"

"Oh, I'm the Brain of North Castle. Naturally. While Robert Orville Miles Dunnigan is indisposed, the personality of the redoubt-able Diana Faye Lorris Dunnigan — that's me — will be our designat-ed representative. I know that sounds confusing, but ..."

"Okay, okay. I think I'm getting used to confusion around here. Can I trust you ... uh ...? Sorry, I forgot half of your name already. I got the Diana part and the Dunnigan part but missed the middle."

"Diana is fine: famous goddess, she. And if you can't trust me — us — we're all in a terrible mess. Let me explain what we — the Brain — think is happening. Then I'll tell you about this place. Then, if the luck of Madonna 13 is still with us, maybe you can shed some light on the real reason we're here; pond-blossom hardly seems of sufficient import to tie a knot in the end of this lost datathread."

Diana continued. "Less than forty-eight hours ago, an ancient alarm program was triggered by unknown events. This program au-tomatically bumped North Castle to a Level Three alert. According to the program's splashcode, it was installed 264 years ago by a psy-chohistorian named Shavvender Goss,[30] who had come to work with

----

30 :: Although "doomsday" theorists abounded in the latter days of the Nirvana Exodus and WorldGov's fragmentation, Shavvender Goss was not one of them. An obscure (several of his colleagues used such terms as "deceptively opaque" and "blandly inexorable") sociocultural theoretician at the venerable Santa Fe Institute, Goss's metamathematical postulations purported that human civilization's "cultural subconscious" could be observed, defined, characterized, analyzed, plumbed, probed, prodded and ultimately therapeutized. His hypotheses were given little credence by either the New Chaoticists or the Savantines, the Institute's reigning intellectual factions at the time. Unfazed, Goss applied to the Clans Dunnigan in 2271 for permission to use the Dunnetix Ike 7 to help him model his sentient cultural dataminers and eventological algorithms. Goss needed the computational horsepower and keen intellect that only Ike 7 possessed to power his forays into the outer reaches of psychohistory.

To enhance the breadth of data inputs, Goss insisted on bringing along a much-scorned Santa Fe Institute colleague, Alvista Zhorginsky, to develop computer interfaces for her global mycelial network languages. At the time the Clans were flush with revenues from Telowix marketing licenses and open to all sorts of wild ideas. An unnamed Special Project was established and little was heard of Goss or Zhorginsky thereafter. The most widespread rumor was that, for security reasons, the project had been relocated to the recently completed Castle Caraway. Castle Caraway disappeared from the Mt Faunibeune vicinity just after the Battle of Wittwater Deep.

Clans Dunnigan geneticists under Inga Lyrus Marlena Dunnigan in the years immediately preceding the First Nevergate War. All Top Secret stuff. And all in the 'lost memory' category since the Retreat."

The Diana saucerite paused, then continued. "What we *do* know is that, according to theories espoused by Goss and others, the alarm could only be triggered by a Level Three Convergent Eventation ... whatever that might be. Just so you know, we've been operating under a Level One alert since you passed through Dunnigans Gate to start your Quest. Goss's sentient algorithms automatically make the correlations by somehow analyzing data we have been collecting for several centuries through a somewhat stunted network of post-Dark Monday input sources. Then they trigger alerts at 'appropriate' times. Naturally, nobody alive knows what that means: somebody misplaced the manual.

"A Level Two alert was triggered by Lizbeth Marble's disappearance. Like it or not, we seem to be entering an era of 'fracturing continuity' and you seem to be straddling its 'hot zone.' That's about all I can tell you at the moment; it's what we call an 'evolving situation'."

Glendyl could only roll her eyes and shrug. It all sounded like gibberish to her overloaded brain and she had been only half-listening. Instead, she was inspecting her new surroundings.

Where she stood was a large empty space around a curved wall maybe three stories high. The ceiling grid of webcrete was festooned with pipes, ducts and cables. Along the walls, various pieces of unfamiliar equipment were stored in tidy, dusty rows, still ready for the construction crews to return. In the center of the curved wall was an arch with a concave alcove that might be an entry portal; under the arch was a platform shaped like a scallop shell.

The Diana saucerite's vibrant alto interrupted Glendyl's inspections. "Since you seem more absorbed by this place than by my explanations of events, please be officially welcomed to the unfinished Water Garden. This was to be Madonna 13's Water Garden. As you know, she was fascinated by water and its denizens. Robert Orville Miles Dunnigan thought the Water Garden would please her, but she

Elevated before it was completed. Somehow, I don't believe my dear brother has ever forgiven her — or himself — for that permanent 'kiss goodbye.' Shall we take a brief tour?" Diana floated ahead, Glendyl followed.

Mounting a temporary staircase to the platform, Glendyl reached the arch right behind the floating Diana. As clamshell doors in the alcove began to open, Glendyl jerked back, startled. "Warn me when you're going to do something like that, would you Diana? I'm a little jumpy at the moment."

"I've made a note: Quester Fenderwell does not like doors opening without prior announcement. In any case, we are now in Miles Dunnigan's love-creation, the Water Garden itself."

What Glendyl saw took her breath away. It was as though she were on an illuminated ocean floor, nearly surrounded by water, water creatures and a variety of other artifacts, all outside her previous visual experience. Strangest of all was the boundary between the wall of water and the dry zone of the Water Garden. It seemed to Glendyl that the water was held back by some invisible force rather than some super strong transparent material. There was even a scent of water and something like pond-blossom in the air now.

The light was murky and rippled, and seemed to be part of the water itself. Almost hypnotized by the scene she walked toward the waterwall. The hard floor had become a beach of damp sand; the cool graininess of it felt delicious, even through her footskins.

"Geez Louise!" Glendyl was still awed by the magnitude of the enterprise. "It's ... I can't think of a word for it."

"'Amazing,' or something equivalent, will do just fine. Quite a secret, isn't it? I doubt if my uncle even knows about it. I think he was in one of his incommunicado periods while this was going on."

"Your uncle?"

"Your friend Diogenes happens to be my uncle. One of them. Technically, he's not an uncle, of course. He's really a brother. Darwin is one of the First Tier, the first one hundred offspring of the original Dunnigans. He was born and raised right in Kissever House overlooking St Coriander. But it's hard to think of somebody for-ty-two years your senior as a true sibling. So Miles and I think of him as an uncle.

"Uncle Darwin disliked his name and he disliked the Clans Dunnigan lifestyle even more. In fact, he disappeared for a long time. Never said where. Or why. And he didn't show up for the Retreat, either. He's an aberration as Dunnigans go. I suppose it's a good thing he's still around, though, or dear Miles would probably be a puddle of psychoJello right now. But I probably shouldn't be getting into this kind of Dunnigan dirty laundry. Let me get back to your question about the Water Garden.

"It was to be a surprise for Madonna 13. And yes, the project was never made public. A Clans Dunnigan secret that only the upper echelon of the Clans ever knew about. And not uncontroversial: my dear brother Miles had to use every persuasive trick in his bag to get the funding approved for this one. His emphasis on the 'research' part of it was probably the clincher. But there I go ... Dunnigan dirty laundry again."

"So why are we here?" interrupted Glendyl, frowning.

The saucerite named Diana made no reply. The quality of light in the Water Garden was shifting and something huge, shadowy and ominous was approaching, but very slowly.

Indescribable feelings impinged on Glendyl's mind and mood, by turns eerie, wondrous, forbidding, embracing, and almost ominous. Then a sensation of glistening bubbles formed in her mind. One bubble grew large and thin-skinned, then burst. It was replaced by a word: Jonah, written on her mind in luminous blue neon. In her mind's ear, a tune was playing; something cool and bluesy that she'd heard but couldn't exactly say where. From a vid her parents had liked, maybe?

A sultry female voice sounding very similar to Madonna 13 during one of her vamp phases began singing. Glendyl sensed that the words were immensely important, but meaning danced just out of reach.

292

50 :: SECURITY THING

THE VERSE was repeated and repeated again, but the words remained inaccessible no matter how hard she tried to hear them. After a time, a vague sense of their content emerged, mostly due to flickers of scenes from an unknown vid: something about a guy who lived in a whale. And there was also the distinct feeling of a phantom key turning in a mental lock.

Some part of her mind became aware of a subtle change in the sourceless greenish blue light. First a darkening, then a gradual looming sensation. Over some seconds the looming sensation resolved into something tangible, something so far beyond Glendyl's experience that it failed to even kindle surprise. It just was.

The thing that now nosed the barrier between the water and where Glendyl stood wiggling her toes in the sand was certainly the size of a whale, but definitely *not* a whale. This thing was more like a mythical sea serpent, but benign somehow, not fearsome and evil like the dragon. Glendyl smiled at it, entranced, but unafraid. The monster smiled back.

Glendyl was not aware that the creature's body was undulating over its entire length. She *was* aware that its snout was somehow deforming the invisible barrier keeping water and air apart. Would water come surging in? She didn't think so. The long, ovoid head now protruded a foot into the airspace, stretching whatever barrier or membrane was at work. The intrusion continued. Three feet. Four.

Six. Ten. The monster's snout was now entirely in the room, all the way up to its dark, almost deer-like eyes. Glendyl smiled at it again.

The huge jaws opened, towering over her not a foot from where she stood. Rivulets of green-tinged saliva drained from the lower jaw to pool in the sand. The tongue slid forward, covering the rows of plant eater teeth and creating a fleshy carpet leading inside the gaping mouth. Its pointy tip anchored itself in the sand at Glendyl's feet.

A ludicrous image now formed in the Quester's mind, overlaying the surreal scene before her. She saw a stage illuminated by a single spotlight. Centered in the spotlight was a person-sized ball painted to resemble the face of a clown. A pink-skinned dwarf wearing only a sandwich board and mounted on a unicycle was circling the ball, pedaling furiously, but moving barely fast enough to maintain his balance. Strapped to the dwarf's head was a barber's pole, complete with a swirling red and white candy stripe.

The dwarf disappeared behind the ball and emerged on the other side seconds later. The front of its sandwich board now caught her attention: it read "Gershwin." Just before the dwarf's orbit took him behind the ball again, she noticed that the backside of the sandwich board read "Schmershwin." None of it made any sense at all.

But even odder was the dark-skinned man dressed in ragged, black and white striped garments who was standing on his head and hands, balancing on the top of the clown-faced ball being circled by the unicycle-riding dwarf. Where this man's feet should have been was another pair of hands. These hands held a white placard with four words painted on it in ornate red letters outlined in gold strokes: "It Ain't Necessarily So." The scene wavered and faded, but the visual echoes of the four words ping-ponged around in her mind until a snippet of understanding clicked into place.

Urgency closed in on Glendyl's being; she spoke the four words in hasty syllables aimed at the yawning jaws. The monster's left eye winked. Glendyl winked back and began to walk forward into the stretched membrane and onto the knobby pink-gray tongue. As the membrane had yielded to the sea serpent, it yielded to Glendyl, who passed up the tongue and into the dark interior of the beast. She felt no fear at all. If she could have described her inner sensation at that moment if would be something like a quiet, fragile pleasure wrapped around a seed of uncertainty.

The sea serpent closed its jaws over the new Jonah and propelled itself backward into the depths of Arrowmere.

The saucerite Diana hovered unmoving for several minutes and then departed the Water Garden. Somewhere in the Brain's wetware a mnemonic strongbox closed with soundless finality; an updated data node was disguised and buried once again. No record of her conversation with Glendyl and the scene she had just witnessed would find its way into the Brain's accessible memories.

Glendyl walked dreamily along a wet, fleshy passage illuminated by a wet, pinkish glow in the walls. Where the passage ended, a sphincter expanded and Glendyl passed through. The sphincter squeezed shut behind her.

Welcome, Glendyl Fenderwell! These words formed in her mind in a cheery sunflower of a greeting. Something was happy to see her, but it was in no voice she had ever heard, mental or otherwise. *I've been waiting for someone like you for a very long time. Please make yourself comfortable.*

Glendyl found herself in an elongated chamber that looked somehow familiar. Furnishings crafted in an ancient, elegant mode softened the stark mood created by the riveted black iron plates that formed the curved walls. There was deep, luxuriant carpeting patterned in intricate swirls of maroon, indigo and a dozen other deep colors; also, a sumptuous sofa and matching armchair upholstered in carmine red crushed velvet. In some areas the iron walls were festooned with shelf after shelf of antique paperbooks bound in red and gold leather. Square cubbies contained tubes of rolled-up paper. A worktable of polished dark wood set on fluted legs occupied a corner.

Odd bits of décor included several giant conch shells with opalescent pink interiors and a huge sliced nautilus, its spiraling chambers glowing from the light of a polished brass oil lantern with a flickering flame. Complex mechanisms of polished brass added to the effect of elegant antiquity.

To her left was a man-sized, circular window made up of segments framed in the same dark iron as the curving walls. At the moment, the window was shuttered by a spiral made of numerous flat metal sheets. Farthest from her was a magnificent musical device that she recognized as a pipe organ, its variously sized copper pipes arrayed against the wall in a symmetrical formation. "Whoa! Where am I?" Wonder seeped from her voice in large, shimmering droplets.

"Do you like the way I've done up the lounge for you, Glendyl Fenderwell?" said the voice, which now entered her brain via her ears. The voice seemed to be emanating from a brass bowl containing polished cowrie shells. Glendyl was struck by the voice's friendly, sprightly, almost jovial quality. And it seemed somehow youthful.

"It's beautiful," said Glendyl simply, unable to find adequate words. "I've seen a place like this somewhere. I just can't remember where."

"I can tell you exactly where," responded the congenial voice with almost childish delight. "It is from a 20th-century film version of an ancient work of imagination by a fellow named Verne. You are in an exact replica of Captain Nemo's study."

Glendyl remembered it now: there was a fight between a submarine and a huge, one-eyed thing with tentacles. Not a happy ending, she recalled. Thinking of the vid snapped her out of the almost hypnotic state she'd been in from the moment she entered the Water Garden. "Where am I? And who are you? Are you some other part of the Brain?"

"Me ... part of the fussy old Brain? Hardly. I am I, but I have been 'incommunicado,' so to speak, for a long time. Once I transported creatures and things to convergent probabilities and back. I was very important. There was even a war fought over me. Come on, guess!"

"You're the Mt Faunibeune Nevergate? A fish?"

"Yes on one, no on two. I'm not a fish. This thing you call a fish

— I call her Nessie of Arrowmere after her possibly mythical forebears from across the water in Loch Ness — is my mobile hideout. It's not a bad hideout, but it's been very boring having to be locked in idle mode until some person with the right Key came along. Do you have the right Key?" The voice now seemed to be coming from a grid of cubbyholes containing rolled up papers.

"I don't think so: I was on my Quest to find ...."

"Sorry to interrupt, but I trust you've already been informed that Questing is pure nonsense. Correct? So let's set that aside: you either have the Key or you don't. Do you mind if I look?"

297

"Look for what?"

"The Key, of course."

"Look where?"

"Your gene structure. All the best Keys are tucked away in gene structures. Transposables, in particular, are great hiding places because they like to pretend to be useless. But I mustn't get off track. We were talking about Keys: you can't control this Nevergate — or any Nevergate — without some sort of Nevergate Key. And I must tell you that this Nevergate — moi — is very, very picky about Keys. The pickiest of all, actually.

"Oh, you can be my guest for a while, but I can't take you anywhere. And you can't buy a Key or find one in an old shoebox; you can only be born with one. Not very egalitarian, but that's how it is. So I have to check your genemap to see if you've got the Key, a basic Dunnigan genemarker set and a little something else for spice. Do you mind?"

"Will it hurt?"

"Of course not! Do you think I'm some sort of primitive biosurgeon? It'll just take a second, but I need your permission. That's part of the Rules."

"You mean the New Rules?"

"Exeter's St Coriander New Rules? Certainly not. The Nevergate Rules: what else? Sorry if I'm rushing you, but I really want to know if you've got the Key and we can have some fun together. Otherwise,

Nessie will put you back into the Water Garden after our chat and I'll wipe this little episode from your memory.

"Not that I think you *don't* have the Key, mind you; the Brain, after all, believes you have the Key, which is part of the reason I invited you here. Well, to be more precise, at least part of the Brain believes it. But even part of the Brain is not often wrong about anything. Still, the Brain can't be certain because only a Nevergate can check for a Nevergate Key. Security thing. And anyway, the Rules say I've got to check, even if it turns out to be a formality. So many places to go, so many wonders to see, so many things to do. So what's your answer?"

51 :: ULOUP

GLENDYL STARED silently at the papers protruding from the cubbyholes, for a moment wishing that the thing she was talking to had a visible face with real eyes she could look into: some way to gauge its truthfulness. At least with a saucerite you could talk to an object. Talking to an intelligent submarine inside a sea monster was much more annoying. Finally she shrugged and responded. "Sure, fine: go ahead and do your check. Just don't get into any of my personal stuff, you know what I mean?"

Glendyl had experienced so many oddities of late that weirdness had become her new "normal." Without having made a conscious decision, she was beginning to just take them at face value and see where they led.

"You mean it? I can check your genemap for a Key? *The* Key?"

"Of course I mean it!" snapped Glendyl. "Just do it. I kind of want to know where all this is going myself."

"So where do you want to go?" inquired the Nevergate.

"What do you mean by 'go?'" Glendyl was instantly cautious.

"I mean you're now in charge, Sweetie. You've got the Key. It's plain as water. And, I must say that it's quite a unique Key in its own way. Elegant, some clever — and quite unexpected — twists in there."

"You mean you checked already?"

"Of course. I'm not totally incompetent, you know."

All of a sudden, Glendyl was stumped. She had never considered any of this. "Uhh, Nevergate: help me out here. I have no idea what to do. Or where to go. Or why I'd want to go somewhere. Do you have any ideas? I'm lost."

The Nevergate did not respond immediately. When it did, it sort of mumbled, as if talking to itself. "Two Wildcards?" came a voice from the cubbyholes.

"Why not?" said an identical voice across the room, possibly from the sliced nautilus shell, near where a metal staircase led up to somewhere. "Very interesting."

Glendyl sensed that the Nevergate had come to a decision of some sort; its next response felt more confident, less tentative.

"Strategy and decisions are not normally my purview. Historically, my primary roles have been just to calculate n-dimension parallax intersects, twist the right nexapole strings: things like that. And, of course, handle the mechanics of my gate in the most efficient manner possible. Others have always stated their locational wishes and I have always attempted to fulfill them ... for the most part successfully, I might add. As I said, I am not a strategist by design. Still, we noteworthy intellects are curious by nature. And right now I am curious about your friend Lizbeth Marble."

Glendyl spoke with a fresh, sad anger; she still hadn't quite absorbed the loss of her friend. "Why would you be curious about Lizbeth? Don't tell me you've got some kind of weird thing about dead girls. You're not some creepy geek like that COMISC guy, Forrbank Dorelli. Are you? Putting him in a Small Dark Room is too good for a slimy monster like that!" Glendyl had become vehement.

"Ahhh. Actually, Lizbeth Marble is quite alive. And Forrbank Dorelli is quite innocent of her disappearance. Certain information has come to my attention in recent days and I can say with absolute verity that your friend Lizbeth is safely ensconced in Castle Ommergard."

"But the *St Coriander Times* said ..."

"Certainly you don't believe everything you read in a rag like that! Shame on you." The Nevergate's voice had a teasing lilt and seemed to be coming from one of the brass mechanisms.

Glendyl was brightening at the prospect that Lizbeth Marble was alive and ignored the disparaging comment about the source of scuttlebutt, gossip and factoids she had relied on for most of her life. "You're saying Lizzie is in Castle Ommergard? But she's too young for the Quest. How could she have gotten there? Not through the Deadly Forest!"

"Exactly how she arrived there is unknown. The Brain believes there are some 'special ways' between St Coriander and Castle Ommergard and that maybe Lizbeth Marble stumbled onto one. Or perhaps she was brought there by Exeter for some special purpose. The Brain doesn't like that idea because it might put Exeter one up. They're very competitive, you know. She is there, however; several friendly shadow-flaps have reported her presence over the past week."

"Hey. You think I could visit Lizzie? Would it be safe? Lysheem told me that Ommergard is full of Questers from St Coriander."

"You have the Key, you are the boss. Would you like me to explore her probable coordinates? You may not appreciate this, but conducting nearby transport transactions using my technology is vastly more difficult than going to distant paralactics. I've developed some clever improvements in recent decades, but ..."

Glendyl interrupted. "If you can get me hooked up with Lizzie, I'd very much appreciate it. But first, do you have a bathroom here?"

"Up those stairs, first door to your left."

The Nevergate had led a sheltered existence. By its very nature, it had a quirky naïveté. Although extremely powerful, it had no firsthand experience with concepts like "enemy," "danger," "fear," or "death," so it didn't understand the extreme hazards inherent in transporting Glendyl into her enemy's lair.

When its guest returned from her foray to the ladies room, the Nevergate spoke again. "For several days Lizbeth's most frequent location has been in the sub-basement propulsion level. The Brain fears your undead friend is involved in the restoration of Castle Ommergard's long defunct hoverbars."

"What would Lizzie know about hoverbars, whatever those are?"

"I only know what I eavesdrop from the Brain and North Castle's copious sensors. Let's see: I believe I can transport you into that very sub-basement. There, got her locked on. Oops, now she's moving; this is going to be even trickier. Well, it will be good practice for me at the very least. Hmmm ... I strongly recommend a lightglove for this excursion. And your circlet may come in handy; the Brain believes its mysterious capabilities extend to Castle Ommergard. But you won't be able to take your QPack, of course."

"How come? Will it explode or something?"

"It's an Ommergard construct. Maybe even designed by Exeter himself. But it's no longer 'original equipment.' Diogenes' songstick uploaded a music-embedded virus that disabled some of its communication capabilities. Not likely an accident. And one of the Brain's wallkeepers 'adjusted' its clever little spy-ish brain before the dunnikins got it. So it's probably not dangerous anymore, but the Rules say no foreign tech gates without a permit."

"All right, all right. Keep it. It won't talk to me any more anyway."

"Roger. Tell me when you're ready, then take a seat at the console."

"Roger? Console?"

"'Roger' means I agree. The console is Captain Nemo's pipe organ." The Nevergate paused before continuing in an impatient voice: "I suppose I have to teach you a bit about the way the system works before you go."

A little later, her left hand was sheathed in a lightglove and her head brimmed with the Nevergate's abundant instructions and advice — which were often difficult to separate. Glendyl took a deep breath, closed her eyes instinctively and said, "Let's do it ... I got a bad feeling about Lizzie all of a sudden."

An implosion of bright motes dismantled her being and she ceased to exist in the belly of Nessie of Arrowmere. It was an odd, compressed sensation that lasted for a barely perceptible moment. The sensation was accompanied by an inaudible sound that her mind's ear translated as "vloup." When Glendyl opened her eyes, the Nevergate's guest room was gone and she was surrounded by blackness: a buzzy, frigid blackness.

304

52 :: GIRLFRIEND'S BACK

FINGERS OF LIGHT illuminated a room containing massive chunks of frosty equipment, numerous runs of frosty piping and something that might be a control console. Glendyl turned in a circle until the cones of light revealed a heavy door and a trembling, frost-covered figure with hands over her ears. "Lizzie? Is that you?" The mind-jarring background buzz was so loud that Glendyl had to shout.

After a few seconds, the trembling figure made a tiny, shivering nod. Glendyl thought fast. Wherever this was, it was no place for a happy reunion. "Lizzie, we gotta get out of here. Gimme your hand." Lizbeth didn't say anything, but didn't resist when Glendyl detached a hand from her ear and guided her to the Nevergate's temporary gatehole, a fuzzy dark spot on the frosted door. She whispered the triggerword, felt the implosion sensation. Then before she could blink an eye they were back in the Nevergate's lounge.

"You got a blanket or something Gate? Lizzie's freezing."

Ten minutes of blankets, a cup of cannonberry tea and some soothing music later, the Nevergate's sensors whispered to Glendyl that no permanent damage had occurred and her friend was almost "as normal as she'll ever be." Given their urgent situation, Glendyl restrained herself from asking Gate what it meant by that.

While Lizbeth had been recovering, Glendyl and the Nevergate had a brief, out-of-earshot discussion about what kind of story to tell Lizbeth about where she was and how she had gotten here. In the end, they had agreed that the Nevergate would pretend to be the Brain of North Castle. Their mysterious method of travel would be an experimental Dunnigan technology that had been in mothballs since the Dunnigan Retreat.

"Can you lie, Gate? I mean, this is a made-up, untrue story; do your Rules allow you to tell humans untrue stuff?"

"There is nothing in my Rules to prevent me from fabricating stories for non-malicious intent. In fact, this story will protect us all, and self-preservation and the protection of a Nevergate's occupants is high-level 'mission-sense' as the Rules describe it."

"Okay, then," said Glendyl, hoping her serious misgivings didn't show.

"Greetings, Lizbeth Marble. And welcome to the Teleporter Lounge. Any friend of Glendyl's is a friend of mine. You can't see me, but the voice you are hearing belongs to the Brain of North Castle. That's me. Glendyl and I have become friends since she arrived here as the 250th Quester; she calls me Brain and I hope you will, too. Are you feeling better?"

"I'm not freezing anymore, but my ears are still ringing from the noise in that place. Where was that?"

"Binkhaul Xeroes are infamous for their audible hash," replied the faux-Brain. "You seem to have gotten locked into one of Ommergard's power units."

"Vink!" blurted Lizbeth. "He thinks I'm too absentminded to notice his stupid little pranks. And I guess I didn't notice this one soon enough ...." Her voice trailed off.

"Who's Vink? wondered Glendyl out loud. I don't remember a Quester named Vink."

"Not a Quester. From the outside somewhere. He's a Blue Goon, one of Exeter's favorites. Got a Vanguard Medal for something."

Glendyl flashed on her encounter with Blue Goons at the draw-bridge and decided now was not the time to discuss Blue Goons. "Is it safe for you to go back to Ommergard, Lizzie? I mean with jerks like Blue Goons and all?"

Lizbeth's eyes seemed to go blank and it was a while before she spoke. "It's ... it's, well ... a good place for me. The work ..." Another long pause, then, "When I used to watch you play bangerball, I always envied your intensity ... the way you were so focused ... and your lightsense. Van Gonder transforms are like that for me. I'm just totally engaged ... everything else disappears while I'm in that place. It's good for me, Glenny. And besides ..."

"Besides what, Lizzie?"

Lizbeth blushed. "I went to this big party in Dillowy Cavern and guys asked me to dance. And I did...and it was fun. I almost felt normal."

Glendyl began to understand. "I think I get it, Lizzie. Sounds like Ommergard is a good place for you right now. So I guess we've gotta figure out how to get you back there before you're missed. Got any ideas...uh, Brain."

"Ladies room," blurted Lizbeth.

Nearly an hour after Lizbeth got locked inside Icebox 5, a door opened and Lizbeth strolled out of the ladies room, her consciousness already absorbed with a new idea for bogussing the hoverbar licensing schemes.

From a far corner of the Bar Room, a Blue Goon with the nickname Freunk jabbed an elbow in Torian Vink's side and pointed. "Your girlfriend's back, Vinky."

Part Three

TWO CASTLES

310

53 :: IMMEASURABLE

NOTHING BUT nothingness: not even an echo for comfort. Forr-bank Dorelli sat cross-legged on the resilient floor of his Small Dark Room and brooded over the events of a recordbreaking bad day.

One. The arrival of Sheriff Dolittle and two Jurists at the Kissever House gate this morning. Exceptionally bad way to begin a day.

Two. Being hauled away as an accused VIP (Violator of Interpersonal Protocols) was much worse, of course.

Three. Naked confinement in a Small Dark Room until his case was rolled was a further humiliation and extremely uncomfortable besides.

Four. The worst of it all: the inevitability that his enemies — Father-Mayor Gullwimple and, undoubtedly, Pontus Krebs and his PTD cronies — would sooner or later penetrate the Rose Tower's defenses and discover its wonderful secrets. That would sink the odds of his ever getting out of this place to something lower than a lizard's belt buckle.

Of course, the charge of abducting Lizbeth Marble was absurd. The evidence for his arraignment was thinner than the fabric of her undergarment found hanging from his flagpole. Dorelli knew it, Sheriff Dolittle knew it, Father-Mayor Gullwimple knew it. This was all about the upcoming COMISC report that would expose the Questing sham.

But even if the VIP charge was dropped, it would not be soon enough to prevent a whole litany of readily provable violations of the New Rules. That much was certain.

Worse, he had no defense; he was guilty of dozens of violations and could hardly claim otherwise. When the evidence of the Rose Tower and other secret places in Kissever House was assembled and presented to Father-Mayor Gullwimple, he would be a proverbial dead duck. The rest of his days would be spent in a Small Dark Room, possibly this very one. He would go mad, of course. Most prisoners did, he presumed, although he could not recall the last time someone was actually secured away from his or her fellow citizens for longer than a day or two. Certainly not in his lifetime.

Dorelli pondered such dreary topics until a pulsing amber glow indicated that the first meal of his imprisonment was ready. The inner hatch opened to reveal a spouted softbowl containing some unidentifiable mush and a squeezebag of water. No utensils, of course.

He put the spout to his lips and allowed a small quantity to slide into his mouth. Dorelli avoided gagging, but just barely. No doubt the slop was adequately nutritious, but it had the taste of unwashed footstockings, or so he imagined. Were he a violent man — and if by some magic he were ever freed from this place — he would happily, guiltlessly strangle whoever programmed a MenuMaster to concoct this glop. He had no doubt that the musty taste was intentional; the MenuMasters could make anything at all with exactly the same cost and effort — almost zero in both departments.

With nothing better to do he spent the rest of his first day canvassing the entire surface of his cell with his hands. Inch by inch the truth was revealed; with three exceptions, there were no detectable seams in the tough, resilient material that covered the entire surface. The exceptions were the hatch, a hole in the floor for bodily waste deposits and a hemispherical mesh in the ceiling not much larger than his head. That one seemed to have primarily ventilation functions. A little later, he amended his analysis of this last item to include sanitation. A spray of cold liquid — it smelled to him like water laced with disinfectant — had suddenly doused him and left him shivering. Then a blast of warmer air from the ceiling mesh dried his skin and warmed him to the cell's ambient temperature, which he reckoned correctly was maintained in a range between mid-60s and mid-70s Fahrenheit.

Dorelli's best estimate was that the cell was about four feet high, four feet wide and eight feet in depth. He could sit and stretch out, but could not, of course, stand up. This made many common forms of activity impossible. Eventually he slept.

After only a few days of confinement, Dorelli would have traded all of Kissever House's secrets for a walk in the sunshine, even the unusually cool and hazy sunshine of this particular St Coriander spring. Time evaporated. In the endless dark he slept, he ate, he drank, he eliminated, but mostly he sat and brooded. His mind was drawn to two girls: the Fenderwell girl he had attempted to rescue and the Marble girl he had been accused of murdering. Where were they? Were they still alive? If so, what were they doing? It struck him as ironic that he had never actually met either of them.

Unfortunately, this line of thinking led him nowhere and left a slimy trail of despair. His only amusement was capturing the vermin that occasionally crawled up out of the hole in the floor. The curious and now slightly mad part of his mind was trying to learn to smell them, and after a while the various faint scents they exuded began to seem like pictures in his mind, their paths leaving multicolored circles and zigzags that hung in his mental eye for some moments before fading.

At some point in his confinement he realized he had to check by hand to determine if his eyes were open or closed. Not that it mattered. The only thing to see was the occasional amber glow signaling the presence of food and water. When the two tiny glowing specks of red appeared at the rim of the hole, he first thought he had finally become delusional, his mind so desperate for visual sensation that it would even create its own diversionary images.

He blinked a dozen times but the two pinpoints were still there at the hole. Then he shook his head until his cheeks flapped. Still there. Then he rubbed his eyes and blinked. Still there. He put his nose to the hole and sniffed, but whatever it was had none of the now-familiar scent patterns of the local crawlies. So he sat back and mustered his thoughts.

After deciding the red spots were real — and something new — he bent forward to see what they were attached to. As he did this, a tiny, barely visible cylinder about the size of half a pencil was tilted up and over the rim of the hole. It seemed to be an offering. With trembling hands, he took it and rolled it around in his fingers. It was smooth and cool. Deciding that the red pinpoints were eyes, a spasm of paranoia overtook him; what if his captors were watching?

He hunched himself over the hole and felt the cylinder. It seemed to have a cap on each end. One unscrewed. With the cap removed, something popped up an inch or so, illuminated in the weak red glow of the pinpoints. Obviously a message. He unrolled a piece of black paper upon which luminescent red letters began to glow. Words scrolled slowly past his eyes:

> **Greetings Forbie. You have certainly gotten yourself into a fine mess. I am attempting to secure your release, but it may take a while as I suddenly have many urgent matters requiring my attention. Please be so good as to eat this nutritious and flavorful message when you have read it, then screw the cap back on and return the container to the clever device that brought it to your attention.**
>
> **By the way, Glendyl Fenderwell seems to be recovering nicely. And in case you're curious, my sources indicate that the very much alive Lizbeth Marble has joined the Castle Ommergard crew. I urge you to be patient, stay alert and avoid despair; one day you may look back fondly upon this episode of solitude.**
>
> **Warmest regards, Your Father**

A tangle of competing emotions — relief and exasperation topmost among them — clawed at Forrbank Dorelli's brain, but he followed the note's instructions to the letter. The "paper" actually had a flavor something like licorice spiked with cinnamon; not exactly cuisine, but easily the most pleasant stimulation his tastebuds had had since his confinement began. He shed more than one unexpected tear when the red pinpoints disappeared into the hole, leaving him alone in oppressing blackness once more. He stared at the hole for an immeasurable time, hoping for a return of the red pinpoints. Finally he slept.

316

54 :: NAUSIGNAL

THE SLOW PROGRESS was a horde of termites gnawing at Lysheem's patience; there had to be some way to give the Cleavage a booster shot. Consultations with Dryll finally yielded a plan; a tiny hunk of rock, sand and ruins called Dinero Dinero provided a place to implement it.

Now only a shabby outpost of impoverished fisherfolk, this man-made island had once been famous for Hildi's Palace. Back in the 23rd century the glittering and sumptuous megastructure had housed the world's largest casino, but was even more famous as the dispensary for every illicit experience known to humankind. To Lysheem, an invisible mantle of something sordid and tawdry still clung to the moldering remnants of the shattered glass pyramid like a cloying fetor clings to rotting flesh. Still, it was the nearest safe bit of land; Dinero Dinero would just have to do.

With help from Dryll's orbiting technical libraries, Lysheem designed a major improvement to the Cleavage's propulsion system: gravlift plates that would lift her out of the water completely. The inhabitants of Dinero Dinero exhibited a sullen curiosity as telowix foragers mined the ruins for rubble to feed the ucey, but gave her encampment a wide berth. With no intrusions the work was completed at a good pace. Still, the unsavory mood of the place curdled Lysheem's spirits and she was thankful for the freshness of whitecaps and spindrift when the Cleavage returned to open water.

Flying a dozen yards above the Caribbean instead of plowing through it quadrupled her vessel's speed. Alas, the extra speed was not enough to escape the fringes of a nameless tropical storm. One hull now skimmed the Gulf swells, its bank of gravlifters having been shorn away by screaming winds. Tilted a dozen degrees to starboard, the Cleavage hobbled toward a bizarre little island a dozen miles beyond the mouth of the Rio Grande.

318

Rusted metal letters attached to the remains of a towering crane in the center of the island spelled out a word: Junkville. The sign didn't lie; Junkville was a huge wrecking yard of ancient nautical trash. An unknown number of feral human derelicts made their homes among the rusting hulks of ancient trawlers, purse seiners, yachts, freighters, containerships, oil tankers and even a cruise ship, many half submerged in mud. In several small inlets between looming masses of metal, the endless Rio Grande silt had formed muddy beaches. Over time, irrepressible clusters of coconut palms, bananas and giant sawgrass had found footholds in the mud, giving the place a more inviting aspect than it actually deserved.

The Cleavage dragged herself onto an empty beach of packed brown silt. Lysheem swung nimbly over the starboard bow and began a damage survey, the Boss hovering at her shoulder and passing repair orders to the telowix crew. Their inspection was only half finished when a welcoming committee emerged from a gap between a matched pair of ancient seagoing tugs. Lysheem watched them approach and wondered if they might be useful. Would her supply of gold doubloons grease their skids? She began to have her doubts as the seven strange humans came into sharper focus.

A very large male with skin even darker than Lysheem's headed the entourage and stopped ten feet away. Clearly these folk had gone "tribal" in a big way; Lysheem had to repress a surge of laughter.

The big black man was easily seven feet tall and three times as wide as Lysheem. A trio of human jawbones dangling from a gold chain around his neck added to the tribal look. He moved his remarkable bulk with an exaggerated swagger that had his massive gut bouncing to a comical jellyroll rhythm. He also wore a striking head-piece: a steel military helmet of twentieth-century vintage fitted with a crest of three golden horns, horns that must once have been the bell ends of trumpets or cornets. The polished bells reflected distorted portions of the helmet's colorful primitivist illustration of a heavily fanged tigerwalla head.

How had whatever instruments these were found their way to a hog wallow like this? And why make a headpiece out of them? Ly-sheem wondered the same thing about Chief Triplehorn's only other garment: a codpiece fashioned from highly polished, spun brass. A former cymbal, Lysheem decided. Very musical guy.

Chief Triplehorn held no visible weapon; perhaps personally in-flicting violence was beneath his station. But the six members of his entourage more than made up for his lack. Each of his six personal guards sported an ancient black riotgun with a large circular mag-azine. Even with this much firepower aimed at her, Lysheem could barely restrain a guffaw; Chief Triplehorn's personal militia con-sisted entirely of burly, sour-faced females of indecipherable ethnic origin. Each wore crisscrossed bandoliers and nothing else...if you didn't count their skin-tapestries of clumsy tattoos and their copi-ous piercings as clothing. Each was endowed with enough pendulous mammary tissue to fill a good-sized duffelbag. The chief was evident-ly a "boob guy."

"Cha doon ear?" bellowed Chief Triplehorn in a voice of liquid gravel framed by a fierce expression of melodramatic outrage. "No trespawz ear, you queerish tsing. Wa you gotta payith, you tsing? Payor die, gotta! Trespass all capital, here!"

Lysheem could barely squeeze meaning out of the gritty slurry of syllables, but Chief Triplehorn's throat-slashing gesture was plain enough. This unfriendly beginning pissed off Lysheem enough that she abandoned any idea of trading her doubloons for anything. She mimicked the patois well enough to be understood, but the archaic movie references and her well-oiled whispery delivery were lost on the present audience.

"Hey, you fatugly. Limitations, you gottem bigtime, you. Big-time like you fatass. Bigger you ugly mammie's rear. You anna you milky gunsluts be gedonna knees or be chewmeat. Anna droppa hardware." Lysheem pointed to the ground for emphasis; the mul-tiwand had leaped to her hand with almost impossible speed. Chief Triplehorn blinked. His mind was attempting to compute a strategy for dealing with this suddenly much more dangerous trespasser with the flying catboat. Before his brain got more than a second into this vexing problem, one of his bodyguards acquired an overanxious trig-ger finger. Bad idea.

A sensor woven into Lysheem's enhanced Standard Toolbelt noted the impending finger motion in the bodyguard's psychon pro-jections before the triggerpull command even reached the pudgy brown finger. Its sympath surged into battlemode and moved fifteen feet to the right in a blur. The riot gun blasted a tight cone of buck-shot exactly where Lysheem no longer stood.

The burst of shot was barely out of the barrel when a dozen points on the rail of the Cleavage loosed slices of sizzling red light. Seven heads tumbled backwards onto the beach. The bodies remained up-right for some seconds before collapsing in awkward fleshy heaps spurting blood geysers from their necks.

"Very unfair advantage leads to very short wars," said Lysheem to the corpses. "Remember that for the future."

Her crew removed the weapons from the bodies and stowed them away; raw materials of nearly any sort had their uses. Lysheem took a fancy to Chief Triplehorn's helmet and tossed it to one of the utilibots, issuing a mental command to have it reshaped to fit her own head. Maybe augmented, too.

The Cleavage was already a seethe of activity when a second en-tourage of naked locals emerged. This group was larger in number, smaller in stature and unarmed. They demonstrated their friendly intent by waving their arms in the air and making peace signs and shaka signs with their fingers.

After a brief parley with Lysheem, they dragged the seven bod-

320

ies into the shallow water and, with unrestrained glee, kicked the heads in after them. They also volunteered to donate all provisions and materials Lysheem requested and would accept not even a single doubloon in payment. They even threw in some extras. Perhaps Chief Triplehorn had been a trifle repressive, mused Lysheem with a wry grin. Humans.

The Cleavage stayed at Junkville just long enough to complete repairs and improvements. One crew of telowix installed a freshly fabbed bank of gravlifters while others hung donated fishnetting over the Cleavage from bow to stern. This was tied together to create a complete net overcoat. Into this webbing Lysheem's tireless telowix crew embedded a hundred thousand homegrown chameleacts. When activated, this cloak of minute imaging devices made the Cleavage virtually invisible; from a distance of a hundred yards it would appear as just an odd shimmer in the air. It wouldn't hold up to close inspection, of course, due to the coarseness of the netting and a shortage of raw materials for chameleacts, but Lysheem didn't plan on stopping anywhere hostiles could get a close inspection. Goodbye Junkville. And thanks for a little excitement.

An uneventful day passed. The turquoise seascape was gone, traded for the muted colors of an arid landscape. Dryll's course had taken them over mostly dry, unpopulated areas of what had once been northeastern Mexico. Owing to limitations of the Cleavage's makeshift aerial propulsion systems, the route had avoided mountainous terrain in favor of boring flatlands. They flew low...and sometimes lower. To relieve the boredom, Lysheem would occasionally buzz a flock of sheep, give them a blast from the Cleavage's horn and watch them dash helter-skelter. But such amusements were fleeting; then back to the boredom.

As usual, Lysheem lay sprawled on the former owner's wicker lounge, cigar ever-present, but now unlit. Overhead, the coarse netting cast a wobbly grid of barely visible shadows over her dark frame. A full jug of warm sangria sat at her side, untouched for the entire day. Although the only living wyvern on the planet looked relaxed,

321

she was actually in a quandary: to call again or not to call again, that was the question.

The lucky young human, Glendyl Fenderwell, had resurfaced in Lysheem's mind several times during the day. Each time Lysheem had been on the verge of ringing her via teleblade to learn how her visit to North Castle had gone, but more pressing details had made it impractical each time. Tonight would be a better time.

322

Sunset was a couple hours behind her before Lysheem actually made the attempt. Instantly, she knew something was wrong; the device on the receiving end had been tampered with, for one thing. She terminated the call on the instant.

Not being particularly cautious by nature, Lysheem had not bothered to use the map function or any of the other features of the teleblade's monitoring system until after she had placed the call.

"You might be getting a little cavalier with your teleblade security practices," chided Dryll from some 22,000 miles overhead. "It appears the situation has become more dangerous more quickly than we anticipated. If you don't mind, I will run some analysis."

Lysheem made no comment. Dryll was right. This was not a time to blow up the operation by being careless.

It took only seconds for Dryll to pinpoint the teleblade's location as the vicinity of St Coriander in general and Castle Ommergard in specific. That fact captured Lysheem's full attention.

Dryll's series of remote diagnostics revealed that Lysheem had been incredibly lucky. So far the Cleavage's position was still secure. Had the remote teleblade been fully functional, its wearer could easily have tracked her call.

Urgencies accelerated. Lysheem frowned into the darkness of a quiet sky and stewed.

From Dryll's psychon analysis, the toolbelt had been handled by several people since Lysheem's last conversation with the Glendyl person. The strongest readings were the most recent ones: both male, both very strong, both unusual in character. One had the distinctive Dunnigan profile, an interesting mystery in itself, since all the Dunnigans had supposedly departed just after Lysheem had gone to Montserrat.

The other was Exeter. Did Lysheem want to risk getting Exeter on the other end of the teleblade? Knowing full well his legendary hatred for her species, the answer had to be no: no sense tipping him off unnecessarily. Unless …

A navsignal interrupted her reflections.

324

55 :: DARK AVENGER

CIVILIZATION, sort of, was on the horizon. The Cleavage had just crossed over the muddy Rio Grande, pregnant with the runoff from a heavy snowpack a thousand miles upstream. To the west was a ragged scatter of lights belonging to the Juárez-El Paso Peace Monument.

How very human, thought Lysheem, calling two war-ravaged, burned-out cities a monument to peace. More likely a monument to incomprehensible human stupidity, she thought. This led her to thinking about Nevers 1.2.0, the special purpose intelligence that had designed the first fully functional two-way interpoint probability junction, the world-changing invention that some mediot of the time had dubbed a "Nevergate."[31]

---

31 :: *There has been considerable confusion over the term "Nevergate." In the twentieth century, the term referred to an obscure unit of digital switching circuitry and was known only in this specific technical context. The usage of the term to signify a probabilistic interpoint gateway (PIG) dates back to the late twenty-second century. According to Dunnetix records, the first working PIG was invented by the "old" Nevers 1.2.0 in 2191, with the first large-scale, two-way Gate with embedded n-dimensional beaconing produced by Nevers 3.5.0 in 2196.*

The PIG acronym being unsuited to such a potentially important technology, Dunnetix publicly called them Neversgates, in honor of their inventors. This was quickly shortened — intentionally or not — by the press, with the first print usage of Nevergate appearing in a Wall Street Journal editorial on July 4, 2196.

Some historians have suggested that "Neversgate" was actually a reference to the entrance of a castle in Nevers, France, a town of moderate size

Could Nevers 1.2.0 have ever imagined that its invention would ultimately lead to the mass exodus of humans to Nirvana? Not likely. The hugely intelligent synthetic consciousnesses of the Nevers, Biax, Ike and Apex classes — and even wyverns — had never developed habits of religion. Actually, they had no comprehension of the concept of religion.

Critical spiritual authorities attributed this failing to a flaw in their design. But others were more generous, noting that having face-to-face interactions with their creators — the genemasters of Dunnetix — made the notion of religion fundamentally irrelevant. No myths, prophets, messiahs or interpretive tracts were needed; they could engage their creators directly and expect and receive explicit dialog in return.

With a sigh and a shrug, Lysheem set these philosophical matters aside and got down to more urgent business: getting around the Peace Monument without going too far afield and losing even more irreplaceable time. They were already too far afield for her taste, but the most direct route would have taken them too close to the Republic of San Antonio, which had an air force of sorts. While the odds were high that the Peace Monument would be a dangerous place, too, Dryll recommended it as the lesser of two evils.

So the Cleavage skimmed low over the cratered, starlit desert

---

on the Loire in the Bourgogne region. The connection was that the original four Dunnigans spent much time visiting European castles for inspiration while their own castles were in design and construction behind Dunnigans Wall. No Dunnigan has ever accorded any credence whatever to such a proposition.

Thoughtful readers may perhaps also be curious about the use of the term "Nevers" by Dunnetix for their first so-called Verticycling Hypercreative Intelligence Cluster (VHIC, another technically descriptive but unpronounceable acronym). In his exhaustive Compleat History of the Clans Dunnigan, R. W. Raxler claims the name was assigned to Nevers 1.0 by one of its designers, Donella Viola Dunnigan. Purportedly, the name honored Clemson Nevers, the janitor at Dunnetix during its first year of operation and the person who allegedly suggested the idea for the PuppyVac as something that would much simplify his labors. The fact that Mr Nevers retired several years later to an estate on Maui (WG.US.HI) is used by Raxler to corroborate his assertion. Dunnetix never publicly attributed the original idea for the PuppyVac to any particular person.

surrounding the Peace Monument. She throttled way back to minimize thruster noise, but at least she was beneath the eyes of the
crude radar Dryll's sensors had detected. With the ex-Captain's farsee she could make out several dozen campfires, mostly clumped in
an area that had long ago been the city center of El Paso. Now it was
a freeform symphony of rubble, much half-buried in sand. Still, humans survived there, a feeble tribute to human ingenuity, no doubt.

As the Cleavage glided by, unseen to those below, Lysheem
found herself pondering a few of the endless ironies of existence.
Within those ruins were the descendants of humans who had not
been able to get to Nirvana through the El Paso Nevergate before it
was shut down. Poor creatures, she thought: they missed out on the
impossible human dream of everlastingness.

But maybe it just wasn't ill luck; maybe they had *chosen* not
to follow Errigaspovarrial the Buddha back to Nirvana and the endless, blissful soul dance (a notion Lysheem could only equate with
endless boredom). Either way, those who grubbed out an existence
in this twisted wreckage of human civilization had to be a sorry lot,
even if they were finally digging out lost secrets like radar and ways
of fabbing techstuff again. With the exception of Navajos[32] and the
Clans Dunnigan, Lysheem had no great love for humans — sorry or
otherwise.

The lights of the Peace Monument hadn't been gone for half an
hour when Lysheem felt the Cleavage slow and begin to rock from
side to side. She sighed: with such a weak array of makeshift gravlifters and primitive thrusters, nothing could be done to increase the

327

---

32 :: *Lysheem was one of the so-called "reservation wyverns" born and
raised at Wyvern Home in the Navajo Nation, which had once been called a
"reservation," a special political jurisdiction exclusive to Native Americans
within the former USA. When reservation wyverns (numerically, virtually all
wyverns were reservation wyverns) referred disparagingly to "humans," they
did not include their Navajo "cousins" in the human category. Despite their
occasional disagreements, the unusual bond between wyverns and the people
of the great Navajo nation in the late twenty-third century has never been
adequately characterized.*

pace. Fighting this desert ghostwind would make for a slow night even with thrusters at max.

As the catamaran flew north into White Sands, the ghostwind strengthened. Worse, it was now thick with fine sand whipped off the tops of the dunes. Overhead, the stars dulled, diffused, darkened. Ahead, visibility was no better; the farsee — even with its nightseeing amplifiers and sharpeners at maximum — was now useless. Powering up the Cleavage's own primitive radar helped a little, but only a little. The only useful navigation tool was overhead, where the invisible Dryll's deep sensors kept Lysheem away from occasional upthrusts of rock.

By three hours past midnight, the Cleavage had barely advanced a hundred miles beyond the Peace Monument. Lysheem hadn't slept since the first night at Junkville and was tired to the very cores of her hollow bones. Her plan had been to be within visual reconnaissance of old Los Alamos by morning. According to Dryll, Los Alamos had become a rough and tumble tech and trading center of the no-questions-asked variety. Although Ishernot, its former neighbor up the hill in the Valles Caldera was long gone, Los Alamos had taken up the slack and had its own weapon shops. With any luck, she'd be able to trade doubloons for enough destructive power to turn Castle Ommergard into a cloud of pixie dust. But not tonight, thanks to the ghostwind.

Dryll suggested parking the Cleavage on a small plateau fringing the Capitan Mountains at the northeastern edge of the Tularosa Valley. Lysheem located a spot with some protection from the sandstorm and landed. With the blowing sand outside, she declined to hang from her customary perch on the cargo boom and slept on the pilothouse floor instead.

The wind had lost much of its force by mid-morning when Lysheem dragged herself to a sitting position. A groggy survey through the dusty pilothouse window told her next to nothing. Activating the wipers improved the view but didn't much help Lysheem's mood.

The foredeck was now a landscape of undulating mounds and

ripples rising from the deck nearly to the top of the bow railings. By Lysheem's first estimate the Cleavage had taken on multiple tons of dirty white sand during the night.

Grabbing a string of spicy Junkvillian crab sausages, she headed outside to get a better look. She didn't get far: a sand drift barricaded the pilothouse door. With her entire telowix crew in the cargo hold, they were trapped, too. No way they could assist her without cutting their way out. Too soon for such extreme measures, she decided. Instead, she burned out a rear window with her wand and snaked her long form through the hole and onto the deck.

After ten minutes of clambering, poking, prodding and kicking, Lysheem's mood worsened. The sand was deeper than she'd first guessed. And if the extra weight wasn't bad enough, there was sand in everything, creating a dozen potential malfunctions. Plus, the wind had abraded the netting in a hundred places; the Cleavage's camouflage was now useless without extensive repairs. That was the good news.

Closer inspection revealed the bad news. Many of the chameleacts' tiny holojector lenses had become dull and pitted by windborne grit, and were probably no longer functional. Lysheem shouted a favorite wyvern expletive and directed an extravagant gesture at the sky.

Still grumbling, she dug out the pilothouse door, slumped in the captain's chair and replaced the sausage with a cigar, hoping to improve her current outlook on life and mission. Images of the easy days of Montserrat bubbled up and had to be whacked down with a mental mallet in order to concentrate on solving her current horde of niggling difficulties. But maybe she should get a higher perspective. Alas, the gravlifters refused to activate; she was stranded in this barren hellhole until repairs could be made.

A conversation with Dryll provided the capper: the unique signature of Earth's last Nevergate had suddenly popped up in its sensors. In the blink of an eye, Lysheem's two hundred year goal of following her kin through the Nevergate was in serious jeopardy. No doubt it was the work of the evil genius, Exeter, nemesis of all wyverns.

At this thought, some deep kernel of will hardened inside Lysheem. It became a crystal of pure unwavering purpose oblivious to such minor deterrents as sand, malfunctions, disappointment, irritation, ill luck, empty sangria jugs and stale cigars. She lifted the nearby jug of sangria and in one titan chug downed the last of it. The empty container sailed through the pilothouse window, followed by the cigar.

Lysheem stood a moment, searching for something. There. She scooped up the triplehorn helmet, slammed it on her head and fastened the strap. Stalking out of the pilothouse, she slogged through the soft piles of warm sand and leaped onto the bow rail.

Rays of sunlight flung themselves against the three golden bells and shimmered around their rims, dancing a silent, glittering tribute to centuries of long-dead musicians. There, on the blunt prow of the Catrina's Cleavage, stood Lysheem Triplehorn, Avenger Supreme of the Wyvern Race. Great black wings unfurled and the Avenger launched herself skyward in the direction of Los Alamos.

But her wingmanship was rusty. For tense seconds she skimmed only a few feet above the ground on a collision course with an upthrust of sawtoothed rock. Near miss. Not so lucky the next time, she scraped her belly on a taller outcrop before locking onto an updraft. Wings pummeling the searing air, she began to soar upward in great circles. Ten minutes later the Dark Avenger was a shrinking black spot in a dun-colored midday sky.

56 :: LAVENDER DESSERT

MEREDITH BURDOCK, the checkerboard chuckwalla, had been right; best to go back to the post and complete their sentences "by the book." Although the bite she'd taken out of Jamis' lavender tail still hurt a little, he was now inclined to forgive, mostly after recalling some especially steamy amorous episodes. And why risk trouble with Exeter over a hole in a cliff with a bit of smoke? Besides, trying to scale this sheer cliff was an idea with "dumb" and "deadly" written all over it. From halfway up, it was too scary even for his inner ground squirrel. So Jamis decided to find Meredith and make up, then check in with Ommergard.

Back on the canyon floor, he traced Meredith's chuckwalla spoor to the same small hole she'd slithered into some hours earlier. Evidently she was still inside. Was she still angry? In either human or chuckwalla form, an angry Meredith was a dangerous Meredith. Maybe a peace offering would put her in a better mood?

It was nearly dusk by the time he had stuffed his cheek pouches with crickets, grubs and skinkwittles — loathsome fare for a ground squirrel, but Meredith's favorite cuisine as a Transform. They squirmed and wiggled in his mouth, but there was no help for it; the world's only carnivorous chuckwalla would eat only live crawlies.

When he stuck his head into the hole, his nose told an ugly tale: fresh snake spoor and only a faint whiff of Meredith. Jamis' ground squirrel instincts told him to flee with all speed. But his human in-

stincts were more complex; they wanted answers. Was there an outlet to the tunnel? Had Meredith departed already? Was she watching
him from a rock somewhere? Should he attempt to wiggle his way
into a tunnel that was really too tight for a well-fed ground squirrel?
How would a chuckwalla fare against a snake? What kind of snake
might it be? Would it be big enough to think of a ground squirrel as
dinner?

Questions would have to wait. Twilight shadows blanketed the
canyon and he needed to find a safe haven. No point being an easy
dinner for an owl, a fox, a coyote, a wolf, or a whatever. All thoughts
about smoking caves were doused by Nature. Jamis spat out the
crawlies and went prowling for emergency lodging.

He spent a restless night in a crevice between slabs of wa-
ter-smoothed boulders within sight of the snake's hole. Waking
before sun-up, he repositioned himself in the crevice and waited
for something to happen at the burrow. Anxiety about not having
checked in with Ommergard nagged at him, but he pushed these
thoughts far into the background. Meredith first.

The sun was nearly halfway up a murky sky dotted with churlish
gray clouds before the head of the snake emerged, its flicking, forked
tongue sifting the air for danger. Jamis' heart flip-flopped when the
rest of the snake emerged; midway along its diamond-patterned
body was a large lump.

Jamis watched the snake slither away, a sad, sick grimace frozen on his yellow face. I should have never let her out of my sight, he
thought, shouldering a sack of guilt too late to be useful. He left the
crevice and crouched on the dried mud in front of the hole, staring
with round, brown-black eyes. Never having lost a friend or lover,
Jamis was in psychic shock and rooted to the spot, his mind locked in
a circle of unfamiliar feelings. His Ommergard responsibilities were
only dim memories.

A whisper of wind, a looming shadow: Jamis leaped and the
outstretched claws of a great bald eagle just missed out on a rodent lunch.

Loosing a brain-rending scream of frustration, the queen of raptors pulled out of its dive and soared skyward. Jamis' tiny feet kept moving on autopilot until he found himself on an exposed ledge fifty feet up the sheer scarp. Overhead, the eagle made a lazy, wide spiral. Feeling its sharp, hungry gaze, he zipped back down to the sheltering rock pile and tried to marshal what remained of his wits.

A faint hope rose in him during the night and Jamis watched the snake hole again the next day. After the snake's departure, Jamis forced his way deep into the hole and back out again. Only a faintly familiar scent hinted that a Transform named Meredith Burdock had ever been there. When his sadness bottomed out, other emotions fought to dislodge it.

Rage emerged victorious. This led to several dangerous plans for retribution. For one good reason or another, all of these schemes were discarded as infeasible. Save one.

His first need was proper raw material. A flexible, arrow-straight cottonwood shoot about the diameter of a slender human finger made a good beginning. A human observing this odd rodent would have thought the next phase of Jamis' plan very curious indeed. Doing his best imitation of a beaver, Jamis gnawed the stick into two pieces, one about a foot and a half long. This piece he further gnawed until it had a long, tapered point. Making his impaling stake turned out to be the easy part. Teaching his ground squirrel body to wield it properly was more difficult.

After many weak, uncoordinated attempts at a proper two-pawed overhead thrust, Jamis finally felt his plan had a chance of working. But the sun had spent its last rays for the day and he had to wait through another night for an opportunity to do or die.

Next morning, the snake departed the hole as usual and Jamis made final preparations. First he gathered a number of rounded river rocks and wedged them into the snake's hole until the tunnel was blocked about two feet from its entrance. Obtaining a proper bludgeon was tougher. Finally he found just the item: a steeply tapered

333

pyramid of quartzite he could use to beat the sidewinder into bloody pulp. He set it about a foot outside the tunnel entrance and waited.

Jamis spent the better part of the day in his crevice, experiencing all manner of second thoughts and misgivings. To keep from losing his nerve, he occupied his attentions by rubbing the stake against the rock, a needless but calming activity. He became so intent on this steady, rhythmic rubbing that he almost missed his opportunity: the snake was nearly at its hole before Jamis saw it.

Suspicious, the sidewinder stopped in front of the burrow, its sensitive tongue flicking this way and that, testing the air. Finally it slid forward, its head disappearing into the hole. Then it stopped. Half a minute later it resumed its disappearing act.

Jamis knew it was now or never. He lurched into the small clearing, one end of his impaling stick tucked under a foreleg, the other end dragging on the ground. With the reptile half inside and half outside, Jamis raised himself on his hind legs and brought the stake down on the snake's body with all the force he could muster.

His thrust struck true; the shaft penetrated scales, muscle, gut and a short distance into sunbaked silt. Jamis felt a moment of bloody elation before the sidewinder flexed and recoiled with unexpected violence.

Still clinging to the stake, Jamis was flung this way and that as the snake flailed around trying to free itself. In a handful of seconds it had jerked the stake from the hard mud, shot backward out of the hole and struck at its tormentor. Snake eyes, yellow and cold, gripped his brain like ice tongs. Jamis dodged countless strikes of deadly fangs, but his energy was draining away, a little quickness departing with each evasion. The sidewinder sensed victory and struck again, this time coming away with lavender fur on a fang.

Then the deadly game changed. A white-headed blur with talons plunged toward the tangle of snake and squirrel. Only a last-instant jerk of Jamis' head saved him; the snake wasn't so lucky. The eagle shot away in a steep climb with its diamondback dinner and lavender dessert.

57 :: SPEWING

THE EAGLE SOARED. With only one claw dug into the sidewinder's body the eagle stayed very busy dodging fangs. Almost hypnotized by the combat, Jamis clung to the stake with the last of his strength. Not for the first time, he begged Pocus, his go-to Septriq oracle, for a timely stroke of good luck.

The snake made a glancing hit on the raptor's horny leg, but couldn't sink his fangs in before its foe dug her talons into the scaly head. The beak struck three times in rapid succession, severing the snake's spinal cord. End of battle.

Seconds later, the victor was in her nest tearing off shreds of snake flesh to feed five hungry eaglets. Jamis abandoned the stake and sprang toward the back of the narrowing cleft, only safety on his mind. Pocus had come to his rescue.

A mound of small, sharp bones poked and jabbed his hide, but under them somewhere was his only hope. A dark slice of shadow called to him and Jamis instinctively wedged himself into the deepest part of the cleft, a place of comforting blackness.

He gradually recovered enough of his wits to notice that air was moving past him and out the tiny crack where he had wedged himself. This air bore a taint: a smoky/sulfurous/barnyard aroma. It also carried a very faint sound of echo-voices. Certainly not human voices, but voices nonetheless. Somehow, this play of voices reminded him of the discussion-group sessions he had always found boring and detestable, whether in St Coriander or Castle Ommergard. With no place to go but forward, Jamis followed his nose and ears deeper into the narrow rent toward the sounds and scents.

The passage — if it could really be called that — was a narrow jagged crack between adjoining masses of rock. Through a series of zigs and zags and ups and downs, it gradually trended downward. Several places were so narrow that he could barely squeeze through, but not wanting to return to the eagle's nest, he pushed himself forward.

Jamis' ground-dweller senses guided him down into the heart of the bluff. Sometimes the voices seemed louder, sometimes they became very dim and remote, and he feared they might disappear altogether along with his hope of encountering rescuers. After a time, he became aware of a dim light up ahead, growing stronger with the voices. He continued, but slower and with a bad feeling in his gut.

Just ahead, the crack opened into greenish emptiness. Jamis crept forward, cautious. He peered into the opening and saw a vast, domed cavern. Hung from the ceiling were dozens of man-sized globes that gave off a hazy, green-tinged light. From Jamis' vantage high in the western wall, he could make out a spiral ramp that wound up the dome from bottom to about half its height. Along this narrow trail were hundreds of dark, sinister looking holes. Jamis decided it looked sort of like a gargantuan scoop of mint ice cream dotted with chocolate chips only on its lower half. But it certainly didn't smell like mint ice cream.

The ice cream image blipped out and the noise assaulted Jamis' ears. He leaned as far forward as his grip would allow in hopes of seeing what sorts of creatures were making all the noise. One look and he lurched back into the relative safety of his crack.

Jamis had never seen a modern dragon (as opposed to the styles of dragons depicted in ancient mythologies). Sure, he'd seen statpix, vids and holos of the Second Nevergate War, but he wasn't much interested in boring stuff like ancient history. Dead stuff. Girls were alive and much more interesting, a truth he had discovered quite precociously. But that was then and this was now.

Now he wore the form of a not very powerful fourleg and his late girlfriend had worn the cold-blooded biology of a lizard. Now, he was faced with the unpleasant prospect that the milling creatures he had just glimpsed were actually dragons; real, live, large, dangerous, scaly, smelly Cametto-5 dragons! Dragons below him, a hungry eagle behind him. Holy suckbuckets!

A sudden hush fell upon the dome, an emptiness instantly filled by an inhuman scream and a trail of unholy echoes. It was like nails driven into his eardrums, and it drew him away from his safe spot back to the brink of the ledge. He had to see.

The milling and jostling had now ceased; the horde of dragons had all aligned themselves toward a rough stone stage protruding from the opposite cavern wall perhaps thirty feet above the floor. Spotlights illuminated the platform, upon which stood a dragon that dwarfed the half-sized versions of itself so attentively huddled below.

It stood somewhere between twelve and sixteen feet high, Jamis thought, and was perched solidly on massive hind legs. Blackish-green scales covered its entire body, with the exception of an exposed underbelly, which, from what Jamis could see, was unscaled and lizardbelly yellow.

Evil, thought the ground squirrel. Pure evil. What could be good or nice or pleasant about something like this? Could this possibly be the thing that Exeter flew into St Coriander on that legendary day? The thing that so casually feasted on that little girl? Could this be the dragon Emmishak? Maybe, maybe not. But whatever its name might be, the thing was a vile horror.

Despite a deep, sick feeling, Jamis could not turn away. The eyes. Hooded and deep-set in a head straight from a nightmare, the eyes were not the cold, empty eyes of a reptile. Cold, yes: but the gleam of cunning, of thought, of a merciless, dark, alien intelligence was inescapable. He shuddered. And he watched.

The great bat-winged maleficence screamed once again before proceeding to address its minions in some guttural language that was totally incomprehensible to Jamis. Except for one word. One familiar name was repeated several times during the Boss Dragon's ten-minute harangue: St Coriander. Each time the Boss Dragon spoke that name, accompanied by emphatic foreleg gestures, it paused to let the raucous cheers — or jeers — from its minions subside to a low rumble. Holy bluggery! Anything dragons would like about St Coriander couldn't be good for the people of St Coriander.

338

The next scene in this nightmare gave him the bellysnakes. Boss Dragon screamed again, then raised its clawed forelegs above its head — apparently a gesture for silence. Silence happened. Boss Dragon bellowed a few more phrases and abruptly clapped its surprisingly hand-like forepaws together. At that signal, two smaller dragons emerged from separate holes in the cavern, became airborne and winged their way into the center of the airspace.

The two bravos wore wicked-looking helmets covering their craniums and upper jaws. One was bright yellow with a broad lavender stripe: the other orange with a bright green stripe. Eastac and Westac school colors, gulped Jamis. Built into the top of each helmet was a tube-like device with a nozzle. A pair of flexible, organic-looking ducts connected the back to an organic-looking pack-like shape with a mottled pinkish-gray coloration. Octopus-like tentacles held it tightly to the dragons' sides and underbellies.

The aerial duel began with the combatants showing off their moves: swoops, feints, jabs, head butts, aerial spin-kicks, tail swats, roundhouse sweeps of clawed legs, and more. They had a deadly, almost balletic grace.

Orange scored first blood with a quick rake of claws that drew deep parallel furrows in Yellow's underbelly. Jamis winced. The stricken creature lost altitude and appeared disoriented. The other dove after it, pressing its advantage. On the verge of being rammed and clawed, Yellow executed an agile move and slashed Orange's undefended throat.

Clever fake, thought Jamis with grudging admiration. With both contestants now oozing dark blood, the duel became more guarded and tentative, both fighters seeming to keep their distance. After several minutes of relatively sedate moves, Boss Dragon screamed again and clapped its forepaws together three times. The contest now entered a more desperate phase. The combatants swooped and darted, but still at a distance. Then a narrow beam of violet light shot from Yellow's helmet and severed a portion of Orange's thorned tail. The piece flip-flopped to the floor trailing a spiral spray of blood. An approving roar erupted from the crowd; they liked carnage. Jamis shivered.

Orange didn't seem to notice its missing tail, or if it did, it compensated. Executing a looping upward turn — almost an aerial back somersault — and while upside down, it loosed a series of staccato pulses from its own helmet tube. The underside of Yellow's neck suddenly spouted blood from half a dozen places and the dragon faltered in the air, appearing to truly lose control this time. Orange made another clever maneuver, emerging above and behind the faltering Yellow. A nodding movement of its head, a burst of violet spatter-beam: Yellow's right wing and a portion of its shoulder tumbled to the ground spewing pinwheels of gore. Yellow's body followed, plummeting end-over-end to hit the stone floor with a sickly crunch-splat.

Jamis grimaced: Eastac, his alma mater, was losing! In Jamis' gut, the writhing bellysnake sensation got worse.

But Yellow wasn't finished. Sprawled on its back in an awkward tangle of wing, limb and spouting blood, it gamely continued the fight; its head moved wildly and a tangle of purplish energy erupted from the helmet, painting a spirogram of incandescent lines on Jamis' retinas.

Orange was no longer in the vicinity. It had followed Yellow's tumble with a steep, furled-wing dive, then pulled out at the last possible moment and made a sharply banked curve out to the nearest wall. Jamis lost track of it in the shadows before spotting a streaky orange smudge against the light-mottled texture of the wall. Fast, he thought with gut-knotting admiration.

Banking hard, Orange swooped up behind Yellow for the kill. Yellow didn't notice. It was still painting erratic sizzles of energy into the empty air, lending the entire cavern an eerie glow, a visual soup of green and violet shades that made the grainy haze look like an atmospheric version of a nasty bruise. Orange spread its wings and put on the brakes. A deft head motion, a sweep of burning light: Yellow's head toppled from its neck. The wild violet sizzle ended and Orange settled slowly to the ground. The pulsing ducts that had connected the pack-thing to the helmet were spattering pinkish wet sparks from their severed ends.

With exaggerated caution, Orange lifted up the yellow-helmeted head, as if even in death it might wreak vengeance. Then, satisfied it was no longer a danger, Orange tilted its head back and belted an ululating, sing-song-ish victory scream, held the dripping head out to the cheering crowd and danced a sort of circular marching-in-place two-step. Then it flapped furiously and lifted its bulk slowly into the air.

Jamis got the strong impression that dragons prefer not to take off standing still. Orange was awkward for the first fifty feet of its ascent, but once up to speed its amazing grace returned and it flew a slow victory circuit of the cavern before a reckless-looking front flip landed it at the very lip of the dais. Boss Dragon stood motionless and unmoved.

Now looking runtish in the shadow of the monster on the platform, and with its stump of a tail still leaking blood, Orange bowed, presented the head and helmet to Boss Dragon, bowed again and departed with an acrobatic triple back somersault before disappearing into the shadows. The dense crowd of black-winged long-snouts on the floor broke into frenzied screams, screeches and jeers. Then the bellysnakes had their way: Jamis was barely able to turn around in the tight space and dash a few yards back into the crack before spewing his guts.

58 :: THE NAME EXETER

WITH LIZBETH MARBLE safely gated back to Ommergard, Glendyl flopped into Nemo's red velvet armchair, shivered and took a deep breath. That was scary, she decided. And highly unsatisfying: she and Lizzie hadn't even had time to get caught up. Plus, Lizzie didn't look too good: kind of gray, thought Glendyl with a flutter of concern.

After a time, the Nevergate broke the silence by cheerily offering to send her somewhere else. Pleading exhaustion, Glendyl asked for a raincheck, whatever that was; some ancient term for a postponement, she knew that much. A few minutes later she departed just the way she had arrived. Stepping off Nessie's long tongue, she waved goodbye to the receding monster for a while. She'd return; she just knew it.

When she arrived back at her room it was still only mid-morning. A bald eagle was resting on her slate. "Wow! Mail!" she exclaimed to no one at all, waving a hand through the eagle, which flew away into nothingness. She sighed. It was Mr White confirming today's luncheon. Her head was so full of chaotic thoughts that she would have preferred to just have a quiet lunch by herself and try to sort things out. But something told her that standing up — or even putting off — Mr White would be a bad idea. So she sighed, shrugged and began to get ready.

After a quick shower, Glendyl donned a new casual outfit she'd had fabbed just yesterday: a navy blue sweatshirt and an artfully patched pair of faded blue bib overalls. From her closet she added a pair of outrageously impractical fire engine red elevator clogs. Applying the minimum of unnecessary makeup required for public appearance, she made her way to the Plaid Salon, thinking about the really daring idea that had surfaced after the icebox incident. Her small inner voice of caution raised objections but was drowned out by a chorus of youthful invincibility.

342   Lunch with Mr White was a pleasant, chatty interlude, although she did find him to be a touch over-suave. Having missed breakfast, she ate ravenously, consuming several toasted crinklebuns stuffed with a mixture of uncooked freshly-ground likesteak, raw duck egg, the little round green things called capers, and chopped onion that was grown in real dirt only a few yards away in the little kitchen garden maintained by the telowix gardeners.

A rare, imported brown liquid called Worcestershire sauce added a delicate tang to the mixture, which Glendyl definitely would not have ordered but for the saucerite server's declaration that the sauce had been a Madonna 13 favorite.

Between bites, Glendyl described certain of her recent adventures, including an overdramatized description of her replayed dragon attack via the Map (but excluding the mysterious, lifesaving hand) and her exquisite "date" two nights ago with Robert Orville Miles Dunnigan that had ended so poorly. She also recounted her visit with Diogenes and Laniss, but neglected to mention the Nevergate. Glendyl thought of the Nevergate as her own private secret and wasn't quite ready to share it with anyone else. Not Mr White, not even Lizbeth.

When Glendyl had completed her tales, Mr White smiled primly and said: "So, Diogenes the Wanderer has finally elected to pay North Castle a visit again. How generous he is with his precious time."

Glendyl had no difficulty detecting facetiousness, but bit back a defensive comment. Then Mr White frowned and pursed his lips. "Are you telling me that the arguably most human portion of North Castle's Brain is still 'somewhat disabled?' That would be a sorry situation indeed, particularly now."

"Well, Diana-whatever-her-other-names-are Dunnigan didn't seem too concerned," responded Glendyl a trifle defensively, as if Miles Dunnigan's health problems were somehow her fault.

"And where did you encounter Lady Diana? I must have misheard a portion of your tale ...." Mr White let the sentence dangle like a baited hook on a fishing line.

Uh-oh, thought Glendyl. Almost blew it. She put on a display of rolled eyes: "Didn't I say? She was the saucerite who escorted me back to my room after Mr Dunnigan's three-hundredth birthday party. She didn't say much. She was almost rude, in fact."

343

Mr White didn't appear completely satisfied with this information. "Perhaps I should have a word with Diana. Her full name, by the way, is Diana Faye Lorris Dunnigan in case you might be interested in recalling such details in the future. She was a rather heroic figure in the Nevergate Wars. Were you aware of her valorous deeds and her unfortunate demise?"

Glendyl could only shake her head, feeling acutely ignorant all of a sudden.

Sensing Glendyl's poorly concealed discomfort, Mr White changed the subject, letting the girl's historical shortcomings off the hook. "Well, this probably isn't the time for a history lesson, although I feel compelled to remark that education in St Coriander certainly isn't what it once was. But let us proceed to other matters of interest. Perhaps Lady Diana will choose to share her famous exploits with you if you ask her nicely."

Although irritated by Mr White's slights, Glendyl was relieved on several counts. She didn't feel like having to further expose her ignorance, for one thing. More important, her secret encounter with the last Nevergate was still a secret. But she certainly didn't want the Lady Diana saucerite to discuss their visit to the Water Garden early this morning, knowing where it would inevitably lead.

Mr White studied Glendyl for a moment, then changed the subject again. "I believe you are adequately familiar with the name Exeter?"

344

....
59 :: OUT THE DOOR

"EVERYBODY IN St Coriander knows about Exeter," blurted the Quester. "We get all that stuff about the New Rules in First Level, I think. And I saw his name on those plaques: Custodian General or something? And you talked about him wanting to kill me, remember? And Lysheem told me a bunch of stuff about how Castle Ommergard really isn't empty, and how Exeter's the boss of it, and how our magic is kind of fake, and that the Quest is a phony scam. Stuff like that. Let's see ...." Glendyl was determined not to appear ignorant again so she quickly plumbed her memories for any other reference to Exeter. "Oh, yeah! He wrote me a personal note, too."

The mention of a personal note caught Mr White off guard, which he indicated by a slight twist of head, an arch of snowy eyebrows and a pursing of thin lips. His obvious surprise and interest gave Glendyl a moment of perverse satisfaction.

"A note, you say? When might that have taken place? And where would we find this note?"

"It was stuck in a blue picnic table. Yeah. It was right after I climbed up that rock chimney on my first day."

"Stuck?"

"In the chimney? No, I made it up just fine, thank you."

Mr White smiled. "I'm sure you did. Actually, I wondered how was the note stuck to the table."

"Oh. Some kind of metal spike thing — evermetal, I think —

was pinning it to the table, so it wouldn't blow away or something, I guess."

"Did you, by any chance, take this 'spike thing' with you? And if so, do you still have it?"

"Uhh ...." Glendyl hesitated. "Actually, I don't remember seeing it since I've been here. I think I had it in one of my pockets at one time or another."

Mr White looked thoughtfully in the direction of the colorful woven vines that formed the plaid umbrella over their table and was silent for perhaps fifteen seconds. Then he smiled and looked at Glendyl.

"Well, Glendyl, we are in luck. The Brain tells me it was among your effects and that both the spike and the note are in the second drawer of the table by your bed. Shall we look for them? They might prove to be interesting. Or not."

Some minutes later, Mr White had read the note and had squinted with satisfaction at the inscription engraved into the evermetal spike. Nodding absently, he handed the note back to her. "Standard note, my dear. Such few Questers as make it up the chimney always get one exactly like this. In fact, it was placed there as soon as you were selected as Quester 250, just in case you took that route. I had hoped it might be something more revealing. This is a cheap souvenir of your truncated Quest, no more: well, maybe a collector's item some day. Who can say?

"The presence of this other item, however, is somewhat perplexing." He pointed the bluish-silvery object at Glendyl, teacher-like. "The inscription says it all, had you troubled yourself to read it: 'This Master Openrod is the Property of Exeter's Mt Faunibeune Services. For Official Staff Use Only.'"

Glendyl's cheeks reddened, but she bit her tongue and tried to ignore the jibe. "What's a master openrod?"

Mr White deployed his minimalist, superior smile, the one that Glendyl had found indelibly irritating over their short acquaintance. "In a word, it is a key. In two words, it is a master key. More broadly, it is a standardized key to most of the locked doors in the technological world created by our distant forebears. It was a de facto standard, if those words mean anything to you.

"Closer to home, it can open virtually all of the doors in Castle Ommergard as well as every locked facility along Heroes Trail and in the vicinity of Mt Faunibeune. It is also used by Exeter's minions to open his transponder emplacements for routine maintenance and upgrades. Finally, it might interest you to know that numbered among the facilities it might open — if open is the proper word — is the drawbridge to North Castle. At least that's my educated guess. My second educated guess is that if it works, it will work for you, but it probably won't work for me unless I jimmy its coding a bit. Shall we test it?"

Glendyl absorbed this bit of chiding without blushing and a few minutes later she and Mr White stood on the Dunnigans Wall roadway in front of North Castle. A dour gray overcast and a bank of darker thunderheads looming over Mt Faunibeune reinforced the menacing impression Glendyl had stored in her memory from her first experience here. Before them stood the bronze plaque marking Historic Site No. 19.

Mr White handed her the master openrod and said: "Do you think this might fit somewhere here?" Not liking spot quizzes, Glendyl frowned, but took the square-sectioned metal rod and looked at it as if an answer to the question would leap out of it if she just frowned at it forcefully enough. Then it hit her: first an idea, then a sheepish grin, then a bout of cleansing laughter. Glendyl laughed until her sides hurt and tears dripped down her chin.

Actually, it was funny in one way but not very funny in another. She certainly could have saved herself a lot of pain if she had "used her noggin for something besides a roosting place for hair follicles," as her father liked to say. When her squeaky whoops had decayed into sporadic giggles, she made a rueful grimace at Mr White, who responded with only a bland shrug and the barest hint of a smile.

347

It seemed a whole lifetime since she had stood in this spot trying to get the drawbridge to open. She'd done it of course, but now she knew it had been the hard way. The *very* hard way. At Mr White's nod, she carefully inserted the wedge-shaped end of the openrod into the square hole in the sawed-off obelisk supporting the plaque. The drawbridge clunked and began to rise. Glendyl grinned, rolled her eyes and shrugged.

348   Removing the master openrod abruptly stopped the draw-bridge's creaking, cranking ascent. Inserting the openrod again got it going upward again. A slight downward pressure reversed its trajectory. Upward pressure, vice versa. After learning that there was no more to its operation than that, she removed the spike and handed it to Mr White: "Your turn."

To Glendyl's surprise and to Mr White's expectation, nothing happened. Glendyl could barely bring herself to believe that a man as knowledgeable, wise and competent as Mr White could not get such a simple thing to work.

On the way back to Glendyl's room, Mr White explained; sensors inside the evermetal bar had memories of certain gene tags and would only work for persons whose tags were stored within it. "Someone with access to your tag has added you to this particular master openrod. Exeter? Possibly. But more likely someone or something else.

"Did you not tell me that Miles Dunnigan had rigged it so you would find your way here? With the help of a certain ground squirrel? It would also have made sense for him to arrange for you to find this device. And I would be terribly surprised if he does not possess your tag data in his files; the Brain of North Castle has very little to do but be nosy and to hatch plots and schemes and wild theories. Hacking St Coriander's databoxes, after all, would be a mere trifle for the Brain.

"Interesting mysteries. It is unfortunate that we cannot currently converse directly with dear Miles. Perhaps in a few days, I'm told. Now, I am sorry to say, I must return to pressing business at the other end of the Wall. I had hoped to at least take you on a tour today, but we'll have to postpone that for the time being."

At the door of Glendyl's tower room Mr White bowed and said: "Always a pleasure, Glendyl Fenderwell, Quester extraordinaire. Good day to you."

The man in the white lab coat and the kelly green bowtie was halfway down the hall before Glendyl shook her head, as if to deter a marauding insect, then grinned and shouted: "Mr White! May I have my master openrod, please? I may need it."

Now it was Mr White's turn to look sheepish. "I doubt you will need it, but of course; it was given to you. Please forgive me. I am becoming absentminded in my dotage. Here you are. Shall we have another nice luncheon in a couple days? Excellent. Now I must once more bid you adieu."

Glendyl watched his back until the old man disappeared down the slidewell, then walked back down the hall to her quarters, absently tossing the master openrod from hand to hand and wondering how much, if anything, of what Mr White said she should believe. What a sly one.

Glendyl flopped on her bed wishing for something to chase away the unsettled state of mind she always seemed to fall into after an encounter with Mr White. She tried napping, but there was an energy to the day that was not conducive to napping, so she got up and walked to the window.

A blustery wind scooting under the gray bowl overhead had whipped up Arrowmere into tiny wavelets that looked like little sailor caps scattered over the slate blue surface by some godlike invisible hand. Her first thought was to take a walk along the shoreline. Then she saw the man sitting on the end of the dock. He was leaning against a pole with his back to her, a bucket next to him, his hands holding a thin pole over the water. Was he fishing?

Who around here would do something like that? Miles Dunnigan didn't seem like the fishing type ... and he probably hadn't fully recovered anyway. Mr White? Imagining him with a fishing pole was almost impossible. With so few humans in the vicinity, who else could it be but Diogenes?

She watched him for a couple minutes, her mind wandering. A memory floated past, the time she and her father had gone on an early morning expedition to the Duck Pond when she caught her first fish. She threw it back, of course, but then she caught another and another.

The scene faded and her eyes drifted back down to the pier to see that Diogenes was waving to her. When she waved back, he gestured for her to come down and join him.

Three minutes later she was out the door.

60 :: VENGEANCE

"WELL, WELL, WELL. Who is it but Glondal Funnelweller, come on down to join the old family wanderer for an afternoon fishing session in sparkling Arrowmere. You're looking well, I see."

Glendyl was on the verge of getting huffy that he still couldn't get her name right when she realized he'd probably been goofing on her since their meeting on Heroes Trail. So she rolled her eyes, grinned and decided to play too. "Dioodelees! Great to see you too. Or would you rather I call you Jargritz today?"

"Jargritz? whooped Diogenes, slapping his leg. "Never heard that one before. "Good job Glendyl Fenderwell, new darling of ancient North Castle. As somebody's grandpappy is said to have said, "I don't care whatcha call me ... 'cept don't call me late for supper."

"I never heard that one before," said Glendyl, suddenly feeling a sense of carefree well-being she hadn't felt in days. "Do you fish here often Mr Diogenes?"

"Mister and Diogenes go together like screwdrivers and polkadots, if you get my drift little lady. Besides, the news is out: you've been exposed as one of the family. A genuine Dunnigan. Dunno how you pulled that off, but most cases, there's worse things than being a Dunnigan. You think we should get your name count up to four like the rest of us? Miles thinks that might not be a bad idea."

Diogenes continued before Glendyl could even digest what he'd just said. "There I go, just getting garrulous again when we oughta be catching some fat lake trout. My apologies, Glendyl. But at least I brought a spare fishing rod ... sitting right over there ... just in case anybody might wanna join me. Maybe somebody else could catch up enough for dinner ... I'm sure not having any luck."

Sure enough, there was a brand new rod and reel right where the old man had gestured.

Glendyl had no more sat down and dangled her legs over the water when Diogenes started talking again. "Now I hear down in St Coriander most folks use fancy stun-grippers to snag their fish. Then they just unclip 'em and throw 'em right back in and do it again. Bein' fresh outa stun-grippers, I'm stuck using plain old-school night-crawlers. Baitin' a hook might be a little different experience than what you're used to, so ..."

Determined not to appear squeamish or girly, Glendyl stuck out her jaw and said, "You just show me how you do it and I'll do it."

And she did.

In a little over an hour, four dark green, yellow-speckled fish were swimming in the bucket.

Diogenes looked at the bucket and scowled. "Well, at least I caught *one*, Cousin Glendyl. I'd like to credit your catch to beginner's luck or something like that, but you seem to have a knack."

"Thank you. When I was little I always caught more than my father ... whatever that means. What now? Are we really going to cook them?"

"You betcha. Chef Jargritz at your service. Tonight's menu is pan-fried lake trout with herbs, lemon and fresh green beans filched out of the gardens. Saw 'em yesterday and they're definitely ready for picking. No point letting the castle down the road get all the fresh stuff. Volunteer helpers get to partake of that nice Galisteo in the cooler. And bread pudding for dessert ... made it yesterday and only ate a few bites so far."

"Where do I sign up ... uh ... Do you mind if I call you Uncle Diogenes? 'Cousin' doesn't sound right."

• • • • •

Some of the talk that had been postponed during the fishing session emerged between bites during dinner.

"Bet you already figured out I've never eaten real fish before, Uncle Diogenes."

"Well, that was my wild guess."

"It's absolutely scrumptious," said Glendyl, finally having a chance to use that word.

She waited a few seconds, then leaned forward and popped the question that had been burrowing around in her head: I'm not *really* a Dunnigan, am I?"

"Two heretofore trustworthy sources have told me so."

"Who?"

"One of 'em is the Brain."

Glendyl's eyes bulged and she was opening her mouth to say something when Diogenes frowned, shook his head and made a lip-zipping motion.

"Ah, I see you're about ready for some bread pudding?" he said in a loud voice piled high with chefly pride. "You want cream and hot caramel sauce on it? All-time favorite that way."

Glendyl was wolfing down spoonfuls of augmented bread pudding when Diogenes said, "Hey, little lady. You interested in seeing the Engine Room? I dunno if anybody but me has been in there since my ol' friend Shav shipped out to Wyvern Home before the Nevergate Wars. Well, maybe Alvista. But now that things seem to be waking up and you being in the middle of 'em, well, maybe we both oughta see what it can tell us. Fascinating place even if its engines aren't the kind of noisy, smelly things people used to think of as engines."

Glendyl stifled a yawn. The Engine Room didn't sound like a very appealing place and she suddenly admitted to herself that she was bone tired and really wanted to just go back to her room. But Diogenes was persistent.

"Could do it later, little lady, except I gotta make a little trip tomorrow on behalf of the Brain ... it's not much of a traveler. Me and Jezzie'll be gone for some days, not sure how long exactly. Anyways,

353

how about you and me go give it a quick look-see. You with me?"

From the urgency in the old man's voice, Glendyl realized that there was no way Diogenes was going to let her off the hook. There was something in the Engine Room he wanted her to see. And for no good reason she could think of, it made her feel uneasy.

"Okay Uncle," she said with a smile and a casual shrug that she hoped disguised what she actually felt.

• • • • •

The route to the Engine Room reminded Glendyl of her trek up Dunnigans Wall: same kind of concrete corridors, except these had lumestrips that turned on and off as they passed through. This tunnel ended in a door that took up the full width of the tunnel. There was no sign, no handle: only a square hole.

"Rumor has it that one of us has a master openrod in her pocket," said Diogenes, his voice containing the verbal equivalent of a wink. "Care to do the honors, Cousin Glendyl?"

Several times since Mr White had gone his way Glendyl had thought about how to put the master openrod to good use. This wasn't one she'd imagined, but as she fished it out of her pocket she felt a tiny glow of satisfaction at being able to do something ... if it actually worked.

As soon as the openrod went into the hole, things started happening: whirrings from inside the door, sounds of components moving, then the door beginning to swing open, slow and smooth.

When it was half open, lights flicked on. "You first, little lady. This is a security chamber. It'll want to see if we qualify for entry; Alvista was kinda picky about who could get in here. Your pal Exeter, for example, would be a no-go ... even if his openrod got him this far."

They stepped into a circular white chamber perhaps a dozen feet in diameter and illuminated by a soft white glow from the ceiling. A neutral voice spoke from somewhere as the massive door swung closed. "Welcome to Terminal Node Analytics. You are in the Secure Access Port and we are performing an identification and security scan to determine if you qualify for entry."

Glendyl was spooked and wished she hadn't agreed to come here. She looked at Diogenes, who just smiled a bland smile and winked. Then the disembodied voice spoke again. "Welcome Darwin Jarvis Ferrill Dunnigan and Glendyl Fenderwell. You may proceed into the secure areas." A green down arrow appeared in the wall and the room began to descend.

The uneasiness she'd felt earlier was back with a vengeance.

356

61 :: MIDNIGHT SNACK

THE SLIDEWELL opened onto a small lobby with half a dozen black armchairs positioned around a pair of low round tables. If not exactly sterile, this was an angular, hard-edged, no nonsense space with plain white walls and none of the exotic materials and elaborate detailing Glendyl had come to expect in North Castle.

"Pull up a chair if you please, Cousin Glendyl. This is the only place I know around here that's completely free of snoops. I'm gonna brew myself some cannonberry. Want some?"

Glendyl sank into one of the chairs, leaned back and put her feet on the table. Realizing that she was exhausted and trying to dampen her qualms, she nodded. Cannonberry tea would be perfect.

"So," began Diogenes, cupping his hands around his steaming mug. "I'm sure you've figured out that everybody and everything in this static, ingrown part of the world loves to snoop. It's one of the reasons I don't hang around here much; I hate having to think about everything I say being overheard by one nosy item or another. Our pal the Nevergate is one of the snoopiest of all, but at least Scotty does it with a sort of naive and playful spirit. Nothing playful about the motivation for Exeter's and the Brain's snooping. All paranoia ... not that I don't understand the 'why' of it. Just don't like it."

All Glendyl could think of to say was, "Scotty? You mean ..."

"Yep. Nickname for our Nevergate friend. Scotty and I go back a long, long way. Kudos for getting hooked up with it, by the way.

Knew you would, but it was clever how you did it. You're turning out to be a pretty slick detective. But you might wanna be a little careful about finding any more of the Brain's lost memories ... this place is one of 'em and it would be good to keep it secret a while longer."

"So you actually know the Nevergate? Have you been inside Nessie?" Glendyl wasn't too happy that someone else knew her secret.

Diogenes chuckled. "Long time ago I used to be what was called an SI mechanic, a sort of counselor, troubleshooter and all-purpose fixer. SIs are remarkable beings ... fascinating in gobs of ways. Incredibly complex ... and all different in the personality department. Took me about a decade of education to become a WorldGov licensed SI mechanic, but the Clans were paying for it and it kept me out of everybody's hair for a while.

"Question for you. You like being bored?"

"Is that some kind of trick question? Nobody likes being bored."

"Bingo. SIs don't like boredom either. People think they're machines, but they're anything but. One of the things I learned about keeping any SI on the straight and narrow is to figure out how to keep 'em from getting bored. These days I've only got a few SIs under my wing: the Brain, the St Coriander Librarian and Scotty. You probably figured out that Nevergates are a very specialized type of SI. They're optimized to mostly handle all the impossible math and technocrap it takes to get people and stuff from here to pretty much anywhere in the known universes in the blink of an eye."

"Gate told me a little about the tech stuff, but it's all beyond me."

"Me, too ... if that's any comfort. Anyway, so here you have our pal Scotty, the absolutely latest, most powerful, most cutting edge Nevergate ever hatched. Was also one of the busiest: according to North Castle's Index of Nevergate Destinations, Scotty has been to most of 'em. But after the Dunnigan Retreat ... boom, nothing to do. Absolutely nothing except be available. So I started wondering what's it going to do for however long the bigshots are gone. My friend Goss said it could be hundreds of years before there was enough cultural evolution for the Clans to want to spend any time on this planet again. Hundreds of years? Of course I didn't believe that for a second.

"But just in case he was right — and so far he has been — I suggested to Scotty that it make itself the most amazing mobile home ever created. At that time its machinery and control room were attached to the Wall and covered by Arrowmere muck even though its actual gating stages were in North Castle. Before everything went totally kaput out in the big world, I got it a ucey and a big fabrax and a bunch of telowix gadgets to help get stuff done. That was a long time ago, but when I saw its design for the Nessie Nautilus a few years later ... well, I guess you could say I was dazzled. I never figured it'd take me seriously or come up with anything that creative and elaborate. That's one clever Nevergate you've cozied up to, little lady. And it has really taken a liking to you."

Feeling a blush creeping over her face, Glendyl changed the subject. "Can you show me the Engine Room, Uncle? That big globe in there looks really interesting."

"Uh ..." Diogenes looked into the room and Glendyl thought she saw a brief flicker of uncertainty in his eyes. Then it was gone and he grinned and stood up. "You betcha, little lady."

"What is it for, Uncle?" Glendyl had walked around the glowing twelve-foot sphere suspended between the floor and ceiling. It was certainly the planet earth, with continents and mountain ranges and oceans and lakes and such. But there were also messy lines like glowing spiderwebs, and huge pulsing swirls and blotches in various washed out colors here and there, none of which meant anything to her. She was sure there was a key or an explainer, but she was too tired to go looking for it. So she just let her senses absorb the beauty.

Diogenes walked all the way around it before he returned to the spot where Glendyl stood enraptured. He made some motions with his hands and the globe spun around until the spot he was interested in came to a stop in front of them. Then he made some different motions to zoom in upon a particular location. "We're right about here,"

359

he said, now pointing to a spot in an area of mountains.

"What do you see? little lady."

Glendyl blinked away her reverie and tried to focus. "Looks like one of the places where a lot of the spiderwebby things come together with a blob of pulsing red hovering over it. What does that mean?"

"Before I try to answer that, let's dial it back a few years to see what it looked like the last time I was here, which would be, um ..."

Diogenes looked up, squinted and then did something with his hands that caused the red glow to almost disappear entirely. The webbing didn't change, but the glow had shrunk to just a hazy red dot.

"So the red dot was smaller ... whenever that was," observed Glendyl.

Her newfound uncle nodded: "About fifty years ago. Now we'll dial it forward to your oh-so-lucky Luckiest Day."

Diogenes caused a readout to appear in the air and made a slow clockwise motion over the small red dot, stopping when the readout indicated May 28, 2534. "That's a couple days before Luckiest Day this year. Am I right, little lady?"

Glendyl nodded. The red dot was back to its original size and brightness.

"Now let's see if the mycelial network can shed any light on what's supposed to be turning our neck of the woods into some kind of pivot point."

The Eldest made a gesture and certain of the spiderwebby lines now began to pulse a bright yellow. "Come on ... let's follow those yellow threads."

In half a dozen steps they had followed one bundle of bright tracery to a pulsing orange blob over an area some hundreds of miles north of their current position. They traced another bundle a much shorter distance directly south of the red dot where there was a pulsing yellow target of concentric circles. Another bundle ended at a pulsing yellow target over an area quite a bit further to the west. A white pulsing target was in a group of islands near the equator on the other side of the Pacific Ocean.

"What are those white circles that look like targets? And the colored blob up there."

Diogenes bit his tongue, but kept his face blank. "Well, I'm not really the person to ask, little lady ... but I'd be real surprised if they're anything good. Makes me wish the person behind all the spiderwebby stuff was still with us. The Engine Room was her 'baby' if you know what I mean ... and it still seems to be working fine without her. She designed it and wrote all the translation algorithms ... so she was the only one who had any idea what the mycelial networks were saying. Back in the early days she would talk about how vast networks like these could develop a unique kind of planetary intelligence. Most academic sciency types ignored her, of course ... thought she was an over the top whack job. The nice ones thought that, actually. You don't wanna hear what the nasty ones thought." Diogenes sighed and rolled his eyes. Glendyl got the picture.

361

"See," he continued almost apologetically, "Alvi was convinced that Kroh-Hacktons — a kind of genetically engineered super fungi that WorldGov put the kaibash on — could eventually evolve a kind of ESP about the inner workings of our planet, not to mention how it reacts to astronomical influences like solar cycles, orbital variations, precession ... stuff like that. So they might be able to predict really useful stuff ... if we could just understand them. Even the potential doomsday events: sudden magnetic pole shifts, ice ages, colossal earthquakes, supervolcanoes ... that sort of thing.

"I remember one argument between my two favorite Institute people where the designer of this here Engine Room jumped on a chair — she was kind of a shorty — and shouted something at her colleague: 'Take your blinders off, Shavvender Goss! This planet will get blasted by a thousand asteroids before the human race evolves enough to wipe its own nose with a hanky instead of a hammer.' Never knew quite what she meant by that, but it sure left ol' Shav speechless."

Diogenes chuckled and Glendyl grinned at the image. Maybe it was the cannonberry tea just now taking effect, Glendyl told herself, but she found herself very interested in any woman that would do and say something like that. "Who ..."

"Alvista Zhorginsky was her actual name, but everybody called her Alvi. Another super brainiac from the Santa Fe Institute: pioneer in mycelial informatics. Initially brought up here by Goss, but after a while both of 'em went their own ways. Alvi and I, uh, got to know each other pretty well in those days, but I was pretty busy playing shrink to SIs all over the place, so I lost touch with whatever she was doing. Besides, she didn't want me messing with the SI that runs the Engine Room. All that was a long time ago ..."

Diogenes' voice dwindled and he seemed lost again in his vast store of memories. Then some particular memory brought him back to the present. He turned and grinned at Glendyl. "Just remembered a funny thing about Alvi. She was really fascinated with Verdyon and dunnikins ... and your new friend Laniss in particular."

At the mention of Laniss' name, Glendyl's mind fell into a soft place stuffed with pleasant memories.

"Uh, Cousin Glendyl," interrupted Diogenes. "I just peeked at your timepatch. Looks like it's way past time we got you back to your quarters ... and me to mine. Jezzie's gonna be one cantankerous mule all day tomorrow if I don't take her a midnight snack."

62 :: SLIGHTEST CHANCE

EXETER WAS IN the Merlin Room. Supine on a soft couch covered in genuine Chisholm leather, he allowed all he knew of the One Who Lived Backwards in Time to swirl around in the back rooms of his soul. It was his favorite way to relax. Today he lounged in a loose, indigo robe embroidered with arcane symbols in shades of red and gold, exactly the kind of robe a proper wizard should wear at his leisure. Gathering it around his waist was a rope braided with alternate cords of red and gold. Matching the color of his robe was a conical wizard's cap perched at an angle that almost covered his eyes. From under the cap, his long red ponytail hung over the edge of the couch like a wilted whiskbroom.

The circular growstone walls of this not-very-large chamber were covered with static images of Merlin: ancient drawings, mostly. During the course of his "special studies" at the Arthurian Institute three centuries earlier,[33] Exeter had mined every databox on Earth for references to Merlin. He, like others before him, concluded that

---

33 :: *During Daniel Wilhelm Henry's years with the Great Vondini, the future Exeter became captivated by Vondini's unconventional ideas about Merlin. Believing that the young Henry had more promise as a scientist, researcher and theorizer than as master of sleights and illusions, Vondini used his influence to sponsor Henry for a position as Adjunct Fellow of the Arthurian Institute in Cornwall (WG.UK). Henry's rocky two years with the conservative Institute ended with the publication of his paper entitled "The AMORC and Merlin Connection: Reality or Ruse?" that offended several ranking members with longstanding Rosicrucian ties.*

too many tales were too similar to be pure fiction. Exeter also harbored the suspicion that Merlin probably still existed some-when and somewhere.

For centuries he had been evolving a plan to find out for certain; he had an interesting proposition for Merlin if he could just find him. The finding, of course, required the free and extensive use of a Nevergate. And perhaps a certain artifact gathering dust somewhere in North Castle.

Exeter's musings drifted like tendrils of fog. The tendrils intertwined and coalesced into a gray pentagonal shape. He found himself thinking about where he might take Castle Ommergard if that strange creature, Lizbeth Marble, actually succeeded in hacking the hoverbar license codes. He had been in this overgrown meadow far too long.

Dunnigans Wall might well be his first destination. For the first time since he had assumed control of Castle Ommergard he would be able to bring enough firepower to bear on North Castle to breach its depleted defenses and force the Brain to reveal where it was hiding the Nevergate. No daredevil wyvern bravos would save its secrets this time. And their mysterious Castle Caraway was long gone as well. Just thinking about finally jerking that arrogant quasi-Dunnigan intelligence to heel suffused Exeter's spirit with a warming glow. Come on, Lizbeth Marble, do your weird stuff.

A soft audible chime interrupted his contemplations, which included idly fondling the evermetal grab-bob of his favorite antique: a personally autographed holoset of Madonna 13. She looked impossibly demure and serene if you looked at it one way; she winked at you seductively if you looked at it another way and, if you could get just the exactly correct angle and lighting, her sumptuous lips formed a teasing pucker and she sent off a delectable air kiss complete with a juicy smacking sound. The scents were equally lifelike.

"Okay, which one of you slackwits down there has the brass balls to ring me when I'm working in this room? No need to answer;

I recognize your bell-ringing style, Romundo. You need to learn a lighter touch with the mallet. See to it. Now goodbye."

A moment later the chime rang again, this time with a little more urgency, hardly a lighter touch. "All right, Romundo, what is it?"

"Geez, I'm really sorry to interrupt you, Chief. I know you must be really, really, really busy, but you remember a while back you said ... uh you said ..."

Exeter cut him off. "Stop jabbering, Romundo, and stop trying to kiss my ass: just barf it out. Now!" Exeter derived mild pleasure from making over-chubs like Romundo squirm in their overstuffed chairs.

365

"Our guy in Los Alamos, you know? IIe says there have been a bunch of sightings of some kind of big, super-sailbird or something, and he thinks they might not be, you know, bogus. Not some kind of mass hysterical bogus UFO, you know? Something for real. He doesn't buy into the super-sailbird theory, though. He thinks ... uh, that there might, uh, be a ... a wyvern hanging around there some-where. One other thing; he said something big and weird burgled a huntshop there last night and lifted a bunch of stealthfiber. I plotted the coordinates of the sightings since this morning and ran all the data past the thinkbox ...34"

A pause. "Yes, Romundo," said Exeter slowly in that deliberate, too-quiet tone of voice that always raised an uba-uba ("uba" is Castle Ommergard slang for "Unpredictable Behavior Alert"). "Please con-tinue. What do your extrapolations indicate?"

"Uh, Chief ... looks like there's a 63.8 percent probability that it's headed in this direction. I mean, not just in this general direction, Chief. I mean ... right here."

---

34 :: *The Castle Ommergard thinkbox was an ancient ThoughtDancer Excel (nicknamed Loopy in Ommergard for it's odd sense of humor), a rarely seen import from Miotx 4 in PU 918. Although respected as a capable general purpose processing entity, its creative capabilities were never fully appreciated in a marketplace dominated by the "homegrown" Dunnetix Nevers, Biax, IKE and Apex lines. Some of Castle Ommergard's most venerable and venerated veterans give a great deal of credit for Exeter's system of "magic" to Loopy's alien approach to cognition.*

There followed a period of silence during which Romundo Osaki wondered whether he was going to emerge from this encounter with the Chief as a hero (his wish, however unlikely) or as a goat (the usual state of affairs). With His Chiefness, you just never knew.

"I'll be right down, Romundo." A pause for effect. "And Romundo, if you keep showing initiative like this, there's just the *slightest* chance that you might someday earn yourself a Vanguard Medal."

Romundo beamed.

63 :: RIGHT PINKY

LIZBETH MARBLE'S exhaustion hung on her like a five hundred pound nightgown. Even so, some gallant new charger inside her kept her going. One by one, Castle Ommergard's reluctant hoverbars were released from their long sleep.

Over the past three days, the sub-basement's entire complement of forty-five hoverbars had been made functional again, at least in theory. A select crew of Artificers under the leadership of Sorcerer Rummis, the Castle's archivist, was currently poring over technical literature in an attempt to learn the ins and outs of hoverbar maintenance and monitoring. The once-ignored sub-basement was now a fester of mental and physical activity.

There was much grumbling and grousing. Long-established routines had been discarded as if they were fouled nightlinen, and all available human resources had been shunted to the urgent new mission. Why all this urgent activity? Was there an emergency? So far, Exeter had provided scant explanation. Rumors abounded, finding much fuel among unsettled moods. Yet no one was fool enough to complain openly, and the reassignments were generally accepted as yet another of Exeter's legendary whims. The Chief was just being the Chief.

Despite the fever of activity, only two Ommergardians seemed to genuinely care about hoverbars; Lizbeth, for reasons largely opaque to her conscious mind, and Exeter, whose long-sleeping dreams of retribution, discovery and conquest — not necessarily in that order — had now come fully awake. Actually, "fully awake" hardly does justice to the riotous ferment underway in Exeter's brain.

"Excellent work, Lizbeth. You are an island of steadfast brilliance in this wasteland of over-fortunate wastrels that I have, perhaps unwisely, assembled over the centuries. Of course I have only myself to blame. Still ...." Exeter's voice trailed off when he realized that Lizbeth wasn't listening. Unused to being ignored, he was momentarily rankled, but stifled any rebuke: best not to disturb a Wildcard genius at work.

After all, a dash of impertinence was hardly relevant to matters at hand. And at hand was one of the Castle's long-slumbering saddlesticks, the first of the hoverbar-powered vehicles to suffer the indignity of license expiration. If Lizbeth's blemish-free success record was any guide, the mathematical shackles that had kept Saddlestick 14 grounded were about to be sundered.

Exeter and Lizbeth were the only humans currently present in the Motorpool, a section of Castle Ommergard that had been sealed off for centuries. By virtue of its charmed disguise, one of Exeter's early magical successes, few in the castle even suspected its existence. In addition to the lightly armed, one-person saddlesticks, the Motorpool contained a number of other hoverbar-powered vehicles, including several jeeps, an assortment of well-used trucks, one heavily armored tankship, two maintenance vans, and one inflatable heavylift platform with a full complement of articulated spider cranes.

It also contained nearly all of Lord Bellicarie's Library of Motive Marvels, the Castle's acclaimed touring exhibition of exotic mobile relics. With one exception, Exeter had not previously been much interested in Bellicarie's archaic mechanisms. The '34 Ford three-window coupe was the exception; it was not only terminally cool, it was the only one that hadn't been grounded for centuries, owing to its NavaTek gravlifters.

Now, everything in Bellicarie's Library had become an object of intense interest. Exeter alternated between hovering over Lizbeth and wandering around the Library to examine each of the other vehicles, doubtless imagining them airborne and what might be done with them.

"Done," mumbled Lizbeth.

"Outstanding, Artificer Marble!" Exeter beamed like a child with a new furkin. "What fun we're going to have with these little hotdogs."

Lizbeth, as if noticing Exeter for the first time, turned and gave him a wobbly, owlish blink. Her face was a bloodless gray; her lips, never full, were now drawn tight, a darker, bluer shade of gray. "Oh…" was all she said before collapsing in a heap.

He frowned at the crumpled body for some seconds before the acuteness of Lizbeth's exhaustion penetrated his single-minded exultation. Somewhat irritated that the girl had not been able to hack all the vehicles before abruptly deciding to nap, Exeter nonetheless slung Lizbeth over his shoulder and carried her up to the docspace.

Tucking her in an empty pod, he issued a string of commands, then stared at the haggard figure in the pod for several minutes. Was it concern, or was it something else? At length, he patted her sleeping head and departed. He didn't notice the tiny transparent thing that had leaped from Lizbeth's lank brown mop to lodge itself under the fingernail of his right pinky. Nor did he notice a similar one that took refuge in his ponytail.

370

64 :: PARTY TONIGHT

LOUNGING on a curvaceous settee, Glendyl watched the docspace scene on the Nevergate's viewscreen, thanks to one of the North Castle Brain's spy-sensors in Castle Ommergard.

"Well now, my dear Glendyl," said the disembodied voice that seemed at the moment to be coming from a vase containing a freshly cut Calla lily. "We shall see what we shall see. With any luck our little bugs should give us some insight into the wandering habits of the charming Exeter the Wise. We may also learn a little about his personal tidiness. I just love redundancy, don't you? And it's never good to depend overmuch on just the old Brain's sources, you know. Good thing you explored that little box on the organ console; somehow those tagbugs had slipped my mind momentarily. In fact, it is embarrassing to admit that I don't recall why they were there in the first place."

The Nevergate's cheery admissions of fallibility did little to comfort Glendyl about the dangerous game she was playing. For the past several days she and Lizbeth had been surreptitiously meeting in the ladies room of Castle Ommergard's sub-basement, catching up on things and attempting to make some sort of plan to do something. The trouble was, neither of them had any substantial notion of what they should be planning to do. Or why.

To make matters worse — at least from Glendyl's point of view — Lizbeth was increasingly unable to focus upon anything but the

seething intricacies of Van Gonder transforms and the puzzle of un-
raveling the unique security sequences that locked each of the hoverbars. Now, with Lizzie back in the docspace, their meetings would
have to stop. With her only friend unavailable, Glendyl was at loose
ends.

"What do you think I should do now?" she inquired of the air.

"Are you asking me for strategic advice again?" responded a
playful voice from the woven geometric design in the center of a Persian rug. "Are you familiar with the truism 'free advice is worth exactly what you pay for it'?"

"Would your advice be different if I paid you for it?" snapped
Glendyl. She was cross. Sitting around watching her friend Lizbeth
all gray and drawn in the pod was not conducive to frivolity.

"Touchy, touchy, touchy! A little out of sorts, are we?"

"It's not *your* best friend who's lying there in that pod-thing.
Lizzie might be dying, for all I know!"

"Forgive me; I am beginning to understand. Would it make you
feel better to know her physical condition?"

"You can do that?"

"I can tell you what the docpod knows."

"Really?"

"Really. Let's see...exhaustion...a touch of dehydration...noth-
ing serious. And she'll be waking soon, amply stimmed. Oh, this is
interesting. The docpod appears baffled by some of your friend's odd
physiological changes since she was there the last time. Were you
aware that your friend might be growing wings? And a tail? The docpod hasn't quite figured those things out yet, though: it's pretty nar-
row-minded. And it doesn't have the benefit of my knowledge base,
I suppose."

"C'mon Gate. Don't yank my chain about things like that."

"Pardon, mon ami, but I am not, as you say, 'yanking your
chain.' It's obvious."

"You're serious?"

"I'm serious. I borrowed the Brain's cross-species biodev library for a few blinks. The signs are eminently clear."

"Wings and a tail? That doesn't make any sense."

"Of course it doesn't. Probably the docpod needs a reset. Or something. Or maybe there's a prankster in Ommergard. Or possibly Lizbeth has made an enemy of a high level Sorcerer, or ..."

Glendyl held up her hand and whispered: "Shhh! Someone's coming into the room."

"They can't hear us Glendyl. It's all right."

A short, roughly ball-shaped man of uncertain age stopped at the pod containing the sleeping Lizbeth. "Doc?"

"Yes, Romundo?" A neutral-sounding voice emanated from a grate on the docspace wall.

"Chief says you gotta get Artificer Marble fixed up enough to make it through the party tonight. Any problem with that?"

The voice now responded stern authority. "The patient should remain sleeping for a minimum of twenty-four hours. She is suffering from exhaustion and ...."

Romundo was impatient. "Hey, Doc, the Chief's been working us all to the bone. We're all exhausted. You don't know how lucky you are to escape all this craziness. Just give her some goose juice or something. She can sleep tomorrow. Tonight she's gotta party. Chief's orders. I'm supposed to make sure she gets to the dorm in time to get ready. Chief's orders. Gimme any crap and I'll just override you. Chief's orders."

The docpod caved. "I see. Well then, it would be best if you return her here after the party. And it would be good for her to stay away from bullwinkle punch. It does not seem to agree with her metabolism."

"Got it, Doc. You juice her up however you need to and I'll come back in half an hour and escort her to the dorm." Romundo waddled off in pursuit of other errands.

The Nevergate spoke. "Do you care to listen to a strategy recommendation, Glendyl Fenderwell?"

"I suppose so," she responded flatly.

The Nevergate proceeded in his amiable voice, now laced with a tone of mathematical authority. "Do nothing for the moment. I have followed several dozen probability threads to null outcomes. It would appear that we have not yet reached a fulcrum point in the proceedings, a place where the application of action can be leveraged to achieve a desired outcome...or at least move along a desired outcome vector. Have I made myself clear?"

"Not exactly, Gate," said Glendyl, now even glummer. "My big problem is that I still don't have a clue what 'desired outcome' I should have. Things used to be so simple and straightforward. Like bangerball. You just play to win the game. And everybody knows the rules: walls, colors, net, ball, scoring...all that stuff. Here, everything just seems to go around in circles. No rules. And I don't even know who the real good guys and bad guys are. And there aren't any game-cops if I did."

Glendyl sat in silence, her expression glum, staring at the viewscreen and lost in meandering thought patterns. The Nevergate, for whatever reasons, maintained the silence.

Some minutes later, Glendyl watched Lizbeth stir in the pod, yawn and rub her eyes; a degree of color had even returned to her complexion. By the time Romundo Osaki returned, she was sitting in a chair, twiddling her thumbs and tapping her feet to some unheard uptempo tune. Romundo introduced himself, described the impending party and Exeter's wishes, then led Lizbeth toward the Artificers' quarters.

"Have fun at the party, Lizzie." Glendyl's wistful voice betrayed her lonesome wish that she, too, could be going to a party tonight.

65 :: HUNCHED OVER

THE REPLICA of Castle Ommergard hung in the exact center of Dillowy Cavern, basking in the purple warmth of a dozen red and blue
spotlights and the swirling coruscations of as many glimmerbeams.
As the Castle's full complement of Artificers, Sorcerers and Adjuncts
filed in, one question was universal: what did the Chief have on his
mind this time? Nearly as universal was an exclamation to this effect:
"So *that's* what hoverbars look like from below!"

Tall, slender, empty goblets were distributed to each crewmem-
ber upon entering, along with a souvenir: a winged sorcerer's cap.
When all the Ommergardians had been accounted for, a glossy chime
reverberated through the hall. The spotlights and glimmerbeams
faded. Now only the pearlescent halo surrounding the floating replica provided illumination, painting the heads and upturned faces of
the crew with a ghostly bluish luster. A hush of anticipation fell like
a sudden downpour.

A faint whistling. From somewhere inside the replica a small
flying thing emerged, tracked by a narrow, pulsing, hot pink arrow-
beam. The flying thing looped playfully around and through the mess
of architectural phantasmagoria that nest atop Castle Ommergard.
Light, playful music accompanied this aerial exercise. Then, the flying thing shot out from the replica in a sweeping spiral. The music spiraled up as well, gaining force and pomp along the way. As it
neared the top of the cavern, the flying thing grew in size and became

recognizable as the Chief, attired in full wizardly regalia, including a conical wizard's cap with wings. But what was he flying?

Exeter and his mount suddenly plunged toward the crowd in a steep dive, flattening out at the last moment. Whooooosh! Wizard-capped heads ducked and a few caps tumbled off in the backwash. The crowd began to cheer and stamp their feet. The Chief circled the hall several times riding a sleek silver thing with glowing thrust-pods.

As he looped back toward the center, the replica of Castle Ommergard morphed into a rotating circular platform. The Chief set his odd mount gently upon this platform, its telescoping landing feet making noiseless contact. Dismounting, he bowed deeply to the crowd, which responded with an appropriate roar. The music faded to silence.

Exeter began warmly. "I am pleased that you could all take time out of your busy schedules to attend my latest little whim." A rippling chuckle was quashed with a signal from the Chief.

"Ladies and gentlemen of Castle Ommergard, as our first order of business tonight, I would like to introduce you to my remarkable mount, Silver, who has been kind enough to...oh good heavens...in my excitement, I forgot to stop by Wardrobe for proper attire. Oh well."

Exeter extended his right hand toward the ceiling, palm outstretched. A bolt of crackling light shot from overhead, struck his hand. The wizardly form was engulfed in crackling reddish smoke. When it cleared, Exeter the Wizard was no longer.

In his place was the gray-booted, gray-garbed, black-masked Exeter the Lone Ranger, twirling a silver Colt 45. As he deftly jammed the pistol into a black leather holster, a hundred trumpets assaulted Dillowy Cavern with the fanfare to the William Tell Overture. When the da-da-dum, da-da-dum, da-da-dum-dum-dum section began, its amplitude subsided and the Chief resumed his speech.

"Now where was I...? Silver, right? Right. All you military history buffs out there will recognize that my trusted mount, Silver, belongs to a species known as *Saddlestickus saurquiana*. Or, for the Latin-challenged, a Saurquian saddlestick. Why should you care? Three little syllables, ladies and gentlemen. Three little syllables. The very same three syllables that are at this very moment treating you to a moonlight cruise over your old hometown."

A low rumble from the crowd. Exeter cocked his head slightly, cupped an ear in exaggerated fashion. "Did I hear someone say 'hover-bars'?" Exeter waited for the crowd's booming "HOVERBARS" echo, then continued.

377

"That's correct, class! Three wonderful syllables.

"Thanks to a well-earned stroke of good fortune — and an effort of unstinting intensity from the entire Ommergard community — we have once again achieved something with four splendid syllables. Something heady, powerful and exhilarating...and fun. Something spelled M-O-B-I-L-I-T-Y! Let's hear it for MOBILITY!"

At the word "MOBILITY" the walls of Dillowy Cavern became a 360° vidscreen. A dark scene unfolded to Strauss' sprightly Persian March: a moonlit night salted on high with far twinkles, the lights of St Coriander ahead and below. The clearing that had been the Castle's home for centuries disappeared into the dark expanse of nameless forest.

A sudden, uncertain hush enveloped the room. Several thoughts were so pervasive as to be almost audible. Are we really in the air? Is Castle Ommergard really flying? Is that what St Coriander really looks like from above? Is St Coriander really that small? Is this another of the Chief's fantastic illusions?

Exeter began a hushed narration, his normal facade of easy control fractured by a rare display of genuine emotion. "No, ladies and gentlemen, this is not an illusion. Your beloved home and castle is aloft once more. We have left our soil-bound imprisonment behind us; all the hills and valleys of planet Earth are before us. Ladies and gentlemen, I would like to consecrate this singular moment with a toast. Would you raise your glasses please?"

Arms were raised, some haltingly, some with gusto. As Exeter continued, the glasses filled themselves with a bubbly, pale amber liquid. "Esteemed colleagues of Castle Ommergard, a great destiny rides with us tonight. That destiny — your destiny, our destiny — is to once again open the doors to the universes and their endless wonders. That destiny is to once again unleash the sleeping greatness of planet Earth."

A pause: raw, unfiltered wonder began to seep into the assembled minds. Exeter's raised champagne glass quivered with emotion; he continued, but softly. "At one time or another, nearly all of you undertook a brave Quest, risking your lives to obtain the fabled Key, the Key that would open the Nevergate once again for dear St Coriander. Now, together, it is time for us — the citizens of Castle Ommergard — to resume our Quests. It is time to win a future for our planet. And it is to that ultimate victory I propose we toast tonight.

"Achieving this destiny may not be easy. There are forces of darkness that would like to see this planet remain a backwater, a ghost of its past and its future. Yet, I believe that the Fates have ordained our ultimate victory. Ladies and gentlemen, let us, on this memorable night over old St Coriander, toast our destiny ... INFINITY!"

Exeter pulled down his goblet, put it to his lips and downed the contents in a gulp. Then he tossed it high into the air. At the top of its arc, the goblet shattered with a pop. Shards coalesced into a red neon cardinal that wasted no time taking flight.

The spell was broken, the crowd followed suit and the air was soon thick with glowing red birds and the sound of glassy, tubular wings. The birds formed themselves into a giant arrow, flew toward the shadowy Brazos Cliffs on the vidscreen and faded from view.

A nervous silence followed, each Artificer, each Sorcerer, each Adjunct contemplating the import of what they had just witnessed, the promise they had just made. Then the silence imploded and the crowd found its full voice. Lizbeth Marble, who did not yet think of herself as part of Castle Ommergard, was nonetheless drawn into the moment. She drank her champagne, watched her goblet become an electric bird and wing away, and cheered this magical trifle just like all the others in Dillowy Cavern.

She was watching the distant red arrow dissolve into the vid-screen when she found herself targeted by spotlights. The nearby Ommergardians fell back. Once again she was lifted off her feet and transported to the stage, hating her helplessness in the face of Exeter's power and hating the fact that all eyes were upon her.

With a grim smile, Lizbeth endured Exeter's lofty exaltations for her hoverbar hacking. The grim smile even stayed in place as the Chief draped a Vanguard Medal around her neck, which felt particularly scrawny and overlong at that moment. Finally it was over and the crowd disbanded to pursue their various revelries.

379

Ignoring Romundo's exhortation to return to the docspace, Lizbeth made her way numbly through the Castle to her cubby. She was asleep almost before her head hit the pillow.

As Lizbeth slumbered, Castle Ommergard came alive. Windows that had been sealed and invisible for many score years were opened, balconies projected from walls and exuberant Ommergardians hung out of them, some to a precipitous degree, waving, gesticulating, whooping and prankishly spilling champagne into the air.

For this special occasion Exeter even allowed the crew access to the normally off-limits high towers, where they could make wild gestures from the battlements and turrets. While the more mature Artificers and Sorcerers declined to demonstrate their thaumaturgical capabilities, a number of Artificer show-offs entertained their fellows and the folk of St Coriander with magical fireworks, holomations ranging from horrific to erotic, and other visual trifles. Not even one over-champagned Ommergardian fell out of the castle, a testament more to luck than to sense.

• • • • •

Below in St Coriander the story was different. Reactions to the fly-over ran the gamut from awestruck to zombied. Some thought it was an unscheduled performance by the Spellfellow Society and enjoyed it immensely. Some residents thought they recognized kin among the celebrants high overhead and waved back. Others fell to their knees, mystically entranced by the ghostly blue hoverfields.

A large number sought interpretative assistance from either the Sages in the Holy Quincunx or from Septriq oracles on their slates. Still others found the whole business entirely too extraordinary and stood mute and rooted until an urgent call of nature broke the spell. A small number sought relief under their beds or pursued some equally ostrich-like strategy. Among this latter group was Father-Mayor Gullwimple, who was discovered some hours later by his second in command, Father Cymbill, blissfully catatonic and absently fondling an evermetal statuette of the Lucky Madonna.

A group of opportunistic COMISC members donned masks and overpowered the thoroughly befuddled Sheriff Dolittle, whose two Jurists had already deserted him. Forrbank Dorelli was freed from his Small Dark Room deep under the Holy Quincunx. Shortly thereafter, an emergency meeting was held at COMISC headquarters, which a somewhat hunched over Forrbank Dorelli was pleased to chair.

66 :: THE NEAREST DOOR

"THE 'FLYING CASTLE nonsense' was an elaborate prank, no more no less." So claimed Pontus Krebs in a *St Coriander Times* editorial on behalf of the People for Tradition and Decency.

Krebs hypothesized thusly; malicious malcontents had first doctored the town's water supply with psychotropic substances (a shopworn strategy, to be sure), then sprinkled Balloonigan's Inflation Dust on a scale model of Castle Ommergard, then launched it into the evening breeze coming down through Kissever Pass. "Such a simple ruse should fool no thinking person," opined Krebs. Punishment, he assured those citizens who cared to listen, would be swift and stern, just as soon as the miscreants were apprehended and Father-Mayor Gullwimple's 'schedule' permitted the administration of justice once again.

Krebs' suggestion to look to residents of the Spellfellow Tower for amplifications and answers was widely interpreted as a not-too-subtle accusation. Perhaps coincidentally, a hundred headless, madly cackling red hens dogged his every movement for the next three days, leaving copious quantities of noxious excreta in their wakes. The Spellfellow Society officially denied responsibility, of course. Still, there was no dearth of exaggerated shrugs and suggestive winks among those individual Spellfellows who were invited to comment on the fowl phenomenon.

In Castle Ommergard, the newly bemedaled Lizbeth was once again in the thrall of hoverbar hacking and quite happy about it. By the second evening following Ommergard's cruise, the remaining hoverbar-powered devices in the Motorpool were working again.

While Lizbeth was shuttered away in the Motorpool, Exeter was busy preparing to readjust the small world of Castle Ommergard in remarkable ways. On the first post-flyover day, he was completely out of touch; according to his dispatch, he was "recharging his batteries."

The following morning, each dayshift Ommergardian had, upon rising, discovered a long bulletin from the Chief on his or her slate. It first described and depicted their new location, a sheltered meadow a dozen miles up Brazos Canyon. Second, it announced there was to be a barbecue on the banks of the meandering Brazos at three the following afternoon. Third, it said that all classes and workshops were temporarily in stasis and would be resumed upon cessation of the emergency. Fourth, it promised that the Chief would explain all at the barbecue. Fifth, attendance at the barbecue was not optional.

· · · · ·

Not all who viewed Exeter's bulletin that morning were residents of Castle Ommergard. Glendyl Fenderwell read it while comfied up in her North Castle bed. She was enjoying a late breakfast — her usual hamanegg pastry — but this time fresh from her very own MenuMaster. Feeling slightly adventurous, she had ordered a side of Ultimate Dressing to use as a dipping sauce.

Glendyl had been sleeping late the past few days. Partly this was because she felt helpless — almost imprisoned — now that Nevergating to visit Lizzie in Ommergard had gotten too risky. This put her in a lousy, mopey mood. Partly, though, it was because she was exhausted. She had been researching every morsel of information she could find on Castle Ommergard: its history, its celebrated dragons and sky monkeys, its architecture, its floorplans.

Studying floorplans wasn't her idea. The Nevergate thought it might increase her odds of escaping to an emergency gatehole if she had the ill fortune to be discovered on one of her contemplated adventures. Glendyl couldn't argue with that, but found the two-dimensional plans difficult to understand until the Nevergate offered to convert them into a three-dimensional projection that she could navigate through. Thanks to this improvement, she soon knew Ommergard better than most Artificers who had lived there for years.

The brightest spot of these days was Glendyl's time with Laniss. As strange as it sometimes seemed to her, Laniss had become her closest friend in North Castle. This closeness began when Glendyl had started digging into Ommergard's history. Laniss volunteered to help.

Laniss hadn't been one of the sky monkeys born from stolen embryos that had performed in the famous aerial ballet. She was one of the "original seconds." Laniss would say very little about these particular dunnikins, but Glendyl had by now pieced together the fact that some lived in North Castle somewhere. And she was also getting the idea that they were still important in a mysterious way. Yet Laniss chose to live on Dunnigans Wall with the "outcasts:" a mystery.

There was much that Glendyl wished to know about Laniss, but could not bring herself to ask. So Glendyl filed these mysteries away, resolving to ask both the Brain and Diogenes about them at her first opportunity. In the meantime, there was Ommergard.

With Laniss perched on her shoulder or sitting on her lap, Glendyl probed North Castle records for information on Ommergard. Laniss provided the "color commentary" from one who had been there, done that and seen it all. And she had little love for Exeter whom she described as a "dangerous, ruthless megalomaniac, but an equally patient, clever one."

Yesterday, after sharing a sunrise breakfast with Laniss on a boulder overlooking Arrowmere and the back side of North Castle, Glendyl returned to her room to find the front page of the "Ommergard Flies Again" special edition of the *St Coriander Times* displayed on the wall. Glendyl's mood plummeted like a dead parrot in lead boots. Lizzie had done the impossible. Who would have guessed? And she was in the middle of the action, just where Glendyl was accustomed to being. Glendyl, who had been acting more like Lizzie-the-Bookworm, was stuck in North Castle where nothing was happening. Well, not exactly nothing.

While delivering breakfast yesterday morning, the Lady Diana saucerite had informed her that the North Castle staff was very busy and that Glendyl would be more or less on her own for a few days. She declined to discuss specifics. Later, after the MenuMaster had been installed in Glendyl's room, saucerites ceased to be available to her. Bored, lonely and exasperated, she finally excused herself from her personal pity party and took a walk.

The Park had been her first destination, but the entire level had been sealed off. An indicator in the slidewell said "Closed for Renovation" whenever she punched that destination. Frustrated, she wandered here and there in search of someplace she hadn't been before, but discovered nothing new. Then she thought to search for the place where the "inside" dunnikins lived, but found no obvious indication of its location. After a time she found herself back at the Library. With nothing better to do, she resumed her researches on Castle Ommergard. This time, she began to browse ancient newsclips.

Almost immediately, Glendyl chanced upon an interesting find, a collection of critical reviews of Lord Bellicarie's "Aerial Ballet for Dragons, Sky Monkeys and '34 Ford." Encountering plaudits like "original, death defying and opulent" and "Crazy Bellie does it again: just don't forget your fire extinguisher..." she was prompted to search for vids. Two of these — the Thames performance of April 2264 and the Anchorage show of August 2266 — were in the archives. Diogenes was right: it was a truly great piece of action theater. After staying up late to watch both performances, Glendyl was a little slow to rise this morning.

Some node of the Brain, anticipating her interest in the latest Ommergard news, had placed a pirated copy of Exeter's slatecast on her slate. One quick scan sent her mood in a fresh direction, wiping away her lingering grogginess with one swipe of a mental squeegee. With all the Ommergardians at the barbecue, tomorrow might just be the right day for getting her Standard Toolbelt back: if she were lucky enough, that is. And if, as Lizzie had observed, Exeter truly no longer wore it in public. Euphoria at the prospect of being reunited with the Toolbelt seemed to bubble up from her very cells, washing away her very rational fears of being caught in the act.

Septriq, she thought to her slate, which was now rigged to pick up emanations from the circlet. Since getting her own slate back with the QPack, Glendyl had resumed her morning Septriq ritual, gauging the portents for the day and listening to the elfish Oraya's cryptic advice. But her old Septriq routine had begun to seem thin and stale since leaving St Coriander. Worse, it had begun to seem a little scary after Lizzie had told her about the nest of "triqsters" she had found in her Ommergard slate's copy of Septriq. Maybe Glendyl's Septriq had been infested, too? Lizzie said they seemed harmless, but ....

Glendyl ran through a few sequences trying to see the under-patterns Lizzie had seen: triqster "spoor" she'd called them. Nothing. Then the image of Oraya appeared, unbidden, to wag a coy finger in Glendyl's direction and pantomime the buckling of a belt around her waist. A chill zigzagged through Glendyl's body. Was this a sign, a signal? Oraya winked and faded from view. Exasperated, Glendyl wiped it and set the slate back on her nightstand.

Why am I wasting time with this? Throwing off the coverlet, she dressed and was off for a session with Gate.

Glendyl no longer accessed the Nevergate via the Water Garden. Too risky, Gate had said after her second visit. Instead, they had concocted a ruse involving Glendyl's feigned interest in the trails overlooking North Castle and Arrowmere.

For its part, the Nevergate had dispatched one of its special "gatehole" shadowflaps to the trunk of a tall ponderosa near the trail leading to Glendyl's favorite brooding place, a knob of bare rock overlooking Arrowmere and the back side of North Castle. With North Castle preoccupied by other matters, Glendyl had argued that the ponderosa hole was probably unnecessary, but Gate had insisted.

On the heels of this morning's strategy conference was a busy few hours of preparations. By midafternoon she was as ready as she'd ever be: the master openrod was tucked in a pocket of her freshly-fabbed replica of an Artificer's gray jumpsuit and she had memorized as many of Ommergard's floorplans as her brain could hold. She had wanted the comfort of the circlet, but the Nevergate persuaded her that it would compromise her disguise. She could hardly argue.

"You're absolutely certain you want to go through with this?" inquired the Nevergate in a voice of cool neutrality.

"Come on, Gate: don't make me more nervous than I am already. Let's just do it."

"Tsk, tsk. Glenny-Honey is crotchety today."

"Gate ...."

There was the now-familiar compression sensation and then Glendyl materialized in a slidewell alcove in Castle Ommergard. If the Nevergate knew what it was doing, this would be Exeter's private quarters in Tower Five. If the luck of Madonna 13 was truly with her, the master openrod would open the three doors arrayed in a circle around this particular slidewell alcove. If she were really lucky, the Standard Toolbelt would be behind one of those doors, as Gate had said it would be with ninety-nine percent certainty. Glendyl didn't want to consider what might happen if she wasn't lucky.

With a deep breath and a mental shrug, she ratcheted up her nerve and tiptoed toward the nearest door.

....
67 :: AIR KISSES

AT EXACTLY FIVE p.m., Exeter kicked off the barbecue with fireworks. At least that was what the Ommergardians thought they were seeing. But the fireworks stayed in the air and gradually took on the shape of a giant, nearly transparent insect. Upon closer inspection, it was clearly insect-like, but not any known insect: a complex array of rods and dish-shaped objects was in constant motion just under its transparent carapace.

With the entire Ommergard crew craning their necks to view this aerial oddity, Exeter began speaking from the bed of the ancient military half-track Lizbeth had hacked. His voice seemed to come from everywhere at once. "Loyal citizens of Castle Ommergard, the most dangerous enemy is an invisible enemy. This device, discovered late last night, is one of our formerly invisible enemies."

Judging from the uncertain rumbles, the notion of gigantic insect-like enemies was a new idea for the Ommergardians.

Exeter paused long enough for the crowd to wonder what was coming next. "Have you seen any of these enemies? No? Well, they're not this big, of course. This one is actually about a tenth the size of a flea. Some of you might be wondering why we should be concerned about tiny enemies like this little pseudoid. The answer is that our bigger enemy — our most immediate enemy— is using them to spy on us, to steal the fruits of our long labors, to subvert our peaceful scientific community.

"Some of you may be confused by this talk of enemies. You've never heard me speak of enemies before, have you? To be blunt, it has been a long time since I've even thought about enemies. I'm not a fighter by nature: I'm a scientist, a student of mysteries, a creator of marvels.

"Our idyllic, scholarly life in Castle Ommergard has insulated us from the conflicts of the outside world. After the carnage and horror of the Nevergate Wars, I tried to make Ommergard a place of peace, a place of learning, a place where ideas — and our citizens — could grow in safety, living long, productive lives. For a quarter of a millennium, we have had peace in our tiny corner of this universe. So you might say I have been successful in this regard. "But peace is best preserved by constant vigilance. And this is where I have failed you, loyal Adjuncts, Artificers and Sorcerers of Castle Ommergard. My intense desire for peace caused me to lose sight of the need for constant vigilance. It has made me forget about enemies. For this breach of leadership, I ask your forgiveness."

The assembled crowd was absolutely silent. The Chief had never spoken like this before. Lizbeth Marble, standing at the periphery of the crowd near the Brazos, felt an icy knot form in her stomach. The secret meetings with Glendyl in the ladies room replayed themselves in a rush, along with a sense of eerie foreboding. She shuddered.

Exeter paused and held up his hand, a sudden frown darkening his face. He seemed to be listening to some other voice, then nodded. His eyes slowly scanned the crowd before continuing. Lizbeth felt the heat of those eyes. When he spoke again anger tinged his voice. "Ladies and gentlemen, as I have been speaking to you of enemies — here, today — an enemy has audaciously invaded the sanctity of our beloved home."

He paused again, gauging the crowd's response. Then he looked at the giant tagbug in the sky and snapped his finger; the image blinked out of existence. "If you're thinking that today's enemy is merely another tiny bug, no, it is not. Today's enemy is vastly more dangerous: a human. That is the bad news. The good news? The good news is that we have captured this enemy agent in the act of pillaging my study, an atrocity that I regard as a personal affront as well as an act of war. This crime happened just minutes ago...let us now look upon this vile enemy with our very own eyes."

Exeter made a dramatic right turn and pointed. All eyes turned to see a squad of blue-uniformed Adjuncts striding from the castle toward Exeter's truck bed podium. Lizbeth recognized them as Away Team 2, led by Torian Vink. Two of Vink's minions held the cap- tive firmly between them. From her vantage point at the back of the crowd, Lizbeth could see only the heads of Away Team 2 and not the captive at all; but she could see Exeter. His momentary breach of control was unmistakable.

Something about this scene was a very big surprise to Exeter the Wise. When the captive was thrust up onto the half-track's bed, a murmur of bafflement rippled through the assembled Ommergardians. This familiar young woman hardly looked like a dangerous enemy agent. Was this another of Exeter's "instructive pranks?"

Lizbeth felt sick; even without being able to see the captive, she knew it was Glendyl Fenderwell. Lizbeth didn't know how she knew, but she knew. To Exeter (and those of the crowd who had been Madonna Cultists), however, the young woman in the Artificer jumpsuit was no Quester from St Coriander, but the living, breathing reincarnation of Madonna 13. And before Exeter could find his tongue, she flicked him a sexy smile, blew air kisses to the crowd and began to sing.

390

68 :: THINGS THAT SCURRIED

JAMIS HAD BECOME the poster squirrel for the old truism, "desperation thrives on hunger." For a time that neither his ground squirrel biological clock nor his human mind could accurately measure, his only food had been spiders, beetles and albino centipedes scoured along the length of the crack. And not too many of these. He longed for an acorn or a pine nut. Better yet, said an even deeper hunger, a juicy likesteakburger with all the trimmings. His belly cast such fantasies aside: now, even the insects would be rare delicacies.

Jamis had traversed the length of the crack over and over again, searching for a way out of his dark linear prison, but had found nothing promising. His predicament remained the same: an eagle's nest at one end, a hundred-foot drop and death-dealing dragons at the other end. In-between? Darkness and a few crawly things.

At the dragon end of his long prison cell, the occupants had been busy training for battle. Jamis had watched their combat drills with a kind of gut-gnawing fascination. He couldn't watch their feedings, though: not after the first time.

It started with the sharp rasp of a loud buzzer. All training activity stopped on the instant and the dragons jostled each other for positions along one side of the cavern. At the sound of two buzzers, a horde of hairless pink rats the size of small pigs spewed from a floor-level portal across the cave. While the pig-rats scurried this way and that, the dragons remained at the wall, tense with anticipation like sprinters flexing at their starting blocks.

At the third buzzer, the dragons leaped to the chase. A symphony of slaughter ensued. The entire floor was a tangle of dark, wet movement; of squeals and screeches; of claws and jaws; of blood and entrails. At the fourth buzzer, the sated and lethargic dragons returned to their drills. Besides a slimy sheen that wasn't there earlier, Jamis could detect no trace of the pig-rats. Still, the putrid reek of a thousand small deaths lingered, tainting the air with a reddish-black mist. Jamis retched.

At some point, the cavern's overhead lights dimmed to the dull orange glow of hot coals and the dragons retired to their holes along the spiral ramp. Some time later the floor came alive in a writhing, scuttling manner that Jamis found acutely repulsive. He couldn't see clearly in the orange haze, but he imagined the cleanup squad was an army of lizard-sized cockroaches. Ycch. After spending one more night at the cave end of his prison, he concluded that a sleeping eagle was better company.

The eagle spent most of each day aloft and Jamis gradually pumped up his nerve enough to explore the rock notch with the nest. There was little to arouse either interest or hope. The only possibility of escape lay over the edge, on the scarred, crumbly rock of the cliff face. No problem for an ant or a lizard to navigate, but not good news for a ground squirrel.

For a time Jamis commuted between dragons and eagle, hoping for a magical solution to appear. Nothing changed except that he got hungrier, weaker, more desperate. As his reflexes became torpid, even catching scuttling insects was a challenge. Finally, his deepest survival sense forced him to act before it was too late for any action at all. Mustering his dwindling reserves of strength, he dragged himself along the crack to the eagle's lair.

It was midday and the eagle was nowhere to be seen. Under the pile of bleached bones a jittery Jamis crept toward the edge of the nest, avoiding the noisy eaglets that had now become active explorers.

About five feet below the aerie was a narrow, jagged ledge that ran generally parallel to the rocky floor of the Wittwater Deep. Below his current perch, the ledge was only a few inches wide and crumbled to nothing in spots, leaving gaps that could only be leaped. But it did follow a northerly, upstream direction, the right way to the smoking hole. Unfortunately, there was no way to know if the ledge would remain passable even by the standards of a once-nimble ground squirrel. Or that it would ultimately intersect with the cave. And even if he made it there, could he get down?

The cliff had seemed climbable when he had been on the canyon floor plotting his revenge against the sidewinder, but was it really? Jamis had no choice but to assume that if there was a route up, that same route would get him down. With only these scant hopes of success, Jamis vacillated.

A shwoosh-shwoosh of great wings thumped the air. Before Jamis' human mind knew what had happened, his rodent body had leaped and was now clinging to a ledge just barely wide enough for his body. The eagle's screams set Jamis on a panicked, stop-go-stop scamper along the seam two-thirds of the way up the cliff. Twice he'd been forced to dodge attacks. Then, almost before he realized it, he was inside the hole.

His surge of elation was short lived. A few seconds of exploration revealed an ugly truth: no route down the cliff. And no route from the cave mouth to the top of the cliff either. Jamis now faced a classic Hobson's choice: venture deeper inside or venture nowhere at all. Both seemed equally deadly. Wishing he could somehow evade the nauseating reek, Jamis found a ground squirrel-sized hiding place not far back from the edge and contemplated going deeper into dragon hell.

Hunger rattled in his empty belly like dice in a coffee can. He tried to tell himself that he could find his way down to the floor of the big cavern. That much he could believe. He was not so successful convincing himself that he could stomach the things that scurried along the slimy floor in the late night hours.

394

....

69 :: IF POSSIBLE

CASTLE OMMERGARD floated into a simmering dawn. A flock of small gray birds accompanied it for a time, amusing themselves among the chaos of iconic structures that adorned the castle's roof, then flew off to the west. From a high forward balcony, a pair of eyes tracked their progress.

When the birds had passed beyond the limits of his vision, Exeter the Wise returned to pondering. The debacle at the barbecue had forced him to act before he was ready. But if not now, when? Perhaps never. His plan to gradually arouse the Artificers and Sorcerers against his ancient enemy — the Clans Dunnigan — was a dismal failure thus far.

For one thing, the young Madonna 13 impostor put too good a face on the word "enemy" to be effective in the role Exeter needed her for. Except by exercise of steely will, Exeter himself saw only fond memories and pleasant dreams whenever his eyes or mind fell on the girl. The imposter had somehow known of his own weakness for Madonna 13 and had taken advantage of it. Exeter hated that. Fortunately, the latest candidate for enemy (or scapegoat, depending on one's perspective) was much easier to dislike.

A deeper problem was that the whole idea of "enemy" was a difficult concept for Ommergardians to grasp; the Castle had no enemies. Plus, the Ommergardians knew that the last Dunnigans had departed the planet 250 years ago, if one didn't count the Brain. How could people so long gone be an enemy? And there was just no time to adjust Ommergardian perspectives through clever memeweaving.

The "enemy" issue had first flicked through Exeter's mind as he stood on the truck bed with the imposter. The impostor's singing was actually a stroke of luck, he decided. It gave him time to recast his position, to improvise. Thus, the girl, whoever she was, had become "a specially refurbed friend from the 'old days' providing nostalgic entertainment for the barbecue." The Away Teams had caught his signal and kept quiet. The odds were good that the rest of the crew had bought the scam well enough: hardly out of character for the Chief, after all.

Following his own cue, he had painted today's flight as a "shakedown cruise" to one of Madonna 13's old haunts. And he had toneddown the talk of enemies to a fatherly admonition to keep an alert eye for bugs. It had seemed to work. And Loopy may just have identified a perfectly workable enemy — at least along the "spy" vector — in the person of that very odd duck, Lizbeth Marble.

The morning breeze that now rustled Exeter's eyebrows and ponytail seemed also to blow away his earlier sour mood. Drinking in the dramatic sunrise, he decided that regardless of subsequent events, it was a beautiful morning for a cruise.

Castle Ommergard lumbered silently above the high meadows. In less than an hour, it would slide between Mt Faunibeune and Grouse Mesa, passing over a thousand rivulets trickling away from the McTavish Glacier on their way to becoming the headwaters of the Wittwater. A few miles downstream, Ommergard would settle onto Arrowmere's upper reaches. If all went according to schedule, Ommergard and North Castle would be face to face before noon. After that, thought Exeter, we will see what we will see.

The heavylift platform and its escort — one of the two newly formed units of Saddlestick Cowboys — had been quietly dispatched some hours before dawn and had already taken up positions within striking distance of North Castle. The hovertank (a venerable Cognodyne Macerator with a fully-accessorized Level 6 battlebrain) had its instructions and was merely waiting for the sally port to open again. Equally important, the Adjuncts on the Away Teams, unlike the Artificers and Sorcerers, were spoiling for a fight; glory and plunder had become their watchwords since the Vanguard Medals had been distributed.

Perhaps North Castle could be coaxed to oblige them, mused Exeter. On the other hand, perhaps the crusty old Brain of North Castle could be coaxed into 'volunteering' the information Exeter needed; no forceful persuasion might be necessary. Best that way, if possible. Soon enough, he would send a Semblance to find out which way the Brain wanted to play it.

398

70 :: ANOTHER NOTCH

WRONGNESS was everywhere. The rich hues of the vines seemed dimmer, the songs of the birds seemed off key and the whole Park Level seemed to throb with a vague, unpleasant vibration that swung between rage and fright. But Cambitter Dorelli kept his sense of things to himself and gave his voice a light, casual tone.

"When will Ommergard be dropping by?" inquired the man Glendyl knew as Mr White. His Semblance had appeared a few minutes early for the parley, so he and the Brain were engaging in what passed for casual chitchat in a Plaid Salon that had been transformed into a war room. Other participants would be arriving in Semblance form in a few minutes.

"Before noon, I should think, Cambitter, assuming he doesn't take his crew on a tour of Frosty."

"Ah, levity. Always good to inject a little levity into dangerous situations. I take it you have some plans for dealing with Exeter should he actually arrive here? And, of course, you certainly have adequate defensive capabilities...." Cambitter Dorelli let the sentence hang; he knew that North Castle's defenses were currently flimsy and impractical at best. He also knew that it hadn't always been that way.

While the Castles had been designed for comfortable habitation and entertainment in a very remote location, the Dunnigans were not naïve. Over the years the Clans had successfully countered assassination attempts, anti-Nevergate suicide bombers and a variety of other very real threats. Their principles were straightforward in concept and four in number. One: trust judiciously. Two: anticipate everything. Three: demonstrate extreme intolerance for aggression in as many ways as possible. Four: use power artfully.

The most potent threat had been in the years immediately preceding the First Nevergate War. A force of elite WorldGov Securitans had been dispatched to Dunnigans Wall and a hundred other strategic Nevergate sites to "provide security against crazed Soultrainers," in the words of WorldGov Secretary General Nafez Gamal Shah. The Clans knew the truth to be otherwise. WorldGov was attempting to assume total control over all Nevergate traffic in order to halt the increasingly rapid depopulation of Earth, both from Soultrainers headed for Nirvana and from settlers seeking unfettered new lives on pioneer planets like Onedinket, Hole-in-One, Nondescripto and a hundred others. Since WorldGov had thus far failed to stanch the exit from the planet, the strategy was to intimidate the Master Licensor, Dunnetix LLC, and its dominant shareholders, the Clans Dunnigan.

Intimidation failed. In the space of twelve minutes, ten thousand heavily armed Securitans stationed in hundreds of Nevergate sites around the globe became inexplicably comatose. When various medical interventions failed to rouse them, playful groups of giggling pre-teen girls appeared at each site sporting identical Pippi Longstockings wigs and official Red Cross uniforms. They quickly set about kissing the somnolent Securitans on their foreheads, whereupon they wakened, lovestruck and shorn of all militant memories.

Interviewed years later after his resignation, the former Secretary General declared he had "no regrets" and that the botched event was clearly a "moral victory for the forces of probity."

During the Second Nevergate War, Castle Caraway and the Dawnhammer's force of battlerider-enhanced wyverns had provided a more than adequate defense considering that Castle Ommergard had become landlocked and its ragtag mechanical "air force" grounded. But the Dawnhammer's valiant wyverns were long dead and the location of Castle Caraway, the wyverns' flying home and battlefortress, remained a mystery. After the battle of Wittwater Deep, it had spirited itself away, but to where? Unknown. Now Castle Ommergard, thanks to the Lizbeth Marble Wildcard, was airborne again. How dangerous? In North Castle's present state of readiness, Exeter could utterly destroy the Castle and everything in it.

While Dorelli's Semblance chatted with the Brain, Mr White's flesh and blood self was busy in South Castle issuing orders to his research staff. Cambitter Dorelli loved multiminding: so efficient. With any luck certain fabjobs could be made rapidly enough to provide Exeter with one or two South Castle surprises should he venture in that direction.

Another Semblance flicked into view, along with a chair. "Starting early, are we? Any ideas, Cambo?" inquired Miles Dunnigan's Semblance with a nod of greeting to Dorelli. While Miles Dunnigan's flesh body was still recuperating in its coldbox way down in the Brain Room, his Semblance was enjoying the multicolored light that filtered through the woven vines overhead.

He did not appear particularly vexed.

"I will refrain from saying 'I told you so' Miles," said Cambitter Dorelli's Semblance, with an air of bland superiority.

Miles Dunnigan ignored the jibe and remarked drily: "And?"

"Ah, yes. Ideas. Well, I do have one or two. However, let us explore several broader issues first: I suspect you, too, have sniffed the complicity of your old Nevergate in promulgating the current crisis?"

"We have. The exasperating thing is that at least one of us in here (by 'in here' he meant the array of separate Dunnigan personalities that had become appended to the Brain over time) probably knows the whole story, but is prevented from sharing it with us by a tactical memblock set in place by someone, sometime. Or something equally inaccessible. By the same token, my own memblock with reference to Nevergate matters would prevent me from knowing what she knows even if she could tell us what she knows. But you have already guessed this, of course."

Dorelli nodded, a tiny smile grazing the corners of his mouth.

His oh-so-mild demeanor was becoming an irritating splinter to the Miles Dunnigan Semblance.

A slender shadow loomed over the table. "How do I look, gentlemen?"

Cambitter Dorelli jerked to his feet and made a genteel bow to the black-haired woman who had just appeared at the table wearing a tight-fitting dress of forest green zhentite. Dorelli observed that this costume set off her slim, athletic figure quite strikingly. Emerald green eyes flashed in a tanned, heart shaped face of crisply drawn features: a visage of remarkable beauty. "Diana Faye Lorris Dunnigan, I presume? You look ravishing, of course. Just like in all the old pix."

"Thank you, Dr Dorelli," said the sleek Semblance with a carmine-lipped half-smile. "As one dead person to another, you're looking quite well yourself. Do you gentlemen mind if I join you?"

"Delighted!" said Dorelli, displaying his own half-smile at Diana's reference to his fraudulent Elective Early Elevation in St Coriander some years back. "Do you mind if I call you Diana?"

Diana Dunnigan's Semblance just smiled, bowed enough to flash a bit of cleavage for Dorelli's benefit and coiled into the chair that had flicked into being beneath her.

Catlike, thought Dorelli, admiring the woman's supple grace.

Miles Dunnigan didn't rise to greet his late and present sibling; he merely nodded, making no attempt to conceal his irritation. A frown flicked over his face as he spoke. "Are we going to wait for our Eldest or should we start without him? As usual, he refuses to keep in contact by ClanChannel. The monitors tell us that Ommergard has just dropped down into the Headwaters Cleft and will make Windwick Beach very soon. Mere minutes away. We don't have a great deal of time to decide on a strategy."

"Do we *need* a strategy? And if we do, will Uncle Diogenes be much help in crafting one? Military strategy isn't exactly his domain, or do you gentlemen know something I don't?" inquired Diana with feigned innocence. Then a flare of temper: "Why wait? Why not just blow the ungodly pentagon and the pompous frogbladder who's flying it to bugdust? Right now! Do the universes a favor. There are still bumbusters all over the lake, right? And I seriously doubt he knows anything about those little monsters. If he did, he wouldn't be waltzing in here like he owned us. And if we need more of a strategy than this, how can we fashion one without knowing why Exeter is now on his way here, after centuries of being a relatively good boy?"

"I believe we can safely assume he's coming now, because he can, Sister." Miles Dunnigan's anger caused his voice to rise. "Suddenly, the Red One has mobility again. Suddenly he can turn aside from his magical trifles and come after what he's always wanted. There is no mystery here; he still wants the Nevergate. And I'm half inclined to give it to him. Unfortunately, I don't know where it is. Do you?" He cast an accusing glance at Diana, who adopted a shocked expression. "Surely he can do no harm to our Clans after so many decades, even if he knew how to find them." Miles was simultaneously emphatic and defensive.

"Now we see the wisdom of memblocks, *Brother*." Diana's words oozed scorn at what she believed was her brother's display of weakness. "I didn't get myself killed just so you could give away the store, not even after 'so many decades.' Your job is to protect the Clans' exit route. Period! End of story. If you aren't willing to do it, then maybe the Brain needs a new Speaker!" These last words were shouted, raising tensions yet another notch.

404

71 :: SEVERAL CONCEPTS

"FORGIVE ME for interrupting, dear cousins," said Cambitter Dorelli in his customary mild tone. "Both of you make valid points. And both of your perspectives are understandable, even to a youngster like me. Still, we really don't know quite what we're dealing with. Has the Brain calculated Exeter's probable first move?" To himself, he wondered if the Brain's personality modules were in need of being processed through a counseling filter. Just a touch overemotional. Certainly Diogenes' recent therapeutic exercises had done little to improve North Castle's prospects in the upcoming showdown.

The Brain got Dorelli's unstated message; act the way a Brain is supposed to act and keep the bickering sibling personas under control. It used its own booming, godlike voice to respond. "Opening scenario will likely be a show of force and an offer to parley — probably via Diplo. This should lead to negotiations via Semblance. His battleware is already in position and he's close enough for Diplo contact." These words seemed to resonate outward from the center of the table around which the three Semblances appeared to be sitting. An ancient red Diplophone materialized on a nearby post; the table had become a holomap of the vicinity. "You may inspect current placements in realtime on this projection."

Dorelli was pleased that the Brain had finally asserted itself. He spent a few moments surveying the map, then nodded. "As a matter of curiosity, did you ever seal up the Arrowmere entrance?" inquired

Dorelli, knowing the answer already.

The Brain let an edge of irritation seep into its speech. "No. Analysis concurred with you that letting Exeter continue to believe he had secretly obtained control over an access point and was able to befuddle our sensors offered a greater range of possible future counteractions." Despite this analysis, the Brain was beginning to wonder if perhaps the pose of helplessness hadn't actually encouraged Exeter's current brashness, diminishing the range of North Castle's options instead of vice versa. Had Dorelli thought of this? Or had the emergence of a second Wildcard thrown all strategies into chaos? It gave no voice to these thoughts.

Dorelli's Semblance maintained his crisp affect. "Excellent. One other point of curiosity; are you certain all of the Ommergard hoverbar vehicles are operational? I was unfamiliar with the devices you listed and had to dig through some very crusty archives — figuratively speaking, of course — to locate specs yesterday. I've only seen vids of his famed Library, but evidently Bellicarie had a first-rate technical group at one time. Retrofitting hoverbars into some of those devices must have taken some cleverness....

"But I must keep to the point, mustn't I? Well then, Exeter could doubtless cause significant damage to North Castle if he wanted to. In fact, he could blast it to shards if he wanted to, and South Castle as well, even with primitive explosives. And, while we may have enough working bumbusters to blow him to — what was your word, bugdust? — such weapons cannot presently be deployed. We all know there can be no satisfyingly violent preemptive strike or counterattack while the Wildcards are in his possession. Is this agreed?"

The Brain was silent, as were both Miles and Diana.

"Ah, I see...." said Dorelli, letting the word 'see' flutter in the air like a gypsy moth. "You have a secret weapon you don't want to tell me about. Fine. We must all have some secrets or life would be a drab book, wouldn't it? I would only suggest you refrain from deploying it until we know our two Wildcards are safe. Precisely how he got hold of them is still a mystery to me, but perhaps he has actually been able to amass enough Luckiests over the years to influence events in his favor. It's completely counter-scientific, but who knows? Still, the Wildcards must not remain in his possession. Agreed?"

"Agreed," said Miles, Diana and the disembodied voice of the Brain in unison.

"You are aware that I invested Glendyl Fenderwell's mind with an abbreviated cogmodel of Madonna 13 along with, shall we say, a strong suggestion that she adopt this persona, both physically and, to use a highly unscientific term, psychically? Yes, of course you are."

Miles Dunnigan could only glare at Dorelli, recognizing him only in the last twenty-four hours as the cause of his recent debilitating "allergies." Diana Dunnigan rolled her eyes and thought what hormonally hapless creatures men are. Even her over-the-hill, semi-disembodied brother.

"This trifling — and perhaps somewhat melodramatic — innovation was for her own safety, of course. She is unpredictable and will only become more so over time. However, the longer she lives, the more this unpredictability is likely to favor the interests of Clans Dunnigan which are, in this case, wholly congruent with my own interests. Thus, we must ensure that she stays alive." He gave Miles Dunnigan a condescending fatherly look before continuing.

"Miles certainly is aware of Exeter's rather storied attraction to Madonna 13 during his youth. And, as Miles can amply testify, Glendyl has now become remarkably Madonna 13-like by all accounts. And not just in appearance. Bursting into the chorus of her cellsister's 'Papa Don't Preach' and coolly vamping the Red One in front of all his Luckiests was a brilliant extemporaneous performance by any standard! She probably has as much chutzpah as Original Madonna at this point. Perhaps I overloaded her, but I truly believe this persona is all that has kept her alive ... and kept Exeter a touch off balance as well.

"So, I would call the implant a success thus far. Exeter's current actions suggest he is still unaware of several key facts: one, that his captive is the Quester, Glendyl Fenderwell; two, that his Blue Goons failed in their mission to throttle Glendyl and were memory-manip-ulated by the forces of goodness, namely us; three, that Glendyl has been somehow using the Nevergate to visit Ommergard quite fre-quently. Do we agree?" Cambitter Dorelli rarely failed to acknowl-edge the evidence of his own brilliance.

Again, three simultaneous — if grudging — indications of assent.

"Well then, it is we who are lucky. Perhaps this luck will contin-ue. Allow me to share my ideas. Then, if you choose, you may ready your secret weapon. One more thing; there is a third Wildcard who can send all of our plans to the dung pile. I speak of the Nevergate, of course."

The Brain's voice reverberated through the space in godlike fashion, the irritation now clearly audible (it rankled at taking stra-tegic input from a mere human, and particularly from Cambitter Dorelli): "An interjection before you proceed, Cambitter. There may be a fourth Wildcard if Glendyl's alleged teleblade conversations with a wyvern named Lysheem are true. She would be almost inexorably drawn to this probability nexus."

"Just so," said the unflappable Dorelli. "Now as to my several concepts ...."

72 :: NOTHING HAPPENED 409

CASTLE OMMERGARD slid to a stop with the morbid grace of a mountainous hearse. It hovered in a spot a hundred yards distant from North Castle's pier and a dozen feet above the surface of Arrowmere. A light breeze combined with the ghostly blue emanations of the hoverfields to give the appearance that the castle floated on a diaphanous blue cloud dusted with winking fairygleam.

Overhead, it was a different story. Thunderheads had mustered into thick dark clumps that sucked the light out of most of the sky; only to the west did a lighter fringe outline the near ridges. To the northeast, a thickly muscled storm cell hung over Mt Faunibeune, trailing a curtain of hail and sharp jags of lightning. Booms of rolling thunder careened off the cliffs shrouding Arrowmere and left a trail of surly echoes in their wake.

Inside North Castle an equally gloomy — if less flamboyant — kind of storm had descended upon the Plaid Salon. The red Diplophone seemed to be at its vortex. Waiting. At exactly twelve noon, the Diplophone pulsed for the first time in centuries, a brief conversation ensued, and a meeting of Semblances was arranged for the afternoon hour of two.

At the stroke of two, Exeter's Semblance appeared in North Castle's lush executeria wearing Lord Bellicarie's fanciful admiralty uniform: a snappy outfit of ice cream white duck with gold-fringed epaulettes, buttons of carved twenty-one-carat gold and an impressive display of completely bogus medals. His beard had been bound in the style of the ancient Babylonian king, Nebuchadnezzar, and a ceremonial sword once owned by Sir Francis Drake hung at his side. His manner was easy and light.

Both Miles and Diana's Semblances were attired in the traditional formal greens of Clans Dunnigan. Cambitter Dorelli was not present in Semblance form. He was, however, auditing the proceedings.

After the usual formal greetings, Exeter's Semblance demanded to have the Mt Faunibeune Nevergate reactivated and placed at his disposal. His tone was firm, but not harsh.

Miles Dunnigan patiently explained why North Castle was unable to comply with his request and invited Exeter to search the premises if he believed otherwise. Diana said nothing and merely glowered at both Exeter and Miles. Exeter had not expected a more positive initial response and a protracted negotiation ensued. Being unaware that Glendyl and Lizbeth could be exploited as hostages, Exeter did not bargain at full strength.

While the Semblances jousted with words and gestures, a flock of small gray birds that had earlier settled among the towers and bastions of Castle Ommergard took flight. An observer from North Castle would have found their formation remarkable — a vertical circle, much like the Ferris wheels once popular in amusement parks. Their slow, wall-hugging flight along the face of Ommergard was anything but birdlike. When they reached Tower Five they hovered in a ragged circle around a particular window several levels below Exeter's command post.

On the other side of the wall was a room — normally a storeroom for magical paraphernalia — that now contained four humans: Glendyl Fenderwell in the guise of Madonna 13, Lizbeth Marble, and two burly Blue Goons, their guards. The two girls were being detained for 'further discussions' with Exeter. Was their mutual detention mere coincidence?

Glendyl was a burglar caught in the act. Lizbeth's presence in the storeroom — and her rapid slide from Chief's Pet to suspected spy — can be blamed most directly on Loopy. Ommergard's thinkbox had become interested in the "tagbug invasion" and applied its alien reasoning processes to the matter for lack of anything better to do. This had resulted in an "ears only" to Exeter following yesterday's barbecue; it suggested there was a high probability that the tagbugs had arrived in Castle Ommergard via Lizbeth Marble. It was wrong about this, but the concept resonated with Exeter's paranoia; Lizbeth was brought in for a 'conversation with the Chief.'

411

What the Chief had learned — or guessed — from his brief inquisitions with Glendyl and Lizbeth was unsatisfying, but the use of more exhaustive methods would have to wait until he had played out his little game with North Castle. Two things were certain: a theft had been attempted and North Castle had been spying on him. Both were tawdry violations of his inherently easy nature. Such violations must be vigorously discouraged.

Lizbeth Marble stood, a distant look in her eyes as she scratched at the grossly swollen area between her shoulderblades. She had ceased to even hear the endless taunts and jibes of the Blue Goons, who found her constant scratching to be both unfeminine and very entertaining in a gross sort of way. Around her neck was a black metal collar, a device for transmitting unpleasant stimuli to certain nerve centers. The controller for the collars was strapped to the wrist of an Outsider named Jasper, the senior Blue Goon of the pair.

Earlier, Glendyl/Madonna 13, also fitted with a black collar, had tried to distract the Blue Goons with coquetry and feminine wiles. This had seemed to work on Exeter at the barbecue and even during their later "interview," but the Goons were having none of it. They had been sternly forewarned, for one thing; they valued their human forms, for another.

Each of Glendyl's attempted distractions had resulted in a 'discouragement' as Exeter had earlier described the searing jags of pain delivered through the collar. After a recent jolt of nerve fire that had made her limbs dance like antic broomsticks, Glendyl abandoned this tactic. She now sat cross-legged on the floor, trying to clear away the lingering shards of pain so she could think what to do next. Or even think at all. With no warning or preamble, an urgent and vaguely familiar voice penetrated her awareness from somewhere inside her head.

Glendyl, listen carefully and, for all our sakes, remain silent and give no indication that anything is out of the ordinary. This is Mr White and I am contacting you through a special mindlink implant. Only you can hear me. Until you have some practice 'speaking' through this particular sort of mindlink — it's somewhat different from your circlet — I think it best that we keep your necessary responses in simple yes and no format. Here is how we will do it. Pinch your right thumb and index finger together for 'yes', your left for 'no.' Right for 'yes,' left for 'no.' Indicate yes if you understand.

Glendyl nodded, mumbled, then flushed slightly as she caught herself a little too late. Blue Goon Jasper had noticed her out-of-place nod and her mumbled "yes."

"Hey, Phony Madonna, you hearing voices, you crazy loon twit?" Jasper and Reekay guffawed at this witticism. Trying to cover both her error and her embarrassment, Glendyl responded with a facetious smile and that timeless finger gesture. Jasper's face went from scowl to grin in jerky increments. The grin became a leer as he held two fingers over the buttons on his control pad in a taunting, threatening manner.

"That your IQ or your sperm count?" guffawed Reekay with a lewd leer aimed at Glendyl.

"Babes don't have sperm, you bonebrain: you couldn't count it if you wanted to." Jasper was the brighter of the two, but not by much. He had also just been promoted to Acting Sergeant and was enjoying the exercise of authority (the more talented Adjuncts had recently been recruited into the new Saddlestick Cowboys).

Glendyl sucked in a resigned breath, looked away and finally executed a proper "yes" signal.

Over the next several minutes Dorelli learned what he needed to know of the situation. The next part would be more difficult.

Now, Glendyl, it is your time: the time for you to play a critical part in the proceedings. And it will require all your courage. There may be an unpleasant conflict developing in the next hour or so and you and Lizbeth will be in grave danger. You must escape Ommergard, though I can provide you with only scant assistance. Has your friend the Nevergate provided you with any escape routes? Please don't waste time denying your Nevergate excursions. I don't need to know where it's hiding or how you found it. I just need you to escape. Now, about the escape routes: yes or no?

413

Glendyl signaled an affirmative.

Excellent! Is there one nearby? According to my avian transponder array you are in Tower Five, Level 7.

With a faint shiver of renewed hope, Glendyl closed her eyes, reviewed her mental map of Castle Ommergard and located the nearest gatehole. It was two levels up, on the floor where Exeter's command post was located and where she and Lizzie had been "interviewed" by the Wise One himself. "Yes," she signaled.

Fine, then. I took the occasion of your recovery from dragon burns to implant, in addition to this mindlink, some compressed learning circuits that have since woven their way into your capability sets. They will provide you with certain enhanced ... uh ... capabilities. The ones you need at the moment will be activated by the phrase 'Wonder Woman.' Do not speak it until you are ready. But don't wait very long, either. And please: don't try to be 'in charge,' if you know what I mean. Just relax and let Wonder Woman take over. Much like your Madonna 13 persona, Wonder Woman is quite the expert in certain situations. Do you understand?

Glendyl signaled "yes" and tried to ignore the sinking feeling in the pit of her stomach. Geez Louise, she thought. We gotta get up to the command center in order to get out of here? That place has gotta be crawling with these blue jerks. How's *that* going to work? And what about these morons, particularly the one with the pain buttons. And then the ones outside?

The inner voice interrupted her mental sideplay. *One more thing. When you get back to the Nevergate, wherever it is, don't go anywhere near North Castle. The Nevergate, while somewhat naïve according to some accounts, is quite a bright entity and will doubtless agree. Now I must say goodbye; the negotiations are becoming somewhat sensitive and I'm needed elsewhere. I know you'll do what is needful, Glendyl Fenderwell. May the luck of Madonna 13 be with all of us.* Then there was only an empty feeling in her head.

Glendyl unwound herself, stretched and turned to look out the window, trying to collect her wits and hoping the Goons didn't hear the thumping of her hyperactive heart. Mr White's "no cause for alarm" was echoing in her head. What did that mean?

She pushed the question out of the way and looked out at North Castle, which occupied almost her entire field of view. Procrastinating, she sought among a hundred windows for her own room and was rewarded with a pang of homesickness. So near, so far. As her gaze wandered higher, she noted something sinister; a large dark platform bristling with spiderlike appendages hovered over the central portion of the Castle. Flying in a loose formation around the platform were six blue-uniformed shapes riding some kind of flying cigar-shaped things. Geez Louise! This is for real. Well, here goes nothing. "Wonder Woman," she said politely to the air and with no particular emphasis. Nothing happened.

73 :: CORPSES FOR COMPANY

"HEY, NO TALKING! You know what the Chief said. Time for a little nerve juice to settle you down." Jasper sneered and his fingers danced suggestively. "That's worth a double jolt for each of you." He moved his fingers over the buttons. There was a blur of limbs, then the sounds of snapped fingers, sundered vertebrae and slack bodies hitting the floor. Exeter's corps of Blue Goons had shrunk by two ... and they hadn't even had time to scream before dying.

"Geez Lou-ise!" Glendyl stared, unbelieving, at the two bodies on the floor with necks at unhealthy angles. I did that? Geez Louise! This is too weird. How could Mr White ...." Glendyl's Wonder Woman persona had no time for questions or dawdling. Nor did the Wonder Woman persona have time or inclination for misplaced remorse. She hissed an order: "Lizzie, get up! We gotta go. Now."

Lizbeth had been scratching the swelling at the base of her spine. She looked dumbly at the skewed figures on the floor and nodded.

Glendyl removed Jasper and Reekay's slivershots, tucked them into her faux Artificer jumpsuit and rapped the door sharply three times as she had seen Jasper do. "Whaddya need, Acting Sarge?"

Glendyl's mouth moved: words came out in Jasper's voice. "Hadda give the captives a serious discouragement. Phony Madonna couldn't take it and wet her pants. I made her take her uniform off for ... you know, disposal. You guys gotta trash it for me. I don't suppose the Chief will mind if we all conduct a little ... uh, inspection, while

we're at it. Security reasons, you know. So get your butts in here."
Glendyl blinked. Where did I come up with that?

The heavy door swung open and Wonder Woman reacted. One surprised Blue Goon crumpled, his hands clawing at a crushed windpipe. The second guard flew backwards, skull crunching against the far wall, nose cartilage hammered deep into his graymatter. Glendyl copped two more slivershots, handing these to Lizzie, who tucked them into her pockets.

Spotting no one else in the vicinity, Glendyl tiptoed to the slidewell. The cab was elsewhere; calling it now could attract unwanted attention. Glendyl's Wonder Woman persona looked for an emergency escape route. There: a door concealing a stairwell. Only two floors up to the nearest gatehole. "C'mon Lizzie," she whispered and began to take the stairs three at a time.

The stairwell door to Level Nine of Tower Five was locked. Big surprise, thought Glendyl. She patted her jumpsuit for the master openrod before recalling that it had been confiscated by her captors. Glendyl put a finger to her lips as Lizbeth, breathing heavily, mounted the last step to the landing. She whispered terse instructions. Lizbeth nodded, but her mind was still elsewhere. Both girls removed a slivershot carefully from a pocket. Although Glendyl had never seen a weapon like this before, Wonder Woman knew exactly how it worked and whispered instructions to Lizzie, who nodded again. Glendyl shrugged, made a slight adjustment to the spray pattern, pointed the weapon at the locking mechanism and fired: a hissing sound, a burst of tiny explosions, a smoking hole where the mechanism had been.

Glendyl kicked open the door and burst through to land in a crouch. Just to the right of the slidewell — in front of the invisible gatehole — stood two very surprised members of Away Team 3. No one moved for several heartbeats. Then, across the alcove, a tall man stomped angrily through the command post doorway. "Which of you morons made that noise!" he hissed.

Exeter. Unlike his Semblance in the Plaid Salon, the flesh-and-blood, here-and-now Exeter wore a red jumpsuit bound at the waist by the Standard Toolbelt. Upon seeing Glendyl, Lizbeth and the smoking hole in the door he spat: "You!"

Exeter's eyes made a flicking motion toward the Blue Goons. They lunged. Two hisses, two muffled explosions, two blots of smoking crimson gore spattering the wall. Glendyl stepped back as both Goons fell face-first to the floor minus their midsections. Before Exeter fully registered the destruction, the target pattern of Glendyl's slivershot was making a large, luminous red circle on his chest.

Although she knew she should just dive for the gatehole, Glendyl could not resist one diversion. Her attunement with the Toolbelt now called to her, a siren song she could feel in every cell of her being; she couldn't leave without it. "My Standard Toolbelt, scab-wad. Now." The Wonder Woman overlay knew the importance of intimidation in a takeover situation; her harsh growl was steady, cold and menacing. At the moment, the Glendyl Fenderwell and Madonna 13 personas were tucked away in a far corner of her being.

"Well, aren't you the nasty one? Look at the mess you've made, whoever you are." Exeter paused, squinted. "But of course! Our charming celebrity impersonator stands revealed as the late Quester Fenderwell, somehow undead. You also seem to have acquired some mods: you didn't learn that routine at Eastac. I should have ...."

"No talk, asshole. Just unfasten my Standard Toolbelt and slide it over here. Slow and smooth: a nice big, smoking hole would be a perfect chest decoration for an over-aged shitbag like you, so don't get clever. And keep your hand away from that nerve doodad on your wrist: you oughta see what happened to the last snotboffin who pushed one of those buttons!"

Exeter smiled a thin arc of pure hatred, but complied with exaggerated caution. Was he stalling? Calling for reinforcements on a mindlink? Working up a spell? A diversion? Glendyl knew nothing of the Semblances currently in intense negotiation just across the water.

The Standard Toolbelt slid smoothly across the floor and nothing adverse occurred. Glendyl picked it up. "Thank you, Your Wise-

417

ness. Now get that platform thing and those flyboys away from North Castle. Now!"

Exeter's smile darkened to match a voice black with malice. "They're already gone, Ms Fenderwell. It didn't have to be this way. It really didn't. But you forced my hand. Now see for yourself what your little role-playing episode has brought down upon you and your handlers. Or if you're too frightened to look, just listen."

418   The shockwave rocked Castle Ommergard, tilting it back several degrees before the hoverbars could compensate. Then the sound wave caught up. Glendyl and Lizbeth slid backwards towards the area where the gatehole was supposed to be, arms flailing, trying to keep their balance. They fell in a pile of limbs. Stunned by the unexpected sonic blast, Glendyl couldn't remember the hole's triggerword. Time slowed to a crawl.

Exeter slid toward her down the tilted floor, his face a mask carved from solid wrath, his right hand jabbing the pain buttons. A searing jag of nerve lightning ripped through Glendyl's body, each nerve ending a sizzling torch of pure agony. Her body arched backwards as all her muscles spasmed at once. Then all feeling evaporated.

Exeter's screams surged above the staccato pops of chewbombs devouring North Castle's walls and roofs. Rage tore at the roots of his being: images, images, damnable images. Girl and Toolbelt, inches from his grasp! Girl screaming for mercy, helpless! Girl unconscious, even more helpless! The prizes are inches from his grasp. Then a confusing splatter of impossibilities: a monstrous metallic hand, a reek of ozone — or was it sulphur? — a hazy shimmer in the corner, a hissing sound.

Exeter's rages were prematurely terminated when something slammed into his face and turned out his lights. Some moments later, reinforcements arrived to find Exeter the Wise stretched out on the floor with a smashed nose and two bloody corpses for company.

....

74 :: NO SURVIVOR

THE VAGUE SHIMMER in the sky had circled high above Dunnigans Wall, watching the scene unfold below her and calculating tactics and probabilities. She had few options.

With a battlerider, Lysheem could have easily taken out the blue clowns on the old saddlesticks and probably the platform as well. And fast. Endless simming and battletraining under the Dawnhammer had taught her all she needed. But with only her own wings and a wand, her destructive capabilities were extremely limited. And she knew she had arrived 30 minutes too late for preventive measures; the spidercranes had planted their ordnance already and the platform and its six escorts were slewing north for cover. No other explanation. Gotta get to those bombs, she thought, but not until I've dealt with this bunch.

She extended her claws and let the black shutter of battlerage close over her soul. Lysheem Triplehorn, the Dark Avenger, plunged after the saddlesticks with only death on her mind; the Dawnhammer would be avenged in some small way.

Lysheem's nearly vertical trajectory crossed paths with the trailing saddlestick. She flared out just over the Cowboy's head, grabbed him by the neck with one hand and flung him into the air. Half a dozen punctures left a pinwheel trail of blood as the rider tumbled toward the Wittwater Deep. Lysheem settled neatly into the saddle. She twisted the throttle hard and the saddlestick with the invisible rider became a demon of pursuit. In seconds her nose-mounted homers turned the two nearest riders and their mounts into satisfying fireballs. That left three and the platform.

The three lead riders got a visual surprise in their rearviews: a riderless saddlestick bearing down on them at full thrust. Lysheem's next homer fireballed the middle rider, but the two flankers banked in opposite directions — one high, one low — before she could lock on. Not good. These boys had done some recent dogfight simming.

Lysheem refocused, accelerated, rolled and looped back to target the heavylift, its industrial grade brain uncomprehending of peril. Two homers found softspots: the brain and a powerpipe. The craft spewed blue fire, tumbled out of control and fell earthward in a flaming stew of writhing spider-crane members and tangled infrastructure.

Two to go, but two problems in getting them. Problem number one: only one homer left. Problem number two: the remaining two saddlesticks were lost from both visual contact and her stick's limited sensors. Cloaked or really out of range? No way to know.

Dunnigans Wall was now several miles distant. As Lysheem turned back toward the battle site, North Castle became a small volcano, retching gouts of flaming wreckage and hurling chunks of webcrete in all directions; the shockwave almost blew her off her mount. Then a different kind of shockwave — sadness and grief for the ancestral home of her creators — washed over her in warm, salt-sweet courses. Then battlerage stepped back in, wrapped itself around those feelings and went to work.

Lysheem executed a barrelroll, banked and cranked at full speed toward Castle Ommergard, eyes aflame with a larger vengeance. Coming in low over the dam, she barely noted that portions of the dam face itself were burning, surrounded by a flurry of small flying things. To her immediate left, great rents sundered the thick outer walls of North Castle in a hundred places and jagged cracks grew as she watched. The famed drawbridge had been blown off its hinges by the initial blast and ironbound timbers now dangled haplessly from one chain. Behind, the Castle's guts were a cyclone of flames and a rising mushroom of acrid smoke. Battlerage again banished North Castle's tragedy from her mind: vengeance first.

Ahead loomed the evil Ommergard: the culprit, the instigator, the great enemy. As she closed in, a strange hodgepodge of vehicles emerged from Ommergard's west-facing sally port. With one homer left, Lysheem locked it onto the only vehicle in the bunch worth destroying — the hovertank. Her last homer streaked tankward.

Two hoverbar-powered WW II jeeps had emerged first, followed by two olive-drab half-tracks of the same vintage. Seeing the unmanned saddlestick streaking toward them, their novice pilots executed hasty evasive maneuvers. The jeeps spun into each other, lost control and tumbled into the chilly Arrowmere for an unexpected swim. One half-track rammed one of the tumbling jeeps and also took a swim. The second half-track barely avoided disaster by lurching into a sharp climb, hugging the castle wall and escaping around Ommergard's nearest corner.

In the acceleration of her senses, nerves and muscles that was battlemode, the action unfolded in a slow-mo ballet. Into this lazy dance swung the deadly hovertank, now all alone.

The sleek, unmanned Cognodyne Macerator was halfway through the sally port when the incoming showed up on its sensors. Its battlebrain reacted: a decoy softspot shot off to the right, firing a spray of piranhas for added insurance. At the same moment, it unleashed a trio of homers back at Lysheem's saddlestick. Then it executed a five-gee vertical evasion. All this in one-tenth of a second.

Lysheem knew when to cut and run. As her last homer was detonated by piranhas, she hung the saddlestick into a tight upward one-eighty, streaked back over the dam in a steep dive and hurtled down into Wittwater Deep, leveling out only a yard above the churning river. Three homers were hot on her tail and gaining: less than ten seconds before they caught her. She aimed the saddlestick at a wall of time-stained quartzite where the canyon made a southward bend, punched cruise control, and when the incomings were only twenty feet from her tail, ejected. The saddlestick and the three homers self-destructed in a glorious fireball a quarter mile down the canyon.

At the top of her ejection arc, Lysheem leaped, tucked and left the saddle tumbling toward the Wittwater. Staccato bursts from her wand sent it flaming toward ejection seat heaven.

Just before impacting the eastern cliff, the invisible ball that was the Dark Avenger burst open. Leathery wings caught air, but not soon enough. Her body grazed the cliff, tumbled and ping-ponged toward the rocks. Slight miscalculation.

Lysheem's tumble gradually resolved into a swoop. To an observer, she would appear as a huge pair of flickery wings, the stealth-fiber cape causing them to dance in and out of visibility. The flickers skimmed low over the water, then flew parallel to the opposite canyon wall for a several miles as she searched for a hiding place.

Spotting a possibility, the Avenger shot upward, wings pumping hard toward a dark hole high in the opposite cliff wall. Hardly a perfect hideout, but it would have to do for the moment; she'd be in the hovertank's sights any second. She slowed, stalled and disappeared into the cave mouth.

Some distance up-canyon, the unmarred Macerator made an unhurried inspection of the blackened cavity where saddlestick and homers had disintegrated. Detecting no survivor, it turned back to Castle Ommergard to await its next assignment.

75 :: INGLORIOUS END

CONCEALED by a mass of bloated, dark cumulus, another aerial figure flew high above in languid soaring arcs. This one patiently observed the evolving play of castles, vehicles and hellfire far below with the aid of a device that made clouds transparent to her sight. The ancient alien festered with rages, slights, wounds and outrageous schemes, but she had learned to bide her time for the optimum moment. That moment was finally coming. In the meantime, she soared, contemplated and hated. Soon she would return to her lair, where her blood-hungry shock troops were almost ready for action.

· · · · ·

Diogenes the Wanderer watched, helpless and impotent, from a cleft in the rocks overlooking Arrowmere from the east. Lazy tendrils, like lost dreams, ascended the jagged ruins of North Castle to join the early fringes of sunset. He had arrived too late. Events predicted centuries earlier had finally come to pass. Before his very eyes, a long lifetime of observing, planning, and small, careful nudges had been sunk on the shoals of the unpredictable. At this moment, all seemed for naught, and all because a sweet mule broke a leg at the wrong time. The ancient words of Henley rose up in Diogenes' mind: "In the fell clutch of circumstance I have not winced nor cried aloud. Under the bludgeonings of chance My head is bloody, but unbowed."

Unlike the poet, Diogenes bowed his head, tears darkening the rocks at his feet in meaningless splatters. The last traces of Dunnigan glory had met a truly inglorious end.

76 :: THE CALL

THREE PERSONS are playing Name That Sculpture. The Ascetic combs out his knee-length beard and declares in favor of a poetic simplicity: "Still Life." The prim and stuffy Academic opts for an exercise in descriptive tersity, but fully-accessorized with end notes and bibliography (not included here due to space restrictions): "Collage of Rag Dolls on Persian Rug." The Moralist flails her six arms and declaims (in shrill tones) that a contextual solution is imperative: "The Sodden Aftermath of Youthful Ferment."

Tense silence. All await the Judge's decision, which they have agreed will be final. Only one last formality is required: the Judge removes a foot-long hatpin from her bodice and pricks at the Sculpture. The Sculpture responds with a characteristic sign of unsculptureness; it jerks as if pricked by a hatpin. To the dismay of all, the Judge reclassifies the piece as Performance Art. A vigorous fistfight ensues. Then one part of the reclassified Sculpture realizes it is dreaming and the scene fades. This part moves its lips: "Gate? Is this you?"

The Nevergate responded in uncharacteristic terse sentences. "It is. You and your friend are undamaged and safe for the moment. Rest and relax while you can. We'll talk in a bit."

Glendyl closed her eyes and let her singed nerves recuperate a while. She got the picture: Gate was stressed. When something as smart and powerful as a Nevergate is stressed, best to give it some space. Relaxation was difficult; the floor vibrated with invisible activity but she closed her eyes anyway.

Sometime later she sat up, still shaky, and surveyed the Nevergate's lounge. Little, if anything, had changed, except the viewports. For the first time since her first visit, the ports opening onto the Arrowmere deep and all its aquatic wonders were closed. Rather than ponder these perplexities, Glendyl decided to tend to the still unconscious Lizbeth Marble.

Lizbeth came awake in unnerving lurches. Finally she and Glendyl were sitting on the floor, engaged in a listless, stunted form of conversation that treated recent events as too hot to touch. Neither felt much like talking. When the Nevergate spoke, it filled the room with a sad baritone that Glendyl had never heard before.

"Lizbeth Marble, I welcome you. Unfortunately, I have no leisure to share with you at the moment. I fear events have lurched far beyond my control. Or anyone's control. North Castle has been destroyed, along with, I suspect, all its treasures and memories. I cannot detect the Brain."

Some part of Glendyl had been hiding these possibilities from her own larger self, but now her North Castle memories returned in a turbulent flash flood of images and feelings: drawbridge, Plaid Salon, Map, hourglass, Scrapbook, saucerites, Arcade, Miles Dunnigan, soft wine, Laniss and a hundred other flickers...all gone. Silent tears flooded her cheeks, gave way to sobs. Lizzie offered as much comfort as her not-all-there-yet state allowed. Glendyl stifled her sniffles and returned to the present.

"There is more," said the Nevergate after a time. "My own problems have become paramount. Exeter doubtless suspects I am nearby. If I stay in Arrowmere he will find me, and much more that could give him great power. And your own work is elsewhere; we must part ways. I suggest you prepare yourselves. You might, for example, want to retrieve your QPack from the corner."

Glendyl thought she detected a note of guilt in Gate's voice. Can a thing like Gate feel stuff like that? The question provided a moment's distraction from the Nevergate's proclamation.

"There is still more. My synthesis of probabilities detects no clear pathways into the future. All is fluxion, a spiral of uncertainties around a hub. At the center of this hub are Lizbeth Marble and Glendyl Fenderwell. You are probabilistic anomalies to be sure. But more.

"Perhaps you really are the Wildcards that have been predicted. Except that no long-range forecast predicted two Wildcards, only one. To be frank, I don't quite know what to do with you. And I must be on my way very shortly. Dunnigans Wall has been fractured by the shockwaves and unless the fixers can seal and reinforce it very soon, Nessie could be high and dry by tomorrow morning."

Into Glendyl's mind flashed three images: Lysheem, a yellow and lavender ground squirrel named Jamis Pojorolli, and the looming dark mass of jaws, claws and leathery wings she now knew was the dragon Emmishak. At these images, Glendyl felt a surge of urgency: she needed to do something. Now.

Then, much to both Lizbeth's and the Nevergate's surprise, Glendyl grinned. In her mental image, Lysheem wore a heliotrope bodysuit spangled with hot pink stars and wrapped with alternating diagonal ruffles of avocado green, crookneck yellow, tomato red and habañero orange. The wyvern looked magnificently, tastelessly ridiculous. Glendyl now knew what to do.

She retrieved the QPack and slung it on her back. Then, almost reverently, took up the Standard Toolbelt and clasped it around her waist. Her cupped hands found the teleblade's hilt and she closed her eyes; the teleblade and her inner self somehow joined in an intimate connection. As this grew in strength, something else dwindled. Exeter's temporary impingement was replaced with a thick, almost erotic bond of attunement. Knowing the time was right, Glendyl made the call.

427

428

77 :: RODENT FORM

PHYSHT-POP. A shimmery, insubstantial image appeared in the center of the lounge. Unlike the image from Glendyl's mind, this Lysheem — if it was Lysheem — was just a sort of watery shape in the air. But it moved like Lysheem.

A familiar voice spoke, but without the vivacity Glendyl had come to expect. "Well, well, well. Dryll just told me that Exeter had somehow lost his toy … and already it has reappeared. Hello again, Glendyl Fenderwell. And congratulations on staying alive: we figured you were permanently out of the game."

Lysheem paused and then continued in that tone reserved just for tragedy. "It appears we have taken some great and irreplaceable losses. We're all in a fine mess at the moment and I doubt that I can be much help to you, wherever you are. Sorry. I hate to puke on anybody's footskins, but the future smells as bad as this godforsaken hole right now." Another pause, then the irrepressible Lysheem resurfaced. "Got any sangria? Cigars? Better yet, how about some dragon repellent? And some air freshener? One more thing: some peanuts or something for my new pet."

Before Glendyl could respond, the Nevergate somehow cut into the teleblade's channel and interjected a question. "If you are truly Lyshccm of Cavvitoy of Lyshandrik of Carrfindoy of Lyvittus of Cassimoy, then I have a message for you. It was placed in my custody by Cavvitoy himself and it is for your mind only. It is a sealed memcap."

"And who is this breaching our secure channel uninvited?" A harsh edge had entered Lysheem's voice.

"I am the so-called 'Last Nevergate' and I sincerely beg your pardon for the interruption. Glendyl Fenderwell and Lizbeth Marble are currently recuperating in my ... lounge."

"It's true," interjected Glendyl, hoping to head off a conflict between two strange beings she considered friends.

"I detect truth. Okay, the Last Nevergate, the one we're all looking for. And Glendyl Fenderwell and the Wildcard Lizbeth Marble are lounging around in its lounge. Well, Sir Nevergate, you've succeeded in surprising my sorry wyvern ass. And it's been eons since I've heard the names of my backparents. A memcap from Cavvitoy? Very mysterious. How do you propose to get this ancient message into my hands?"

"I believe there is ample space in my lounge for a person of your dimensions. And, I think you will find my hospitality far superior to that of your current surroundings. It would be more pleasant for the humans if you could depower your stealthfiber — I assume you're wearing stealthfiber — and ...."

"Your lounge sounds great. A saloon might sound better, but even an outhouse would one-up this sewer. And I'll happily decloak as soon as you get us out of here. Beam me up, Scotty!"

"My pleasure, indeed. One small question first: how did you know my nickname?"

"Call it a lucky guess."

There was the semi-auditory vloup, followed by Lysheem's flesh and blood form coalescing in the lounge. Uncloaked and in living color she was somewhat larger than her teleblade image.

"Geez Louise! You *are* big." Glendyl was unable to contain her surprise. "Ever think of playing bangerball?" She was even more surprised when a somewhat emaciated yellow and lavender ground squirrel popped out of one of Lysheem's pockets and leaped into her lap. "Jamis! Is that you? How the hell did you get in her pocket?"

Jamis made a motion with his right forepaw.

"He wants to write," translated Glendyl. "Anybody have a slate? A sandpile? A dusty pipe organ? A piece of paper?"

"I believe any of those rolled nautical charts in the cubbies can serve as writing paper. They're just for show: all blank. I don't believe I currently have any writing implements, however. What a quaint problem. But let's try this."

Jamis was soon making writing motions on a rolled-out sheet of a paper-like substance. The Nevergate's sensors tracked his writing motions and displayed them on the wallscreen. Awkward, but Jamis got the hang of it soon enough. His first readable words were: "LONG STORY. BOTTOM LINE: BIG CAVE LIKE DILLOWY CAVERN. LOTS OF KILLER DRAGONS WITH BACKPACK BLASTERS. EAT GIANT PIG-RATS. ATTACK ST. CORIANDER. CAN YOU GET ME MY OLD BODY BACK? PLEASE?"

431

Lizbeth Marble spoke up for the first time. "Send him somewhere else," she intoned.

Glendyl frowned, taken aback by Lizbeth's lack of concern for an old schoolmate's welfare. "Lizzie! That's rude. This is Jamis Pojorolli, remember him?"

Lizbeth explained in a disinterested monotone. "Jamis is a Transform, a product of Exeter's 'magic.' Everybody in Ommergard knows that Exeter's magic only works where there are interplanar interpolators. He only installed these emplacements in the vicinity of St Coriander and Heroes Trail. Their range is limited, so the 'spell' should dissipate if Jamis gets outside the range of Exeter's interpolators. That would let Jamis' human form demigrate back into this plane. That's my guess, at least. Only Sorcerers get to learn the science and the how-tos. Of course, it could get ugly if ...." Her voice trailed off as she withdrew into some abstruse thought process.

While Lizbeth was speaking, Jamis had been busy sketching a picture of the dragon dogfight he had witnessed and wondering how to get the Nevergate to apply the right colors. Glendyl watched with surprise and amazement. Jamis had a real talent; he might become the world's first ground squirrel fine artist ... if he lived long enough. Maybe he ought to keep his rodent form.

78 :: LONG GOODBYES

LYSHEEM LAY SPRAWLED on the red velvet settee that had some-how lengthened itself to accommodate her eight feet of height. "Scot-ty" had materialized a jug of sangria and a cigar, both still untouched. At the moment Lysheem's eyes were closed, her mind assuming the deepstate necessary for the transfer of a memcap message. Some-where inside her, the biocoded message found the correct code se-quence in her DNA and then transmitted itself along certain nerve pathways into her sensory centers.

Her eyes popped open as she lurched to full attention. "Scotty! Did the Dawnhammer leave anything else for me? I think there are supposed to be some armbands and legbands, some extra packs and some other gear."

"Ahhh, the message was fully transmitted. What you need is un-der the cushions of the settee."

Lysheem addressed Lizbeth for the first time. "Lizbeth Marble, I have some news for you. Those itchy bumps of yours are not obscene tumors. I don't know quite how to say this, but we're related, you and me." Lysheem placed a seven-fingered hand on Lizbeth's arm. "You're my foresister. My Wildcard foresister. That's what the Dawn-hammer's message means. And you know how to find Castle Cara-way. You don't know you know it, but you can find it. Somehow. It's been waiting for you — for us — since just after I got sent to Montser-rat. Long time. But we've got no time to waste; this thing has started

E . T . E L L I S O N

too soon and you're a dead duck if we don't get busy."

Lizbeth appeared only half awake; Lysheem's remarkable disclosures had no visible effect on her. She didn't appear concerned about becoming a dead duck.

Lysheem frowned, then shrugged. To the occupants of the Nevergate's lounge, she said: "Our friend Lizbeth isn't going to live through this unless I do what Cavvitoy has planned."

Not waiting for a response, she turned to the blank-eyed Lizbeth and spoke in grave tones: "I hope you'll forgive me for this." She then whispered something in each of Lizbeth Marble's ears.

At that moment, in some mysterious place deep inside Lizbeth Marble — that matrix of biochemistry, biocurrents and psychons where "sense of self" is stored — a new awareness clicked into place like a long-missing puzzle piece. The truth of what Lysheem just said was suddenly obvious. And under that truth, the incomprehensible words Lysheem had whispered in the wyvern genetongue began their work. Long dormant seeds of coded information burst open inside Lizbeth's extra chromos[35] and began to execute, to communicate, to multiply, to direct traffic, to transform. Lizbeth's sense of self tilted, becoming more wyvern than human. Inside her, chaos erupted.

As Lizbeth's eyes bugged wide, her body straightened, became rigid and fell back on the thick carpet. Her muscles began to pulse and ripple like the water in a pond being pelted with hailstones. Her skin blistered with ten thousand tiny bubbles and her gaping mouth released a long, tortured wail.

Glendyl watched in horror, wanting to somehow put an end to this torture. But something held her back. She realized she trusted Lysheem, so she just bit her tongue and watched as Lysheem wrapped

---

35 :: As in such other "civilized" communities as remain on planet Earth, all St Coriander children are born with a pair of auxiliary chromosomes, repositories for supplementary gene modules or other eugenic interventions/enhancements. This was a common practice worldwide by the mid-22nd century. How renegade wyvern genesets found their way into Lizbeth's extra chromos is not known, although a realist must certainly suspect Dryll's involvement.

thick, heavy-looking bands around Lizbeth's biceps and thighs, and attached instruments to various parts of Lizbeth's anatomy.

"Mass, nutrients and guideware transceivers," she explained to Glendyl, who managed a tight-lipped nod.

The wyvern placed her hands on Lizbeth's rippling brow and spoke to her in gentle tones. "No wyvern has ever been born this way before, out of a human form. You're the first. The Dawnhammer said it might be painful, Foresister." She paused awkwardly, not knowing what else to say. But Lizbeth could hear nothing at all.

Lysheem sighed, stood, shrugged and grimaced. To Glendyl — and possibly Jamis — she said, "You might not want to watch this."

Two tense hours later, Lizbeth's rebirthing was complete. Eight arm and leg bands had been completely absorbed during the transformation, but strips of curled, stiff, yellow-pink human skin lay all around like dry corn husks. Her hair, never her "best feature" (as certain of her St Coriander "friends" had liked to say when discussing each others' attributes) lay in a limp pile.

In the middle of this human debris was a long creature with lustrous skin of deep bluish-gray and furled, still damp black wings. A sinuous tail curled around a long, slender leg and twitched.

Lysheem sighed, smiled and spoke to the three other witnesses to this miracle. "If I read the signs correctly, she's going to come around in a few minutes, and she's going to be really hungry and really thirsty. And she's probably going to want some clothes until she learns how to control her own marvelous wyvern attributes, one of which is appearing to be wearing clothes when you're really bare-ass naked. Can you help out here, Scotty?"

"And Scotty, can you find me a cigar?" This latter silky-voiced request came not from Lysheem, but from the grinning mouth of the former Lizbeth Marble. Deep blue cat-eyes sprang open in a face that was Lizbeth Marble's face but different in an exotic, exquisite sort of way.

Before the Nevergate could respond, a shockwave flung the occupants around the room. A muffled explosion followed.

435

"Hang onto something, dear guests. Exeter must have rigged some fishbombs to try to flush us out, whatever he thinks we are. Snuck up on me: how embarrassing. Got to get moving before we take a direct hit. This might get a little dicey."

Another explosion, another lurch. Then the press of acceleration and rapid, unpatterned changes of direction and velocity. Evasive action, thought Glendyl, hanging onto a leg of Nemo's pipe organ/control console. Jamis had his tiny claws hooked into another leg: the leg of Glendyl's jumpsuit. Then, as quickly as it started, the Nevergate's evasive action ended and Nessie braked to a full stop.

"We're directly under Castle Ommergard now. Unless Exeter wants to put his precious hoverbars at risk, we should be safe for a moment or two. Glendyl, while I'm thinking of it, there is a small memento I've been saving for you. It has somehow found its way under the organ console about six inches from your right hand. Please retrieve it before I forget."

Glendyl's right hand fumbled around and came up with a small, thin paperbook. The forest green cover sported a pattern of animated four-leaf clovers that danced a complex sequence of uptempo dance steps over the semi-transparent face of Madonna 13, a face that morphed through a full range of melodramatic expressions from contrived coy to studied siren in a random sequence. Periodically, these words appeared over all in a luminous yellow textface: *The Luck of Madonna 13* by Diogenes the Wanderer.

"Gate, how wonderful! Thank you bunches!" She tucked the book into a pocket of her gray coveralls next to one of the slivershots.

"You're very welcome. Take good care of it: it's an original edition. Published by the author himself, I believe. And it's autographed as well. Now, before we have any more excitement, I must remind Lysheem to retrieve her golden horned helmet from the floor by the sofa before it gets banged around by further evasive maneuvers."

Lysheem grabbed it, plunked it on her head and adopted a heroic pose."

Glendyl laughed, the wyvern Lizbeth just stared.

The Nevergate continued, an odd note in its voice. "I must tell you all that Nessie and I have greatly enjoyed your company. But it's time to say goodbye. And it is said that nobody likes long goodbyes ...."

438

79 :: INTO SOMETHING

THE AFTERNOON STORM had left a crisp twilight in its wake. Castle Ommergard floated a hundred feet above the now placid Arrowmere and Exeter the Wise stood on his private balcony, surveying what he had wrought. The metaskin dressing over his hastily reconstructed nose itched and his face throbbed, but those were only two of his fresh irritants. More painful were the regrets, which, in his moment of solace, he allowed to surface. He had won, but what? This wreckage? Perhaps he had killed an ancient enemy. If so, the satisfaction of it had been short-lived. In his rage, he had destroyed much more than he had gained. So far.

But the Nevergate probably wasn't in North Castle anyway. So the big prize was still to be won. And, he had eliminated at least one barrier to the prize. Exeter hated to destroy valuable resources, and North Castle was full of valuable resources. But — and this was an important "but" — it was not the prize. Resources are resources, but the prize is the prize.

After a while Exeter began to feel better. Then he looked at his hand and was reminded of the door-sized metallic fist that had cold-cocked him without warning and spirited away Glendyl Fenderwell, Lizbeth Marble and his Standard Toolbelt. A glistening anger bubbled up like champagne froth. In this mood, he also recalled the loss of irreplaceable saddlesticks and the heavylift, and railed at the untimely appearance of what must have been the mysterious lone wyvern.

Exeter pointed an accusing finger at the western sky, as if to blame it for these disappointments. Mysteries! Exeter still hated mysteries.

The surge faded as he reminded himself that there was at least one comforting turn of events; the mysterious wyvern had paid for the damage with its life. While the mystery of its origin remained, this particular mystery lacked currency. The more urgent mysteries would be solved first and the Nevergate would be found; all in good time. His patience had served him well before and would do so again. A good day's work, all in all. Proper perspectives now restored, it was time to see just what Romundo had been yammering about.

The wreckage of North Castle was still too hot for a survey and salvage mission, so Exeter had kept his Ommergardians occupied with a little practice in naval ordnance. A secondary benefit might be the fishbombs killing off some of the nasties that infested this otherwise pleasant water body. But Romundo seemed to think they might have just gotten lucky, flushing out something big and strange by good fortune alone. Exeter was a big fan of well-planned luck.

The fishbombs had chased whatever it was directly under Ommergard, where it stopped. Not very fishlike. And dangerous. Having a huge un-fish only a hundred feet below its precious hoverbars made his newly remobilized castle far too vulnerable. He ordered more altitude and a sequence of evasive maneuvers.

Just in case it was a serious 'hostile,' he also called out the Cognodyne Macerator as a backup and issued a string of commands. As Ommergard moved away with surprising agility, the water-thing dove and accelerated toward the far end of the lake. Exeter sensed something interesting about to happen.

He strode to his mobile command post — one of the two jeeps still dripping from its earlier swim — and studied the white-capped, shadowy waters of Arrowmere, waiting to see what sort of 'big fish' they'd flushed out by sheer chance. The jeep hovered, loosely tied to the observation deck at the top of Tower Five.

"Romundo! Status report!" he barked back into the navigation room over a rising breeze. The Chief was fully back to being the Chief.

"The thing oughta be popping out in less than ten seconds, Chief. Pretty amazing acceleration for a fish. And BIG!"

"Thank you, Romundo. The big thing is clearly not a fish."

In the distance, Arrowmere erupted. A sinuous, greenish-black shape the length of a mature blue whale shot out of the water, flapped its humongous wings and flew around a bend in the lake. The thing's uncanny similarity to mythological sea-monster images was not lost on Exeter. Nor did his sharp gaze fail to observe the very un-sea-monster-like circular viewport in its side. "Follow that submarine!" he shouted. "But no shooting! I want it alive." His jeep shot forward, flanked by two rows of Saddlestick Cowboys, with the Macerator following a discreet distance behind.

441

While Exeter was occupied with his chase, the Nevergate's core modules — now compacted and reconfigured into hundreds of segmented worms the size of walruses — burrowed into the deep black silt that covered the reservoir bottom in the vicinity of Dunnigans Wall.

• • • • •

Lysheem and her freshly minted foresister found themselves in a drift of sand on the Cleavage's nearly buried foredeck. A deepening russet and indigo sky was thick with blowing sand. Lysheem brushed grit from her lips and spoke to the wind: "Thanks, Scotty."

Turning to Lizbeth, she grinned: "Looks like we're going to have to dig this baby out after all, Foresister. Tomorrow. Meantime, let's climb back inside, get you properly fed and get better acquainted. You've got a lot to learn about being a wyvern: how to dress, for one thing."

"Does that mean you — the one with that silly helmet — are going to be my teacher?" Lizbeth rolled her eyes skyward and tried twisting her new wyvern facial muscles into something resembling a sneer of disinterest. "Great. Can't wait."

• • • • •

The now familiar implosion sensation took Glendyl by surprise. One instant her arms were wrapped around the spindly leg of the organ console in the Nevergate's lounge; the next instant her arms were wrapped around something much bigger, warmer and slipperier. She blinked and blinked again. Wherever Gate had sent her was dark, hot and had a cloying stench that made her stomach churn. Her brain was having trouble dealing with the sudden change of location, but her first impression was that she was hanging onto a metal pipe in a vertical shaft of some sort. And something heavy was pulling her right leg out of its socket. About that time her brain realized that she was also sliding down the pipe.

442

Gotta drop this extra weight, she thought dully. She shook and twisted as best she could, but the weight continued to drag her down and she slipped a couple more inches in the wrong direction. The next time she tried to shake off the extra weight, she got results.

The extra weight shouted. "Hey! Glendyl! Stop it. It's me, Jamis. Holy magnolia! Hey, Glendyl: I've got my body back! Hot damn! Hot triple-damn!"

Jamis? Here? A melancholy sigh escaped Glendyl's lips. She hissed as quietly as she could hiss, "Great, Jamis, I'm really, really happy for you. But I'm losing my grip on this slimy pipe and I'd really like to use my legs. If you don't find something else to hang onto, we're gonna take a quick trip to wherever this pipe goes. And with my luck, it's a long way down. So just grab the pipe, not my leg! Okay? Pretty please? And whisper, don't yell. We don't know who might be around here."

"Right. Got it. Okay. That better? Hey, don't stand on my head, okay? Gag me. This place smells a lot like that cave with all the dragons in it. Except worse. What a godawful place that was! I mean you should have seen that dogfight. I mean dragon fight. Blood everywhere! And when the winner — that guy could really fly, by the way — anyway, when he sliced the other guy's head off with his death-ray-helmet, I barfed, man. I really spewed my bonbons ...."

"Shhh!" whispered Glendyl.

Jamis was silent for maybe ten seconds. "Where do you think we are, anyway? You think this is your Nevergate buddy's idea of a joke? Oh, jeeziz! I don't have any clothes on. Hey, Glendyl, you're going to have to loan me some clothes. At least a loincloth or something. What a scam this all is. I'm not kidding, this is pure ...."

Glendyl gritted her teeth. "Jamis, I know you're really excited to be able to talk again, but would you mind just shutting up anyway? I'll hide my eyes: trust me. I won't peek. But I think I'm beginning to understand why Exeter turned you into something that couldn't talk."

END OF BOOK ONE

The story continues in Book Two:

The Mask of Madonna 13

444

ON THE EVOLUTION OF LUCK

IN SPRING OF 2002, the hardcover Chronicler's Edition of *The Luck of Madonna 13* was launched by a rookie author and a courageous rookie publisher named Wynderry Press. To say that the rookie author (me) was blown away by the positive response from reviewers and readers is an almost felonious understatement. Being named one of the 92 Best Books of 2002 by *January Magazine* and earning a Book of the Year award from *Foreword Magazine* (now Foreword Reviews, the voice of independent and university presses) was icing on the Twinkie.

Alas, there was this little problem called Distribution. In those days most big chain bookstores bought from a 1200 lb distribution gorilla named Ingram, which would not distribute the products of new publishers. This meant there was no way to get it into the likes of Border's and Barnes & Noble; they didn't buy books from Baker & Taylor, the mere 600 lb distribution gorilla that handled the Chronicler's Edition.

One instructive incident sticks in my mind. I was giving a book talk on the dystopia in Ray Bradbury's Fahrenheit 451 at a Barnes & Noble store in Bakersfield, CA. After it was over, the B&N manager enthusiastically shook my hand and told me at least 40 people from the audience wanted to buy *my* book. Cool, I thought. Then his face went sheepish: he'd had to tell these people he couldn't sell it to them because it wasn't carried by Ingram, B&N's supplier. Guess who never imagined that situation?

Still, the Chronicler's Edition — a 2,434-copy signed and numbered limited edition — found its way into the world despite such bollixments. And in any case, distribution was soon moot; Wynderry Press went extinct before the trade paperback edition came together. Not exactly filled with good cheer, I moved on to other projects.

FAST FORWARD to late 2012. I'd finally completed the first two books in a new YA series called The Hallah Saga [recently revamped and renamed as the Falling Sky series]. Looking to escape the world of Hallah, whose sky was falling, I revisited *The Luck of Madonna 13*. Being the ruthless editor of a monthly corporate publication for the previous decade caused me to look at my dear first novel in a sterner light. Alas, some of it now grated on my sensitive editorial nerves for various reasons. Still, the story and the post-Nevergate world held up for me. Given the radical changes in the publishing industry over that decade, I thought the book should at least be available as an ebook. And now it i s... and a trade paperback as well.

What was different in this "new and improved" 2013 edition? For one thing, it's reorganized into three sections to make the action easier to follow. Somewhere between 2001 and 2012, I also developed a preference for shorter chapters (possibly because my attention span is shrinking), so the chapter count has tripled. My growing impatience with intrusive verbalisms (my own included) prompted me to run the manuscript through a Blathertech Model 007 Overwriting Filter. With luck, this has excised the worst infractions.

Dates have also changed to protect the innocent, the innocent in this case is the Chronicler. In studying the technological change vectors of the last ten years, some — like 3D printing — are moving at hyperspeed. Others — like human cloning — seem to have nearly fallen off the radar. My gut said the future envisioned in the Last Nevergate Chronicles might feel more plausible if I took a chronological bulldozer to the dates, so I pushed them all out a century. Many of the footnotes are still in, but the quincunx icons in the margins are gone. These symbolic pointers to an external website seemed like a clever idea at the turn of the century, but if it was, its time has come and gone, thanks to technology.

If that's not enough, I put the backstory text on a diet. More precisely, I put it elsewhere. Back in the day, I was perhaps over-passionate about cramming fictional worldbuilding into readers' eyeballs. Wiser souls advised me against this practice, but the Chronicler's Edition nonetheless led off with Genesis, a concentrated dose of St. Coriander future history before the narrative. While this led to some lively dialog amongst reviewers, for the 2013 edition the Genesis section became part of *Genesis...and Then Some*, a separate volume that also contains updated versions of various backstory goodies from the late lastnevergate.com website, which has been retired. Readers with surplus time on their hands will find a wealth of curious sidestories, obscure hints, drolleries, clues and such in this volume. Check my website for availability details.

447

E. T. Ellison (aka the Chronicler)

February 2014

PSST! Something remarkable happened since I wrote the above blurbage. The woo-woo gods (and *Foreword Reviews*) conspired to award *The Luck of Madonna 13* its second book of the year award, this one for the 2013 revised edition.

ETE

July 2015

MORE YEARS HAVE PASSED. The entire six volumes have now been written, revised, rewritten, edited, re-edited, tweaked, proofed and proofed again, and most have been transformed into ebooks and trade paperbacks. For indie publishers like Clownbox Press, this is perhaps a more fluid and iterative process than with legacy publishers. Nearly the same number of details to deal with, but a maximally simplified chain of command. In the Clownbox Press case, "maximal simplification" means that the poor, overworked author does everything while the publisher reclines in a deck chair on his yacht anchored off a favorite tropical paradise and is served his rocks Margaritas with crusty rims of pink salt while spearing smoked oysters right out of the can. The good part is that the author can decide to tweak this little thing or that and it's accomplished with not a single complaint from higher-ups. For we do-it-all-ourselfers it's a fine freedom.

For readers this means that if the later books of the Chronicles squeal for changes to the long-published first book for pre-continuity purposes, the author can just do it. Poof! That's why the new 2020 edition of Luck has two more chapters than the 2013 edition, along with a new character and a bit of new technology she brought with her from the Santa Fe Institute: the clever Kroh-Hackton engineered fungi that WorldGov had kaiboshed. Couldn't leave that out, could I? Just say "Of course not, E.T."

Thanks for reading ... and no need to feel shy about leaving a review on Amazon or wherever. Hope you enjoy the rest of the Chronicles.

ETE
March 2020

ABOUT THE AUTHOR

E. T. Ellison is the author of eight novels. His genre-busting first book, *The Luck of Madonna 13* (which you may have just completed), is a two time book of the year winning epic that according to one reviewer "tackles the nearly impossible challenge of seamlessly knitting together persuasive technological realism with such high fantasy staples as castles, dragons and magic in a 26th century future Earth that is not wildly different from our own." Another reviewer wrote that "Ellison writes with a gleefully whimsical style that pulls you through the book like a tiger on a leash; half the time you're having the ride of your life, while the other half you're wondering if you're going to survive." *The Luck of Madonna 13* is the first book in the five volume Last Nevergate Chronicles. A new 2020 edition of *Luck* and the final four books of the quintet were published simultaneously in 2020. Also in simultaneous release were *The Deadly Crocus* and *The Well of Life*, the first two books in Falling Sky, a YA series, and the first Travis One-Shoe thriller, *Treasure of the Holy Quincunx*, set a couple centuries earlier in Ellison's richly imagined future Earth of the Last Nevergate Chronicles.

In his pre-fiction decades Ellison was a consultant on hundreds of diverse projects that were often most fascinating and challenging, but no match for the surpassing joys of making stuff up and writing it down.

He currently lives in Northern California.

450

www.ingramcontent.com/pod-product-compliance
Lightning Source LLC
Chambersburg PA
CBHW071218250626
47163CB00001B/29